MARGARET OLIPHANT

(1828-1897) was born in Wall[...] Scotland until the age of ten w[...] and then Birkenhead. Her mot[...] little is known of her father, F[...] "took affidavits" in a Liverpool [...] novel at the age of sixteen whil[...] [...]er through an illness, but her first published work was *Passages in the Life of Mrs Margaret Maitland* (1849), and in 1851 she was introduced to the Scottish firm of Blackwoods, who were to be her principal publishers, and to whose *Blackwood's Magazine* she remained a regular contributor until her death.

In 1852 she married her cousin Francis Oliphant, an architectural glass painter and associate of Pugin. The greater part of the family income, however, came from her journalism and Scottish regional novels such as *Katie Stewart* and *The Quiet Heart* (1854). In 1859 she found herself a widow with three small children and £1000 in debt: from then on she was always under pressure to write to educate her sons (her daughter died in 1864), and also to support her brothers, nephew and nieces.

One of the greatest women of the Victorian Age, Mrs Oliphant eventually published almost 100 novels, of which the best known are the "Carlingford Chronicles": *The Rector and The Doctor's Family* (1863), *Salem Chapel* (1863), *The Perpetual Curate* (1864), *Miss Marjoribanks* (1866), and *Phoebe Junior* (1876). Other important works include *Harry Joscelyn* (1881), *The Ladies Lindores* (1883), *Hester* (1883), *A Country Gentleman and His Family* (1886), *Lady Car* (1889), *Kirsteen (1890)* and *Sir Robert's Fortune* (1895). She also wrote supernatural tales, biographies, literary histories, translations and travel books. Her last years were overshadowed by the deaths of her nephew Frank in 1879, and her sons Cyril and "Cecco" in 1890 and 1895. Remembered by J.M. Barrie as "of an intellect so alert that one wondered she ever fell asleep", Mrs Oliphant died in Wimbledon at the age of sixty-nine.

Virago also publishes *Hester, The Rector & The Doctor's Family, Salem Chapel, The Perpetual Curate* and *Miss Marjoribanks*.

Chronicles of Carlingford

PHOEBE, JUNIOR

MRS OLIPHANT

WITH A NEW INTRODUCTION BY
PENELOPE FITZGERALD

Virago

Published by VIRAGO PRESS Limited 1989
20-23 Mandela Street, Camden Town, London NW1 OHQ

First published in Great Britain by Hurst and Blackett Limited 1876
Introduction Copyright © Penelope Fitzgerald 1989

A CIP catalogue record for this book is available from the British Library

Printed in Finland by Werner Söderström Oy

INTRODUCTION

From the time when she was left a widow at the age of thirty-one Mrs Oliphant never, she said, had five pounds which she didn't earn for herself by writing. By 1872 it became clear that she would have to support her brother and his family in addition to her own three children. This duty she took on with her usual reckless generosity and total inability to save a penny. Together with what she called "a lightly-flowing stream of articles" for the magazines, she published two three-volume novels, wrote two more and produced a biography of Montalembert, the Catholic social reformer, which meant staying in the icy family château in the Côte d'Or while the family read aloud to her from his papers, but refused to let her see them. On 22 October she wrote to her publisher, John Blackwood, "I have begun, partly to amuse myself, and on a sudden impulse, a new series of the Chronicles of Carlingford." The fact that it amused her, at such a moment, to go back to her place of the imagination says a great deal for Carlingford.

The first five Chronicles had appeared between 1863 and 1866.[1] They were not arranged in order of time, and she could have taken up the story wherever she pleased — in respectable Grange Lane, with the doctor on his rounds, even with the brickworkers on Wharfside. She chose to return to the Dissenters of Salem Chapel, and the parsonage of St Roque's.

The author of *Everywhere Spoken Against*[2] was surely wrong to speak of Mrs Oliphant's "simplifed view of Church and Dissent" in *Phoebe Junior* and her "absurd solution" to the division between them. Although in Chapter XXVII there is a hard-hitting dispute between the young minister and the young Anglican on their duties to the old, the young, the poor and the unemployed, "women who take in washing, and men who go about hunting for a day's work", Mrs Oliphant is not offering a solution as such. The crisis of the novel is emotional, social and moral. For the first time, too, in the "Chronicles", she is deeply concerned with the power of money. Mr Copperfield, the vastly successful contractor, is Golden Gain itself, a broad mid-Victorian caricature. He is not only rich but able to create wealth with "that kind of faculty which is in practical life what genius is in literature". He has bought a Turner ("I like a thing that costs a deal, and is of no use — that's what I call luxury"), and the whole room seems to feel a "definable relief" when he goes out of it. But his money is real, like the savings of old Tozer, the retired grocer. On the other hand Mr May, the incumbent of St Roque's, exists in a kind of world of visionary money, "which was borrowed here to-day, and paid there to-morrow . . . never reaching anybody's pocket, and representing anything but that one thing which money is supposed to be able to extinguish — debt". Betsy, the parsonage maid-of-all-work, says "I've had a deal of experience of gentlefolk, and it's always money as is the thing that sets them off their head." It acts (which is perhaps what Betsy means) as a test for all of them. Reginald May is tormented by the offer of a sinecure — "not honest work" he thinks. His innocent younger sister, dazed by a visit to London, tells him "If I had a chance of two hundred and fifty a year! There is nothing I would not do for it!" But she has no idea what she is talking about. She only feels her own helplessness. "How is a girl to earn any money? I wish I knew how." Phoebe, however, Mrs Oliphant's heroine, sets herself to marry money because, as she frankly admits, it is more agreeable to have money than not to have it, and above all because it is a necessary condition of power and influence. She sets about this with perfect candour and good sense, and, what is more, she is never proved wrong. I cannot bring to mind any other novelist of that date who would have dared to make a heroine out of Phoebe, junior.

Phoebe senior, her mother, is the daughter of old Tozer — that is to say, she comes from the disgraceful background of a shop, and a shop reeking of cheese and bacon at that. She has married a Dissenting minister, Henry Beecham (Beecher in *Salem Chapel*, but Mrs Oliphant is often reckless about names). They have bettered themselves by moving to London and to a chapel which is supported by a wealthy congregation, in particular by Mr Copperhead. To Phoebe they have given every advantage — not too much education, though, or the congregation "would think they meant to make a schoolmistress of her, which they thanked Providence they had no need to do". Phoebe is not the sort of girl to reject her family, even when she finds out that her grandfather, "fond and greasy" is a retired butterman. True, it means one more obstacle on the climb upwards, but "giving in was not in her". The man she has selected is the blundering young oaf of a Clarence Copperhead, referred to as "her dull companion" and "no great thing", but ready with wealth and obstinate devotion. Mr Copperhead, of course, demands something much better as a match for his son. As adversaries, Phoebe and he understand each other perfectly. In the final showdown they confront each other as business rivals. But Phoebe's bid is infinitely higher because she has a genuine sense of honour and duty. "Honour! that's for men," says Copperhead, but "the big, rich, noisy man was silenced". He can only recover his self-esteem by reckoning the value of Phoebe's cleverness as a commodity. "It was brains I wanted," he reflects, "and I've bought 'em dear."

Phoebe is determined to be herself. Perhaps she chooses the only way open to her in her time and place. It was not until much later (in *Kirsteen*, 1891) that Mrs Oliphant allowed herself a heroine who stays unmarried and opens a successful business. *Phoebe Junior*, however, goes deeper than *Miss Marjoribanks*, the fourth of the "Chronicles", which is also about a strong-willed young woman. This is because we are allowed to know what Phoebe is giving up in her pursuit of success, and so is she. When she dismisses Reginald May "her heart contracted with a real pain . . . she went in with a sense in her mind that she had never touched so close upon a higher kind of existence, and perhaps never again might have the opportunity". But this, like the grocer's shop, is an impediment to be put behind her.

Surely it is to emphasise this point that Mrs Oliphant introduces her counter-heroine, Ursula May. The two of them are brought together by a neat turn in the plot — Phoebe comes to Carlingford to look after her grand-mother, Clarence Copperhead has been sent for tuition to Mr May. The contrast between the two girls is made at once, Phoebe strikingly dressed in black, Ursula in white, "a pale little maiden", almost shrinking out of sight. Phoebe serenely takes command in any situation, Ursula is hard put to it to manage the motherless, penniless house-hold. She is a troubled peacemaker, daunted by "all the mendings, all the keepings in order, the tradespeople to be kept in good humour" and a father more difficult than any of them. But awkward as she is, innocent, "refreshing" to her knowledgeable cousins, she has a day-to-day courage which can be compared to Phoebe's. Mrs Oliphant takes a novelist's risk that Ursula may in the end prove the more sympathetic of the two. Courage, certainly, is needed for the ordeal of giving her first dinner party. Mrs Oliphant puts all her comic skill into the disaster of the entrées, perhaps because she had once, when entertaining Major Blackwood, failed terribly with her own.[3] Poor Ursula has none of Phoebe's almost royal self-possession. But when she discovers, later in the story, that she loves and is loved, the "passion which had got possession of her" gives Ursula an unexpected authority which takes all the rest of them aback.

Ursula's threadbare home is a battleground, compared with the complacent and cosy life of the Beechams and the Tozers. There are continual shifts of front, the whole family united against the tradesmen, Ursula either in alliance or at odds with her wild younger sister, all the children in wary conflict with their father. Although this is a large claim to make, I think St Roque's can take its place with any of the parsonages of Victorian fiction. Bitterly true to life is Mr May's indulgent welcome to the little ones (which he hopes will be noticed by the passers-by) changing within the space of two pages to a furious row and withdrawal to that forbidden ground, his study. A bad temper, Mrs Oliphant points out, is a possession like any other, and Mr May makes effective use of his. And yet St Roque's parsonage, in its way, is a house of mercies. "We are not very tidy or comfortable, perhaps, but we all beong to each other, at least," says Reginald to his sisters. And the neglected shrubbery is the setting for the moonlit love scenes of Chapter XXXII.

The character of Mr May is peculiar, and yet recognisable at once to anyone who prefers not to face their own shortcomings. Mrs Oliphant lets us know him painfully well. He is not a noble unfortunate, like Trollope's Mr Crawley, nor is he a monster. He lives, as indeed he has to do, by self-delusion. His inability to make ends meet appears to him an injustice done by the world to a scholar and gentleman. If one of his humbler parishioners has become involved in his doubtful transactions, well, that is to be regretted, but Cotsdean, after all, is only a tradesman. "He must be sacrificed, if it came to that." In the masterly opening to Chapter XXXIX, Mr May's sanity, threatened by his suppressed conscience, wavers a little. Although his affairs are at crisis point, he has had a pleasant day out, and is walking back to the station, fortified by sherry and a biscuit.

As he went along, he felt himself fall into a curious dreamy state of mind, which was partly fatigue perhaps, but was not at all unpleasant. Sometimes he almost seemed to himself to be asleep as he trudged on, and woke up with a start, thinking that he saw indistinct figures, the skirt of a dress or the tail of a long coat, disappearing past him, just gone before he was fully awake to what it was. He knew there was no one on the lonely road, and . . . these vanishings of indistinct wayfarers . . . half-amused him in the curious state of his brain. He had got rid of his anxiety. It was all quite plain before him what to do, — to go to the Bank, to tell them what he had coming in, and to settle everything as easily as possible . . . when he got to the railway station, and got into a carriage, he seemed to be floating somehow in a prolonged vision of light and streaks of darkness, not quite aware how far he was going, or where he was going . . . "If Sir Robert's sherry had been better, I should have blamed that," he said to himself.

Self-deception, on the edge of disorder, could hardly be better described, or more gently. And, as Mrs Oliphant once said, "Tragedy is terrible, but when it drops into tragi-comedy, tragi-farce at the end, that is the most terrible of all."

Mr May's final reckoning — the tragi-farce — is with Tozer. By attempting, as he does, to forge Tozer's name on a bill he might seem to be challenging the spirit of Carlingford itself. Ruin must follow. Mrs Oliphant has judged exactly the effect of age and retirement on the old butterman. Homely and decent as always, but less control-led and more easily flustered, he is still conditioned by the shop and the chapel. The very idea of his name being used makes him bristle like a wild animal. Money, for the moment, doesn't matter to him, nor the Bible's teaching on forgiveness. "The Bible's spiritual; but there's trade, and there's justice." But, just as in *Salem Chapel*, (where he first makes his appearance), Tozer has depths we could hardly have guessed at. Mr May, humbled and half mad, has, after all, been his customer, and beyond that he is a clergyman. And "the terrible mystery of human wicked-ness and guilt prostrated his common soul with as sharp an anguish of pity and shame as could have befallen the most heroic". If Mrs Oliphant had not been a mid-Victorian she would not have called Tozer common. If she hadn't recognised him as heroic, she would not have been Mrs Oliphant. James Barrie thought that she did not know how to finish off her great scenes, and that someone else ought to have been sent in to do it for her, but this one she ends without hesitation. "'I'll not say no to that money, not now, Mr Northcote, sir.'" At this point, Mrs Oliphant says, "Nature awoke in the old butterman," as though grocery was not a trade, but an instinct.

In giving this book the subtitle *A Last Chronicle of Carlingford* Mrs Oliphant acknowledged what she owed to Trollope. In her rapid, capacious way she had undoubtedly helped herself to details. The election in *Miss Marjoribanks* owes something to *Dr Thorne*, the brickworks in Carling-

owes something to *Dr Thorne*, the brickworks in Carlingford recall the brickworks in Hogglestock, the name Tozer
must surely come from the bill-broker in *Framley
Parsonage*. In *Phoebe Junior* the whole question of the
chaplaincy at the old mens' retreat suggests *The Warden*.
Whether this disturbed Trollope at all I do not know. Mrs
Oliphant is not one of the lady writers of whom he would
"fain say a word" in his *Autobiography*. But certainly it
didn't disturb Mrs Oliphant. The great natural story-teller
knew herself secure in the world of her own creation.
Indeed, Phoebe herself is said to enjoy reading the Barchester novels.

At the end of his series Trollope had written a moving
farewell to Barchester. Mrs Oliphant does nothing of the
kind. During the course of *Phoebe Junior*, however, a
number of judgements are passed on Carlingford. The
Dorsets — the Mays' London cousins — call it "a pretty,
sleepy country place", but Ursula's comment, when she
comes back from her visit, is "Oh, Janey, is everybody
dead? How dull it is!" To Phoebe's mother, who has
escaped from the close atmosphere of Salem Chapel, it is
"an old-fashioned, conceited, Tory town", a kind of trap,
and those who doubt this "don't know Carlingford, or the
folks there". Clarence Copperhead, to be sure, approves of
it because there are no museums, and "the worst of going
abroad is that you've always got to look at things of that
sort. To have to do it at home would be beyond a joke."
To Mr Copperhead, however, it is "a bit of a little
piggery", and indeed he is in favour of getting rid of it
altogether. "A country town is a mistake, in my opinion
. . . I'd raze them all to the ground, and have one London
and the rest green fields." Certainly Carlingford, in the
space of twenty years, has grown no more used than ever it
was to new ideas — Phoebe causes consternation by
playing Beethoven and having "ideas of her own" about

Wagner, and by wearing an "aesthetic" dress to the meeting of the Dis-establishment Society. Even the town itself seems not to have expanded very much. We hear no more of its becoming a bishopric. The roads still peter out beyond St Roque's into fields of cabbages and potatoes. The Tozers' fierce daughter-in-law is improving the shop — ("more than was wanted, or was thought upon in my time," Mrs Tozer says) — but even she has to admit that "folks can't do everything at once".

Mrs Oliphant, I believe, thought of the town as unchangeable, or rather that if it changed it would no longer be Carlingford. It is not so much a matter of streets and houses as a moral climate. In its obstinacy there is a certain magnificence. In the whole extent of the "Chronicles" only Dr Rider (of *The Doctor's Family*) and Frank Wentworth (of *The Perpetual Curate*) have been able, with the help of their wives, to challenge Carlingford and get the better of it, and yet continue to live there. Bright spirits have come, in their time, as ministers to Salem Chapel, as Horace Northcote does in *Phoebe Junior*, but Tozer concludes,

"If any more o' them young intellectuals turns up at Carlingford, I'll tell him right out, 'You ain't the man for my money.' I'll say to him as bold as brass, 'I've been young, and now I'm old, and it's my conviction as clever young men ain't the sort for Salem.'"

Phoebe, of course, will seek her fortunes elsewhere, but so, too will Ursula. And for those who remain behind there are no conventional endings. Mrs Oliphant did not see it as her duty, as a novelist, to put things tidily to rights. Life in the "Chronicles" is not a matter of transformation, but of adaptation and survival. Mr May will never be called up to admit what he has done, or to face the truth about himself. Janey, left in charge of the housekeeping, is as wild as ever. Reginald has called a truce with his conscience, but not, when the story ends, with his feelings. "However he is young, and things may mend."

So Mrs Oliphant takes her leave of Carlingford.

Penelope Fitzgerald, London, 1987

1. *The Rector*, 1863; *The Doctor's Family*, 1863; *Salem Chapel*, 1863; *Miss Marjoribanks*, 1866; all published by W. Blackwood & Sons. *Phoebe Junior* was eventually published by Hurst & Blackett in 1876.
2. Valentine Cunningham, *Everywhere Spoken Against: Dissent in the Victorian Novel*, Clarenden Press, Oxford, 1977.
3. They were chicken cutlets. "Let us not dwell on such horrors, even in recollection." Margaret Oliphant, *Annals of a Publishing House*, W. Blackwood & Sons, London, 1897.

CONTENTS.

PHŒBE, JUNIOR.

A Last Chronicle of Carlingford.

CHAPTER I.

THE PASTOR'S PROGRESS.

MISS PHŒBE TOZER, the only daughter of the chief deacon and leading member of the Dissenting connection in Carlingford, married, shortly after his appointment to the charge of Salem Chapel, in that town, the Reverend Mr. Beecham, one of the most rising young men in the denomination. The marriage was in many ways satisfactory to the young lady's family, for Mr. Beecham was himself the son of respectable people in a good way of business, and not destitute of means; and the position was one which they had always felt most suitable for their daughter, and to which she had been almost, it may be said, brought up. It is, however, scarcely necessary to add that it was not quite so agreeable to the other leading members of the congregation. I should be very sorry to say that each family wished that preferment for its own favourite daughter; for indeed there can be no doubt, as Mrs. Pigeon asserted vigorously, that a substantial grocer, whose father before him had established an excellent business, and who had paid for his pew in Salem as long as any one could recollect, and supported every charity, and paid up on all occasions when extra expense was necessary, was in every way a more desirable son-in-law than a poor minister who was always dependent on pleasing the chapel folks, and might have to turn out any day. Notwithstanding, however, the evident superiority of the establishment tnus attained by Maria Pigeon, there is a certain something attached to the position of a clerical caste, even among such an independent body as the congregation at Salem Chapel, which has its own especial charms, and neither the

1

young people who had been her companions nor the old people who had patronized and snubbed her, felt any satisfaction in seeing Phœbe thus advanced over them to the honours and glories inalienable from the position of minister's wife. All her little airs of bridal vanity were considered as so many offensive manifestations of delight and exultation in her rise in life. Her *trousseau*, though pronounced by all competent judges not half so abundant or fine as Maria Pigeon's, still called forth comments which nobody ventured to indulge in, in respect to the grocer's blooming bride. A grocer's lady has a right to anything her parents can afford; but to see a minister's wife swelling herself up, and trying to ape the quality, filled the town with virtuous indignation. The sight of young Mrs. Beecham walking about with her card-case in her hand, calling on the Miss Hemmingses, shaking hands with Mrs. Rider the doctor's wife, caused unmitigated disgust throughout all the back streets of Carlingford; and "*that* Phœbe a-sweeping in as if the chapel belonged to her," was almost more than the oldest sitter could bear. Phœbe, it must be added, felt her elevation to the full, and did not spare her congregation. Sometimes she would have the audacity to walk from the vestry to the pew, as if she were an office-bearer, instead of coming in humbly by the door as became a woman. She would sit still ostentatiously until every one had gone, waiting for her husband. She quite led the singing, everybody remarked, paying no more attention to the choir than if it did not exist; and once she had even paused on her way to her seat, and turned down the gas, which was blazing too high, with an air of proprietorship that nobody could endure.

"Does Salem belong to them Tozers, I should like to know?" said Mrs. Brown. "Brown would never be outdone by him in subscriptions you may be sure, nor Mr. Pigeon neither, if the truth was known. I never gave my money to build a castle for the Tozers."

Thus the whole congregation expressed itself with more or less eloquence, and though the attendance never diminished, everybody being too anxious to see "what they would do next," the feeling could not be ignored. Phœbe herself, with a courage which developed from the moment of her marriage, took the initiative.

"It never answers," she said, solemnly, "to marry one of the flock; I knew it, Henery, and I told you so; and if you would be so infatuated, and marry me when I told you not, for your own interests—"

"They're all jealous of you, my pet, that's what it is," said

Mr. Beecham, and laughed. He could bear the annoyance in consideration of that sweet consciousness of its cause which stole over all his being. Phœbe laughed, too, but not with so delicious a gratification. She felt that there were people, even in Salem, who might be jealous of him.

"The end of it all is, we must not stay here," she said. "You must find another sphere for your talents, Henery, and I'm sure it will not be difficult. If you get put on that deputation that is going down to the North, suppose you take a few of your best sermons, dear. That can never do any harm—indeed it's sure to do good, to some poor benighted soul at least, that perhaps never heard the truth before. And likewise, perhaps, to some vacant congregation. I have always heard that chapels in the North were very superior to here. A different class of society, and better altogether. These Pigeons and Browns, and people are not the sort of society for you."

"Well, there's truth in that," said Mr. Beecham, pulling up his shirt-collar. "Certainly it isn't the sort of thing one was accustomed to." And he lent a serious ear to the suggestion about the sermons. The consequence was that an invitation followed from a chapel in the North, where indeed Mrs. Phœbe found herself in much finer society, and grew rapidly in importance and in ideas. After this favourable start, the process went on for many years by which a young man from Homerton was then developed into the influential and highly esteemed pastor of an important flock. Things may be, and probably are, differently managed now-a-days. Mr. Beecham had unbounded fluency and an unctuous manner of treating his subjects. It was eloquence of a kind, though not of an elevated kind. Never to be at a loss for what you have to say is a prodigious advantage to all men in all positions, but doubly so to a popular minister. He had an unbounded wealth of phraseology. Sentences seemed to melt out of his mouth without any apparent effort, all set in a certain cadence. He had not, perhaps, much power of thought, but it is easy to make up for such a secondary want when the gift of expression is so strong. Mr. Beecham rose, like an actor, from a long and successful career in the provinces, to what might be called the Surrey side of congregational eminence in London; and from thence attained his final apotheosis in a handsome chapel near Regent's Park, built of the whitest stone, and cushioned with the reddest damask, where a very large congregation sat in great comfort and listened to his sermons with a satisfaction no doubt increased by the fact that the cushions were soft as

their own easy-chairs, and that carpets and hot-water pipes
kept everything snug under foot.

It was the most comfortable chapel in the whole connection.
The seats, were arranged like those of an amphitheatre, each
line on a slightly higher level than the one in front of it, so
that everybody saw everything that was going on.   No dim-
ness or mystery was wanted there ; everything was bright daylight, bright paint, red cushions, comfort and respectability.
It might not be a place very well adapted for saying your
prayers in, but then you could say your prayers at home—
and it was a place admirably adapted for hearing sermons in,
which you could not do at home ; and all the arrangements
were such that you could hear in the greatest comfort, not
to say luxury.   I wonder, for my own part, that the poor
folk about did not seize upon the Crescent Chapel on the
cold Sunday mornings, and make themselves happy in those
warm and ruddy pews.   It would be a little amusing to
speculate what all the well-dressed pew-holders would have
done had this unexpected answer to the appeal which Mr.
Beecham believed himself to make every Sunday to the world
in general, been literally given.   It would have been extremely embarrassing to the Managing Committee and all
the office-bearers, and would have, I fear, deeply exasperated
and offended the occupants of those family pews ; but fortunately this difficulty never did occur.   The proletariat of
Marylebone had not the sense or the courage, or the profanity,
which you will, to hit upon this mode of warming themselves.
The real congregation embraced none of the unwashed multitude.   Its value in mere velvet, silk, lace, trinkets, and furs
was something amazing, and the amount these comfortable
people represented in the way of income would have amounted
to a most princely revenue.   The little Salems and Bethesdas,
with their humble flocks, could not be supposed to belong to
the same species ; and the difference was almost equally marked
between such a place of worship as the Crescent Chapel and
the parish churches, which are like the nets in the Gospel, and
take in all kinds of fish, bad and good.   The pew-holders in the
Crescent Chapel were universally well off ; they subscribed
liberally to missionary societies, far more liberally than the
people in St. Paul's close by did to the S. P. G.   They had
everything of the best in the chapel, as they had in their houses.
They no more economized on their minister than they did on
their pew-cushions, and they spent an amount of money on
their choir which made the singing-people at St. Paul's gnash
their teeth.   From all this it will be seen that the atmosphere

of the Crescent Chapel was of a very distinct and individual
kind. It was a warm, luxurious air, perfumy, breathing of
that refinement which is possible to mere wealth. I do not
say there might not be true refinement besides, but the surface
kind, that which you buy from upholsterers and tailors and
dressmakers, which you procure ready made at schools, and
which can only be kept up at a very high cost, abounded and
pervaded the place. Badly dressed people felt themselves out
of place in that brilliant sanctuary; a muddy footprint upon
the thick matting in the passages was looked at as a crime.
Clean dry feet issuing out of carriage or cab kept the aisles
unstained, even on the wettest day. We say cab, because
many of the people who went to the Crescent Chapel objected
to take out their own carriages or work their own horses on
Sunday; and there were many more who, though they did not
possess carriages, used cabs with a freedom incompatible with
poverty. As a general rule, they were much better off than
the people at St. Paul's, more universally prosperous and well-
to-do. And they were at the same time what you might safely
call well-informed people—people who read the newspapers,
and sometimes the magazines, and knew what was going on.
The men were almost all liberal in politics, and believed in Mr.
Gladstone with enthusiasm; the women often "took an interest" in public movements, especially of a charitable character.
There was less mental stagnation among them probably than
among many of their neighbours. Their life was not profound
nor high, but still it was life after a sort. Such was the flock
which had invited Mr. Beecham to become their pastor when
he reached the climax of his career. They gave him a very
good salary, enough to enable him to have a handsome house in
one of the terraces overlooking Regent's Park. It is not a
fashionable quarter, but it is not to be despised in any way.
The rooms were good-sized and lofty, and sometimes have been
known to suffice for very fine people indeed, a fact which the
Beechams were well aware of; and they were not above the
amiable weakness of making it known that their house was in
a line with that of Lady Cecilia Burleigh. This single fact of
itself might suffice to mark the incalculable distance between
the Reverend Mr. Beecham of the Crescent Chapel, and the
young man who began life as minister of Salem in Carlingford.
And the development outside was not less remarkable than the
development within.

It is astonishing how our prejudices change from youth to
middle age, even without any remarkable interposition of
fortune; I do not say dissipate, or even dispel, which is much

more doubtful — but they change. When Mr. and Mrs.
Beecham commenced life, they had both the warmest feeling
of opposition to the Church and everything churchy. All the
circumstances of their lives had encouraged this feeling. The
dislike of the little for the great, the instinctive opposition of a
lower class towards the higher, intensified that natural essence
of separatism, that determination to be wiser than one's neighbour, which in the common mind lies at the bottom of all
dissent. In saying this we no more accuse Dissenters in
religion than Dissenters in politics, or in art, or in criticism.
The first dissenter in most cases is an original thinker, to
whom his enforced departure from the ways of his fathers is
misery and pain. Generally he has a hard struggle with himself before he can give up, for the superlative truth which has
taken possession of him, all the habits, the pious traditions of
his life. He is the real Nonconformist—half martyr, half
victim, of his convictions. But that Nonconformity which has
come to be the faith in which a large number of people are
trained is a totally different business, and affects a very different kind of sentiments. Personal and independent conviction
has no more to do with it than it has to do with the ardour of
a Breton peasant trained in deepest zeal of Romanism, or the
unbounded certainty of any other traditionary believer. For
this reason we may be allowed to discuss the changes of feeling
which manifested themselves in Mr. and Mrs. Beecham without
anything disrespectful to Nonconformity. Not being persons
of original mind, they were what their training and circumstances, and a flood of natural influences, made them. They
began life, feeling themselves to be of a hopelessly low social
caste, and believing themselves to be superior to their superiors
in that enlightenment which they had been brought up to believe
distinguished the connection. The first thing which opened
their minds to a dawning doubt whether their enlightenment
was, in reality, so much greater than that of their neighbours,
was the social change worked in their position by their removal
from Carlingford. In the great towns of the North, Dissent
attains its highest social elevation, and Chapel people are no
longer to be distinguished from Church people except by the
fact that they go to Chapel instead of Church, a definition so
simple as to be quite overwhelming to the unprepared dissenting intelligence, brought up in a little Tory borough, still
holding for Church and Queen. The amazing difference which
this made in the sentiments of Mrs. Phœbe Beecham, *née*
Tozer, it is quite impossible to describe. Her sudden introduction to "circles" which Mrs. Pigeon had never entered, and

to houses at the area-door of which Mr. Brown, the dairyman, would have humbly waited, would have turned the young woman's head, had she not felt the overpowering necessity of keeping that organ as steady as possible, to help her to hold her position in the new world. Phœbe was a girl of spirit, and though her head went round and round, and everything felt confused about her, she did manage desperately to hold her own and to avoid committing herself; but I cannot attempt to tell how much her social elevation modified her sectarian zeal. Phœbe was only a woman, so that I am free to assign such motives as having a serious power over her. Let us hope Mr. Beecham, being a man and a pastor, was moved in a more lofty, intellectual, and spiritual way.

But however that may be, the pair went conjugally together in this modification of sentiment, and by the time they reached the lofty eminence of the Crescent Chapel, were as liberal-minded Nonconformists as heart could desire. Mr. Beecham indeed had many friends in the Low, and even some in the Broad Church. He appeared on platforms, to promote various public movements, along with clergymen of the Church. He spoke of " our brethren within the pale of the Establishment " always with respect, sometimes even with enthusiasm. "Depend upon it, my dear Sir," he would even say sometimes to a liberal brother, " the Establishment is not such an unmitigated evil as some people consider it. What should we do in country parishes where the people are not awakened? They do the dirty work for us, my dear brother—the dirty work." These sentiments were shared, but perhaps not warmly, by Mr. Beecham's congregation, some of whom were hot Voluntaries, and gave their ministers a little trouble. But the most part took their Nonconformity very quietly, and were satisfied to know that their chapel was the first in the connection, and their minister justly esteemed as one of the most eloquent. The Liberation Society held one meeting at the Crescent Chapel, but it was not considered a great success. At the best, they were no more than lukewarm Crescent-Chapelites, not political dissenters. Both minister and people were Liberal, that was the creed they professed. Some of the congregations Citywards, and the smaller chapels about Hampstead and Islington, used the word Latitudinarian instead ; but that, as the Crescent Chapel people said, was a word always applied by the bigoted and ignorant to those who held in high regard the doctrines of Christian charity. They were indeed somewhat proud of their tolerance, their impartiality, their freedom from old prejudices. " That sort of thing will not do now-a-days," said Mr. Copperhead, who was a great railway contractor and one of the deacons, and who had himself a son at Oxford. If there had been any bigotry in the Crescent, Mr. Copperhead would have had little difficulty in transferring himself over the way to St. Paul's Church, and it is astonishing what an effect that fact had upon the mind of Mr. Beecham's flock.

Mr. Beecham's house was situated in Regent's Park, and was constructed on the ordinary model of such houses. On the ground-floor was a handsome dining-room, a room which both Mr. and Mrs. Beecham twenty years before would have considered splendid, but which now they condescended to, as not so large as they could wish, but still comfortable. The drawing-room above was larger, a bright and pleasant room, furnished with considerable " taste." Behind the dining-room, a smaller room was Mr. Beecham's study, or the library, as it was sometimes called. It was lined with book-cases containing a very fair collection of books, and ornamented with portraits (chiefly engravings) of celebrated ministers and laymen in the connection, with a bust of Mr. Copperhead over the mantelpiece. This bust had been done by a young sculptor whom he patronized, for the great man's own house. When it was nearly completed, however, a flaw was found in the marble, which somewhat detracted from its perfection. The flaw was in the shoulder of the image, and by no means serious; but Mr. Copperhead was not the man to pass over any such defect. After a long and serious consultation over it, which made the young artist shake in his shoes, a solution was found for the difficulty.

" Tell you what, Sir," said Mr. Copperhead; " I'll give it to the minister. It'll look famous in his little study. Works of art don't often come his way; and you'll get a block of the best, Mr. Chipstone—the very best, Sir, no expense spared— and begin another for me."

This arrangement was perfectly satisfactory to all parties, though I will not say that it was not instrumental in bringing about certain other combinations which will be fully discussed in this history. The Beechams were mightily suprised when the huge marble head, almost as large as a Jupiter, though perhaps not otherwise so imposing, arrived at the Terrace; but they were also gratified.

" It is quite like receiving us into his own family circle," Mrs. Beecham said with a glance at her daughter, Phœbe, junior, who, with all her pink fingers outspread, was standing in adoration before that image of wealth and fabulous luxury.

"What a grand head it is!" cried the young enthusiast, gazing rapt upon the complacent marble whisker so delightfully curled and bristling with realistic force.

"It looks well, I must say, it looks well," said Mr. Beecham himself, rubbing his hands, "to receive such a token of respect from the leading member of the flock." And certainly no more perfect representation of a bell-wether ever adorned any shepherd's sanctuary.

CHAPTER II.

THE LEADING MEMBER.

MR. COPPERHEAD, to whom so much allusion has been made, was a well-known man in other regions besides that of the Crescent Chapel. His name, indeed, may be said to have gone to the ends of the earth, from whence he had conducted lines of railway, and where he had left docks, bridges, and lighthouses to make him illustrious. He was one of the greatest contractors for railways and other public works in England, and, by consequence, in the world. He had no more than a very ordinary education, and no manners to speak of; but at the same time he had that kind of faculty which is in practical work what genius is in literature, and, indeed, in its kind is genius too, though it neither refines nor even (oddly enough) enlarges the mind to which it belongs. He saw the right track for a road through a country with a glance of his eye; he mastered all the points of nature which were opposed to him in the rapidest survey, though scientifically he was great in no branch of knowledge. He could rule his men as easily as if they were so many children; and, indeed, they were children in his hands. All these gifts made it apparent that he must have been a remarkable and able man; but no stranger would have guessed as much from his appearance or his talk. There were people, indeed, who knew him well, and who remained incredulous and bewildered, trying to persuade themselves that his success must be owing to pure luck, for that he had nothing else to secure it. The cause of this, perhaps, was that he knew nothing about books, and was one of those jeering cynics who are so common under one guise or another. Fine cynics are endurable, and give a certain zest often to society, which might become too civil without them; but your coarse cynic is not pleasant. Mr. Copperhead's eye was as effectual in quenching emotion of any but the coarsest kind as water is against fire. People might be angry in his presence—it was the only passion he comprehended; but tenderness, sympathy, sorrow, all the more generous sentiments, fled and concealed themselves when this large, rich, costly man came by. People who were brought much in contact with him became ashamed of having any feelings at all; his eye upon them seemed to convict them of humbug. Those eyes were very light grey, prominent, with a jeer in them which was a very powerful moral instrument. His own belief was that he could "spot" humbug wherever he saw it, and that nothing could escape him; and, I suppose, so much humbug is there in this world that his belief was justified. But there are few more awful people than those ignoble spectators whose jeer arrests the moisture in the eye, and strangles the outcry on their neighbour's lip.

Mr. Copperhead had risen from the ranks; yet not altogether from the ranks. His father before him had been a contractor, dealing chiefly with canals and roads, and the old kind of public works; a very rough personage indeed, but one to whose fingers gold had stuck, perhaps because of the clay with which they were always more or less smeared. This ancestor had made a beginning to the family, and given his son a name to start with. *Our* Mr. Copperhead had married young, and had several sons, who were all in business, and all doing well; less vigorous, but still moderately successful copies of their father. When, however, he had thus done his duty to the State, the first Mrs. Copperhead having died, he did the only incomprehensible action of his life—he married a second time, a feeble, pretty, pink-and-white little woman, who had been his daughter's governess; married her without rhyme or reason, as all his friends and connections said. The only feasible motive for this second union seemed to be a desire on Mr. Copperhead's part to have something belonging to him which he could always jeer at, and in this way the match was highly successful. Mrs. Copperhead the second was gushing and susceptible, and as good a butt as could be imagined. She kept him in practice when nobody else was at hand. She was one of those naturally refined but less than half-educated, timid creatures who are to be found now and then painfully earning the bread which is very bitter to them in richer people's houses, and preserving in their little silent souls some fetish in the shape of a scrap of gentility, which is their sole comfort, or almost their sole comfort. Mrs. Copperhead's fetish was the dear recollection that she was "an officer's daughter;" or rather this had been her fetish in the days when she had nothing, and was free to plume herself on the reflected glory. Whether in the depths of her luxurious abode, at the height of her good fortune, she still found comfort in the thought, it would be hard to tell. Everybody who had known her in her youth thought her the most fortunate of women. Her old school companions told her story for the encouragement of their daughters, as they might have told a fairy tale. To see her rolling in her gorgeous carriage, or bowed out of a shop where all the daintiest devices of fashion had been placed at her feet, filled passers-by with awe and envy. She could buy whatever she liked, festoon herself with finery, surround herself with the costliest knick-knacks; the more there were of them, and the costlier they were, the better was Mr. Copperhead pleased. She had everything that heart could desire. Poor little woman! What a change from the governess-chrysalis who was snubbed by her pupil and neglected by everybody! and yet I am not sure that she did not—so inconsistent is human nature—look back to those melancholy days with a sigh.

This lady was the mother of Clarence Copperhead, the young man who was at Oxford, her only child, upon whom (of course) she doted with the fondest folly; and whom his father jeered at more than at any one else in the world, more even than at his mother, yet was prouder of than of all his other sons and all his possessions put together. Clarence, whom I will not describe, as he will, I trust, show himself more effectually by his actions, was like his mother in disposition, or so, at least, she made herself happy by thinking; but by some freak of nature he was like his father in person, and carried his mouse's heart in a huge frame, somewhat hulking and heavy-shouldered, with the same roll which distinguished Mr. Copperhead, and which betrayed something of the original navvy who was the root of the race. He had his father's large face too, and a tendency towards those demonstrative and offensive whiskers which are the special inheritance of the British Philistine. But instead of the large goggle eyes, always jeering and impudent, which lighted up the paternal countenance, Clarence had a pair of mild brown orbs, repeated from his mother's faded face, which introduced the oddest discord into his physiognomy generally. In the family, that is to say among the step-brothers and step-sisters who formed Mr. Copperhead's first family, the young fellow bore no other name than that of the curled darling, though, indeed, he was as far from being curled as any one could be. He was not clever; he had none of the energy of his race, and promised to be as useless in an office as he would have been in a cutting or a yard full of men. I am not sure that this fact did not increase secretly his father's exultation and pride in him. Mr. Copperhead was fond of costly and useless things; he liked them for their cost, with an additional zest in his sense of the huge vulgar use and profit of most things in his own life. This tendency, more than any appreciation of the beautiful, made him what is called a patron of art. It swelled his personal importance to think that he was able to hang up thousands of pounds, so to speak, on his walls, knowing all the time that he could make thousands more by the money had he invested it in more useful ways. The very fact that he could afford to refrain from investing it, that he could let it lie there useless, hanging by so many cords and ribbons, was sweet to him. And so also it was sweet to him to possess a perfectly useless specimen of humanity, which had cost him a great deal, and promised to cost him still more. He had plenty of useful sons as he had of useful money. The one who was of no use was the apex and glory of the whole.

But these three made up a strange enough family party, as may be supposed. The original Copperheads, the first family, who were all of the same class and nature, would have made a much noisier, less peaceable household; but they would have been a much jollier and really more harmonious one. Mr. Copperhead himself somewhat despised his elder sons, who were like himself, only less rich, less vigorous, and less self-assertive. He saw, oddly enough, the coarseness of their manners, and even of their ways of thinking; but yet he was a great deal more comfortable, more at his ease among them, than he was when seated opposite his trembling, deprecating, frightened little wife, or that huge youth who cost him so much and returned him so little. Now and then, at regular periodical intervals, the head of the family would go down to Blackheath to dine and spend the night with his son Joe, the second and the favourite, where there were romping children and a portly, rosy young matron, and loud talk about City dinners, contracts, and estimates. This refreshed him, and he came home with many chuckles over the imperfections of the family.

"My sons buy their wives by the hundred-weight," he would say jocularly at breakfast the day after; "thirteen stone if she is a pound, is Mrs. Joe. Expensive to keep up in velvet and satin, not to speak of mutton and beef. Your mother comes cheap," be would add aside to Clarence, with a rolling laugh. Thus he did not in the least exempt his descendants from the universal ridicule which he poured on all the world; but when he sat down opposite his timid little delicate wife, and by his University man, who had very little on the whole to say for himself, Mr. Copperhead felt the increase in gentility as well as the failure in jollity. "You are a couple of ghosts after Joe and his belongings, you two. Speak louder, I say, young fellow. You don't expect me to hear that penny-whistle of yours," he would say, chuckling at them, with a mixture of pride and disdain. They amused him by their dulness and silence, and personal awe of him. He was quite out of his element between these two, and yet the very fact pleasantly excited his pride.

"I speak as gentlemen generally speak," said Clarence, who was sometimes sullen when attacked, and who knew by experience that his father was rarely offended by such an argument.

"And I am sure, dear, your papa would never wish you to do otherwise," said anxious Mrs. Copperhead, casting a furtive frightened glance at her husband. He rolled out a mighty laugh from the head of the table where he was sitting. He contemplated them with a leer that would have been insulting, had he not been the husband of one and the father of the other. The laugh and the look called forth some colour on Mrs. Copperhead's cheek, well as she was used to them; but her son was less susceptible, and ate his breakfast steadily, and did not care.

"A pretty pair you are," said Mr. Copperhead. "I like your gentility. How much *foie gras* would you eat for breakfast, I wonder, my lad, if you had to work for it ? Luckily for you, I wasn't brought up to talk, as you say, like a gentleman. I'd like to see you managing a field of navvies with that nice little voice of yours—ay, or a mob before the hustings, my boy. You're good for nothing, you are; a nice delicate piece of china for a cupboard, like your mother before you. However, thank Heaven, we've got the cupboard," he said with a laugh, looking round him; "a nice big 'un, too, well painted and gilded; and the time has come, through not talking like a gentleman, that I can afford you. You should hear Joe. When that fellow talks, his house shakes. Confounded bad style of house, walls like gingerbread. How the boards don't break like pie-crust under Mrs. Joe's fairy foot, I can't make out. By Jove, ma'am, one would think I starved you, to see you beside your daughter-in-law. Always had a fine healthy appetite had Mrs. Joe."

There was nothing to answer to this speech, and therefore a dead silence ensued. When the master of the house is so distinctly the master, silence is apt to ensue after his remarks. Mrs. Copperhead sipped her tea, and Clarence worked steadily through his breakfast, and the head of the family crumpled the Times, which he read at intervals. All sorts of jokes had gone

on at Joe's table the morning before, and there had been peals
of laughter, and Mrs. Joe had even administered a slap upon
her husband's ruddy cheek for some pleasantry or other. Mr.
Copperhead, as he looked at his son and his wife, chuckled behind the Times. When they thought he was occupied they
made a few gentle remarks to each other. They had soft voices,
with that indescribable resemblance in tone which so often
exists between mother and son. Dresden china; yes, that was
the word; and to see his own resemblance made in that delicate
pâte, and elevated into that region of superlative costliness,
tickled Mr. Copperhead, and in the most delightful way.

"How about your ball?" was his next question, "or Clarence's ball, as you don't seem to take much interest in it,
ma'am? You are afraid of being brought in contact with the
iron pots, eh? You might crack or go to pieces, who knows,
and what would become of me, a wretched widower." Mr.
Copperhead himself laughed loudly at this joke, which did not
excite any mirth from the others, and then he repeated his
question, "How about the ball?"

"The invitations are all sent out, Mr. Copperhead; ninety-
five—I—I mean a hundred and thirty-five. I—I beg your
pardon, they were in two lots," answered the poor woman nervously. "A hundred and thirty-eight—and there is—a few
more—"

"Take your time, ma'am, take your time, we'll get at the
truth at last," said her husband; and he laid down his paper
and looked at her. He was not angry nor impatient. The
twinkle in his eye was purely humorous. Her stumblings
amused him, and her nervousness. But oddly enough, the most
furious impatience could not have more deeply disconcerted her.

"There are a few more—some old friends of mine," she went
on, confused. "They were once rather—kind—took an interest; that is—"

"Oh, the baronet and his daughters," said Mr. Copperhead,
"by all means let's have the baronet and his daughters.
Though as for their taking an interest—if you had not been a
rich man's wife, ma'am, living in a grand house in Portland
Place—"

"It was not now," she said, hurriedly. "I do not suppose
that any one takes an interest—in me now—"

Mr. Copperhead laughed, and nodded his head. "Not
many, ma'am, I should think—not many. You women must
make up your minds to that. It's all very well to take an interest in a pretty girl; but when you come to a certain age—
Well, let's proceed, the baronet—"

" And his two girls—"

" Ah, there's two girls! that's for you, Clarence, my boy. I thought there must be a motive. Think that fellow a good *parti*, eh? And I would not say they were far wrong if he behaves himself. Make a note of the baronet's daughter, young man. Lord, what a world it is!" said Mr. Copperhead, reflectively. " I should not wonder if you had been scheming, too."

" I would not for the world!" cried the poor little woman, roused for once. " I would not for anything interfere with a marriage. That is the last thing you need fear from me. Whether it was a girl I was fond of, or a girl I disliked—so long as she was Clarence's choice. Oh, I know the harm that is done by other people's meddling—nothing, nothing, would induce me to interfere."

Mr. Copperhead laid down his paper, and looked at her. I suppose, however little a man may care for his wife, he does not relish the idea that she married him for anything but love. He contemplated her still with amused ridicule, but with something fiercer in his eyes. " Oh—h!" he said, " you don't like other people to interfere? not so much as to say, it's a capital match, eh? You'll get so and so, and so and so, that you couldn't have otherwise—carriages perhaps, and plenty of money in your pocket (which it may be you never had in your life before), and consideration, and one of the finest houses in London, let us say in Portland Place. You don't like that amount of good advice, eh? Well, I do—I mean to interfere with my son, to that extent at least—you can do what you like. But as you're a person of prodigious influence, and strong will, and a great deal of character, and all that," Mr. Copperhead broke out with a rude laugh, " I'm afraid of you, I am—quite afraid."

Fortunately, just at this moment his brougham came round, and the great man finished his coffee at a gulp, and got up. " You look out for the baronet's daughters, then—" he said, " and see all's ready for this ball of yours; while I go and work to pay the bills, that's my share. You do the ornamental, and I do the useful, ha, ha! I'll keep up my share."

It was astonishing what a difference came upon the room the moment he disappeared. Somehow it had been out of harmony. His voice, his look, his heavy person, even his whiskers had been out of character. Now the air seemed to flutter after the closing of the door like water into which something offensive has sunk, and when the ripples of movement were over the large handsome room had toned down into perfect accord with its remaining inhabitants. Mrs. Copperhead's eyes were rather red—not with tears, but with the inclination to shed tears, which she carefully restrained in her son's presence. He still continued to eat steadily—he had an admirable appetite. But when he had finished everything on his plate, he looked up and said, "I hope you don't mind, mamma; I don't suppose you do; but I don't like the way my father speaks to you."

"Oh, my dear!" cried the mother, with an affected little smile, "why should I mind? I ought to know by this time that it's only your papa's way."

"I suppose so—but I don't like it," said the young man, decisively. He did not notice, however, as after second thoughts he returned to the game-pie, that his mother's eyes were redder than ever.

CHAPTER III.

MR. COPPERHEAD'S BALL.

THIS ball was an event, not only in Mr. Copperhead's household, but even in the connection itself, to which the idea of balls, as given by leading members of the flock, was somewhat novel. Not that the young people were debarred from that amusement, but it was generally attained in a more or less accidental manner, and few professing Christians connected with the management of the chapel had gone the length of giving such an entertainment openly and with design. Mr. Copperhead, however, was in a position to triumph over all such prejudices. He was so rich that any community would have felt it ought to extend a certain measure of indulgence to such a man. Very wealthy persons are like spoilt children, their caprices are allowed to be natural, and even when we are angry with them we excuse the vagaries to which money has a right. This feeling of indulgence goes a very great way, especially among the classes engaged in money-making, who generally recognize a man's right to spend, and feel the sweetness of spending more acutely than the hereditary possessors of wealth. I do not believe that his superior knowledge of the best ways of using money profitably ever hinders a money-making man from lavish expenditure; but it gives him a double zest in spending, and it makes him, generally, charitable towards the extravagances of persons still richer than himself. A ball, there was no doubt, was a worldly-minded entertainment, but still, the chapel re-

flected, it is almost impossible not to be a little worldly-minded
when you possess such a great share of the world's goods, and
that, of course, it could not be for himself that Mr. Copperhead
was doing this, but for his son. His son, these amiable casuists
proceeded, was being brought up to fill a great position, and no
doubt society did exact something, and as Mr. Copperhead had
asked all the chief chapel people, his ball was looked upon with
very indulgent eyes. The fact that the minister and his family
were going staggered some of the more particular members a
little, but Mr. Beecham took high ground on the subject and
silenced the flock. "The fact that a minister of religion is one
of the first persons invited, is sufficient proof of the way our
friend means to manage everything," said the pastor. "Depend
upon it, it would be good for the social relations of the country
if your pastors and teachers were always present. It gives at
once a character to all the proceedings." This, like every other
lofty assertion, stilled the multitude. Some of the elder ladies,
indeed, groaned to hear, even at the prayer-meetings, a whisper
between the girls about this ball and what they were going to
wear; but still it was Christmas, and all the newspapers, and
a good deal of the light literature which is especially current
at that season, persistently represented all the world as in a
state of imbecile joviality, and thus, for the moment, every ob
jection was put down.

To nobody, however, was the question, what to wear, more
interesting than to Phœbe, junior, who was a very well-instructed
young woman, and even on the point of dress had theories of
her own. Phœbe had, as her parents were happy to think,
had every advantage in her education. She had possessed a
German governess all to herself, by which means, even Mr.
Beecham himself supposed, a certain amount of that philosophy
which Germans communicate by their very touch must have got
into her, besides her music and the language which was her
primary study. And she had attended lectures at the ladies'
college close by, and heard a great many eminent men on a
great many different subjects. She had read, too, a great deal.
She was very well got up in the subject of education for women,
and lamented often and pathetically the difficulty they lay under
of acquiring the highest instruction; but at the same time she
patronized Mr. Ruskin's theory that dancing, drawing, and
cooking were three of the higher arts which ought to be studied
by girls. It is not necessary for me to account for the dis-
crepancies between those two systems, in the first place because
I cannot, and in the second place, because there is in the
mind of the age some ineffable way of harmonizing them

which makes their conjunction common. Phœbe was restrained from carrying out either to its full extent. She was not allowed to go in for the Cambridge examinations because Mr. Beecham felt the connection might think it strange to see his daughter's name in the papers, and, probably, would imagine he meant to make a schoolmistress of her, which he thanked Providence he had no need to do. And she was not allowed to educate herself in the department of cooking, to which Mrs. Beecham objected, saying likewise, thank Heaven, they had no need of such messings; that she did not wish her daughter to make a slave of herself, and that Cook would not put up with it. Between these two limits Phœbe's noble ambition was confined, which was a " trial" to her. But she did what she could, bating neither heart nor hope. She read Virgil at least, if not Sophocles, and she danced and dressed though she was not allowed to cook.

As she took the matter in this serious way, it will be understood that the question of dress was not a mere frivolity with her. A week before the ball she stood in front of the large glass in her mother's room, contemplating herself, not with that satisfaction which it is generally supposed a pretty young woman has in contemplating her own image. She was decidedly a pretty young woman. She had a great deal of the hair of the period, nature in her case, as (curiously, yet very truly) in so many others, having lent herself to the prevailing fashion. How it comes about I cannot tell, but it is certain that there does exist at this present moment, a proportion of golden-haired girls which very much exceeds the number we used to see when golden hair had not become fashionable—a freak of nature which is altogether independent of dyes and auriferous fluid, and which probably has influenced fashion unawares. To be sure the pomades of twenty years ago are, Heaven be praised! unknown to this generation, and washing also has become the fashion, which accounts for something, Anyhow, Phœbe, junior, possessed in perfection the hair of the period. She had, too, the complexion which goes naturally with those sunny locks—a warm pink and white, which, had the boundaries between the pink and the white been a little more distinct, would have approached perfection too. This was what she was thinking when she looked at herself in her mother's great glass. Mrs. Beecham stood behind her, more full-blown and more highly-coloured than she, but very evidently the rose to which this bud would come in time. Phœbe looked at her own reflection, and then at her mother's, and sighed such a profound sigh as only lungs in the most excellent condition could produce.

"Mamma," she said, with an accent of despair, "I am too pink, a great deal too pink! What am I to do?"

"Nonsense, my pet," said Mrs. Beecham; "you have a lovely complexion;" and she threw a quantity of green ribbons which lay by over her child's hair and shoulders. A cloud crossed the blooming countenance of Phœbe, junior. She disembarrassed herself of the ribbons with another sigh.

"Dear mamma," she said, "I wish you would let me read with you now and then, about the theory of colours, for instance. Green is the complementary of red. If you want to bring out my pink and make it more conspicuous than ever, of course you will put me in a green dress. No, mamma, dear, not that—I should look a fright; and though I dare say it does not matter much, I object to looking a fright. Women are, I suppose, more ornamental than men, or, at least, everybody says so; and in that case it is our duty to keep it up."

"You are a funny girl, with your theories of colour," said Mrs. Beecham. "In my time, fair girls wore greens and blues, and dark girls wore reds and yellows. It was quite simple. Have a white tarlatan, then; every girl looks well in that."

"You don't see, mamma," said Phœbe, softly, suppressing in the most admirable manner the delicate trouble of not being understood, "that a thing every girl looks well in, is just the sort of thing that no one looks *very* well in. White shows no invention. It is as if one took no trouble about one's dress."

"And neither one ought, Phœbe," said her mother. "That is very true. It is sinful to waste time thinking of colours and ribbons, when we might be occupied about much more important matters."

"That is not my opinion at all," said Phœbe. "I should like people to think I had taken a great deal of trouble. Think of all the trouble that has to be taken to get up this ball!"

"I fear so, indeed; and a great deal of expense," said Mrs. Beecham, shaking her head. "Yes, when one comes to think of that. But then, you see, wealth has its duties. I don't defend Mr. Copperhead—"

"I don't think he wants to be defended, mamma. I think it is all nonsense about wasting time. What I incline to, if you won't be shocked, is black."

"Black!" The suggestion took away Mrs. Beecham's breath. "As if you were fifty! Why, I don't consider myself old enough for black."

"It is a pity," said Phœbe, with a glance at her mother's full colours; but that was really of so much less importance. "Black would throw me up," she added seriously, turning to the glass. "It would take off this pink look. I don't mind it in the cheeks, but I am pink all over; my white is pink. Black would be a great deal the best for both of us. It would tone us down," said Phœbe, decisively, "and it would throw. us up."

"But for you, a girl under twenty, my dear—"

"Mamma, what does it matter? The question is, am I to look my best? which I think is my duty to you and to Providence; or am I just," said Phœbe, with indignation, "to look a little insipidity—a creature with no character—a little girl like everybody else?"

The consequence of this solemn appeal was that both the Phœbes went to Mr. Copperhead's ball in black; the elder in velvet, with Honiton lace (point, which Phœbe, with her artistic instincts, would have much preferred, being unattainable); the younger in tulle, flounced to distraction, and largely relieved with blue. And the consequence of this toilette, and of the fact that Phœbe did her duty by her parents and by Providence, and looked her very best, was that Clarence Copperhead fell a hopeless victim to her fascinations, and scarcely could be induced to leave her side all night. The ball was about as remarkable a ball as could have been seen in London. The son of the house had contemplated with absolute despair the list of invitations. He had deprecated the entertainment altogether. He had said, "We know nobody," with a despairing impertinence which called forth one of his father's roars of laughter. And though Mr. Copperhead had done all he could to assume the position of that typical Paterfamilias who is condemned to pay for those pleasures of his family which are no pleasure to him, yet common-sense was too much for him, and everybody felt that he was in reality the giver and enjoyer of the entertainment. It was Mr., not Mrs. Copperhead's ball. It was the first of the kind which had ever taken place in his house; the beginning of a new chapter in his social existence. Up to this moment he had not shown any signs of being smitten with that craze for "Society," which so often and so sorely affects the millionnaire. He had contented himself hitherto with heavy and showy dinners, costing Heaven knows how much a head (Mr. Copperhead knew, and swelled visibly in pride and pleasure as the cost increased), which he consumed in company with twenty people or so of kindred tastes to himself, who appreciated the cost and understood his feelings. On such people, however, his Dresden china was thrown away. Joe and Mrs. Joe were much more in their way than the elegant University man and the well-bred mother, who was "a poor little dowdy," they all said. Therefore the fact had been forced upon Mr. Copperhead that his circle must be widened and advanced, if his crowning glories were to be appreciated as they deserved.

The hunger of wealth for that something above wealth which the bewildered rich man only discovers the existence of when he has struggled to the highest pinnacle of advancement in his own way, began to seize this wealthy neophyte. To be sure, in this first essay, the company which he assembled in his fine rooms in Portland Place, to see all his fine things and celebrate his glory, was not a fine company, but they afforded more gratification to Mr. Copperhead than if they had been ever so fine. They were people of his own class, his old friends, invited to be dazzled, though standing out to the utmost of their power, and refusing, so far as in them lay, to admit how much dazzled they were. It was a more reasonable sort of vanity than the commoner kind, which aims at displaying its riches to great personages, people who are not dazzled by any extent of grandeur, and in whose bosoms no jealousy is excited towards the giver of the feast. Mr. Copperhead's friends had much more lively feelings; they walked about through the great rooms, with their wives on their arms, in a state of semi-defiance, expressing no admiration, saying to each other, "This must have cost Copperhead a pretty penny," as they met in doorways; while the ladies put their flowery and jewelled heads together and whispered, "Did you ever see such extravagance? And what a dowdy *she* is with it all!" This was the under-current of sentiment which flowed strong in all the passages, and down the rapids of the great staircase; a stream of vigorous human feeling, the existence of which was as deeply gratifying to the entertainer as the sweetest flattery. The lord and the ladies who might have been tempted to his great house would not have had a thought to spare for Mr. Copperhead; but the unwilling applause of his own class afforded him a true triumph.

Amid this throng of people, however, there could be little doubt that the one young lady who attracted his son was the least eligible person there, being no other than Phœbe Beecham, the pastor's daughter. Almost the only other utterly ineligible girl was a pale little maiden who accompanied Sir Robert Dorset and his daughters, and who was supposed to be either their governess or their humble companion. The Dorsets were the only people who had any pretensions to belong to "society," in all those crowded rooms. They were distantly related to Mrs. Copperhead, and

had been, she gratefully thought, kind to her in her youth, and
they had no particular objection to be kind to her now that she
was rich, though the Baronet, as Mr. Copperhead always called
him, winced at so rampant a specimen of wealth, and "the
girls" did not see what good it was to keep up relations with
a distant cousin, who though so prodigiously rich was of no
possible use, and could neither make parties for them, nor
chaperon them to the houses of the great. When they had
received her present invitation, they had accepted it with
surprise and hesitation. Chance only had brought them to
London at that time of the year, the most curious time surely
to choose for a ball, but convenient enough as affording a little
amusement at a season when little amusement was ordinarily
to be had. Sir Robert had consented to go, as a man with no
occupation elsewhere might consent to go to the Cannibal
Islands, to see how the savages comported themselves. And
little Ursula May, another poor relative on the other side of
the house, whom they had charitably brought up to town with
them, might go too, they decided, to such a gathering. There
was no Lady Dorset, and the girls were "girls" only by
courtesy, having passed the age to which that title refers.
Such good looks as they had were faded, and they were indif-
ferently dressed. This last circumstance arose partly from the
fact that they never dressed very well, and partly because they
did not think it necessary to put themselves to much trouble
for poor Mrs. Copperhead's ball. Their little companion,
Ursula, was in a white frock, the sort of dress which Phœbe
had rebelled against. She was all white and had never been
to a ball before. This little party, which represented the
aristocracy at the Copperhead's ball, went to the entertainment
with a little expectation in their minds: What sort of people
would be there? Would they be "frights?" They were not
likely to be interesting in any other way, the Miss Dorsets
knew; but to little Ursula a ball was a ball, and meant delight
and glory she was aware, though she did not quite know how.
The expectations of the party, however, were strangely disappointed. Instead of being "a set of frights," Mrs. Copperhead's guests were found to be resplendent in toilette. Never,
even under a ducal roof, had these ladies found themselves in
such a gorgeous assembly, and never before, perhaps, even at
the Duchess's grandest receptions, had they been unable to
discover a single face they knew. Sir Robert was even more
appalled by this discovery than his daughters were. He put
up his glass and peered more and more wistfully into the
crowd. "Don't know a soul," he repeated at intervals. Poor

Sir Robert! he had not thought it possible that such an event could happen to him within the four seas. Accordingly the Dorsets clung, somewhat scared, to Mrs. Copperhead's side, and Ursula along with them, who looked at the crowd still more wistfully than Sir Robert did, and thought how nice it would be to know somebody. Unfortunately the Miss Dorsets were not attractive in personal appearance. Clarence Copperhead, though he was not indifferent to a baronet, was yet not sufficiently devoted to the aristocracy to do more than dance once, as was his bounden duty, with each of the sisters. "It seems so strange not to know any one," these ladies said. "Isn't it?" said Clarence. "*I* don't know a soul." But then he went off and danced wtth Phœbe Beecham, and the Miss Dorsets stood by Mrs. Copperhead, almost concealing behind them the slight little snow-white figure of little Ursula May.

Clarence was a very well-behaved young man on the whole. He knew his duty, and did it with a steady industry, working off his dances in the spirit of his navvy forefather. But he returned between each duty dance to the young lady in black, who was always distinguishable among so many young ladies in white, and pink, and green, and blue. The Miss Dorsets and Ursula looked with interest and something like envy at that young lady in black. She had so many partners that she scarcely knew how to manage them all, and the son of the house returned to her side with a pertinacity that could not pass unremarked. "Why should one girl have so much and another girl so little?" Ursula said to herself; but, to be sure, she knew nobody, and the young lady in black knew everybody. On the whole, however, it became evident to Ursula that a ball was not always a scene of unmixed delight.

"It is very kind of you to remember what old friends we are," said Phœbe. "But, Mr. Clarence, don't be more good to me than you ought to be. I see your mother looking for you, and Mr. Copperhead might not like it. Another time, perhaps, we shall be able to talk of old days."

"There is no time like the present," said the young man, who liked his own way. I do not mean to say that it was right of Phœbe to dance with him, especially dances she had promised to other people. But he was the personage of the evening, and that is a great temptation. Mr. Copperhead himself came up to them more than once, with meaning in his eyes.

"Don't be too entertaining, Miss Phœbe," he said; for he saw no reason why he should not speak plainly in his own house, especially to the minister's daughter. "Don't be too entertaining. This is Clarence's ball, and he ought to be civil to other people too."

"Oh, please go away!" cried Phœbe, after this admonition. But Clarence was sullen, and stood his ground.

"We are going to have our waltz out," he said. "It is not my ball a bit—let him entertain his people himself. How should I know such a set of guys? I know nobody but you and the Dorset girls, who are in society. Parents are a mistake," said the young man, half rebellious, half sullen, "they never understand. Perhaps you don't feel that, but I should think girls must see it sometimes as well as men."

"Girls don't use such strong expressions," said Phœbe, smiling, as they flew off in the uncompleted waltz. She danced very well, better than most of the ladies present, and that was the reason Clarence assigned to his mother for his preference of her. But when Mr. Copperhead saw that his remonstrance was unheeded by the young people, he went up to Mrs. Beecham, with a rich man's noble frankness and courage. "I am delighted to see you here, ma'am, and I hope you have remarked how well Miss Phœbe is entertaining my boy. Do you see them dancing? She's been away from you a long time, Mrs. Beecham, as girls will when they get hold of somebody that pleases them. Shouldn't you like me to go and fetch her back?" Mrs. Beecham, with cheeks that were very full blown indeed, and required a great deal of fanning, called back her child to her side at the end of that dance. She scolded Phœbe behind her fan, and recalled her to a sense of duty. "A pastor's daughter has to be doubly particular," she said; "what if your poor papa was to get into trouble through your thoughtlessness?"

"I was not thoughtless, mamma; forgive me for answering back," said Phœbe, very meekly; and she showed no signs of sulkiness, though Clarence was carried off and kept from approaching her again.

Unfortunately, however, when Clarence was removed from Phœbe, he fell into still greater peril. The eldest Miss Dorset and her mother, both of them with equally benevolent intentions, introduced him simultaneously to Ursula May. "The poor little girl has not danced once," Mrs. Copperhead, who had recollections of standing by herself for a whole evening, unnoticed, whispered in his ear, and Miss Dorset spoke to him still more plainly. "We brought her," she said, "but I cannot get her partners, for I don't know anybody." And what could Clarence do but offer himself? And Ursula, too, was a good dancer, and very pretty—far prettier than Phœbe.

"Confound him! there he is now for ever with that girl in white," said his father to himself, with great rage. Dozens of good partners in pink and blue were going about the room. What did the boy mean by bestowing himself upon the two poor ones, the black and the white. This disturbed Mr. Copperhead's enjoyment, as he stood in the doorway of the ball-room, looking round upon all the splendour that was his, and feeling disposed, like Nebuchadnezzar, to call upon everybody to come and worship him. He expanded and swelled out with pride and complacency, as he looked round upon his own greatness, and perceived the effect made upon the beholders. When that effect did not seem sufficiently deep, he called here and there upon a lingerer for applause. "That's considered a very fine Turner," he said, taking one of them into a smaller room. "Come along here, you know about that sort of thing —I don't. I should be ashamed to tell you how much I gave for it; all that money hanging there useless, bringing in nothing! But when I do buy anything I like it to be the very best that is to be had."

"I'd as soon have a good chromo," said the person addressed, "which costs a matter of a five-pound note, and enough too, to hang up against a wall. But you can afford it, Copperhead. You've the best right of any man I know to be a fool if you like."

The great man laughed, but he scarcely liked the compliment. "I am a fool if you like," he said, "the biggest fool going. I like a thing that costs a deal, and is of no use. That's what I call luxury. My boy, Clarence, and my big picture, they're dear; but I can afford 'em, if they were double the price."

"If I were you," said his friend, "I wouldn't hang my picture in this little bit of a hole, nor let my boy waste his time with all the riff-raff in the room. There's Smith's girl and Robinson's niece, both of them worth a cool hundred thousand; and you leave him to flourish about all over the place with a chit in a white frock, and another in a black one. I call that waste, not luxury, for my part."

"I don't want to sell either the boy or the picture," said the rich man, with a laugh. But nevertheless he was annoyed that his son should be such an ass. Miss Smith and Miss Robinson were as fine as their milliners could make them. The first of these ladies had an emerald locket almost as big as a warming-pan, and Miss Robinson's pearls were a little fortune in themselves; but the chosen objects of that young idiot's attentions wore nothing but trumpery twopenny-halfpenny trinkets, and gowns which had been made at home for all Mr. Copperhead knew. Confound him! the father breathed hotly to himself. Thus it will be seen that unmixed pleasure is not to be had in this world, even in the midst of envious friends and the most splendid entertainment which money could supply.

CHAPTER IV.

A COUNTRY PARTY.

"VERY funny, now," said Sir Robert. "I don't know that such a thing ever happened to me before. Give you my word for it, I didn't know a single soul, not one; and there must have been a couple of hundred or so there. Jove! I never thought there were as many people in England that I didn't know."

"How could you know Mr. Copperhead's friends?" said Sophy Dorset. "What I wonder is, that she should have asked us. Not but that it was amusing enough, once in a way, just to see how such people look."

"They looked very much like other people, my dear. Finer, though. I haven't seen so many jewels at an evening party for ages. Very much like other people. Fatter, perhaps, the men, but not the women. I notice," said Sir Robert, who himself was spare, "that City men generally have a tendency to fat."

"They are so rich," said Miss Dorset, with gentle disgust.

She was the quiet one, never saying much. Sophy, who was lively, conducted the conversation. They were all seated at breakfast, later than usual, on the morning after the Copperheads' ball. It was a hazy morning, and the party were seated in a large sitting-room in the "very central" locality of Suffolk Street, looking down that straight little street upon the stream of carriages and omnibuses in the foggy distance. It was not for pleasure that this country party had come to London. Sir Robert's second son, who was in India, had sent his eldest children home to the care of his father and sisters. They were expected at Portsmouth daily, and the aunts, somewhat excited by the prospect of their charge, had insisted upon coming to town to receive them. As for Ursula May, who was a poor relation on the late Lady Dorset's side, as Mrs. Copperhead had been a poor relation on Sir Robert's, London at any season was a wonder and excitement to her, and she could not sufficiently thank the kind relations who had given her this holiday in her humdrum life. She was the daughter of a poor clergyman in the little town of Carlingford, a widower with a large family. Ursula was the eldest daughter, with the duties of a mother on her much burdened hands; and she had no special inclination towards these duties, so that a week's escape from them was a relief to her at any time. And a ball! But the ball had not been so beatific as Ursula hoped. In her dark blue serge dress, close up to the throat and down to the wrists, she did not look so pale as she had done in her snow-white garments on the previous night; but she was at the best of times a shadowy little person, with soft, dark brown hair, dark brown eyes, and no more colour than the faintest of wild rose tints; but the youthfulness, and softness, and roundness of the girl showed to full advantage beside the more angular development of the Miss Dorsets, who were tall, and had lost the first smooth curves of youth. To Ursula, not yet twenty, these ladies looked very mature, almost aged, being one of them ten, and the other eight years older than herself. She looked up to them with great respect; but she felt, all the same—how could she help it?—that in some things, though the Miss Dorsets were her superiors, it was best to be Ursula May.

"Poor Clara!" said Sir Robert. 'She was always a frightened creature. When I recollect her, a poor little governess, keeping behind backs at the nursery parties—and to see her in all her splendour now!"

"She would keep behind backs still, if she could," said Miss Dorset.

"Think of that, Ursula," cried Sophy; "there is an example for you. She was a great deal worse off than you are; and to see her now, as papa says! You may have a house in Portland Place too, and ask us to balls, and wear diamonds. Think of that! Though last night you looked as frightened as she."

"Don't put such demoralizing ideas into the child's head. How it is that girls are not ruined," said Miss Dorset, shaking her head, "ruined! by such examples, I cannot tell. They must have stronger heads than we think. As poor as Cinderella one day, and the next as rich as the Queen—without any merit of theirs, all because some chance man happens to take a fancy to them."

"Quite right," said Sir Robert; "quite right, my dear. It is the natural course of affairs."

Miss Dorset shook her head. She went on shaking her head

as she poured out the tea. She was not given to eloquence, but the subject inspired her.

"Don't think of it, Ursula; it is not the sort of thing that good girls ought to think of," and the elder sister made signs to Sophy, who was reckless, and did not mind the moral effect' of the suggestion.

"Poor Mrs. Copperhead! I shall never have a house in Portland Place, nor any diamonds, except Aunt Mary's old brooch. I shall live and die an old maid, and nobody will waste a thought upon me," said Sophy, who made this prophecy at her ease, not expecting it to come true; "but I don't envy poor Clara, and if you marry such a man as Mr. Copperhead, though I shall admire you very much, Ursula, I shan't envy you."

"Is young Mr. Copperhead as bad as his father?" said Ursula, simply.

She was so far from thinking what meaning could be attached to her words, that she stopped and looked, wondering, from one to another when they laughed.

"Ha! ha! ha!" said Sir Robert; "not so bad, either!"

Poor Ursula was extremely serious. She turned with relief to Miss Dorset, who was serious too.

"My dear, we don't know much about Clarence; he is a heavy young man. I don't think he is attractive. Have you had a letter from the Parsonage this morning?" said Anne Dorset, with a very grave face; and as it turned out that Ursula had a letter, Miss Dorset immediately plunged into discussion of it. The girl did not understand why the simple little epistle should be so interesting, nor did she perceive yet what the laughter was about. To tell the truth, Ursula, who was not clever, had thought young Mr. Copperhead very *nice*. He had asked her to dance when nobody else did; he had talked to her as much as he could have talked to Sophy Dorset herself. He had rehabilitated her in her own eyes after the first disappointment and failure of the evening, and she was prepared to think, whatever might be said about the father, that the son was "very kind" and very agreeable. Why should they laugh? Ursula concluded that there must be some private joke of their own about Clarence (what a pretty, interesting, superior name Clarence was!) which she could not be permitted to know.

"If you talk like that," said Anne Dorset to Sophy, "you will set her little head afloat about good matches, and spoil her too."

"And a very good thing," said Sophy. "If you had put the

idea into my head, I should not be Sophy Dorset now. Why shouldn't she think of a good match? Can she live there for ever in that dreadful Parsonage, among all those children whom she does not know how to manage? Don't be absurd, Anne; except an elder daughter like you here and there, you know, girls must marry if they are to be of any consequence in the world. Let them get it into their heads; we can't change what is the course of nature, as papa says."

"Oh, Sophy! it is so unwomanly."

'Never mind; when a man chuckles and jeers at me because I am unmarried, I think it is unmanly; but they all do it, and no one finds any fault."

"Not all surely; not near *all*."

"Don't they? Not to our faces, perhaps; but whenever they write, whenever they speak in public. When men are so mean, why should we train girls up to unnatural high-mindedness? Why, that is the sort of girl who ought to make a good marriage; to 'catch' somebody, or have somebody 'hooked' for her. She is pretty, and soft, and not very wise. I am doing the very best thing in the world for her, when I laugh at love and all that nonsense, and put a good match into her mind."

Miss Dorset turned away with a sigh, and shook her head. It was all she could do. To encounter Sophy in argument was beyond her power, and if it had not been beyond her power, what would have been the good of it? Sophy had a story which, unfortunately, most people knew. She had been romantic, and she had been disappointed. Five or six years before, she had been engaged to a clergyman, who, finding that the good living he was waiting for in order to marry was not likely to come through Sir Robert's influence, intimated to his betrothed his serious doubt whether they were likely to be happy together, and broke off the engagement. He married somebody else in six months, and Sophy was left to bear the shame as she might. To be sure, a great many people were highly indignant with him at the moment; his sin, however, was forgotten long ago, so far as he was concerned; but nobody forgot that Sophy had been jilted, and she did not forget it herself, which was worse. Therefore Miss Dorset attempted no argument with her sister. She shook her gentle head, and said nothing. Anne was the elder sister born, the maiden-mother, who is a clearly defined type of humanity, though rare, perhaps, like all the finer sorts. She resolved in her own mind to take private means for the fortification and preservation of Ursula, whose position, as elder sister of a motherless family, interested her especially as being like her own; but Anne owned within

herself that she had never been so young as little Ursula
May.

Ursula, for her part, thought very little about the question
which had thus moved her cousins. She thought Mr. Clarence
Copperhead was very nice, and that if she had but known as
many people, and had as many partners as that young lady in
black, she would have enjoyed the ball very much. After all,
now that it was over, she felt that she had enjoyed it. Three
dances were a great deal better than none at all, and to have
that pretty white frock given to her by Sir Robert was no
small matter. Besides, for in this as in other things the uses
of adversity are sometimes sweet, the pretty dress, which no
doubt would have been torn and crumpled had she danced
much, was almost quite fresh now, and would do very well at
Carlingford if there should be any balls there—events which
happened occasionally, though Ursula had never been lucky
enough to go to any of them. And Cousin Sophy had given
her a set of Venetian beads and Cousin Anne a bracelet. This
good fortune was quite enough to fill her mind with satisfaction,
and prevent any undue meditation upon good matches or the
attentions of Clarence Copperhead. Ursula was as different
as possible from Phœbe Beecham. She had no pretensions to
be intellectual. She preferred the company even of her very
smallest brothers and sisters to the conversation of her papa,
though he was known to be one of the most superior men in
the diocese. Even when her elder brother Reginald, of whom
she was very fond, came home from college, Ursula was more
than indifferent to the privileged position of elder sister, by
which she was permitted to sit up and assist at the talks which
were carried on between him and his father. Reginald was
very clever too ; he was making his own way at the university
by means of scholarships, the only way in which a son of Mr.
May's was likely to get to the university at all, and to hear
him talk with his father about Greek poetry and philosophy
was a very fine thing indeed; how Phœbe Beecham, if the
chance had been hers, would have prized it; but Ursula did
not enjoy the privilege. She preferred a pantomime, or the
poorest performance in a theatre, or even Madame Tussaud's
exhibition. She preferred even to walk about the gay streets
with Miss Dorset's maid, and look into the shop-windows and
speculate what was going to be worn next season. Poor little
girl ! with such innocent and frivolous tastes, it may be supposed she did not find her position as elder sister and housekeeper a very congenial one. Her father was no more than
Incumbent of St. Roque, an old perpetual curacy merged in a

district church, which was a poor appointment for an elderly man with a family; he was very clever and superior, but not a man who got on, or who did much to help his children to get on; and had Ursula been of the kind of those who suffer and deny themselves by nature, she would have had her hands full, and abundant opportunity afforded her to exercise those faculties. But she was not of this frame of mind. She did what she was obliged to do as well as time and opportunity permitted; but she did not throw herself with any enthusiasm into her duties. To keep seven children in good condition and discipline in a small house, on a small income, is more, it must be allowed, than most girls of twenty are equal to; only enthusiasm and self-devotion could make such a task possible, and these qualifications poor little Ursula did not possess. Oh! how glad she was to get away from it all, from having to think of Janey and Johnny, and Amy and little Robin. She was not anxious about how things might be going on in her absence, as kind Miss Dorset thought she must be. The happiness of escaping was first and foremost in her thoughts.

CHAPTER V.

SELF-DEVOTION.

" MR. COPPERHEAD's manner is not pleasant sometimes, that is quite true. We must make allowances, my dear. Great wealth, you know, has its temptations. You can't expect a man with so much money and so many people under him to have the same consideration for other people's feelings. He says to this man go and he goeth, and to that man come and he cometh."

" That is all very well," said Phœbe; " but he has no right, that I can think of, to be rude to mamma and me."

" He was not exactly rude, my dear," said Mrs. Beecham. "We must not say he was rude. Clarence ought to have divided his attentions more equally, we must admit, and his father was annoyed—for the moment. I have no doubt he has forgotten all about it long ago, and will be as pleasant as ever next time we meet."

" I am quite sure of it," said the pastor, " and at the worst it was but his manner—only his manner. In short, at the committee meeting yesterday nothing could have been nicer.

He went even out of his way to send, as it were, a kind message to Phœbe. 'I needn't ask if Miss Phœbe enjoyed herself,' he said. Depend upon it, my dear, if there was a temporary annoyance it is both forgotten and forgiven, so far as Mr. Copperhead is concerned."

"Forgiven!" Phœbe said to herself; but she thought it wiser to say nothing audible on the subject. Her father and mother, it was evident, were both disposed to extend any amount of toleration to the leading member. It was he who was the best judge as to what he had a right to be annoyed about. The family party were in Mr. Beecham's study, where the large bust of Mr. Copperhead stood on the mantelpiece, the chief decoration. How could any one be so wicked as to rebel against the influence of so great a personage? Phœbe had her own ideas, but she was wise and kept them to herself.

"And now," said Mrs. Beecham, solemnly, "what is to be done, my dear, about this letter from my good papa?"

Phœbe was standing in front of a book-case, apparently looking for a book. She said nothing; but it was easy to perceive by the erectness of her shoulders, and the slight movement that ran through her, that her attention was fully engaged.

"Ah, yes indeed, what about it?" the pastor said. He put down the pen, which he had been holding in his hand by way of symbol that, amiable as he was, his attention to his womankind was an encroachment upon time which might be more usefully employed. But this was a serious question; he had no suggestion to offer, but he sat and twiddled his thumbs, and looked at his wife with interest suddenly aroused.

"There is a great deal to be thought of," said Mrs. Beecham, "it is not a simple matter of family devotion. Of course if I had no other ties, nor other duties, everything would be easy. I should go at once to my poor suffering mamma."

Mrs. Beecham was a clever woman, but she had not been able to get it out of her mind, owing to the imperfections of her education in youth, that it was a vulgar thing to say father and mother. "But in the present circumstances," she continued, her husband having given his assent to this speech, "it is clear that I cannot do what I wish. I have you to think of, my dear, and the children, and the duties of my position. On the other hand, of course I could not wish, as poor mamma's only daughter, to have my sister-in-law called in. She is not the kind of person; she is underbred, uneducated. Of course she would be thinking of her own children, and what would be best for them. My parents have done all that ought to be expected from them for Tom. Considering all things, what they have to dispose of ought to go to Phœbe and Tozer. But Mrs. Tom would not see that."

"It is very true, my dear; I don't suppose she would," said Mr. Beecham, with an anxious air.

"Mrs. Tom," said his wife, with some heat, "would think her own had the first claim. She maintained it to my very face, and after that what have we to expect? It's us that are Tozers," she said; "as for you, Phœbe, you belong to another family. I put it in my own language of course, not in her vulgar way."

"It is a very serious question altogether," said the pastor, with some solemnity. "I don't see how you can get away, and I don't know what is to be done."

"Whatever is to be done, I won't leave poor mamma in the hands of Mrs. Tom," cries Mrs. Beecham, "not whatever it costs me. She's capable of anything, that woman is. To have her in the same town is bad enough, but in the same house nursing poor mamma! You and I would never see a penny of the money, Henery, nor our children—not a penny! besides the vexation of seeing one's own parents turned against one. I know very well how it would be."

Mr. Beecham ceased twiddling his thumbs. The crisis was too serious for that indulgence. "The position is most difficult," he said, "I see it all. It is easy to see it for that matter, but to decide what are we to do is not easy. To go back to Carlingford after so many changes, would it be good for you?"

"It would kill me," said Mrs. Beecham, with energy, "you know it would kill me. Envy drove us out, and envy would bring me to the grave. I don't deceive myself, that is what I see before me, if I tear myself from all my duties and go. But on the other hand——"

"Listen, mamma!" cried Phœbe, turning round suddenly; "if grandmamma is ill, and you are afraid to leave her alone, why not send me?"

Both her parents turned towards Phœbe, as she spoke; they listened to her with wonder and consternation, yet with admiring looks. Then they looked at each other consulting, alarmed. "You!" said Mrs. Beecham, and "You!" echoed the pastor, repeating in his great astonishment what his wife said.

"Yes, indeed, me—why not me? it would be only my duty," said Phœbe, with great composure. "And there is nothing to keep me from going. I almost think I should like it—but anyhow, mamma, if you think it necessary, whether I like it or not—"

"Phœbe, my darling, you are the best child in the world," cried her mother, rising up, and going to her hastily. She gave her a kiss of maternal enthusiasm, and then she looked at her husband. "But should we take advantage of it?" she said.

"You see, my dear," said Mr. Beecham, hesitating, "you might find many things different from what you are used to. Your grandpapa Tozer is an excellent man—a most excellent man—"

"Yes, yes," said his wife, with some impatience. She was as conscious as he was of the great elevation in the social scale that had occurred to both of them since they left Carlingford, and knew as well as he did that the old people had remained stationary, while the younger ones had made such advances; but still she did not like to hear her husband criticize her father. What there was to be said, she preferred to say herself. "Yes, yes," she said, "Phœbe knows there is a difference; they are old-fashioned folks, and don't live quite as we live. Some things would strike you very strangely, my dear, some things you would not like; and then Phœbe may be, for anything I can tell, at a turning-point in her own life."

"If you mean about the Copperheads, mamma, dismiss that from your mind," said Phœbe. "There is no sort of hurry. We may be thrown together in after-life, and of course no one can tell what may happen, but in the mean time there is nothing of the sort in my mind—nor in any one else's. Do not think of that for a moment. I am at no turning-point. I am quite ready and quite willing to go wherever you please."

Once more the parent pair looked at each other. They had been very careful not to bring their children into contact, since they were children, with the homelier circumstances of the life in which they themselves had both taken their origin. They had managed this really with great skill and discretion. Instead of visiting the Tozers at Carlingford, they had appointed meetings at the sea-side, by means of which the children were trained in affectionate acquaintance with their grandparents, without any knowledge of the shop. And Mr. Tozer, who was only a butterman at Carlingford, presented all the appearance of an old Dissenting minister out of it—old-fashioned, not very refined perhaps, as Mrs. Beecham allowed, but very kind, and the most doting of grandfathers. The wisp of white neck-cloth round his neck, and his black coat, and a certain unction of manner all favoured the idea. Theoretically, the young people knew it was not so, but the impression on their imagination was to this effect. Mrs. Tozer was only "grandmamma." She was kind too, and if rather gorgeous in the way of ribbons, and dressing generally in a manner which Phœbe's taste condemned, yet she came quite within the range of that affectionate contempt with which youth tolerates the disadvantages of its seniors. But the butterman's shop! and the entire cutting off from everything superior to the grocers and poulterers of Carlingford—how would Phœbe support it? This was what Mr. and Mrs. Beecham asked each other with their eyes—and there was a pause. For the question was a tremendous one, and neither knew in what way to reply.

"Phœbe, you are a very sensible girl—" said her father at last, faltering.

"I beg your pardon, papa. I don't think you are treating me as if I were sensible," said Phœbe. "I know well enough that grandpapa is in business—if that is what you are·afraid of—"

"Has been in business," said Mrs. Beecham. "Your grandpapa has retired for some time. To be sure," she added, turning to her husband, "it is only Tom that has the business, and as I consider Mrs. Tom objectionable, Phœbe need not be brought in contact—"

"If Phœbe goes to Carlingford," said the pastor, "she must not be disagreeable to any one. We must make up our minds to that. They must not call her stuck up and proud."

"Henery," said Mrs. Beecham, "I can put up with a great deal; but to think of a child of mine being exposed to the tongues of those Browns and Pigeons and Mrs. Tom, is more than I can bear. What I went through myself, you never knew, nor any one breathing—the looks they gave me, the things they kept saying, the little nods at one another every time I passed! Was it my fault that I was better educated, and more refined like, than they were? In Mr. Vincent's time, before you came, Henery, he was a very gentleman-like young man, and he used to come to the —— High Street constantly to supper. It wasn't·my doing. I never asked him —no more than I did you!"

"Your father used to ask me," said Mr. Beecham, doubtfully. "It was very kind. A young pastor expects it in a new place; and a great many things arise, there is no doubt, in that way."

"Not by my doing," said the lady; "and when we were married, Henery, the things I did to please them! Thank Heaven, they know the difference now; but if they were to set themselves, as I could quite expect of them, against my child—"

"Mamma," said Phœbe, tranquilly, "I think you forget that it is me you are talking of. I hope I know what a pastor's

daughter owes to herself. I have had my training. I don't
think you need be frightened for me."

"No; I think Phœbe could manage them if any one could,"
said her father, complacently.

She smiled with a gracious response to this approval. She
had a book in her hand, which of itself was a proof of Phœbe's
pretensions. It was, I think, one of the volumes of Mr. Stuart
Mill's "Dissertations." Phœbe was not above reading novels
or other light literature, but this only in the moments dedicated
to amusement, and the present hour was morning, a time not
for amusement, but for work.

"Phœbe don't know Carlingford, nor the folks there," said
Mrs. Beecham, flushed by the thought, and too much excited to
think of the elegancies of diction. She had suffered more than
her husband had, and retained a more forcible idea of the
perils; and in the pause which ensued, all these perils crowded
into her mind. As her own ambition rose, she had felt how
dreadful it was to be shut in to one small circle of very small
folks. She had felt the injurious line of separation between
the shopkeepers and the rest of the world; at least she thought
she had felt it. As a matter of fact, I think it very doubtful
whether Phœbe Tozer had felt anything of the kind; but she
thought so now; and then it was a fact that she was born
Phœbe Tozer, and was used to that life, whereas Phœbe Beecham
had no such knowledge. She had never been aware of the
limitations of a small Dissenting community in a small town,
and though she knew how much the Crescent congregation
thought of a stray millionnaire like Mr. Copperhead (a thing
which seemed too natural to Miss Beecham to leave any room
for remark), her mother thought that it might have a bad effect
upon Phœbe's principles in every way, should she find out the
lowly place held by the connection in such an old-fashioned,
self-conceited, Tory town as Carlingford. What would Phœbe
think? how would she manage to associate with the Browns
and the Pigeons? Fortunately, Mr. and Mrs. Tozer had
retired from the shop; but the shop was still there, greasy
and buttery as ever, and Mrs. Beecham's own respected papa
was still "the butterman." How would Phœbe bear it? This
was the uppermost thought in her mind.

"You know, my darling," she said afterwards, when they had
left the study, and were seated, talking it over, in the drawing-
room, "there will be a great deal to put up with. I am silly;
I don't like even to hear your papa say anything about dear
old grandpapa. He is my own, and I ought to stand up for
him; but even with grandpapa, you will have a great deal to

put up with. They don't understand our ways. They are used to have things so different. They think differently, and they talk differently. Even with your sense, Phœbe, you will find it hard to get on."

"I am not at all afraid, I assure you, mamma."

"You are not afraid, because you don't know. I know, and I am afraid. You know, we are not great people, Phœbe. I have always let you know that—and that it is far finer to elevate yourself than to be born to a good position. But when you see really the place which poor dear grandpapa and grandmamma think so much of, I am sure I don't know what you will say."

"I shall not say much. I shall not say anything, mamma. I am not prejudiced," said Phœbe. "So long as an occupation is honest and honourable, and you can do your duty in it, what does it matter? One kind of work is just as good as another. It is the spirit in which it is done."

"Oh, honest!" said Mrs. Beecham, half relieved, half affronted. "Of course, it was all that. Nothing else would have answered papa. Your uncle Tom has the—business now. You need not go there, my dear, unless you like. I am not fond of Mrs. Tom. We were always, so to speak, above our station; but she is not at all above it. She is just adapted for it; and I don't think she would suit you in the least. So except just for a formal call, I don't think you need go there, and even that only if grandmamma can spare you. You must be civil to everybody, I suppose; but you need not go further; they are not society for you. You will hear people talk of me by my Christian name, as if we were most intimate; but don't believe it, Phœbe. I always felt aspirations towards a very different kind of life."

"Oh, don't be afraid, mamma," said Phœbe, calmly; "I shall be able to keep them at a distance. You need not fear."

"Yes, my dear," said the anxious mother; "but not too much at a distance either. That is just what is so difficult. If they can find an excuse for saying that my child is stuck up! Oh! nothing would please them more than to be able to find out something against my child. When you have apparently belonged to that low level, and then have risen," said Mrs. Beecham, with a hot colour on her cheek, "there is nothing these kind of people will not say."

These conversations raised a great deal of thought in Phœbe's mind; but they did not change her resolution. If it was necessary that some one should go to look after her grandmamma, and keep all those vulgar people at bay, and show to

the admiring world what a Dissenting minister's daughter
could be, and what a dutiful daughter was, then who so fit as
herself to be the example? This gave her even a certain
tragical sense of heroism, which was exhilarating, though serious.
She thought of what she would have to "put up with," as of
something much more solemn than the reality; more solemn,
but alas! not so troublesome. Phœbe felt herself something
like a Joan of Arc as she packed her clothes and made her
preparations. She was going among barbarians, a set of people
who would not understand her, probably, and whom she would
have to "put up with." But what of that? Strong in a sense
of duty, and superior to all lesser inducements, she felt herself
able to triumph. Mrs. Beecham assisted with very divided
feelings at the preparations. It was on her lips to say, "Never
mind the evening dresses; you will not want them." But then
the thought occurred to her that to let the Carlingford folks
see what her daughter had been used to, even if she had no use
for such things, would be sweet.

"No, Henery; she shall take them all," she said to her husband. "They shall see the kind of society my child is in;
very different from their trumpery little teas! They shall see
that you and I, we grudge nothing for Phœbe—and I dare be
sworn there is not one of them like her, not even among the
quality! I mean," said Mrs. Beecham, hastily, with a flush of
distress at her own failure in gentility, "among those who
think themselves better than we are. But Phœbe will let them
see what a pastor's family is out of their dirty little town. She
will bring them to their senses. Though I hesitated at first
when it was spoken of, I am very glad now."

"Yes; Phœbe is a girl to find her level anywhere," said the
pastor, complacently. And they forgot what she would have
to put up with in their satisfaction and admiration for herself.

CHAPTER VI.

A MORNING CALL.

SIR ROBERT DORSET and his daughter called, as in duty
bound, upon their relation two days after her ball. "You had
better come with us, Ursula," said Miss Dorset. "Sophy does
not care about visits, and Mrs. Copperhead asked a great many
questions about you. She is very tender-hearted to the——
young." Anne had almost said to the poor, for it is difficult to

remember always that the qualifications by which we distinguish our friends when they are not present, are not always satisfactory to their own ears. "She was like you once, you know," she added, half apologetically. Ursula, who was not in the least disposed to take offence, did not ask how, but assented, as she would have assented had Cousin Anne told her to get ready to go to the moon. She went upstairs and put on her little felt hat, which had been made handsome by the long drooping feather bestowed upon her by Sophy, and the blue serge jacket which corresponded with her dress. She had not any great opinion of her own good looks, but she hoped that she was "lady-like," notwithstanding the simplicity of her costume. This was her only aspiration. In her heart she admired the tall straight angular kind of beauty possessed by her cousins, and did not think much of her own roundness and softness, which seemed to Ursula a very inferior "style;" but yet if she looked lady-like that was always something, and both Sir Robert and his daughter looked at her approvingly as she stood buttoning her gloves, waiting for them.

"If there are other city gentlemen there mind you make yourself very agreeable, Ursula," said Cousin Sophy, which vexed the girl a little. Whether the people were city gentlemen or not, of course, she said to herself, she would try to be *nice*—was not that a girl's first duty? She tried for her part to be *nice* to everybody, to talk when she could, and receive the recompense of pleased looks. To walk with her friends up the long line of Regent Street, with many a sidelong glance into the shop-windows, was very pleasant to Ursula. Sometimes even Cousin Anne would be tempted to stop and look, and point things out to her father. Unfortunately, the things Miss Dorset remarked were chiefly handsome pieces of furniture, beautiful carpets, and the like, which were totally out of Ursula's way.

"There is just the kind of carpet I want for the drawing-room," Anne said, looking at something so splendid that Ursula thought it was good enough for the Queen. But Sir Robert shook his head.

"The drawing-room carpet will do very well," he said. "It will last out my day, and your brother will prefer to please himself."

This brought a little cloud upon Anne Dorset's placid face, for she too, like Mr. Beecham, had a brother whose wife it was not agreeable to think of as mistress in the old house. She went on quickly after that looking in at no more shops. Perhaps she who could buy everything she wanted (as Ursula

thought) had on the whole more painful feelings in looking at
them, than had the little girl beside her, whose whole thoughts
were occupied by the question whether she would have enough
money left to buy her sister Janey one of those new neckties
which were " the fashion." Janey did not often get anything
that was the fashion. But at any rate Ursula made notes and
laid up a great many things in her mind to tell Janey of—which
would be next best.

Mrs. Copperhead was seated in a corner of her vast drawing-
room when her visitors arrived, and her pale little countenance
brightened at sight of them. They were the nearest approach
to "her own people" that the poor soul possessed. She received
their compliments upon her ball with deprecating looks.

" I am sure you are very good—very good to say so. I am
afraid it was not much amusement to you. They were not the
kind of people—"

" I scarcely knew a soul," said Sir Robert; " it was a curious
sensation. It does one good now and then to have a sensation
like that. It shows you that after all you are not such a fine
fellow as you thought yourself. Once before I experienced
something of the same feeling. It was at a ball at the Tuileries—
but even then, after a while, I found English people I knew,
though I didn't know the French grandees; but, by Jove ! except yourself and Mr. Copperhead, Clara, I knew nobody here."

Mrs. Copperhead felt the implied censure more than she was
intended to feel it.

" Mr. Copperhead does not care about cultivating fashionable
people," she said, with a little spirit. " He prefers his old
friends."

"That is very nice of him," cried Anne, "so much the kindest
way. I liked it so much. At most balls we go to, people
come and ask me to dance for duty, pretending not to see that
my dancing days are over."

" She talks nonsense," said Sir Robert. " Clara, I must
trust to you to put this notion out of Anne's head. Why
should her dancing days be over ? I am not a Methuselah, I
hope. She has no right to shelve herself so early, has she ?
I hope to see her make a good match before I die."

" So long as she is happy—" said Mrs. Copperhead, faltering.
She was not any advocate for good matches. "Oh, there is
Mr. Copperhead!" she added, with a little start, as a resounding
knock was heard. "He does not often come home so early; he
will be very glad to see you, Sir Robert. Are you going to stay
long in town, Miss May ? "

" Not long, only till the children arrive," said Anne, looking compassionately at the rich man's nervous wife. She had been quiet enough, so long as she was alone. Now a little fever seemed to be awakened in her. She turned to Ursula and began to talk to her quickly—

"Do you like being in town? It is not a good time of the year. It is nicer in May, when everything looks cheerful; but I always live in London. You will come back for the season, I suppose?"

"Oh no," said Ursula. "I never was in London before. Cousin Anne brought me for a great pleasure. I have been twice to the theatre, and at the ball here."

"Oh yes, I forgot, you were at the ball—and you danced, did you dance? I cannot remember. There were so many people. Oh yes, I recollect. I spoke to Clarence—"

"I danced three times," said Ursula. "I never was at a ball before. It was very nice. Mr. Copperhead was so kind—"

"What is that about Mr. Copperhead being kind? Was I kind? I am always kind—ask my wife, she will give me a good character," said the master of the house, coming up to them. "Ah, the Baronet! how do you do, Sir Robert? I don't often see you in my house."

"You saw us the other evening," said Sir Robert, courteously, "and we have just come, Anne and I, to let Clara know how much we enjoyed it. It was really splendid. I don't know when I have seen so much—um—luxury—so great a display of —of—beautiful things—and—and wealth."

"Glad to hear you were pleased," said Mr. Copperhead, "no expense was spared at least. I don't often throw away my money in that way, but when I do I like things to be regardless of expense. That is our way in the city; other people have to make a deal of gentility go a long way, but with us, who don't stand on our gentility—"

"It is not much to stand upon, certainly, in the way of giving balls," said Sir Robert. "I quite agree with you that money should not be spared when a good effect is to be produced. Anne, my dear, if you have said all you have to say to Clara, you must recollect that we have a great deal to do—"

"You are not going the moment I come in," said Mr. Copperhead. "Come, we must have some tea or something. Not that I care very much for tea, but I suppose you'll be shocked if I offer you anything else in the afternoon. Haven't you ordered tea, Mrs. Copperhead? I can't teach my wife hospitality, Sir Robert—not as I understand it. She'd see you come and go a dozen times, I'll be bound, without once thinking of offering anything. That ain't my way. Tea! and directly, do you hear."

"Yes," said Mrs. Copperhead, in a nervous tremor; "bring tea, Burton, please. It is rather early, but I do so hope you will stay." She gave Miss Dorset an appealing glance, and Anne was too kind to resist the appeal.

"To be sure they'll stay," said Mr. Copperhead. "Ladies never say no to a cup of tea, and ours ought to be good if there's any virtue in money. Come and look at my Turner, Sir Robert. I ain't a judge of art, but it cost a precious lot, if that is any test. They tell me it's one of the best specimens going. Come this way."

"You won't mind?" said poor Mrs. Copperhead. "He is very hospitable, he cannot bear that any one should go without taking something. It is old-fashioned, but then Mr. Copperhead—"

"It is a most kind fashion, I think," said Anne Dorset, who had a superstitious regard for other people's feelings, "and Mr. Copperhead is quite right, I never say no to a cup of tea."

Just then Clarence came in with his hands in his pockets, so curiously like his father in his large somewhat loose figure, as unlike him in aspect and expression, that even the gentle Anne could scarcely help smiling. When he had shaken hands with Miss Dorset he dropped naturally into a seat beside Ursula, who, dazzled by his position as son of the house, and flattered by what she called his "kindness," was as much pleased by this sign of preference as if Clarence Copperhead had been a hero.

"I hope you have recovered my father's ball," he said.

"Recovered! Mr. Copperhead."

"Yes, you think it uncivil; but I myself have scarcely recovered yet. The sort of people he chose to collect—people whom nobody knew."

"But, Mr. Copperhead," said Ursula, "if it was his old friends, as your mother says, how much more noble of him than if they had been fine people he did not care for! As for me, I don't know any one anywhere. It was all the same to me."

"That was very lucky for you," said the young man. "My good cousins did not take it so easily. They are your cousins, too?"

"Oh, yes—they are so good," cried Ursula. "Cousin Sophy laughs at me sometimes, but Cousin Anne is as kind as an angel. They have always been good to us all our lives."

"You live near them, perhaps? Sir Robert has been kind enough to ask me to the Hall."

"No, not near. We live at Carlingford. It is not a place

like the Dorsets'; it is a poor little town where papa is one of
the clergymen. We are not county people like them," said
Ursula, with anxious honesty, that he might not have a false
idea of her pretensions. "I have never been anywhere all my
life, and that is why they brought me here. It was by far the
most beautiful party I ever saw," she added, with a little
enthusiasm. "I never was at a real dance before."

"I am glad you thought it pretty," said Clarence. "I
suppose it was pretty; when the rooms are nice," and he
looked round the handsome room, not without a little complacency, "and when there is plenty of light and flowers, and
well-dressed people, I suppose no dance can help being a
pretty sight. That was about all. There was no one worth
pointing out."

"Oh, there were some very pretty people," said Ursula;
"there was a young lady in black. She was always dancing.
I should have liked to know her. You danced with her a
great many times, Mr. Copperhead."

"Ah!" said Clarence. He was not more foolish than his
neighbours, but it flattered him that his dancing with one
person should have been noticed, especially by a pretty creature, who herself had attracted him and shared the privilege.
"That was Miss Beecham. I did not dance with her above
three or four times. Of course," he said, apologetically, "we
are old friends."

Ursula did not know why he should apologize. She did not
intend to flirt, not having any knowledge of that pastime as
yet. She was quite simple in her mention of the other girl,
who had attracted her attention. Now having said all she
could remember to say, she stopped talking, and her eyes
turned to the elder Mr. Copperhead, who came back, followed
by Sir Robert. There was a largeness about the rich man,
which Ursula, not used to rich men, gazed at with surprise.
He seemed to expand himself upon the air, and spread out his
large person, as she had never known any one else do. And
Sir Robert, following him, looked so strangely different. He
was very reluctant to be so led about, and, as it were, patronized
by the master of the house, and his repugnance took a curious
form. His nose was slightly drawn up, as if an odour of
something disagreeable had reached him. Ursula, in her innocence, wondered what it was.

"Here's the Baronet, Clarence," said Mr. Copperhead, who
was slightly flushed; "and he doubts the Turner being
genuine. My Turner! Go off at once to those picture people,
Christie, whatever you call them, and tell them I want proofs

that it's genuine. I am not the sort of man, by George! to be cheated, and they ought to know that. They have had many a hundred pounds of my money, but they shall never have another penny if I don't get proofs. It ain't pleasant, I can tell you, to hear the Baronet, or any one else for that matter, running down my pictures."

"I did not run it down," said Sir Robert, with another little curl of his nostrils. (What could there be in this grand big house that could make a disagreeable smell?) "I only said that I had seen copies that were so wonderfully good that none but an expert could tell the difference; that was all. I don't say that yours is one of them."

"No; nor no one shall!" cried Mr. Copperhead. "We shall have the experts, as you call them, and settle it. By George! there shall be nothing uncertain in my house. You can tell the men it is Sir Robert Dorset who suggested it. There's nothing like a title (even when it isn't much of a title) to keep people up to their work. Not meaning any disrespect to Sir Robert, I could buy him and his up five times over. But I ain't Sir Robert, and never will be. Say Sir Robert, Clarence, my boy; that'll bear weight."

"It was an unfortunate observation on my part," said Sir Robert, stiffly. "I have a picture myself, which I bought for a Correggio, and which is a mere copy, I believe, though a very nice one. I hold my tongue on the subject, and nobody is the wiser. Anne, my dear, I think we must go now."

"That would never suit me," said the rich man; "holding my tongue ain't my way, is it, Mrs. Copperhead? What! going, after all, without your tea? I am afraid, ma'am, the Baronet is touchy, and doesn't like what I said. But nobody minds me, I assure you. I say what I think, but I don't mean any harm."

"Oh, no," said Anne, drawing herself up, while her father took leave of poor little tremulous Mrs. Copperhead. "We really must go; we have stayed longer than we meant to stay. Ursula—"

"Your little companion?" said Mr. Copperhead. "Ah; you should take care, Miss Dorset, of these little persons. They stand in the way of the young ladies themselves often enough, I can tell you. And so can Mrs. Copperhead; she knows."

He laughed, and both Anne and Ursula became aware that something offensive was meant; but what it was, neither of them could make out. Mrs. Copperhead, whose intelligence had been quickened on that point, perceived it, and trembled more and more.

"Good-bye, dear," she said to Ursula in an agony. "Though we are not cousins, we are connections, through your kind Cousin Anne; for she lets me call her my Cousin Anne too. Perhaps you will come and pay me a visit sometimes, if—if you can be spared."

"Oh, yes; I should be very glad," said Ursula, confused.

She did not understand why Sir Robert should be in such a hurry, when both young Mr. Copperhead and his mother were so kind. As for the other Mr. Copperhead, he did not interest Ursula. But he went down to the door with them in an excess of civility, offering Anne his arm, which she was obliged to take, much against her will; and even Ursula felt a passing pang of humiliation when the footman threw open the great door before them, and no carriage was visible.

"Oh, you are walking!" said Mr. Copperhead, with one of his big laughs.

After all, a laugh could hurt nobody. Why was it that they all felt irritated and injured? Even Sir Robert grew scarlet, and when they were outside on the broad pavement turned almost angrily upon his daughter.

"I tell you what, Anne," he said; "not if it was to save my life, shall I ever enter that brute's doors again."

"Oh, papa; poor Mrs. Copperhead!" cried kind Anne, with a wail in her voice. That was all the reply she made.

CHAPTER VII.

SHOPPING.

NEXT day a telegram came from Southampton, announcing the arrival of the little Dorsets, which Ursula rejoiced over with the rest, yet was dreadfully sorry for in her heart. "Now we shall be able to get home," the sisters said, and she did her best to smile; but to say that she was glad to leave London, with all its delights, the bright streets and the shop-windows, and the theatres, and the excitement of being "on a visit," would be a great deal more than the truth. She was glad, sympathetically, and to please the others; but for herself, her heart fell. It was still winter, and winter is not lively in

Carlingford ; and there was a great deal to do at home, and
many things " to put up with." To be sure, that was her duty,
this was only her pleasure ; but at twenty, pleasure is so much
more pleasant than duty. Ursula did not at all rebel, nor did
she make painful contrasts in her mind, as so many young people
do ; asking why are others so well off, and I so badly off ? but
her heart sank. All the mendings, all the keepings in order, the
dinners to be invented with a due regard for the butcher's bill,
the tradespeople to be kept in good humour, the servant to be
managed, and papa, who was more difficult than the servant,
and more troublesome than the children ! If Ursula sighed
over the prospect, I don't think the severest of recording angels
would put a very bad mark against her. She had been free of
all this for ten wonderful days. No torn frocks, no unpleasant
baker, no hole in the carpet, no spoiled mutton-chops, had disturbed her repose. All these troubles, no doubt, were going
on as usual at home, and Janey and the maid were struggling
with them as best they could. Had Ursula been very high-
minded and given up to her duty, no doubt she would have
been too much moved by the thought of what her young sister
might be enduring in her absence, to get the good of her holiday ; but I fear this was not how she felt it. Janey, no doubt,
would get through somehow ; and it was very sweet to escape
for ever so short a time, and have a real rest. Therefore, it
must be allowed that, when Ursula went to her bed-room after
this news arrived, she relieved herself by " a good cry." Two
or three days longer, what difference could that have made to
those children ? But after her headache was relieved in this
way, the cloud dispersed a little. The thought of all she had to
tell Janey consoled her. She counted over the spare contents of
her purse, and calculated that, after all, she would have enough
to buy the necktie ; and she had all her presents to exhibit ;
the ball-dress, that unhoped-for acquisition ; the Venetian
beads ; the bracelet, " Which is really good—*good* gold ; fancy ! "
said Ursula to herself, weighing it in her hand. How Janey
would be interested, how she would be dazzled ! There was a
great deal of consolation in this thought. In the afternoon her
cousins took her out " shopping," an occupation which all young
girls and women like. They bought a great many things " for
the spring," and " for the children," while Ursula looked on
with admiration. To be able to buy things three months in
advance, three months before they could possibly be wanted,
what luxury ! and yet the Dorsets were not rich, or so, at least,
people said.

" Now, Ursula," said Cousin Anne, " we have made all our

purchases. Suppose you choose frocks for the children at home."

"Oh, me?" cried poor Ursula, forgetting grammar. She blushed very red, and looked, not without indignation, into Anne Dorset's mild eyes. "You know I have not any money; you know we can't afford it!" she cried, with starting tears.

"But I can," said Cousin Anne; "at least, I have some money just now. Money always goes, whether one buys things or not," she added, with a little sigh. "It runs through one's fingers. When one has something to show for it, that is always a satisfaction. Come, this would be pretty for little Amy; but it is you who must choose."

"But, Cousin Anne! Dresses! If it was a necktie or a ribbon; but frocks—"

"Frocks would be most useful, wouldn't they? One for Amy, and one for Janey. I suppose Robin does not wear frocks now?"

"He has been in knickerbockers these two years," said Ursula, half proud, half sorry; "and the worst of it is, they can't be made at home. Papa says, boys' clothes made at home are always spoiled, and the tailor is so dear. Oh, Cousin Anne, are you really, really going to be so very, very good—!"

Mrs. Copperhead came into the shop while they were choosing. Poor little woman! she who trembled so in her own house, how everybody bowed down before her at Messrs. Margrove and Snelcher's! It was all she could do to extricate herself from a crowd of anxious officials, all eager to supply her with everything that heart could desire, when she saw the little party. She came up to them, almost running in her eagerness, her small pale face flushed, and leaned on Anne Dorset's chair and whispered to her.

"You will not be angry, dear kind Anne. You are always so good to everybody. Oh, forgive me! forgive me!"

Ursula could not help hearing what she said.

"There is nothing to forgive you, Mrs. Copperhead."

"Oh, dear Anne! But I am more than myself, you know! He does not mean it; he never was brought up to know better. He thinks that is how people behave—"

"Please don't say anything, dear Mrs. Copperhead."

"Not if you will forgive—not if you will promise to forgive. Poor Clarence is heart-broken!" cried the poor woman. "He is so frightened for what you must think."

"We don't think anything," said Sophy, breaking in; "it is one of our good qualities as a family that we never think. Come and help us; we are choosing frocks for Ursula's sisters.

She has two. What are their ages, Ursula? You, who live in town, and know the fashions, come and help us to choose."

And how respectful all the shopmen grew when the nameless country party was joined by the great Mrs. Copperhead—or rather the great Mr. Copperhead's wife, at whose command was unlimited credit, and all the contents of the shop if she chose. One hurried forward to give her a chair, and quite a grand personage, a "head man," came from another counter to take the charge of pleasing such a customer. Ursula could not but look upon the whole transaction with awe. Mrs. Copperhead was a very humble, timid woman, and Mr. Copperhead was not *nice;* but it was something to command the reverence of all the people in such a grand shop—a shop which Ursula by herself would scarcely have ventured to enter, and in which she felt timid and overwhelmed, saying, "Sir" to the gentleman who was so good as to ask what she wanted. But here Mrs. Copperhead was not afraid. She gave herself up with her whole heart to the delightful perplexity of choice, and when that matter was settled, looked round with searching eyes.

"Don't they want something else?" she said, "it is so long since I have bought any children's things. It reminds me of the days when Clarence was little, when I took such pride in his dress. Come with me into the cloak room, my dear, I am sure they must want jackets or something."

Ursula resisted with pitiful looks at Cousin Anne, and Sophy whispered into Mrs. Copperhead's ear an explanation, which, instead of quenching her ardour, brought it up instantly to boiling point. Her pale little languid countenance glowed and shone. She took both Ursula's hands in hers, half smiling, half crying.

"Oh, my dear," she said, "you can give me such a pleasure, if you will! You know we are connections, almost relations. Let me send them something. Dear children, I wish I could see them. Come and look at the little jackets and mantles. I have often thought, if Providence had given me a little girl, what pleasure I should have had in dressing her. Hats too! I am sure they must want hats. Come, my dear, come and look at them." Ursula did not know what to do. A little pride and a great deal of shyness kept her back, but Mrs. Copperhead was too much in earnest to be crossed. She bought a couple of very smart little upper garments for Amy and Janey, and then, clandestinely taking no one into her confidence, for Ursula herself, and gave secret orders to have them all sent to the Dorsets' lodgings that night. She was quite transformed so long as this transaction lasted. Her languid countenance grew bright, her pale eyes lighted up.

"You have given me such a pleasure," she said, holding Ursula's hands, and standing up on tiptoe to kiss her. "I am so much obliged to you. I could almost think that Clarence was little again, or that he had got a little sister, which was always my heart's desire. Ah, well! often, often, it seems better for us not to have our heart's desire, my dear; at least I suppose that is how it must be."

"I do not know how to thank you," said Ursula, "you have been so kind—so very kind."

"I have been kind to myself," said Mrs. Copperhead, "I have so enjoyed it; and, my dear," she added, with some solemnity, still holding Ursula by the hands, "promise you will do me one favour more. It will be such a favour. Whenever you want anything for yourself or your sister will you write to me? I am always in London except in autumn, and I should so like to do your commissions. People who live in London know how to get bargains, my dear. You must promise to let me do them for you. It will make me so happy. Promise!" cried the little woman, quite bright in her excitement. Ursula looked at the two others who were looking on, and did not know what to say.

"She thinks you are too expensive an agent for her," said Sophy Dorset, "and I think so too."

Mrs. Copperhead's face faded out of its pleasant glow.

"There are two things I have a great deal too much of," she said, "money and time. I am never so happy as when I am buying things for children, and I can see that she will trust me —won't you, my dear? Must we say good-bye now? Couldn't I take you anywhere? Look at that big carriage, all for me alone, a little light woman. Let me take you somewhere. No! Ah, Cousin Anne, you have not forgiven us for all you said."

"We have some other things to do," said Anne, drawing back. As for Ursula, she would not at all have objected to the splendour of the carriage. And her heart was melted by the lonely little woman's pathetic looks. But the other ladies stood out. They stood by while poor Mrs. Copperhead got into the carriage and drove off, her pale reproachful little face looking at them wistfully from the window. It was afternoon by this time, getting dark, and it was a tolerably long walk along the lighted, crowded streets.

"Cousin Anne, I am afraid we have hurt her feelings," said Ursula; "why wouldn't you go?"

"Go!" cried mild Anne Dorset; "get into that man's carriage after yesterday? Not for the world! I can put up with a great deal, but I can't go so far as that."

"She never did any harm," said Sophy, "poor little soul! You see now, Ursula, don't you, how fine it is to marry a rich man, and have everything that your heart can desire?"

Ursula looked at her wondering. To tell the truth, Mrs. Copperhead's eagerness to buy everything she could think of for the unknown children at Carlingford, the manner with which she was regarded in the great shop, her lavish liberality, her beautiful carriage, and all the fine things about her, had brought Ursula to this very thought, that it was extremely fine to marry a rich man. Sophy's irony was lost upon her simple-minded cousin, and so indeed was Mrs. Copperhead's pathos. That she was very kind, and that she was not very happy, were both apparent, but Ursula did not connect the unhappiness with the fact that she was a rich man's wife. Mr. Copperhead certainly was not very *nice;* but when people got so old as that, they never were very happy, Ursula thought, and what had the money to do with it? She looked confused and puzzled at Sophy, wondering what she meant. Yes, indeed, to marry a rich man, to be able to buy presents for everyone, to make the children at home perfectly happy without any trouble to one's self! Could any one doubt that it was very nice? Alas! Ursula did not think it at all likely that this would ever be in her power.

"Poor Mrs. Copperhead!" said Anne, as they made their way along the crowded street, where it was difficult for them to walk together, much less to maintain any conversation. And presently Ursula, keeping as close as possible to her cousin's side, but compelled to make way continually for other passers-by, lost herself in a maze of fancies, to which the misty afternoon atmosphere, and the twinkling lights, and the quickly passing crowds lent a confused but not unpleasing background. She was glad that the noise made all talk impossible, and that she could dream on quietly as they glided and pressed their way through the current of people in Oxford Street and Regent Street, as undisturbed as if she had been shut up in her own room—nay, more so—for the external sights and sounds which flitted vaguely by her, disguised those dreams even from herself. Mrs. Copperhead had once been poorer than she was, a poor little governess. What if somewhere about, in some beautiful house, with just such a carriage at the door, a beautiful young hero should be waiting who would give all those dazzling delights to Ursula? Then what frocks she would buy, what toys, what ornaments! She would not stop at the girls, but drive to the best tailor's boldly, and bid him send down some one to take Johnnie's measure, and Robin's, and even Reginald's; and then she would go to the toy-shop, and to the bookseller, and I can't tell where besides; and finally drive down in the fairy chariot laden with everything that was delightful, to the very door. She would not go in any vulgar railway. She would keep everything in her own possession, and give each present with her own hands—a crowning delight which was impossible to Mrs. Copperhead—and how clearly she seemed to see herself drawing up, with panting horses, high-stepping and splendid, to the dull door of the poor parsonage, where scarcely anything better than a pony-carriage ever came! How the children would rush to the window, and "even papa," out of his study; and what a commotion would run through Grange Lane, and even up into the High Street, where the butcher and the baker would remember with a shiver how saucy they had sometimes been—when they saw what a great lady she was.

A dreamy smile hovered upon Ursula's face as she saw all the little scenes of this little drama, mixed up with gleams of the shop-windows, and noises of the streets, and great ghosts of passing omnibuses, and horses steaming in the frosty air. How many girls, like her, go dreaming about the prosaic streets? It was not, perhaps, a very elevated or heroic dream, but the visionary chariot full of fine things for the children, was better than Cinderella's pumpkin carriage, or many another chariot of romance. Her cousins, who were so much her elders, and who shuddered in their very souls at the thought of poor Mrs. Copperhead, and who were talking earnestly about the children they expected next morning, and what was to be done with them, had no clue to Ursula's thoughts. They did not think much of them, one way or another, but took great care not to lose her from their side, and that she should not be frightened by the crowding, which, after all, was the great matter. And they were very glad to get back to the comparative quiet of Suffolk Street, and to take off their bonnets and take their cup of tea. But Ursula, for her part, was sorry when the walk was over. She had enjoyed it so much. It was half Regent Street and half Carlingford, with the pleasure of both mixed up together; and she was half little Ursula May with her head in the air, and half that very great lady in the dream-chariot, who had it in her power to make everybody so happy. Between poor Mrs. Copperhead, who was the most miserable, frightened little slave in the world, with nothing, as she said, but time and money, and Ursula without a penny, and who always had so much to do, what a gulf there was! a gulf, however, which fancy could bridge over so easily. But the dream was broken when she got indoors; not even the quiet of her own little room could bring back in all their glory the disturbed images that had floated before her in the street.

This was Ursula's last day in town, and there can be no doubt that it was of a nature, without any aid from Sophy's suggestion, to put a great many ideas into her mind.

CHAPTER VIII.

THE DORSETS.

Next day the little Dorsets came, an odd little pair of shivering babies, with a still more shivering Ayah. It was the failing health of the little exotic creatures, endangered by their English blood, though they had never seen England, and talked nothing but Hindostanee, which had brought them " home " at this inhospitable time of the year; and to get the rooms warm enough for them became the entire thought of the anxious aunts, who contemplated these wan babies with a curious mixture of emotions, anxious to be " very fond " of them, yet feeling difficulties in the way. They were very white, as Indian children so often are, with big blue veins meandering over them, distinct as if traced with colour. They were frightened by all the novelty round them, and the strange faces, whose very anxiety increased their alarming aspect; they did not understand more than a few words of English, and shrank back in a little heap, leaning against their dark nurse, and clinging to her when their new relations made overtures of kindness. Children are less easily conciliated in real life than superficial observers suppose. The obstinate resistance they made to all Anne Dorset's attempts to win their confidence, was enough to have discouraged the most patient, and poor Anne cried over her failure when those atoms of humanity, so strangely individual and distinct in their utter weakness, helplessness, and dependence, were carried off to bed, gazing distrustfully at her still with big blue eyes; creatures whom any moderately strong hand could have crushed like flies, but whose little minds not all the power on earth could command or move. Strange contrast! Anne cried when they were carried off to bed. Sir Robert had escaped from the hot room, which stifled him, long before; and Sophy, half angry in spite of herself, had made up her mind to "take no notice of the little wretches."

"Fancy!" she said; "shrinking at Anne—Anne, of all people in the world! There is not a little puppy or kitten but knows better. Little disagreeable things! Oh, love them! Why should I love them? They are John's children, I believe; but they are not a bit like him; they must be like their mother. I don't see, for my part, what there is in them to love."

"Oh, much, Sophy," said Anne, drying her eyes; "they are our own flesh and blood."

"I suppose so. They are certainly Mrs. John's flesh and blood; at least, they are not a bit like us, and I cannot love them for being like her, can I?—whom I never saw?"

The illogicality of this curious argument did not strike Anne.

"I hope they will get to like us," she said. "Poor little darlings! everything strange about them, new faces and places. I don't wonder that they are frightened, and cry when any one comes near them. We must trust to time. If they only knew how I want to love them, to pet them—"

"I am going to help little Ursula with her packing," said Sophy hastily; and she hurried to Ursula's room, where all was in disorder, and threw herself down in a chair by the fire. "Anne is too good to live," she cried. "She makes me angry with her goodness. Little white-faced things like nobody I know of, certainly not like our family, shrinking away and clinging to that black woman as if Anne was an ogre—*Anne!* why, a little dog knows better—as I said before."

"I don't think they are very pretty children," said Ursula, not knowing how to reply.

"Why should we be supposed to be fond of them?" said Sophy, who was relieving her own mind, not expecting any help from Ursula. "The whole question of children is one that puzzles me; a little helpless wax image that does not know you, that can't respond to you, and won't perhaps when it can; that has nothing interesting in it, that is not amusing like a kitten, or even pretty. Well! let us suppose the people it belongs to like it by instinct—but the rest of the world—"

"Oh, Cousin Sophy!" cried Ursula, her eyes round with alarm and horror.

"You think I ought to be fond of them because they are my brother's children? We are not always very fond even of our brothers, Ursula. Don't scream; at your age it is different; but when they marry and have separate interests—if these mites go on looking at me with those big scared eyes as if they expected me to box their ears, I shall do it some day—I know

I shall; instead of going on my knees to them, like Anne, to curry favour. If they had been like our family, why, that would have been some attraction. Are you pleased to go home, or would you prefer to stay here?"

"In London?" said Ursula, with a long-drawn breath, her hands involuntarily clasping each other. "Oh! I hope you won't think me very silly, but I do like London. Yes, I am pleased—I have so many presents to take to them, thanks to you and to Cousin Anne, and to Mrs. Copperhead. I am ashamed to be carrying away so much. But Carlingford is not like London," she added, with a sigh.

"No, it is a pretty soft friendly country place, not a great cold-hearted wilderness."

"Oh, Cousin Sophy!"

"My poor little innocent girl! Don't you think it is desolate and cold-hearted, this great sea of people who none of them care one straw for you?"

"I have seen nothing but kindness," said Ursula, with a little heat of virtuous indignation; "there is you, and Mrs. Copperhead; and even the gentlemen were kind—or at least they meant to be kind."

"The gentlemen?" said Sophy, amused. "Do you mean the Copperheads? Clarence perhaps? He is coming to Easton, Ursula. Shall I bring him into Carlingford to see you?"

"If you please, Cousin Sophy," said the girl, simply. She had not been thinking any thoughts of "the gentlemen" which could make her blush, but somehow her cousin's tone jarred upon her, and she turned round to her packing. The room was littered with the things which she was putting into her box, that box which had grown a great deal too small now, though it was quite roomy enough when Ursula left home.

"Ursula, I think you are a good little thing on the whole—"

"Oh, Cousin Sophy, forgive me! No, I am not good."

"Forgive you! for what? Yes, you are on the whole a good little thing; not a saint, like Anne; but then you have perhaps more to try your temper. We were always very obedient to her, though we worried her, and papa always believed in her with all his heart. Perhaps you have more to put up with. But, my dear, think of poor Mrs. Copperhead, for example—"

"Why do you always call her poor Mrs. Copperhead? she is very rich. She can make other people happy when she pleases. She has a beautiful house, and everything—"

"And a bear, a brute of a husband."

"Ah! Does she mind very much?" asked Ursula, with composure. This drawback seemed to her insignificant, in comparison with Mrs. Copperhead's greatness. It was only Sophy's laugh that brought her to herself. She said with some haste, putting in her dresses, with her back turned, "I do not mean to say anything silly. When people are as old as she is, do they mind? It cannot matter so much what happens when you are old."

"Why? but never mind, the theory is as good as many others," said Sophy. "You would not mind then marrying a man like that, to have everything that your heart could desire?"

"Cousin Sophy, I am not going to—marry any one," said Ursula, loftily, carrying her head erect. "I hope I am not like that, thinking of such things. I am very, very sorry that you should have such an opinion of me, after living together ten days."

She turned away with all the forlorn pride of injury, and there were tears in her voice. Sophy, who dared not laugh in reply, to make the young heroine more angry, hastened to apologize.

"It was a silly question," she said. "I have a very good opinion of you, Ursula. Ten days is a long time, and I know you as if we had been together all your life. I am sure you do not think anything a nice girl ought not to think; but I hope you will never be deceived and persuaded to marry any one who is like Mr. Copperhead. I mean who is not nice and young, and good, like yourself."

"Oh, no!" cried the girl, with energy. "But most likely I shall not marry any one," she added, with a half sigh; "Janey may, but the eldest has so much to do, and so much to think of. Cousin Anne has never married."

"Nor Cousin Sophy either." Sophy's laugh sounded hard to the girl. "Never mind, you will not be like us. You will marry, most likely, a clergyman, in a pretty parsonage in the country."

"I do not think I am very fond of clergymen," said Ursula, recovering her ease and composure. "They are always in and about, and everything has to be kept so quiet when they are studying; and then the parish people are always coming tramping upstairs with their dirty feet. When you have only one servant it is very, very troublesome. Sir Robert never gives any trouble," she said, once more, with a soft little sigh.

"Papa?" said Sophy, somewhat surprised; "but you would not—" she was going to say, marry papa; but when she looked at Ursula's innocent gravity, her absolute unconsciousness of the meanings which her chance words might bear, she refrained.

"I think I must send Seton to help you," she said, " you can not get through all that packing by yourself."

"Oh yes, I am not tired. I have put in all my old things. The rest are your presents. Oh, Cousin Sophy!" said the girl, coming quickly to her and stealing two arms round her, "you have been so good to me! as if it was not enough to give me this holiday, the most delightful I ever had in my life—to send me home loaded with all these beautiful things! I shall never forget it, never, never, if I were to live a hundred years!"

"My dear!" cried Sophy, startled by the sudden energy of this embrace. Sophy was not emotional, but her eyes moistened and her voice softened in spite of herself. "But you must let me send Seton to you," she said, hurrying away. She was excited by the day's events, and did not trust herself to make any further response ; for if she "gave way" at all, who could tell how far the giving way might go? Her brother John had been married at the time when Sophy too ought to have been married, had all gone well—and, perhaps, some keen-piercing thought that she too might have had little children belonging to her, had given force and sharpness to her objections to the pale little distrustful Indian children who had shrunk from her overtures of affection. She went to her room and bathed her eyes, which were hot and painful, and then she went back to Anne in the sitting-room, who had opened the window to reduce the temperature, and was resting in an easy chair, and pondering what she could do to make the children love her, and to be a mother to them in the absence of Mrs. John.

"I have been talking to Ursula, who is always refreshing," said Sophy. "I wonder whom that child will marry. She gave me to understand, in her awkward, innocent way, that she preferred papa. A laugh does one good," Sophy added, slightly rubbing her eyes. Anne made no immediate answer. She scarcely heard indeed what her sister said.

"I think we shall get on after a while," she said, softly. "They said their prayers very prettily, poor darlings, and let me kiss them without crying. After a while we shall get on, I don't fear."

"Anne!" cried Sophy, "you are too much for mere human nature : you are too bad or too good for anything. I begin to hate these little wretches when I hear you speak of them so."

"Hush!" said Anne, "I know you don't mean it. Easton will be very strange to them at first. I could not go to India for my part. A crust of bread at home would be better. Think of parting with your children just when they come to an age to understand?"

"John, I suppose, did not take children into consideration when he went away. You speak as if children were all one's life."

"A great part of it," said Anne, gently. "No, dear, I am not clever like you, and perhaps it is what you will call a low view; but after all it runs through everything. The flowers are used for the seed, and everything in the world is intended to keep the world going. Yes, even I, that is the good of me. I shall never be a mother, but what does that matter? There are so many children left on the world whom somebody must bring up."

"And who are brought to you when they need you, and taken from you when they need you no longer," said Sophy, indignantly; "you are left to bear the trouble—others have the recompense."

"It is so in this world, my dear, all the way down, from God himself. Always looking for reward is mean and mercenary. When we do nothing, when we are of no use, what a poor thing life is," said Anne, with a little colour rising in her cheeks, "not worth having. I think we have only a right to our existence when we are doing something. And I have my wages; I like to be of a little consequence," she said, laughing. "Nobody is of any consequence who does not do something."

"In that case, the ayah, the housemaid is of more consequence than you."

"So be it—I don't object," said Anne; "but I don't think so, for they have to be directed and guided. To be without a housemaid is dreadful. The moment you think of that, you see how important the people who work are; everything comes to a standstill without Mary, whereas there are ladies whose absence would make no difference."

"I, for instance."

"You are very unkind to say so, Sophy; all the same, if you were to do more, you would be happier, my dear."

"To do what? go on my knees to those wax dolls, and entreat them to let me pet them and make idols of them—as you will do?"

"Well, how are you getting on now?" said Sir Robert, coming in. "Ah! I see, you have the window open; but the room is still very warm. When they get to Easton they will have their own rooms of course. I don't want to reflect upon John, but it is rather a burden this he has saddled us with. Mrs. John's mother is living, isn't she? I think something might have been *said* at least, on her part, some offer to take her share."

Sophy gave her sister a malicious glance, but promptly changed her tone, and took up her position in defence of the arrangement, with that ease which is natural in a family question.

"Of course," she said, "your grandchildren, Dorsets, and the heir, probably, as Robert has no boy, could go nowhere, papa, but to us. It may be a bore, but at least John showed so much sense; for nothing else could be——"

"John does not show very much sense in an ordinary way. What did he want with a wife and children at his age? The boy is five, isn't he? and the father only thirty—absurd! I did not marry till I was thirty, though I had succeeded before that time, and was the only son and the head of the family. John was always an ass," said Sir Robert, with a crossness which sprang chiefly from the fact that the temperature of the room was higher than usual, and the habits of his evening interfered with. He was capable of sacrificing something of much more importance to his family, but scarcely of sacrificing his comfort, which is the last and most painful of efforts.

"That may be very true," said Sophy, "but all the same, it is only right that the children should be with us. Mrs. John's people are not well off. Her mother has a large family of her own. The little things would have been spoiled, or they would have been neglected; and after all, they are Dorsets, though they are not like John."

"Well, well, I suppose you are right," said Sir Robert, grumbling, "and, thank Heaven, to-morrow we shall be at home."

Anne had scarcely said a word, though it was she who was most deeply concerned about the children. She gave her sister a hug when Sir Robert relapsed into the evening paper, and then stole upstairs to look at the poor babies as they lay asleep. She was not a mother, and never would be. People, indeed, called her an old maid, and with reason enough, though she was little over thirty; for had she been seventy, she could not have been more unlikely to marry. It was not her vocation. She had plenty to do in the world without that, and was satisfied with her life. The sad reflection that the children whom she tended were not her own, did not visit her mind, as, perhaps, it had visited Sophy's, making her angry through the very yearning of nature. Anne was of a different temperament, she said a little prayer softly in her heart for the children and for her sister as she stooped over the small beds. "God bless the children—and, oh, make my Sophy happy!" she said. She had never asked for nor thought of happiness to herself.

It had come to her unconsciously, in her occupations, in her duties, as natural as the soft daylight, and as little sought after. But Sophy was different. Sophy wanted material for happiness—something to make her glad; she did not possess it, like her sister, in the quiet of her own heart And from the children's room Anne went to Ursula's, where the girl, tired with her packing, was brushing her pretty hair out before she went to bed. Everything was ready, the drawers all empty, the box full to overflowing, and supplemented by a large parcel in brown paper; and what with the fatigue and the tumult of feeling in her simple soul, Ursula was ready to cry when her cousin came in and sat down beside her.

"I have been so happy, Cousin Anne. You have been so good to me," she said.

"My dear, everybody will be good to you," said Miss Dorset, "so long as you trust everybody, Ursula. People are more good than bad. I hope when you come to Easton you will be still happier."

Ursula demurred a little to this, though she was too shy to say much. "Town is so cheerful," she said. It was not Sir Robert's way of looking at affairs.

"There is very little difference in places," said Anne, "when your heart is light you are happy everywhere." Ursula felt that it was somewhat derogatory to her dignity to have her enjoyment set down to the score of a light heart. But against such an assertion what could she say?

CHAPTER IX.

COMING HOME.

THE party which set out from Suffolk Street next morning was a mighty one; there were the children, the ayah, the new nurse whom Anne had engaged in town, to take charge of her little nephews as soon as they got accustomed to their new life; and Seton, the ancient serving-woman, whom the sisters shared between them; and Sir Robert's man, not to speak of Sir Robert himself and the Miss Dorsets and Ursula. Easton was within a dozen miles of Carlingford, so that they all travelled together as far as that town. The Dorset party went farther on to the next station, from which they had still six miles to travel by carriage. They set down Ursula on the platform with her box and her parcel, and took leave of her, and swept out of the station again, leaving her rather forlorn and solitary among the crowd. " Disgraceful of May not to send some one to meet the child. I suppose he knew she was coming," said Sir Robert. And Ursula had something of the same feeling, as she stood looking wistfully about her. But as soon as the train was gone, her name was called in a somewhat high-pitched voice, and turning round she found herself hugged by Janey, while Johnnie, fresh from school, seized her bag out of her hand by way of showing his satisfaction.

" We didn't come up till we could make sure that the Dorsets were out of the way," said Janey, "and, oh, is it really you ? I am so glad to get you home."

" Why didn't you want to see the Dorsets ? They are the kindest friends we have in the world," said Ursula. " How is papa ? Is he in a good humour ? And the rest ? Why did not some more come to meet me ? I made sure there would be four at least."

" Amy and Robin have gone out to tea—they didn't want to go ; but papa insisted. Oh, he is very well on the whole. And Reginald is at home, of course, but I thought you would like me best. Johnnie came to carry the bag," said Janey with a natural contempt for her younger brother. " What a big parcel ! You must have been getting quantities of presents, or else you must have packed very badly, for I am sure there was lots of room in the trunk when you went away."

" Oh, Janey, if you only knew what I have got there ! "

" What ? " said Janey, with quiet but composed interest. It never occurred to her that she could have any individual concern in the contents of the parcels. She was a tall girl who had outgrown all her frocks, or rather did outgrow them periodically, with dark elf locks about her shoulders, which would not curl or *créper*, or do anything that hair ought to do. She had her thoughts always in the clouds, forming all sorts of impossible plans, as was natural to her age, and was just the kind of angular, jerky school-girl, very well intentioned, but very maladroit, who is a greater nuisance to herself and everybody else than even a school-boy, which is saying a good deal. Things broke in her hands as they never broke in anybody else's ; stuffs tore, furniture fell to the ground as she passed by. Ursula carefully kept her off the parcel and gave it to Johnnie. One of the railway porters, when all the rest of the passengers were disposed of, condescended to carry her trunk, and thus they set out on their way home. The parsonage was close to St. Roque, at the other end of Grange Lane. They had to walk all the way down that genteel and quiet suburban road, by the garden walls over which, at this season, no scent of flowers came, or blossomed branches hung forth. There were red holly-berries visible, and upon one mossy old tree a gray bunch of mistletoe could be seen on the other side of the street. But how quiet it was! They scarcely met a dozen people between the station and St. Roque.

"Oh, Janey, is everybody dead?" said Ursula. "How dull it is! You should see London——"

"Ursula," said Janey firmly, "once for all, I am not going to stand this London! A nasty, smoky, muddy place, no more like Carlingford than—I am like you. You forget I have been in London; you are not speaking to ignorant ears," said Janey, drawing herself up, "and your letters were quite bad enough. You are not going to talk of nothing but your disagreeable London here. Talk to people who have never seen it!" said the girl, elevating her shoulders with the contempt of knowledge.

"That time you were at the dentist's—" said Ursula, "and call that seeing London! Cousin Anne and Cousin Sophy took me everywhere. We went to drive in the Park. We went to the Museum and the National Gallery. And, oh! Janey, listen! we went to the theatre: think of that!"

"Well, I should like to go to the theatre," said Janey, with a sigh. "But you told me in your letter. That's what comes of being the eldest. Unless you get married, or something, nobody will ever think of taking *me*."

"You are five years younger than I am," said Ursula, with dignity. "Naturally, people don't think of a girl at your age. You must wait till you are older, as I have had to do. Janey! guess what is in *that?*"

"Your new dress—your ball-dress. If it isn't crumpled as you said, you can't have danced very much. I know my dress will be in tatters if I ever go to a ball."

"I danced as much as I wished. I did not know many people," said Ursula, drawing herself up. "Of course at this time of the year nobody is in town, and we hardly knew any one —and of course—"

"Of course, you only knew the fashionable people who are out of town in winter," cried Janey, with a laugh which echoed along the street. Ursula had not come home from London to be laughed at by her younger sister, she who had been petted by the Dorsets, and whose opinion even Sir Robert had asked on various occasions. She felt this downfall all the more deeply that she had been looking forward to so many long talks with Janey, and expected to live all her brief ten days' holiday over again, and to instruct her young sister's mind by the many experiences acquired in that momentous time.   Poor Ursula! ten days is quite long enough to form habits at her age, and she had been taken care of, as young ladies are taken care of in society; accompanied or attended wherever she went, and made much of.   To find herself thus left to arrive and get home as she pleased, with nobody but Janey to meet her, was a terrible falling-off; and to be laughed at by Janey was the last step of all.   Tears filled her eyes, she turned her shoulder to her companion, averting her head; and this was all poor Ursula had to look to.   The dreary Carlingford street, papa finding fault, everything going wrong, and Janey laughing at her!   To be Cousin Anne's maid, or governess to the little Indian children would be better than this.   For five minutes more she walked on in offended silence, saying nothing, though Janey, like the school-girl she was, made frequent use of her elbow to move her sister.

"Ursula!" the girl said at last, with a more potent nudge, "what's the matter? won't you speak to me?"   And Janey, who had her own disappointment too, and had expected to be received with enthusiasm, burst out crying, regardless of appearances, in the middle of the street.

"Janey, for Heaven's sake—people will see you!   I am sure it is I who should cry, not you," said Ursula, in sudden distress.

"I don't care who sees me," sobbed Janey.   "You have been enjoying yourself while we have stayed at home, and instead of being pleased to come back, or glad to see us—   Oh, how can you be so cold-hearted?" she said with a fresh burst of tears.

Here the other side of the question suddenly dawned upon Ursula.   She had been enjoying herself while the others stayed at home.   It was quite true.   Instead of feeling the shock of difference she should have thought of those who had never been so lucky as she was, who had never seen anything out of Carlingford.   "Don't be so foolish, Janey," she said, "I *am* glad;—and I have brought you such beautiful presents.   But when you do nothing but laugh——"

"I am sure I didn't laugh to hurt.   I only laughed for fun!" cried Janey, drying her eyes not without a little indignation; and thus peace was made, for indeed one was dying to tell all that happened, and the other dying to hear.   They walked the rest of the way with their heads very close together, so absorbed that the eldest brother, coming out of the gate as they approached, stood looking at them with a smile on his face for some time before they saw him.   A slight young man, not very tall, with dark hair, like Ursula's, and a somewhat anxious expression, in correct English clerical dress.

"Has it all begun already?" he said, when they came close up to him, but without perceiving him, Ursula's face inspired with the pleasure of talking, as Janey's was with the eager delight of listening. The house was built in the ecclesiastical style, with gables and mullioned windows, which excluded the light, at least, whether or not they inspired passers-by with a sense of correct art, as they were intended to do. It was next door to the church, and had a narrow strip of shrubbery in front, planted with somewhat gloomy evergreens. The gate and door stood always open, except when Mr. May himself, coming or going, closed them momentarily, and it cannot be denied that there were outward and visible signs of a large, somewhat unruly family inside.

"Oh, Reginald!" cried Ursula. "You have come home!"

"Yes—for good," he said with a half-laugh, half-sigh. "Or for bad—who can tell? At all events, here I am."

"Why should it be for bad?" cried Janey, whose voice was always audible half-way up the street. "Oh, Ursula, something very nice has happened. He is to be warden of the old college, fancy! That *is* being provided for, papa says; and a beautiful old house."

"Warden of the old college! I thought it was always some old person who was chosen."

"But papa says he can live at home and let the house," cried Janey. "There is no reason why it should be an old gentleman, papa thinks; it is nice, because there is no work—but look at Reginald, he does not like it a bit; he is never satisfied, I am sure, I wish it was me—"

"Come in," said Reginald hastily, "I don't want all my affairs, and my character besides, to be proclaimed from the house-tops." Janey stopped indignant, to make some reply, and Ursula, grasping her arm, as she feared, with an energetic pinch, went in quickly. Little Amy had been playing in the little square hall, which was strewed with doll's clothes, and with two or three dolls in various stages of dilapidation. Some old, ragged school-books lay in a corner, the leaves out of one of which were blowing about in the wind. Even ten days of Anne Dorset's orderly reign had opened Ursula's eyes to these imperfections.

"Oh, what a muddle!" she cried; "I don't wonder that Reginald does not care for living at home."

"Oh, I wish papa heard you!" cried Janey loudly, as Ursula led the way into the drawing-room, which was not much tidier than the hall. There was a basket-full of stockings to be mended, standing on the old work-table. Ursula felt, with a sinking of the heart, that they were waiting for her arrival, and that Janey had done nothing to them. More toys and more old school-books were tossed about upon the faded old carpet. The table-cover hung uneven, one end of it dragging upon the floor. The fire was burning very low, stifled in dust and white ashes. How dismal it looked! not like a place to come home to. "Oh, I don't wonder Reginald is vexed to be made to live at home," she said once again to herself, with tears in her eyes.

"I hope you have enjoyed yourself," her brother said, as she dropped wearily into the old easy-chair. "We have missed you very much; but I don't suppose you missed us. London was very pleasant, I suppose, even at this time of the year?"

"Oh, pleasant!" said Ursula. "If you had been with me, how you would have liked it! Suffolk Street is only an inn, but it is a very nice inn, what they call a private hotel. Far better than the great big places on the American principle, Sir Robert says. But we dined at one of those big places one day, and it was very amusing. Scores of people, and great mirrors that made them look hundreds. And such quantities of lights and servants; but Sir Robert thought Suffolk Street very much the best. And I went to two theatres and to a ball. They were so kind. Sophy Dorset laughs at me sometimes, but Anne is an angel," said Ursula fervently. "I never knew any one so good in my life."

"That is not saying much," said Janey, "for none of us are very good, and you know nobody else. Anne Dorset is an old maid."

"Oh, Janey! how dare you?"

"And, for that matter, so is Sophy. Papa says so. He says she was jilted, and that she will never get a husband."

"Hold your tongue," said Reginald fiercely, "if we are to hear what my father says at second hand through an imp like you—"

"Oh, yes," said Janey, mocking, "that is because you are not friends with papa."

"Janey, come and help me to take off my things," said Ursula, seeing that Reginald would probably proceed to strong measures and box his sister's ears. "If you were older, you would not talk like that," she said, with dignity, as they went upstairs. "Oh, dear Janey, you can't think how different Cousin Anne and Sophy are, who are not girls, like us. They never talk unkindly of other people. You would get to think it childish, as I do, if you had been living with Cousin Anne."

"Stuff!" said Janey. "Papa is not childish, I hope. And it was he who said all that. I don't care what your fine Cousin Anne does."

Notwithstanding, the reproof thus administered went to Janey's heart; for to a girl of fifteen, whose next sister is almost twenty, the reproach of being childish is worse than any other. She blushed fiery-red, and though she scoffed, was moved. Besides, though it suited her to quote him for the moment, she was very far from putting any unbounded faith in papa.

"Just wait a moment! See what Cousin Anne, whom you think so little of, has sent you," said Ursula, sitting down on the floor with the great parcel in her lap, carefully undoing the knots; for she had read Miss Edgeworth's stories in her youth, and would not have cut the strings for the world; and when the new dresses, in all their gloss and softness, were spread out upon the old carpet, which scarcely retained one trace of colour, Janey was struck dumb.

"Is that," she said, faltering and conscience-stricken, "for me?"

"This is for you; though you think them old maids—and that they will never get husbands," said Ursula, indignantly. "What a thing for a girl to say! And, indeed, I don't think Cousin Anne will ever get a husband. There is not one in the world half good enough for her—not one! Yes, this is for you. They went themselves, and looked over half the things in the shop before they could get one to please them. They did not say, 'Janey is an unkind little thing, that will repeat all she hears about us, and does not care for us a bit.' They said, 'Ursula, we must choose frocks for Janey and Amy. Come and help us to get what they will like best.'"

Janey's lips quivered, and two very big tears came into her eyes. She was stricken with the deepest compunction, but her pride did not permit her to give in all at once.

"I dare say you told her how badly off we were," she said.

"I told her nothing about it, and she did not say a word—not a word, as if it were a charity—only to please you—to let you see that you were remembered; but I dare say it is quite true after all," said Ursula, with lofty irony, "that Cousin Anne will never get a husband, and that they are old maids."

"Oh, you know I didn't mean it!" said Janey, giving way to her tears.

Then Ursula got up and took off her hat and smoothed her hair, feeling satisfied with her success, and went downstairs again to Reginald, who was seated on the dingy sofa waiting for her, to answer her questions about the great event which had happened since she had been away. Ursula's mind was full of the shock of the sharp impression made by her return, though the impression itself began to wear away.

"I can understand why you don't care about living at home," she said. "Oh I wonder if I could do anything to mend it! I am so glad you have got something, Reginald. If you have a good servant, you might be quite comfortable by yourself, and we could come and see you. I should not feel it a bit—not a single bit; and it would be so much nicer for you."

"You are mistaken," said her brother. "It is not staying at home I object to. We are not very tidy or very comfortable, perhaps, but we all belong to each other, at least. It is not that, Ursula."

"What is it, then? Janey says," said Ursula, drawing a long breath of awe and admiration, "that you are to have two hundred and fifty pounds a year."

"For doing nothing," he said.

"For doing nothing?" She looked up at him a little bewildered, for his tone struck Ursula as not at all corresponding with the delightful character of the words he said. "But, Reginald, how nice, how very nice it sounds! How lucky you must have been! How could it happen that such a delightful thing should come to one of us? We are always so unlucky, papa says."

"If you think this luck—" said Reginald. "He does, and he is quite pleased; but how do you suppose I can be pleased? Thrust into a place where I am not wanted—where I can be of no use. A dummy, a practical falsehood. How can I accept it, Ursula? I tell you it is a sinecure!"

Ursula looked at him with eyes round with wonder. He seemed to be speaking in some different language of which she understood nothing. "What is a sinecure?" she said.

CHAPTER X.

PAPA.

"Ursula has come back!" cried the little ones, who had returned from their tea-party, running to meet their father at the door.

Mr. May was very good, except by moments, to his younger children. He was not, indeed, an unkind father to any of them; but he had never forgiven Providence for leaving him with his motherless family upon his hands, a man so utterly unfit for the task. Perhaps he did not put this exactly into words, but he felt it deeply, and had never got over it. There were so many things that he could have done better, and there were so many people who could have done this better; and yet it was precisely to him, not a person adapted to the charge of children, that it had been given to do it! This seemed to argue a want of judgment in the regulation of mortal affairs, which irritated him all the more because he was a clergyman, and had to persuade other people that everything that happened to them was for the best. He was a man of some culture, and literary power, and wrote very pleasant "thoughtful" papers for some of the Church magazines; but these compositions, though very easy to read, were only brought into the world by elaborate precautions on the part of the family, which scarcely dared to speak above its breath when papa was "writing;" for on such occasions he could be very savage, as the occasional offender knew. He was a man with an imposing person, good-looking, and of very bland and delightful manners, when he chose. But yet he had never made friends, and was now at fifty-five the incumbent of St. Roque, with a small income and a humble position in the church hierarchy of Carlingford. He preached better than any other of the Carlingford clergymen, looked better, had more reputation out of the place; and was of sufficiently good family, and tolerably well connected. Yet he never got on, never made any real advance in life. Nobody could tell what was the cause of this, for his opinions were moderate and did not stand in his way—indeed within the limits of moderation he had been known to modify his principles, now inclining towards the high, then towards the low, according as circumstances required, though never going

too far in either direction. Such a man ought to have been
successful, according to all rules, but he was not. He was
generally in debt and always needy. His eldest son, James,
was in India, doing well, and had often sent a contribution
towards the comfort of the family, and especially to help Reginald at College. But James had married a year before, and
accordingly was in a less favourable position for sending help.
And indeed these windfalls had never produced much effect
upon the family, who heard of James' gifts vaguely without
profiting by them. All this *donna à penser* to the elder children.
Having no softening medium of a mother's eyes to look at
their father through, they were more bold in judging him than,
perhaps, they ought to have been; and he did not take pains
to fascinate his children, or throw the glamour of love into
their eyes. He took it for granted, frankly and as a part of
nature, that he himself was the first person to be considered
in all matters. So he was, of course—so the father, the bread-
winner, the head of the family, ought to be; and when he has
a wife to keep him upon that pedestal, and to secure that his
worship shall be respected, it becomes natural, and the first
article of the family creed; but somehow when a man has to
set forth and uphold this principle himself, it is less successful;
and in Mr. May's case it was not successful at all. He was
not severe or tyrannical, so that they might have rebelled. He
only held the conviction quite honestly and ingeniously, that
his affairs came first, and were always to be attended to. Nothing could be said against this principle—but it tells badly in
the management of a family unless, indeed, as we have said, it
is managed through the medium of the mother, who takes away
all imputation of selfishness by throwing an awful importance
and tender sanctity over all that happens to be desirable or
necessary for " papa."

Mr. May had no wife to watch over the approaches of his
study, and talk of him with reverential importance to her
children. This was not his fault, but his misfortune. Bitterly
had he mourned and resented the blow which took her from
him, and deeply felt the loss she was to him. This was how
he spoke of it always, the loss to him; and probably poor Mrs.
May, who had adored and admired her husband to the last day
of her life, would have been more satisfied with this way of
mourning for her than any other; but naturally Ursula, who
thought of the loss to herself and the other children, found
fault with this limitation of the misfortune. A an who has
thus to fight for himself does not appear in an amiable aspect
to his family, to whom, as to all young creatures, it seemed

natural that *they* should be the first objects; and as they were
a great trouble and burden to him, perhaps the children did not
always bear their most amiable aspect to their father. Both
looked selfish to the other, and Mr. May, no doubt, could have
made out quite as good a case as the children did. He thought
all young people were selfish, taking everything they could, trying to extract even the impossible from the empty purse and
strained patience of their elders; and they thought that he
was indifferent to them, thinking about himself, as it is a
capital sin in a parent to do; and both of them were right and
both wrong, as indeed may be said in every case to which there
are two sides.

"Ursula has come!" cried the two little ones. Amy and
Robin could read their father's face better than they could read
those instruments of torture called printed books, and they saw
that he was in a good humour, and that they were safe to venture upon the playful liberty of seizing him, one by each hand,
and dragging him in. He was a tall man, and the sight of
him triumphantly dragged in by these imps, the youngest of
whom was about up to his knees, was pretty, and would have
gone to the heart of any spectator. He was not himself unconscious of this, and when he was in a good humour, and the
children were neat and tolerably dressed, he did not object to
being seen by the passers-by dragged up his own steps by those
two little ones. The only passers-by, however, on this occasion were a retired shopkeeper and his wife, who had lately
bought one of the oldest houses in Grange Lane, and who had
come out for a walk as the day was fine. " Mark my words,
Tozer," the lady was saying, " that's a good man though he's
a church parson. Them as children hangs on to like that, ain't
got no harm in them."

" He's a rum un, he is," said Mr. Tozer in reply. It was
a pity that the pretty spectacle of the clergyman with his
little boy and girl should have been thus thrown away upon a
couple of Dissenters, yet it was not without its effect. Amy
pulled one arm and Robin pulled the other. They were dark-
haired children like all the Mays, and as this peculiarity is
rare among children, it gave these two a certain piquancy.

" Well, well," he said, " take me to Ursula," and after he had
kissed his newly-arrived daughter, he sat down in the faded drawing-room with much geniality, and took one child on each knee.

" I hope you have enjoyed yourself, Ursula," he said; " of
course, we have missed you. Janey has done her best, but she
is not very clever at housekeeping, nor does she understand
many things that people require, as you have learned to do."

" Oh, I am so glad you have missed me ! " said Ursula, " I
mean sorry; I have enjoyed myself very, very much. The
Dorsets were so kind, kinder than anybody ever was before."

" And, papa, they have sent me a new dress."

" And me too, papa," chirruped little Amy on his knee."

" You too, Mouse! it was very kind of them; and you went to
the Tower and did all the lions, Ursula? that is the lot of country
cousins, and the Dorsets would spare you nothing, I suppose."

" We went to much better things," said Ursula, producing
her theatres and her ball as she had done before. " And, oh,
papa, I like them so much. I wish we lived a little nearer.
Those poor little Indian children, I fear they will be too much
for Cousin Anne; they look so pale and so peevish, not like
our children here."

" Well, they are not pale at all events," said Mr. May, putting them down; " run and play like good children. You will
have heard that we have had something happening to us, even in
this quiet place, while you were away."

" Oh, I was so astonished," said Ursula, " but Reginald
doesn't seem to like it. That is so odd; I should have thought
he would have been overjoyed to get something. He used to
talk so about having no interest."

" Reginald is like a great many other people. He does not
know his own mind," said Mr. May, his countenance overcast-
ing. Ursula knew that sign of coming storms well enough,
but she was too much interested to forbear.

" What is a sinecure, papa ? " she asked, her brother's last
word still dwelling in her mind.

" A piece of outrageous folly," he cried, getting up and
striding about the room, " all springing from the foolish books
boys read now-a-days, and the nonsense that is put into their
minds. Mean! it means that your brother is an ass, that is what
it means. After all the money that has been spent upon him—"

" But, papa, we have not spent much, have we ? I thought
it was his scholarship? " said Ursula with injudicious honesty.
Her father turned upon her indignantly.

" I am not aware that I said we. *We* have nothing to spend
upon any one, so far as I know. I said I—the only person
in the house who earns any money or is likely to do so, if
Reginald goes on in this idiotical way."

Ursula grew red. She was Mr. May's own daughter, and
had a temper too. " If I could earn any money I am sure I
would," she cried, " and only too glad. I am sure it is wanted
badly enough. But how is a girl to earn any money ? I wish
I knew how."

"You little fool, no one was thinking of you. Do a little more in the house, and nobody will ask you to earn money. Yes, this is the shape things are taking now-a-days," said Mr. May, "the girls are mad to earn anyhow, and the boys, forsooth, have a hundred scruples. If women would hold their tongues and attend to their own business, I have no doubt we should have less of the other nonsense. The fact is everything is getting into an unnatural state. But if Reginald thinks I am going to maintain him in idleness at his age—"

"Papa, for Heaven's sake don't speak so loud, he will hear you!" said Ursula, letting her fears of a domestic disturbance overweigh her prudence.

"He will hear me? I wish him to hear me," said Mr. May, raising his voice. "Am I to be kept from saying what I like, how I like, in my own house, for fear that Reginald should hear me, forsooth! Ursula, I am glad to have you at home; but if you take Reginald's part in his folly, and set yourself against the head of the family, you had better go back again and at once. *He* may defy me, but I shall not be contradicted by a chit of a girl, I give you my word for that."

Ursula was silent; she grew pale now after her redness of hasty and unconsidered self-defence. Oh, for Cousin Anne to shield and calm her; what a difference it made to plunge back again thus into trouble and strife.

"He thinks it better to be idle at his father's expense than to do a little work for a handsome salary," said Mr. May; "everything is right that is extracted from his father's pocket, though it is contrary to a high code of honour to accept a sinecure. Fine reasoning that, is it not? The one wrongs nobody, while the other wrongs you and me and all the children, who want every penny I have to spend; but Reginald is much too fine to think of that. He thinks it quite natural that I should go on toiling and stinting myself."

"Papa, it may be very wrong what he is doing; but if you think he wants to take anything from you—"

"Hold your tongue," said her father; "I believe in deeds, not in words. He has it in his power to help me, and he chooses instead, for a miserable fantastic notion of his own, to balk all my care for him. Of course the hospital was offered to him out of respect for me. No one cares for *him*. He is about as much known in Carlingford as—little Amy is. Of course it is to show their respect to me. And here he comes with his fantastic nonsense about a sinecure! Who is he that he should make such a fuss? Better men than he is have held them, and will to the end of the chapter. A sinecure! what does he call a sinecure?"

"That is just what I want to know," said Ursula under her breath, but her father did not, fortunately, hear this ejaculation. Reginald had gone out, and happily was not within hearing, and Mr. May calmed down by degrees, and told Ursula various circumstances about the parish and the people which brought him down out of his anger and comforted her after that passage of arms. But the commotion left him in an excitable state, a state in which he was very apt to say things that were disagreeable, and to provoke his children to wrath in a way which Ursula thought was very much against the scriptural rule.

"Things in the parish are going on much as usual," he said, "Mrs. Sam Hurst is as kind as ever."

"Indeed!" said Ursula with a suppressed snort of anger. Mr. May gave the kind of offensive laugh, doubly offensive to every woman, which men give when their vanity is excited, and when there is, according to the common expression, a lady in the case.

"Yes, she is very kind," he said with a twinkle in his eye. "She has had the children to tea a great many times since you have been away. To show my sense of her kindness, you must ask her one of these days. A woman who understands children is always a valuable friend for a man in my position— and also, Ursula, for a girl in yours."

"She may understand children, but they are not fond of her," said Ursula, with a gleam of malice which restored her father to good humour. He had no more idea of marrying a second time than of flying. He was tenderly attached in his way to his wife's memory, and quite sufficiently troubled by the number of dwellers in his house already; but he rather liked, as a good-looking man in his wane generally does, to think that he could marry if he pleased, and to hold the possibility over the heads of his household, as a chastisement of all their sins against him which he could use at any time. All the Mays grew hot and angry at the name of Mrs. Sam Hurst, and their fear and anger delighted their father. He liked to speak of her to provoke them, and partly for that, partly for other reasons of his own, kept up a decorous semi-flirtation with his neighbour who lived next door, and thus excited the apprehensions and resentment of the girls every day of their lives. When Ursula thought of Mrs. Sam Hurst she wished for the Dorsets no more. It was above all things, she felt, her duty to be here on the spot to defend the family from that woman's machinations. The idea put energy into her. She ceased to be tired, ceased to feel herself, " after her journey," capable of nothing but sitting still and hearing of all that had been done since she went away.

In the course of the evening, however, Ursula took advantage of a quiet moment to look into the dictionary and make herself quite safe about the meaning of the word sinecure. It was not the first time she had heard it, as may be supposed. She had heard of lucky people who held sinecures, and she had heard them denounced as evil things, but without entering closely into the meaning. Now she had a more direct interest in it, and it must be confessed that she was not at all frightened by the idea, or disposed to reject it as Reginald did. Ursula had not learnt much about public virtue, and to get a good income for doing nothing, or next to nothing, seemed to her an ideal sort of way of getting one's livelihood. She wished with a sigh that there were sinecures which could be held by girls. But no, in that as in other things " gentlemen " kept all that was good to themselves; and Ursula was disposed to treat Reginald's scruples with a very high hand. But she did not choose that her father should attack him with all these disagreeable speeches about maintaining him in idleness, and taunts about the money that had been spent on his education. That was not the way to manage him, the girl felt ; but Ursula resolved to take her brother in hand herself, to argue with him how foolish it was, to point out to him that if he did not take it some one else would, and that the country would not gain anything while he would lose, to laugh at his over delicacy, to show him how delightful it would be if he was independent, and what a help to all his brothers and sisters. In short, it seemed quite simple to Ursula, and she felt her path mapped out before her, and triumphed in every stage of her argument, inventing the very weakest replies for Reginald to make. Full of the inspiration of this purpose, she felt that it was in every way well that she had come home. With Reginald settled close by, going away no longer, standing by her in her difficulties, and even perhaps, who could tell ? taking her to parties, and affording her the means now and then of asking two or three people to tea, the whole horizon of her life brightened for Ursula. She became reconciled to Carlingford. All that had to be done was to show Reginald what his duty was, and how foolish he was to hesitate, and she could not allow herself to suppose that *when it was put before him properly* there could long remain much difficulty upon that score.

CHAPTER XI.

PHŒBE'S PREPARATIONS.

A FEW days after Ursula's return home, another arrival took place in Carlingford. Phœbe Beecham, after considering the case fully, and listening with keen interest to all the indications she could pick up as to the peculiarities of her grandfather's house, and the many things in life at Carlingford which were "unlike what she had been used to," had fully made up her mind to dare the difficulties of that unknown existence, and to devote herself in her mother's place to the care of her grandmother and the confusion of Mrs. Tom. This was partly undertaken out of a sense of duty, partly out of that desire for change and the unknown, which has to content itself in many cases with the very mildest provision, and partly because Phœbe's good sense perceived the necessity of the matter. She was by no means sure what were the special circumstances that made "Mrs. Tom" disagreeable to her mother, but she was deeply sensible of the importance of preventing Mrs. Tom from securing to herself and her family all that Mr. and Mrs. Tozer had to leave. Phœbe was not mercenary in her own person, but she had no idea of giving up any "rights," and she felt it of the utmost importance that her brother, who was unfortunately by no means so clever as herself, should be fully provided against all the contingencies of life. She was not concerned about herself in that particular. Phœbe felt it a matter of course that she should marry, and marry well. Self-confidence of this assured and tranquil sort serves a great many excellent purposes—it made her even generous in her way. She believed in her star, in her own certain good-fortune, in herself; and therefore her mind was free to think and to work for other people. She knew very well by all her mother said, and by all the hesitations of both her parents, that she would have many disagreeable things to encounter in Carlingford, but she felt so sure that nothing could really humiliate *her*, or pull her down from her real eminence, that the knowledge conveyed no fears to her mind. When this confidence in her own superiority to all debasing influences is held by the spotless princess in the poem, it is the most beautiful of human sentiments, and why it should not be equally elevated when entertained by a pink and plump modern young woman, well up in all nineteenth century refinements, and the daughter of the minister of the Crescent Chapel, it would be hard to say. Phœbe held it with the strongest faith.

"Their ways of thinking, perhaps, and their ways of living, are not those which I have been used to," she said; "but how does that affect me? I am myself whatever happens; even if poor dear grandmamma's habits are not refined, which I suppose is what you mean, mamma, that does not make me unrefined. A lady must always be a lady wherever she is—Una," she continued, using strangely enough the same argument which has occurred to her historian, "is not less a princess when she is living among the satyrs. Of course, I am not like Una—and neither are they like the wild people in the wood."

Mrs. Beecham did not know much about Una, except that she was somebody in a book; but she kissed her daughter, and assured her that she was "a real comfort," and devoted herself to her comfort for the few days that remained, doing everything that it was possible to do to show her love, and, so to speak, gratitude to the good child who was thus throwing herself into the breach. The Beechams were in no want of money to buy what pleased them, and the mother made many additions to Phœbe's wardrobe which that young lady herself thought quite unnecessary, not reflecting that other sentiments besides that of simple love for herself were involved.

"They shall see that my daughter is not just like one of their common-looking girls," Mrs. Beecham said to her husband; and he shared the feeling, though he could not but think within himself that her aspect was of very much more importance than the appearance of Phœbe Tozer's child could possibly be as *his* daughter.

"You are quite right, my dear," he replied, "vulgar people of that sort are but too ready to look down upon a pastor's family. They ought to be made to see the difference."

The consequence of this was that Phœbe was fitted out like a young princess going on her travels. Ursula May would have been out of her wits with delight, had half these fine things come her way; but Phœbe took them very calmly.

"I have never undervalued dress," she said, "as some girls do; I think it is a very important social influence. And even without that, mamma, so long as it pleases you—" So with this mixture of philosophy and affection all went well.

"We must call on Mrs. Copperhead before you go; they would think it strange, after all the interest they have shown in us."

"Have they shown an interest in us?" said Phœbe. "Of course we must call—and Mrs. Copperhead is a lady, but as for Mr. Copperhead, mamma—"

"Hush! he is the leading member, and very influential in the connection. A pastor's family must not be touchy, Phœbe. We must put up with a great many things. There ought to be peace among brethren, you know, and harmony is the first thing that is essential in a church—"

"I wonder if harmony would be as essential, supposing Mr. Copperhead to come to grief, mamma."

"Phœbe! slang from you—who have always set your face against it."

"What can one talk but slang when one thinks of such a person?" said Phœbe gravely; and thus saying she opened the door for her mother, and they went out in their best gowns to pay their visit. Mrs. Copperhead was very civil to the pastor's family. It was not in her to be uncivil to any one; but in her soft heart she despised them a little, and comported herself to them with that special good behaviour and dignified restraint which the best natured people reserve for their inferiors. For though she went to chapel, taken there by Mr. Copperhead, she was "church" at heart. The interest which Mrs. Beecham took in everything, and the praises she bestowed on the ball, did not relax her coldness. They were too well off, too warm and silken to call forth her sympathies, and there was little in common between them to afford any ground for meeting.

Yes, Mr. Copperhead was quite well—she was quite well— her son was quite well. She hoped Mr. Beecham was well. She had heard that most people were pleased with the ball, thank you. Oh, Miss Beecham was going away—indeed! She hoped the weather would be good; and then Mrs. Copperhead sat erect upon her sofa, and did not try to say any more. Though she had not the heart of a mouse, she too could play the great lady when occasion served. Clarence, however, was much more hospitable than his mother. He liked Phœbe, who could talk almost as if she was in society, as girls talk in novels. He knew, of course, that she was not in society, but she was a girl whom a fellow could get on with, who had plenty to say for herself, who was not a lay figure like many young ladies; and then she was pretty, pink, and golden, "a piece of colour" which was attractive to the eye. He soon found out where she was going, and let her know that he himself intended a visit to the neighbourhood.

"The Dorsets live near," he said. "Relations of my mother. You saw them at the ball. I dare say you will meet them

somewhere about." This, it is to be feared, Clarence said in
something of his mother's spirit, with a warm sense of superiority, for he knew that the pastor's daughter was very unlikely
to meet the Dorsets. Phœbe, however, was equal to the occasion.

"I am not at all likely to meet them," she said with a gracious smile. "For one thing, I am not going to enjoy myself,
but to nurse a sick person. And sick people don't go to parties.
Besides, you know the foolish prejudices of society, properly
so called. I think them foolish because they affect me," said
Phœbe, with engaging frankness. "If they did not affect me,
probably I should think them all right."

"What foolish prejudices?" said Clarence, thinking she was
about to say something about her inferior position, and already
feeling flattered before she spoke.

"About Dissenters, you know," she said; "of course, you
must be aware that we are looked down upon in society. It
does not matter, for when people have any sense, as soon as they
know us they do us justice; but of course you must be aware that
the prejudice exists."

Clarence did know, and with some bitterness; for Mr.
Copperhead, though he did not care much, perhaps, about
religion, cared for his chapel, and stood by it with unswerving
strictness. His son, who was an Oxford man, and respectful
of all the prejudices of society, did not like this. But what
could he do against the obstinate dissentership of his father?
This, as much as anything else, had acted upon the crowd the
night of the ball, and made them all nobodies. He hesitated
to make any reply, and his face flushed with shame and displeasure. Phœbe felt that she had avenged upon Clarence his
mother's haughty politeness. She had brought home to him a
sense of the social inferiority which was common to them both.
Having done this, she was satisfied, and proceeded to soften
the blow.

"It cannot fall upon you, who are in so much better a
position, as it does upon us," said Phœbe. "We are the very
head and front of the offending, a Dissenting minister's family!
—Society and its charms are not for us. And I hope we know
our place," she said, with mock humility; "when people have
any sense and come to know us it is different; and for the
foolish ones I don't care. But you see from that, I am not
likely to meet your cousins, am I?" she added with a laugh.

"If you mean that they are among the foolish ones——"

"Oh, no.; I don't. But you can't suppose they will take
the trouble to find *me* out. Why should they? People entirely

out of my range, and that have nothing to do with me. So you may be quite sure I am right when I say we sha'n't meet."

"Well," said Clarence, piqued, "I am going to Easton, and I shall see you, if Mrs. Beecham will give me permission to call."

"She will give you the address along with that; but till then, good-bye," said Phœbe. To tell the truth, she had no desire to see Clarence Copperhead in Carlingford. Perhaps he meant something, perhaps he did not—at this stage of the proceedings it was a matter of indifference to Phœbe, who certainly had not allowed "her affections" to become engaged. If he did mean anything, was it likely that he could support unmoved the grandfather and grandmother who were, or had been, "in trade?" On the other hand, was it not better that he should know the worst? Phœbe was no husband-hunter. She contemplated the issue with calm and composure, however it might turn out.

"He asked me if he might call," said Mrs. Beecham, in some excitement. "I don't care much to have you seen, my darling, out of your own father's house."

"Just as you please, mamma—just as it suits best," said Phœbe, dismissing the subject. She was not anxious. A good deal depended on whether he meant anything or nothing, but even that did not conclude the subject, for she had not made up her own mind.

"Why didn't you tell them about the Mays?" said Clarence, as the two ladies went out. "They live in Carlingford, and I should think it would be pleasant on both sides."

"My dear boy, you forget the difference of position," said Mrs. Copperhead. "They are Dissenters."

"Oh, I like that," cried Clarence, half angry, as himself sharing the disadvantages of the connection. "A needy beggar like May has a great deal to stand upon. I like that."

"But it is true all the same," said Mrs. Copperhead, shaking her head. "And you can see the difference at once. I dare say Miss Beecham is a very clever young woman, but between her and Miss May what a difference there is! Any one can see it—"

"I am afraid then I am stupid, for I can't see it, mother. They are both pretty girls, but for amusing you and that sort of thing give me Phœbe. She is worth twenty of the other. As sharp as a needle, and plenty to say for herself. This is the kind of girl I like."

"I am very sorry for it. I hope that is not the kind of wife you will like," said Mrs. Copperhead, with a sigh.

" Oh, wife! they haven't a penny, either the one or the other," said Clarence, with delightful openness, " and we may be sure that would not suit the governor even if it suited me."

In the mean time Mrs. Beecham and Phœbe were walking up the broad pavement of Portland Place towards their home.

" It is pleasant to see the mother and the son together," said Mrs. Beecham, who was determined to see everything in the best light that concerned the Copperheads. " They are so devoted to each other, and, Phœbe, dear—I don't like to talk in this way to a sensible girl like you, but you must see it with your own eyes. You have certainly made a great impression upon Clarence Copperhead. When he said he hoped to see you in Carlingford, and asked, might he call? it was exactly like asking my permission to pay you his addresses; it is very flattering, but it is embarrassing as well."

" I do not feel particularly flattered, mamma; and I think if I were you I would not give him the address."

Mrs. Beecham looked anxiously in her daughter's face.

" Is it from prudence, Phœbe, or is it that you don't like him, that you wouldn't have him if he asked you? "

" We must wait till he does ask me," said Phœbe, decisively. " Till then I can't possibly tell. But I don't want him at Carlingford. I know that grandpapa and grandmamma are— in trade."

" Yes, dear," said Mrs. Beecham, in a subdued voice.

" Dissenters, and in trade; and he is going to stay with the Dorsets, fine county people. Don't give him the address; if we meet by chance, there is no harm done. I am not ashamed of any one belonging to me. But you can say that you don't think his father would like him to be visiting me at Carlingford —which I am sure would be quite true."

" Indeed he might go much farther without finding any one so well worth visiting," said the mother, indignant, to which Phœbe nodded her head in tranquil assent.

" That is neither here nor there," she said; " you can always tell him so, and that will please Mr. Copperhead, if ever he comes to bear of it. He thought at one time that I was too entertaining. One knows what that means. I should like him to see how little I cared."

" But, my dear, Clarence Copperhead would be worth—a little attention. He could give a girl—a very nice position," Mrs. Beecham faltered, looking at her daughter between every word.

" I am not saying anything against Clarence Copperhead," said Phœbe, with composure, " but I should like his dear papa to know how little I care, and that you have refused him my address."

This was all she said on the subject. Phœbe was quite ready to allow that Clarence was everything that her mother had said, and she had fully worked out her own theory on marriage, which will probably be hereafter expounded in these pages, so that she was not at all shocked by having his advantages thus pointed out to her. But there was no hurry, she said to herself. If it was not Clarence Copperhead, it would be some one else, and why should she, at this early stage of her career, attempt to precipitate the designs of Providence? She had plenty of time before her, and was in no hurry for any change; and a genuine touch of nature in her heart made her anxious for an opportunity of showing her independence to that arrogant and offensive "leading member," who made the life of the office-bearers in the Crescent a burden to them. If she could only so drive him into a corner, that he should be obliged to come to her in his despair, and beg her to accept his son's hand to save him from going off in a galloping consumption, that would have been a triumph after Phœbe's heart. To be sure this was a perfectly vain and wildly romantic hope—it was the only bit of wild and girlish romance in the bosom of a very well-educated, well-intentioned, and sensible young woman. She had seen her parents put up with the arrogance of the millionnaire for a long time without rebelling any more than they did; but Mr. Copperhead had gone further than Phœbe could bear; and thoroughly as she understood her own position, and all its interests, this one vain fancy had found a footing in her mind. If she could but humble him and make him sue to her. It was not likely, but for such a triumph the sensible Phœbe would have done much. It was the one point on which she was silly, but on that she was as silly as any cynic could desire.

And thus with a huge trunk full of charming dresses, a dressing-case fit for any bride, the prettiest travelling costume imaginable, and everything about her fit, Mrs. Beecham fondly thought, for a duke's daughter, Phœbe junior took her departure, to be the comfort of her grandmamma, and to dazzle Carlingford. Her fond parents accompanied her to the station and placed her in a carriage, and fee'd a guard heavily to take care of and watch over her. "Not but that Phœbe might be safely trusted to take care of herself anywhere," they said. In which expression of their pride in their daughter, the observant reader may see a proof of their own origin from the humbler classes. They would probably have prided themselves on her timidity and helplessness had they been a little better born.

CHAPTER XII.

GRANGE LANE.

Mr. and Mrs. Tozer had retired from business several years before. They had given up the shop with its long established connection, and all its advantages, to Tom, their son, finding themselves to have enough to live upon in ease, and indeed luxury; and though Mrs. Tozer found the house in Grange Lane shut in by the garden walls to be much duller than her rooms over the shop in High Street, where she saw everything that was going on, yet the increase in gentility was unquestionable. The house which they were fortunate enough to secure in this desirable locality had been once in the occupation of Lady Weston, and there was accordingly an aroma of high life about it, although somebody less important had lived in it in the mean time, and it had fallen into a state of considerable dilapidation, which naturally made it cheaper. Mr. Tozer had solidly repaired all that was necessary for comfort, but he had not done anything in those external points of paint and decoration, which tells so much in the aspect of a house. Lady Weston's taste had been florid, and the walls continued as she had left them, painted and papered with faded wreaths, which were apt to look dissipated, as they ought to have been refreshed and renewed years before. But outside, where the wreaths do not fade, there was a delightful garden charmingly laid out, in which Lady Weston had once held her garden parties, and where the crocuses and other spring bulbs, which had been put in with a lavish hand, during Lady Weston's extravagant reign, had already begun to blow. The violets were peeping out from among their leaves on a sheltered bank, and Christmas roses, overblown, making a great show with their great white stars, in a corner. Tozer himself soon took a great interest in this little domain out of doors, and was for ever pottering about the flowers, obeying, with the servility of ignorance, the gardener's injunctions. Mrs. Tozer, however, who was in weak health, and consequently permitted to be somewhat cross and contradictory, regretted the High Street.

"Talk of a garden," she said, "a thing as never changes except according to the seasons! Up in the town there was never a day the same, something always happening—Soldiers marching through, or Punch and Judy, or a row at the least. It is the cheerfullest place in the whole world, I do believe; shut up here may do for the gentry, but I likes the streets and what's going on. You may call me vulgar if you please, but so I do."

Tozer prudently said nothing to such outbursts except a soothing exhortation to wait till summer, when she would find the benefit of the fresh air, not to speak of the early vegetables; and he himself found the garden an unspeakable resource. At first, indeed, he would stroll up to the shop of a morning, especially if any new consignment of first-rate York hams, or cheese, was coming in, which he loved to turn over and test by smell and touch; but by and by the ancient butterman made a discovery, such as we are all apt to make when we get old and step out of the high road of life. He found out that his son did not appreciate his advice, and that Mrs. Tom cared still less for his frequent appearances. Indeed, he himself once saw her bounce out of the shop as he entered, exclaiming audibly, "Here's that fussy old man again." Tozer was an old man, it is true, but nobody (under eighty) cares to have the epithet flung in his teeth; and to be in the way is always unpleasant. He had self-command enough to say nothing about it, except in a very modified shape to his wife, who was ready enough to believe anything unpleasant about Mrs. Tom; but he took to gardening with ardour from that day; and learned all about the succession of the flowers, and how long one set lasted, and which kind should be put into the ground next. He would even take off his coat and do a tolerable day's work under the gardener's direction, to the great advantage of his health and temper, while Mrs. Tozer grumbled upstairs. She was getting more and more helpless about the house, unable to see after the stout maid-of-all-work, who in her turn grumbled much at the large house, for which one maid was not enough. Many altercations took place in consequence between the mistress and servant.

"The ungrateful hussy hasn't even as many rooms to do as she had in the High Street, when there was the 'prentices' beds to make," Mrs. Tozer said indignantly to her husband; but Jane on her side pointed to the length of passage, the stairs, the dining and drawing-rooms, where there had once only been a parlour.

"Cook and 'ousemaid's little enough," said Jane; "there did ought to be a man in this kind of 'ouse; but as there's only two in family, . shouldn't say nothing if I had a girl under me."

Things were gravitating towards this girl at the time of Phœbe's arrival; but nothing had as yet been finally decided upon. Jane, however, had bestirred herself to get the young lady's room ready with something like alacrity. A young person coming to the house promised a little movement and change, which was always something, and Jane had no doubt that Phœbe would be on her side in respect to the "girl." "She'll want waiting upon, and there'll always be sending of errands," Jane said to herself. She knew by experience " what young 'uns is in a house."

There was something, perhaps, in all the preparations for her departure which had thrown dust in Phœbe Beecham's eyes. She had been too sharp-sighted not to see into her mother's qualms and hesitations about her visit to Carlingford, and the repeated warnings of both parents as to the " difference from what she had been accustomed to;" and she thought she had fully prepared herself for what she was to encounter. But probably the elaborate outfit provided by her mother and the importance attached to her journey had to some degree obliterated this impression, for it is certain that when Phœbe saw an old man in a shabby coat, with a wisp of a large white neckcloth round his throat, watching anxiously for the arrival of the train as it came up, she sustained a shock which she had not anticipated. It was about five years since she had seen her grandfather, an interval due to hazard rather than purpose, though, on the whole, the elder Beechams had not been sorry to keep their parents and their children apart. Phœbe, how-ever, knew her grandfather perfectly well as soon as she saw him, though he had not perceived her, and was wandering anxiously up and down in search of her. She held back in her corner for the moment, to overcome the shock. Yes, there could be no doubt about it; there he was, he whom she was going to visit, under whose auspices she was about to appear in Carlingford. He was not even like an old Dissenting minister, which had been her childish notion of him. He looked neither more nor less than what he was, an old shopkeeper, very decent and respectable, but a little shabby and greasy, like the men whose weekly bills she had been accustomed to pay for her mother. She felt an instant conviction that he would call her " Ma'am," if she went up to him, and think her one of the quality. Poor Phœbe! she sat back in her corner and gave a gasp of horror and dismay, but having done this, she was her-self again. She gave herself a shake, like one who is about to take a plunge, rose lightly to her feet, took up her bag, and stepped out of the carriage, just as Mr. Tozer strolled anxiously past for the third time.

"Grandpapa!" she cried with a smile. Mr. Tozer was almost as much taken aback by this apparition as Phœbe herself had been. He knew that his daughter had made great strides in social elevation, and that her children, when he had seen them last, had been quite like "gentlefolk's children;" but to see this young princess step forth graciously out of a first-class carriage, and address him as "grandpapa," took away his breath.

"Why—why—why, Miss! you ain't little Phœbe?" he cried, scared out of his seven senses, as he afterwards said.

"Yes, indeed, I am little Phœbe," she said, coming up and kissing him dutifully. She was half-disgusted, he half-frightened; but yet it was right, and Phœbe did it. "I have only two boxes and a bag," she said, "besides my dressing-case. If you will get a cab, grandpapa, I will go and see after the luggage."

Old Tozer thought he could have carried the bag himself, and left the boxes to follow; but he succumbed humbly and obeyed.

"She don't seem a bit proud," he said to himself; "but, good Lord, what'll she ever say to my old woman?"

He saw the contrast very clearly between his wife and this splendid grandchild. It did not strike him so much in his own case.

"How is grandmamma?" said Phœbe, blandly; "better, I hope? Mamma was so sorry not to come herself; but you know, of course, she has a great many things to do. People in town are obliged to keep up certain appearances. You are a great deal better off in the country, grandpapa."

"Lord bless you, my dear, do you call Carlingford the country?" said Mr. Tozer. "That is all you know about it. Your granny and I are humble folks, but the new minister at Salem is one as keeps up appearances with the best. Your mother was always inclined for that. I hope she has not brought you up too fine for the likes of us."

"I hope not, indeed," said Phœbe. "No fear of my being too fine for my duty, grandpapa. Do you live down this nice road? How pretty it is! how delightful these gardens must be in summer. I beg your pardon for calling it the country. It is so quiet and so nice, it seems the country to me."

"Ah, to be sure; brought up in the London smoke," said Mr. Tozer. "I don't suppose, now, you see a bit of green from year's end to year's end? Very bad for the 'ealth, that is;

but I can't say you look poorly on it. Your colour's fresh, so was your mother's before you. To be sure, she wasn't cooped up like you."

" Oh, we do get a little fresh air sometimes—in the parks, for instance," said Phœbe. She was somewhat piqued by the idea that she was supposed to live in London smoke.

" Ah, the parks are always something ; but I suppose it takes you a day's journey to get at them," said Mr. Tozer, shaking his head. " You mustn't mind your grandmother's temper just at first, my dear. She's old, poor soul, and she ain't well, and she's sometimes cross above a bit. But she'll be that proud of you, she won't know if she's on her 'eels or 'er 'ead ; and as for a cross word now and again, I hope as you won't mind—"

" I shan't mind anything, grandpapa," said Phœbe, sweetly, " so long as I can be of use."

And these were, indeed, the dutiful sentiments with which she made her entry upon this passage in her life, not minding anything but to be of use. The first glimpse of old Tozer, indeed, made it quite evident to Phœbe that nothing but duty could be within her reach. Pleasure, friends, society, the thought of all such delights must be abandoned. And as for Clarence Copperhead and the Miss Dorsets, the notion of meeting or receiving them was too absurd. But Duty remained, and Phœbe felt herself capable of the sacrifice demanded from her. That confidence in herself which we have already indicated as a marked feature in her character, gave her the consoling certainty that she could not suffer from association with her humble relations. Whosoever saw her must do her justice, and that serene conviction preserved her from all the throes of uneasy pride which afflict inferior minds in similar circumstances. She had no wish to exhibit her grandfather and grandmother in their lowliness, nor to be ostentatious of her homely origin, as some people are in the very soreness of wounded pride ; but if hazard produced the butterman in the midst of the finest of her acquaintances, Phœbe would still have been perfectly at her ease. She would be herself, whatever happened.

In the mean time, however, it was apparent that Duty was what she had to look to ; Duty, and that alone. She had come here, not to amuse herself, not to please herself, but to do her duty ; and having thus concluded upon her object, she felt comparatively happy, and at her ease.

Mrs. Tozer had put on her best cap, which was a very gorgeous creation. She had dressed herself as if for a party, with a large brooch, enclosing a curl of various coloured hair cut

from the heads of her children in early life, which fastened a
large worked collar over a dress of copper-coloured silk, and
she rustled and shook a good deal as she came downstairs into
the garden to meet her grandchild, with some excitement and
sense of the "difference" which could not but be felt on one
side as well as on the other. She, too, was somewhat frightened
by the appearance of the young lady, who was her Phœbe's
child, yet was so unlike any other scion of the Tozer race; and
felt greatly disposed to curtsey and say "Ma'am" to her.

"You've grown a deal and changed a deal since I saw you
last," she said, restraining this impression, and receiving
Phœbe's kiss with gratified, yet awe-struck feeling; and then
her respectful alarm getting too much for her, she added, faltering, "You'll find us but humble folks; perhaps not altogether what you've been used to—"

Phœbe did not think it expedient to make any reply to this
outburst of humility.

"Grandmamma, I am afraid you have over-exerted yourself,
coming downstairs to meet me," she said, taking the old lady's
hand, and drawing it within her arm. "Yes, I have grown; I
am tall enough to be of some use; but you must not treat me
as if I were a stranger. No, no; never mind my room. I am
not tired; the journey is nothing. Let me take you back to
your chair and make you comfortable. I feel myself quite at
home already. The only odd thing is that I have never been
here before."

"Ah, my dear, your mother thought too much of you to
send you to the likes of us; that's the secret of it. She was
always fond of fine folks, was my Phœbe; and I don't blame
her, bringing you up quite the lady as she's done."

"You must not find fault with mamma," said Phœbe, smiling.
"What a nice cozy room! This is the dining-room, I suppose;
and here is your cushion, and your footstool at this nice window.
How pleasant it is, with the crocuses in all the borders already!
I am not at all tired; but I am sure it must be tea-time, and I
should so like a cup of tea."

"We thought," said Mrs. Tozer, "as perhaps you mightn't
be used to tea at this time of day."

"Oh, it is the right time; it is the fashionable hour," said
Phœbe; "everybody has tea at five. I will run upstairs first,
and take off my hat, and make myself tidy. Jane—is that her
name?—don't trouble, grandmamma; Jane will show me the
way."

"Well?" said Mr. Tozer to Mrs. Tozer, as Phœbe disappeared. The two old people looked at each other with a little

awe; but she, as was her nature, took the most depressing view. She shook her head.

"She is a deal too fine for us, Tozer," she said. "She'll never make herself 'appy in our quiet way. Phœbe's been and brought her up quite the lady. It ain't as her dress is much matter. I'd have given her a silk myself, and never thought of it twice; and something lively like for a young person, 'stead of that gray stuff, as her mother might wear. But all the same, she ain't one of our sort. She'll never make herself 'appy with you and me."

"Well," said Tozer, who was more cheerful, "she ain't proud, not a bit; and as for manners, you don't pay no more for manners. She came up and give me a kiss in the station, as affectionate as possible. All I can say for her is as she ain't proud."

Mrs. Tozer shook her head; but even while she did so, pleasanter dreams stole into her soul.

"I hope I'll be well enough to get to chapel on Sunday," she said, "just to see the folk's looks. The minister needn't expect much attention to his sermon. 'There's Phœbe Tozer's daughter!' they'll all be saying, and a-staring, and a-whispering. It ain't often as anything like her is seen in chapel, that's a fact," said the old lady, warming into the exultation of natural pride.

Phœbe, it must be allowed, had a good cry when she got within the shelter of her own room, which had been very carefully prepared for her, with everything that was necessary for comfort, according to her grandmother's standard; but where the "tent" bed hung with old-fashioned red and brown chintz, and the moreen curtains drooping over the window, and the gigantic flowers on the carpet, made Phœbe's soul sick within her. Notwithstanding all her courage, her heart sank. She had expected "a difference," but she had not looked for her grandfather's greasy coat and wisp of neckcloth, or her grandmother's amazing cap, or the grammatical peculiarities in which both indulged. She had a good hot fit of crying, and for the moment felt so discouraged and depressed, that the only impulse in her mind was to run away. But her temperament did not favour panics, and giving in was not in her. If somebody must do it, why should not she do it? she said to herself. How many times had she heard in sermons and otherwise that no one ought to look for the sweet without the bitter, and that duty should never be avoided or refused because it is unpleasant? Now was the time to put her principles to the test; and the tears relieved her, and gave her something of the feeling of a martyr, which is always consolatory and sweet; so she dried her eyes, and bathed her face, and went downstairs cheerful and smiling, resolved that, at all costs, her duty should be done, however disagreeable it might be. What a good thing the new fashion of five o'clock tea is for people who have connections in an inferior path of life who make tea a meal, and don't dine, or dine in the middle of the day! This was the thought that passed through Phœbe's mind as she went into the dining-room, and found the table covered, not to say groaning under good things. She took her place at it, and poured out tea for the old people, and cut bread-and-butter with the most gracious philosophy. Duchesses did the same every day; the tea-table had renewed its ancient sway, even in fashionable life. It cannot be told what a help and refreshment this thought was to Phœbe's courageous heart.

CHAPTER XIII.

THE TOZER FAMILY.

WHEN Phœbe woke next morning, under the huge flowers of the old fashioned cotton drapery of her "tent" bed, to see the faint daylight struggling in through the heavy curtains which would not draw back from the window, the discouragement of her first arrival for a moment overpowered her again—and with even more reason—for she had more fully ascertained the resources of the place in which she found herself. There were no books, except some old volumes of sermons and a few back numbers of the Congregational Magazine, no visitors, so far as she could make out, no newspaper but the Carlingford Weekly Gazette, nothing but her grandmother's gossip about the chapel and Mrs. Tom to pass the weary hours away. Even last night Mrs. Tozer had asked her whether she had not any work to beguile the long evening, which Phœbe occupied much more virtuously, from her own point of view, in endeavouring to amuse the old people by talking to them. Though it was morning, and she ought to have been refreshed and encouraged by the repose of the night, it was again with a few hot tears that Phœbe contemplated her prospects. But this was only a passing weakness. When she went down to breakfast, she was again cheerful as the crocuses that raised their heads along the borders with the promise of summer in them. The sun was shining, the sky was frosty, but blue. After all, her present sufferings could not endure for ever. Phœbe hurried to get dressed, to get her blue fingers warmed by the dining-room fire. It is needless to say that there was no fire, or thought of a fire in the chilly room, with its red and brown hangings, in which Mrs. Tozer last night had hoped she would be happy. "No fear of that, grandmamma," she had answered cheerfully. This was as much a lie, she felt, as if it had been said with the wickedest intentions—was it as wrong? How cold it was, and yet how stifling! She could scarcely fasten the ribbon at her neck, her fingers were so cold.

"Yes, grandpapa, it is brighter than in London. We don't live in the city, you know. We live in rather a pretty neighbourhood looking out on Regent's Park, but it is seldom so bright as the country. Sometimes the fog blows up our way, when the wind is in the east; but it is warmer, I think," said Phœbe, with a little shiver, stooping over the dining-room fire.

"Ah!" said Mrs. Tozer, shaking her head, "it's your mother as has spoilt you, I don't make no doubt, with fires and things. That takes the hardiness out of young folks. A little bit of cold is wholesome, it stirs up the blood. Them as is used to fires is always taking cold. One good fire in the sitting-room, that's always been my principle, and them as is cold if they can't warm theirselves with movin' about, which is far the best, let them come and warm their fingers when they please —as you may be doing now."

"Perhaps it is a very good principle, grandmamma," said Phœbe, "when one is used to it; but the country is colder than town. Where there are fires on every side you must have more warmth than in a detached house like this. But it is only my hands after all. Shall I make the tea?"

"You should wear mittens like me—I always did in the High Street, especial when I was going and coming to the shop, helping serve, when the children were young and I had the time for it. Ah! we've done with all that now. We're more at our ease, but I can't say as we're much happier. A shop is a cheerful sort of thing. I dare say your mother has told you—"

"No," said Phœbe, under her breath; but the reply was not noticed. She nearly dropped the teapot out of her hand when she heard the word—Shop! Yes, to be sure, that was what being "in trade" meant, but she had never quite realized it till now. Phœbe was going through a tremendous piece of mental discipline in these first days. She writhed secretly, and moaned to herself—why did not mamma tell me? but she sat quite still outside, and smiled as if it was all quite ordinary and natural, and she had heard about the shop all her life. It seemed cruel and unkind to have sent her here without distinct warning of what she was going to meet. But Phœbe was a good girl, and would not blame her father and mother. No doubt they meant it " for the best."

" Is Uncle Tom," she said, faltering somewhat, " in the—shop now ? "

" If I'm able," said Mrs. Tozer, " I'll walk that far with you this morning—or Tozer, I mean your grandfather, will go. It's a tidy house o' business, though I say it as shouldn't, seeing it was him and me as made it all ; though I don't hold with Mrs. Tom's nonsense about the new windows. Your Uncle Tom is as innocent as innocent, but as for her, she ain't no favourite of mine, and I makes no bones about saying so, I don't mind who hears."

" She ain't so bad as you make her out," said Tozer. " She's kind enough in her way. Your grandmother is a-going to show you off—that's it, my dear. She can't abide Tom's wife, and she wants to show her as you're far finer than her girls. I don't say no. It's nat'ral, and I'm not one as stands against nature ; but don't you be prejudiced by my old woman there. She *is* a prejudiced one. Nothing in the world will make her give up a notion when she's took it into her head."

" No, nothing ; and ain't I always right in the end ? I should think you've proved that times enough," said the old woman. " Yes, I'll take a little, my dear, since you press me so pretty. Folks take many a thing when they're pressed as they wouldn't touch if there was no one to say, take a bit. Tozer, he never thinks of that ; he's always had the best o' appetites ; but as for me, if I get's a cup o' tea that's all as I cares for. You'll see as she'll take my view, when she's once been to the High Street. She's her mother's daughter, and Phœbe can't abide that woman, no more than me."

" Have they got many children ? " said Phœbe. " I know there are two girls, but as I have never seen them—Are they as old as I am ? " she asked, with a tremulous feeling at her heart. If there were girls in the shop in the High Street, with whom she would have to be on familiar terms, as her cousins and equals, Phœbe did not feel that she could put up with that.

" The eldest, Polly, is only twelve," said Tozer ; " but never you mind, my dear, for you shan't be without company. There's a deal of families with daughters like yourself. Your grand-mother won't say nothing against it ; and as for me, I think there's nought so cheery as young folks. You shall have a fire in the drawing-room, and as many tea-parties as you like. For the young men, I can't say as there's many, but girls is plenty, and as long as you're content with that—"

Mrs. Tozer regarded him with withering contempt across the table.

"You're clever ones, you men," she said. "Families with daughters! Do you think the Greens and the Robbins is company for *her*? I dare say as you've heard your mother speak of Maria Pigeon, my dear? She married John Green the grocer, and very well to do and respectable they may be, but nobody but the likes of your grandfather would think of you and them making friends."

"Indeed I don't care for making friends," said Phœbe, "you must remember that I came not for society, but to wait upon you, dear grandmamma. I don't want young friends. At home I always go out with my mother; let me take walks with you, when you are able. I am glad Uncle Tom's children are little. I don't want company. My work—and the garden —and to sit with grandmamma, that is all I care for. I shall be as happy as the day is long," said this martyr, smiling benignly over the aches in her heart.

Her grandparents looked at her with ever-growing pride. Was not this the ideal young woman, the girl of the story-books, who cared about nothing but her duty?

"That's very nice of you, my dear; but you ain't going to hide yourself up in a corner," said Tozer. And, "Never fear, I'll take her wherever it's fit for her to go to," his wife added, looking at her with pride. Phœbe felt, in addition to all the rest, that she was to be made a show of to all the connection, as a specimen of what the Tozer blood could come to, and she did not even feel sure that something of the same feeling had not been in her mother's bosom when she fitted her out so perfectly. Phœbe Tozer had left contemporaries and rivals in Carlingford, and the thought of dazzling and surpassing them in her off-spring as in her good fortune had still some sweetness for her mind. "Mamma meant it too!" Phœbe junior said to herself with a sigh. Unfortunately for her, she did everybody credit who belonged to her, and she must resign herself to pay the penalty. Perhaps there was some compensation in that thought.

And indeed Phœbe did not wonder at her grandmother's pride when she walked up with her to High Street, supporting her on her arm. She recognised frankly that there were not many people like herself about, few who had so much the air of good society, and not one who was so well dressed. There were excuses to be made then for the anxiety of the old people to produce her in the little world which was everything to them, and with her usual candour and good sense she acknowledged this, though she winced a little when an occasional acquaintance drifted across Mrs. Tozer's path, and was introduced with pride to "my granddaughter," and thrust forth an ungloved hand, with an exclamation of, "Lord bless us, Phœbe's eldest! I hope I see you well, Miss." Phœbe continued urbane, though it cost her many a pang. She had to keep on a perpetual argument with herself as she went along slowly, holding up her poor grandmother's tottering steps. "If this is what we have really sprung from, this is my own class, and I ought to like it; if I don't like it, it must be my fault. I have no right to feel myself better than they are. It is not position that makes any difference, but individual character," Phœbe said to herself. She got as much consolation out of this as is to be extracted from such rueful arguments in general; but it was after all indifferent comfort, and had not her temperament given her a strong hold of herself, and power of subduing her impulses, it is much to be feared that Phœbe would have dropped her grandmother's arm as they approached the station, and run away. She did waver for a moment as she came in sight of it. On that side lay freedom, comfort, the life she had been used to, which was not very elevated indeed, but felt like high rank in comparison with this. And she knew her parents would forgive her and defend her if she went back to them, unable to support the martyrdom which she had rashly taken upon herself. But then how weak that would be, Phœbe thought to herself, drawing Mrs. Tozer's arm more tightly within her own—how small! how it would hurt the feelings of the old people, how it would vex and embarrass her father and mother! Lastly, it might peril her brother's interests and her own, which, to do her justice, was the last thing she thought of, and yet was not undeserving of notice in its way.

"Lean on me more heavily, grandmamma," she said at last, finally concluding and throwing off this self-discussion. She could not prolong it further. It was unworthy of her. Henceforward she had made up her mind to set her face like a flint, and no longer leave the question of her persistence in her domestic mission an open question. Whatever she might have "to put up with," it was now decided once for all.

"Bless us all, if this ain't grandmamma," said Mrs. Tom. It was not often, as she herself said with pride, that she required to be in the shop, which was very much improved now from its old aspect. Ill luck, however, brought her here to-day. She stood at the door which led from the shop to the house, dividing the counter, talking to a lady who was making a complaint upon the quality of cheese or butter. Mrs. Tozer had led Phœbe that way in order to point out to her the plate-glass windows and marble slabs for the cheese, of which, though they were one of her grievances against Mrs. Tom, she was secretly proud.

"I don't deny but what they've done a deal," said the old woman, "show and vanity as I call it. I wish they may do as well for themselves with all their plate-glass as me and Tozer did without it; but it ain't often as you'll see a handsomer shop," she added, contemplating fondly the scene of her early labours. If a squire looks fondly at his land, and a sailor at his ship (when ships were worth looking at), why should not a shopkeeper regard his shop with the same affectionate feelings? Mrs. Tom Tozer had just taken leave of her remonstrant customer with a curtsey, and an assurance that the faults complained of should be remedied, when she caught sight of the infirm old woman leaning on Phœbe's arm, and made the exclamation already quoted.

"Lord bless us all! if it ain't grandmamma, and Phœbe's daughter along o' her, I'll lay you sixpence," said Mrs. Tom in the extremity of her surprise, and at the highest pitch of her voice. The lady customer was still in the shop, and when she heard this she turned round and gave the newcomers a stare. (It was not very wonderful, Phœbe allowed to herself with secret anguish). She gave old Mrs. Tozer a familiar nod. "This is quite a long walk for you now-a-days," she said, gazing at Phœbe, though she addressed the old woman.

"Thank ye, ma'am, I am a deal better," said Mrs. Tozer, "especially as I've got my granddaughter to take care of me."

"Oh! is this young—person your granddaughter," said the customer with another stare, and then she nodded again and went away wondering. "Well," Phœbe said to herself, "one little sting more or less what did it matter?" and she went on through the shop supporting her grandmother, keenly sensible of the looks that encountered her on every side. Mrs. Tom stood leaning against the counter, waiting for them without making any advance. She was smart and good-looking, with a malicious gleam in a pair of bright black beady eyes.

"How are you, granny?" she said, "I declare you're looking quite young again, and as spry as twenty. Come in and rest; and this young lady as is with you, I don't think as I need ask her name, the likeness speaks for itself. It's Phœbe Beecham, ain't it? Bless us all! I'd have known her anywhere, I would;

the very moral of her mother, and of you too, granny. As you stand there now, you're as like as two peas."

Unconsciously Phœbe cast a look upon her grandmother. She did not think she was vain. To be unconscious that she had some personal advantages would, of course, be impossible; but a thrill crept through her when she looked at the old woman by her side, wrinkled and red, in her copper-coloured gown. As like as two peas! was that possible? Phœbe's heart sank for the moment to her shoes, and a pitiful look of restrained pain came to her face. This was assailing her in her tenderest point.

"Am I so like you, grandmamma?" she said, faltering; but added quickly, "then I cannot be like mamma. How do you do? My mother wished me to come at once, to bring her kind regards. Is my uncle at home?"

"No, Miss, your uncle ain't at home," said Mrs. Tom, "but you might be civil, all the same, and put a name to me, more nor if I was a dog. I'm your aunt, I am—and I likes all my titles, I do—and proper respect."

"Surely," said Phœbe, with a bow and a gracious smile—but she did not add that name. She was pleased to think that "Tom's wife" was her mother's favourite aversion, and that a dignified resistance to her claims was, so to speak, her duty. It even amused her to think of the ingenuity required throughout a long conversation for the clever and polite eluding of this claim.

"I hope as you mean to let us in, Amelia," said Mrs. Tozer, "for it ain't often as I takes so long a walk. I would never have thought of it but for Phœbe—Phœbe junior, as Tozer calls her. She's been used to things very different, but I'm thankful to say she ain't a bit proud. She couldn't be more attentive to me if I was the queen, and talks of your children as pretty as possible, without no nonsense. It ain't often as you see that in a girl brought up like she's been."

"I don't pretend to know nothing of how she's been brought up," said Mrs. Tom, "and I don't think as there's no occasion for pride here. We're all well-to-do, and getting on in the world—thanks to Him as gives the increase. I don't see no opening for pride here. Me and your mother were never very good friends, Phœbe, since that's your name; but if there's anything I can do for you, or my family, you won't ask twice. Grandmother's ain't a very lively house, not like mine, as is full of children. Come in, Granny. I'm always speaking of making the stairs wider, and a big window on the landing; but folks can't do everything at once, and we'll have to do with it a bit longer. We've done a deal already to the old place."

"More than was wanted, or was thought upon in my time," said the old lady, to whom this was as the trumpet of battle. "The stairs did well enough for me, and I can't think what Tom can want changing things as he's been used to all his life."

"Oh, it ain't Tom," said his wife, her face lighting up with satisfaction. "Tom wouldn't mind if the place was to come to bits about our ears. He's like you, granny, he's one of the stand-still ones. It ain't Tom, it's me."

This little passage of arms took place as they were going up-stairs, which cost poor Mrs. Tozer many pantings and groanings, and placed Phœbe for once on Mrs. Tom's side, for a window on the landing would have been a wonderful improvement, there was no denying. When, at last, they had toiled to the top, fighting their way, not only through the obscurity, but through an atmosphere of ham and cheese which almost choked Phœbe, the old lady was speechless with the exertion, though the air was to her as the air of Paradise. Phœbe placed her on a chair and undid her bonnet-strings, and for a minute was really alarmed. Mrs. Tom, however, took it with perfect equanimity.

"She's blown a bit; she ain't as young as she was, nor even as she thinks for," said that sympathetic person. "Come, Granny, cheer up. Them stairs ain't strange to you. What's the good of making a fuss? Sit down and get your breath," she went on, pulling forward a chair; then turning to Phœbe, she shrugged her shoulders and raised her eyebrows. "She's breaking fast, that's what it is," said Mrs. Tom under her breath, with a nod of her head.

"This is the room as your mother spent most of her life in when she was like you," said Mrs. Tozer, when she regained her breath. "It was here as she met your father first. The first time I set my eyes on him, 'That's the man for my Phœbe,' I said to myself; and sure enough, so it turned out."

"You didn't miss no way of helping it on, neither, granny, if folks do you justice," said Mrs. Tom. "Mothers can do a deal when they exerts themselves; and now Phœbe has a daughter of her own, I dare be sworn she's just as clever, throwing the nice ones and the well-off ones in her way. It's a wonder to me as she hasn't gone off yet, with all her oppor-tunities—two or three and twenty, ain't you, Miss Phœbe? I should have thought you'd have married long afore now."

" I shall be twenty my next birth-day," said Phœbe. "My cousins are a great deal younger, I hear; are they at school? I hope I shall see them before I go."

" Oh, you'll see 'em fast enough," said their mother, "they're 'aving their music lesson. I don't hold with sending girls to school. I likes to keep them under my own eye. I suppose I needn't ask you now if you play?"

" A very little," said Phœbe, who rather piqued herself upon her music, and who was learned in Bach and Beethoven, and had an opinion of her own about Wagner. Mrs. Tom brightened visibly, for her girls played not a little, but a great deal.

" And draw?—but I needn't ask, for living in London, you've got masters at your very door."

" Not at all, I am sorry to say," said Phœbe, with a pathetic tone of regret in her voice.

" Lord bless us! Now who'd have thought it? I think nothing a sacrifice to give mine the best of education," said Mrs. Tom.

CHAPTER XIV.

STRANGERS.

" WELL, Ursula, how do you do?" said Mrs. Sam Hurst, meeting her young neighbour with outstretched hands. She was a portly good-looking woman with an active mind, and nothing, or next to nothing to do, and instead of being affronted as some persons might have been, she was amused, and indeed flattered, by the suspicion and alarm with which all the young Mays regarded her. Whether she had the least intention of ever giving any justification to their alarms it would be impossible to say, for indeed to a sensible woman of forty-five, well to do and comfortable, a husband with " a temper of his own," and a large poor unruly family, was, perhaps, not so tempting as he appeared to be to his jealous children. Anyhow she was not at all angry with them for being jealous and afraid of her. She was cordial in her manner to the Mays as to everybody she knew. She asked how Ursula had enjoyed herself, where she had been, what she had seen, and a hundred questions more.

" It is quite delightful to see somebody who has something to tell," she said when the interrogation was over. " I ask everybody what news, and no one has any news, which is dreadful for me."

"How can you care for news?" said Ursula, "news! what interest can there be in mere news that doesn't concern us?"

"You are very foolish, my dear," said Mrs. Hurst; "what's to become of you when you're old, if you don't like to hear what's going on? I'm thankful to say I take a great deal of interest in my fellow-creatures for my part. Now listen, I'll tell you a piece of news in return for all your information about London. When I was in Tozer's shop to-day—I always go there, though they are Dissenters; after all, you know, most tradespeople are Dissenters; some are sorry for it, some think it quite natural that gentle-people and tradespeople should think differently in religious matters; however, what I say is, you can't tell the difference in butter and bacon between church and dissent, can you now? and Tozer's is the best shop in the town, certainly the best shop. So as I was in Tozer's as I tell you, who should come in but old Mrs. Tozer, who once kept it herself—and by her side, figure my astonishment, a young lady! yes, my dear, actually a young lady, in appearance, of course—I mean in appearance—for, as you shall hear, it could be no more than that. So nicely dressed, nothing vulgar or showy, a gown that Elise might have made, and everything to correspond, in perfect taste. Fancy! and you may imagine how I stared. I could not take my eyes off her. I was so astonished that I rubbed up my old acquaintance with the old woman, and asked her how her rheumatism was. I *hope* it is rheumatism. At all events I called it so, and then she told me as proud as a peacock that it was her granddaughter; fancy, her granddaughter! did you ever hear of such a thing? The other woman in the shop, the present Tozer, called out to her by name. Phœbe they called her. Poor girl, I was so sorry for her. A lady in appearance, and to have to submit to that!"

"Oughtn't ladies to be called Phœbe?" asked Janey. "Why not? It's rather a pretty name."

"That is so like Janey," said Mrs. Hurst; "I know she is the clever one; but she never can see what one means. It is not being called Phœbe, it is because of her relations that I am sorry for her. Poor girl! educating people out of their sphere does far more harm than good, I always maintain. To see that nice-looking, well-dressed girl in Tozer's shop, with all the butter boys calling her Phœbe—"

"The butter boys are as good as any one else," cried Janey, whose tendencies were democratic. "I dare say she likes her relations as well as we like ours, and better, though they do keep a shop."

"Oh, Janey!" cried Ursula, whose feelings were touched; then she remembered that her sympathies ought not to flow in the same channel with those of Mrs. Sam Hurst, and continued coldly, "If she had not liked them she need not have come to see them."

"That is all you know, you girls. You don't know the plague of relations, and how people have got to humble themselves to keep money in the family, or keep up appearances, especially people that have risen in the world. I declare I think they pay dear for rising in the world, or their poor children pay dear—"

"You seem to take a great deal of interest in the Tozers," said Ursula, glad to administer a little correction; "even if they came to St. Roque's I could understand it—but Dissenters!" This arrow struck home.

"Well," said Mrs. Hurst, colouring, "of all people to take an interest in Dissenters I am the last; but I was struck, I must admit, to see that old Mrs. Tozer, looking like an old washerwoman, with a girl in a twenty-guinea dress, you may take my word for it, though as plain as that little brown frock of yours, Ursula. That was a sight to wake any one up."

Ursula looked down at the little brown frock thus contemptuously referred to, with mingled offence and consciousness of inferiority. It had not cost as many shillings, and had been made up at home, and was not a shining example of the dressmaker's art. "If you value people according to what their dress costs—"

"I can't know much about her moral qualities, can I?" said Mrs. Hurst, "and I don't suppose she has any position, being old Tozer's grandchild. But she wasn't amiss in her looks, and I declare I should have taken her for a lady if I had met her in the street. It shows how one may be taken in. And this is a lesson for you, young girls; you must never trust to appearances. I confess I'd like to find out some more about her. Going in, Ursula? Well, my dear, perhaps I'll step in for a talk in the evening. You must be dull after your gaiety. Tell your dear papa," said Mrs. Hurst with a laugh, "that I am coming to sit with you after tea. Now mind you give him my message. He does not like to miss me when I come to the Parsonage, does he now? Good-bye for the present. Till eight o'clock."

"Oh, how I hate her," cried Janey, "except sometimes when

she makes me laugh and I feel tempted to like her; but I always resist it. Do you think really, Ursula, that papa could be—such a—stupid—"

"Oh, please don't ask me," cried Ursula. "How can I tell? I don't know what he may do; but if he does—and if she does —oh, then, Janey—"

"Yes, indeed, then!" said Janey, breathing hard. This mysterious threat seemed very horrible to both of them, though what they meant by it, it would have been very hard for either of them to tell. They waited within the little shrubbery whispering to each other till they heard Mrs. Hurst close her own door, for they did not want any more of her society, though they had no intention of going in. When she was safe out of the way, they stole out and continued their walk in the opposite direction.

"I wanted to have gone into the town," said Ursula. "It *is* hard to have that woman next door; one can't go anywhere or do anything! I wanted some braid for your new frock, Janey, and twist to make the button-holes; but if we had said we were going up into Carlingford, she would have come too. Never mind; a walk is better than nothing. Walk fast, and let us try how far we can go before tea."

Upon this idea the two girls set out walking as if for a race, which did them all the good in the world, quickening the blood in their veins, sending the colour to their cheeks, and dispersing all the cobwebs from their minds, since they soon got into the spirit of the race, and pursued it with eagerness, with little outbursts of laughter, and breathless adjurations to each other to keep within the proper pace, and not to run. It was not a very inviting road along which they took their walk. Beyond St. Roque the land was divided into allotments for the working people, not very tidily kept, and rough with cut cabbages, plants, and dug-up potatoes. Beyond this lay a great turnip-field, somewhat rank in smell, and the east wind swept chill along the open road, which was not sheltered by a single tree, so that the attractions of the way soon palled upon pedestrians. Looking back to Grange Lane, the snug and sheltered look of that genteel adjunct to the town was comforting to behold. Even Grange Lane was not gay; a line of garden walls, however they may shelter and comfort the gardens within, are not lovely without; but yet the trees, though leafless, waved over the red lines of brick, and the big laurels hung out bushes of dark verdure and long floating sprays of ivy.

"Let's turn back; perhaps she may not be at the window," cried Ursula. "It is so dull here."

Janey stopped short in the heat of the walk, objecting for the moment.

"I wish you had not gone to London. You never used to care for the streets and the shops; now a regular good walk is too much for you," cried Janey.

"With a turnip-field on one side and a potato-field on the other!" said Ursula, in high disdain.

"I tell you what!" cried Janey. "I don't think I like you since you came back. The Dorsets are fine people, and we are not fine. There are no grand parties, nor theatres, nor balls at Carlingford. When we go out here, we go to walk, not to see things, as you have been used to doing. I don't know what you mean by it; nineteen years with us, and one fortnight with them! and the fortnight counts for more than all the years!"

Janey was not in the habit of restraining her voice any more than anything else about her, and she spoke this out with loud school-girl tones, reckless who might hear her. In most cases she might have done this with the utmost impunity, and how was she to know, as she said to her sister afterwards, in self-defence, that any one, especially any gentleman, could be lurking about, spying upon people, among those nasty allotments? There was some one there, however, who came down the muddy path, all cut up by the wheel-barrows, with a smile upon his face. A gentleman? Janey called him so without a doubt on the subject; but Ursula, more enlightened and slightly irritated, had her doubts. He was dressed, not with any care of morning costume, but wore a black frock-coat of the most formal description, with a white cravat carelessly tied, semi-clerical, and yet not clerical. He had a smile on his face, which, on the whole, was rather a handsome face, and looked at them, showing evident signs of having heard what Janey said. To be sure, he did not say anything, but Ursula felt that his look was just the same as if he had spoken, and coloured high, resenting the intrusion. By this stranger's side was one of the men who had been working at the allotments, whose hands were not clean, and whose boots were heavy with the clinging, clayey soil. When they had nearly reached the road, the gentleman turned round and shook hands with his companion, and then walked on towards Carlingford, throwing another look towards the girls as he passed. It would be hard to say whether curiosity or anger was strongest in Ursula. In Janey, the former sentiment carried everything before it.

"Oh, I wonder who he is?" she cried, low, but eager, in

her sister's ear. "Who can he be, Ursula, who can he be?
We know all the men about here, every one, as well as we know
Reginald. Oh, Ursula, who do you think he can be?"

"He is very impertinent," cried Ursula, with an angry
blush. "How should I know? And oh! how very silly of
you, Janey, to talk so loud, and make impudent men stare at
us so."

"Impudent!" cried Janey. "I didn't talk loud. He
looked rather nice, on the contrary. Why, he laughed! Do
you call that impudent? It can't be anybody from the town,
because we know everybody; and did you see him shaking
hands with that man? How very funny! Let us run in and
tell Mrs. Sam Hurst, and ask her who she thinks he is. She
is sure to know."

"Janey," said Ursula, severely, "if you live very long, you
will be as great a gossip and as fond of news as Mrs. Sam
Hurst herself."

"I don't care," cried Janey; "you're just as fond of news as
I am, only you won't confess it. I am dying to know who he
is. He is quite nice-looking, and tall and grand. A new
gentleman! Come, quick, Ursula; let us get back and see
where he goes."

"Janey!" cried the elder sister. She was half curious herself, but Ursula was old enough to know better, and to be
ashamed of the other's naïve and undisguised curiosity. "Oh,
what would Cousin Anne say! A girl running after a gentleman (even if he is a gentleman), to see where he goes!"

"Well!" cried Janey, "if she wants to know, what else is
she to do? Who cares for Cousin Anne? She is an old maid.
Why, if it had been a lady, I shouldn't have minded. There
are so many ladies; but a new gentleman! If you won't come
on, I will run by myself. How pleased Mrs. Sam Hurst will
be!"

"I thought you hated Mrs. Sam Hurst?"

"So I do when I think of papa; but when there's anything
going on, or anything to find out, I like her dearly. She's such
fun! She never shilly-shallies, like you. She's not an old
maid like your Cousin Anne that you are always talking of.
Come along! if anybody else finds out who he is before we do,"
cried Janey, with almost despairing energy, "I shall break my
heart!"

Ursula stoically resisted the tug upon her, but she went back
to Grange Lane, to which, indeed, she had turned her face
before they met the stranger, and she could not help seeing
the tall black figure in front of her which Janey watched so

eagerly. Ursula was not eager, but she could not help seeing him. He walked up the street quickly, not as if he thought himself of interest to any one, but when he had got half way up Grange Lane, crossed to speak to somebody. This filled Janey with consternation.

"He is not such a stranger after all," she cried. "He knows some one. He will not be quite a discovery. Who is it he is talking to, I wonder? He is standing at one of the doors, but it is not Miss Humphreys, nor Miss Griffiths, nor any of the Charters. Perhaps she is a stranger too. If he is married he won't be half so interesting, for there are always plenty of ladies. Perhaps he has just come by the railway to spend the day—but then there is nothing to see in Carlingford, and how did he know that man at the lots? Oh, Ursula, why don't you answer me? why don't you say something? have you no feeling? I am sure it don't matter a bit to me, for I am not out; I am never asked to parties—but I take an interest for you other girls' sake."

Before this time, however, Ursula had found a new object of interest. She had not been quite so unmoved as Janey supposed. A new gentleman was a thing to awaken anybody who knew Carlingford, for, indeed, gentlemen were scarce in the society of the little town, and even at the most mild of tea-parties it is ludicrous to see one man (and that most likely a curate) among a dozen ladies—so that even when she appeared to Janey to wonder, she felt that her sister's curiosity was not unjustifiable. But while thus engaged in the enterprise of discovering "a new gentleman" for the good of society, Ursula's eyes and her attention were caught by another interest. The stranger had crossed the street to talk to a lady, who had been walking down the Lane, and whom Ursula felt she had seen somewhere. Who was it? Certainly not Miss Humphreys, nor Miss Griffiths, nor any other of the well-known young ladies of Grange Lane. The setting sun, which had come out suddenly after a dull day, threw a slanting, long-drawn ray up the street, which fell upon the strangers, as they stood talking. This ray caught the young lady's hair, and flashed back a reflection out of the shining coils which looked to Ursula (being dark herself, she admired golden hair more than anything) as bright as the sunshine. And in the light she caught the outline of a pretty head, and of a nose slightly "tip-tilted," according to the model which the Laureate has brought into fashion. Where had she seen her before? She remembered all at once with a rush of bewildered pleasure.

"Janey! Oh, Janey!" she cried, "Listen! This is too extraordinary. There is the young lady in black!"

Janey, as may be supposed, had heard every detail of Mrs. Copperhead's ball, and knew what Ursula meant as well as Ursula herself did. She grew pale with excitement and curiosity. "No!" she said, "you can't mean it. Are you sure, are you quite sure? Two new people in one day! Why, everybody must be coming to Carlingford. It makes me feel quite strange!" said this susceptible young woman; "the young lady in black!"

"Oh, yes, there can't be any mistake," said Ursula, hurrying on in her excitement, "I looked at her so much. I couldn't mistake her. Oh, I wonder if she will know me, I wonder if she will speak to me! or if she is going to see the Dorsets, or what has brought her to Carlingford. Only fancy, Janey, the young lady in black whom I have talked so much of; oh, I wonder, I do wonder what has brought her here."

They were on the opposite side of the lane, so that their hurried approach did not startle the strangers; but Phœbe, looking up at the sound of the footsteps, saw a face she knew looking wistfully, eagerly at her, with evident recognition. Phœbe had a faculty quite royal of remembering faces, and it took but a moment to recall Ursula's to her. Another moment was spent in a rapid discussion with herself, as to whether she should give or withhold the salutation which the girl evidently sought. But what harm could it do? and it would be pleasant to know some one; and if on finding out who she was, Miss Dorset's little relation shrank from her acquaintance, why then, Phœbe said to herself, "I shall be no worse than before." So she sent a smile and a bow across the road and said, "How do you do?" in a pause of her conversation. Ursula was too shy to feel on equal terms with the young lady in black, who was so much more self-possessed than she was. She blushed and smiled, answered, "Quite well, thank you," across the lane like a child, and notwithstanding a great many pokes from Janey's energetic elbow, went on without further response.

"Oh, why can't you run across and speak to her?" cried Janey, "oh, how funny you are, and how disagreeable! would I pass any one I knew, like that!"

"You don't understand, you are only a child," said Ursula, frightened and agitated, yet full of dignity, "we have only met —in society. When you are introduced to any one in society it does not count. Perhaps they might not want to know you; perhaps—but anyhow you can't rush up to them like two girls at school. You have to wait and see what they will do."

"Well, I declare!" cried Janey; "then what is the good of society? You know them, and yet you mustn't know them. I would never be such a fool as that. Fancy looking at her across the lane and saying 'quite well, thank you,' after she had begun to speak. I suppose that's Cousin Anne's way? I should have rushed across and asked where she was staying, and when she would come to see us. Ursula, oh," cried Janey, suddenly changing her tone, and looking at her sister with eyes which had widened to twice their natural size with the grandeur of the idea, "you will have to ask her to tea!"

"Oh, you silly girl, do you think she would come? you should have seen her at the ball. She knew everybody, and had such quantities of partners. Mr. Clarence Copperhead was always dancing with her. Fancy her coming to tea with us." But Ursula herself was somewhat breathless with the suggestion. When a thing has been once said, there is always a chance that it may be done, and the two girls walked up very quickly into the High Street after this, silent, with a certain awe of themselves and their possibilities. It might be done, now that it had been said.

CHAPTER XV.

A DOMESTIC CRISIS.

THE interest shown by the two girls in the stranger whom they had noted with so much attention was not destined to meet with any immediate reward. Neither he, nor "the young lady in black," whom he hurried across the street to meet, could be heard of, or was seen for full two days afterwards, to the great disappointment of the young Mays. Ursula, especially, who had been entertaining vague but dazzling thoughts of a companionship more interesting than Janey's, more novel and at the same time more equal than that which was extended to her by the Miss Griffiths in Grange Lane, who were so much better off and had so much less to do than she. Ursula did not recollect the name of the fortunate girl who was so much in the ascendant at Mr. Copperhead's ball, though Phœbe had been introduced to her; but she did recollect her popularity and general friendliness, and the number of partners she had, and all those delightful signs of greatness which impress a poor

little stranger, to whom her first dance is not unmingled pleasure
She whispered to Janey about her even in the drawing-room
when all the family were assembled.

"Do you think she will call?" said Ursula, asking counsel
even of Janey's inexperience, of which she was so contemptuous
on other occasions.

"Call! how can she, if she is a stranger?" said Janey.

"As if you knew anything about it!" Ursula retorted with
great injustice.

"If I don't know, then why do you ask me?" complained
Janey with reason. The room looked more cheerful since
Ursula had come home. The fire, no longer choked with cinders,
burned clear and red. The lamp, though it was a cheap one,
and burned paraffin oil, did not smell. The old curtains were
nicely drawn, and the old covers smoothed over the chairs. All
this did not make them look less old; but it made their antiquity
natural and becoming. Johnnie, the schoolboy, was learning
his lessons on the rug before the fire. Reginald sat writing,
with a candle all to himself, at a writing-table in a corner.
Ursula and Janey were working at the centre table by the
light of the lamp. They had no time, you may imagine, for
fancy-work. Janey, with many contortions of her person,
especially of her mouth, with which she seemed to follow the
movements of her needle, was stitching up a sleeve of her new
frock which Miss Dorset had sent her, and which a poor dressmaker, who "went out," was at this moment making up in the
schoolroom; while Ursula was still busy with the basket of
stockings which she had found awaiting her on their return.
What Reginald was doing at the writing-table was probably
a great deal less useful, but the girls respected his occupation
as no one ever thought of respecting theirs, and carried on their
conversation under their breath, not to interrupt him. The
little children had gone to bed, tea was over, and several hours
of the long winter evening still before them. Janey had given
over lessons, partly because there was no one to insist upon her
doing them. Once in a week or so her father gave her a lecture
for her ignorance, and ordered her into his study to do a long
sum in arithmetic out of the first old "Colenso" that could be
picked up; and about once a week too, awakening suddenly to
a sense of her own deficiencies, she would "practise" energetically on the old piano. This was all that was being done
for Janey in the way of education. She was fifteen, and as
Johnnie, and Amy, and Robin were at an age when school is a
necessity, the only retrenchment possible was to keep Janey
at home. Ursula had got what education she possessed in the

same irregular way. It was not much. Besides reading and
writing, she had pretty manners, which came by nature like
those other gifts. A girl is not so badly off who can read and
write and has pretty manners. Janey possessed the two first
faculties, but neither had nor apparently could acquire the third.
The two dark brown heads were close together as they
worked—Ursula's shining and neat, and carefully arranged,
Janey's rough with elf-locks; but they were more interesting
than Reginald, though he was so much better informed. As
for Johnnie, he lay extended on the rug, his head slightly raised
on his two hands, his book on a level with the rest of his person,
saying over his lesson to himself with moving lips. And now
and then, when the girls' whispered chatter was silent, the sound
of Reginald's pen scratching across the paper would fill up the
interval; it was a sound which filled them all with respect.

This peaceful domestic scene was broken in upon by the
entry of Mr. May. From the moment that he closed the hall-
door behind him, coming in, a little thrill ran through the
family party. The girls looked at each other when they heard
that sound, and Johnnie, without stopping his inward repetition,
shifted himself and his book adroitly, with the cleverness of
practice, to the side instead of the front of the fire. Reginald's
pen stopped its scratching, and he wheeled round on his chair
to give an appealing glance at his sisters.

"What is it now?" he said hurriedly. Every one knew that
when the door was closed like that it meant something like a
declaration of war. But they had not much time to wait and
wonder. Mr. May came in, pushing the door wide open before
him, and admitting a gust of chill air of the January night.
He looked at the peaceable domestic scene with a "humph"
of dissatisfaction, because there was nothing to find fault with,
which is as great a grievance as another when one is in the
mood for grievances. He had come in cross and out of sorts,
with a private cause for his ill-temper, which he did not choose
to reveal, and it would have been a relief to him had he found
them all chattering or wasting their time, instead of being
occupied in this perfectly dutiful way—even Johnnie at his
lessons, repeating them over under his breath. What was the
world coming to? Mr. May was disappointed. Instead of
leading up to it gradually by a general *battue* of his children
all round, he had to open upon his chief subject at once, which
was not nearly so agreeable a way.

"What are you doing, Reginald?" he asked, roughly, pulling his chair to the other side of the fire, opposite the corner
to which Johnnie had scuffled out of the way. "I have come

in especially to speak to you. It is time this shilly-shallying was done with. Do you mean to accept the College chaplaincy or not? an answer must be given, and that at once. Are you so busy that you can't attend to what I say?"

"I am not busy at all, sir," said Reginald, in a subdued voice, while his sisters cast sympathetic looks at him. Both the girls, it is true, thought him extremely foolish, but what of that? Necessarily they were on his side against papa.

"I thought as much; indeed it would be hard to say what you could find to be busy at. But look here, this must come to an end one way or another. You know my opinion on the subject."

"And you know mine, sir," said Reginald, rising and coming forward to the fire. "I don't say anything against the old College. For an old man it might be quite a justifiable arrangement—one who had already spent his strength in work—but for me—of course there is nothing in the world to do."

"And two hundred and fifty a year for the doing of it—not to speak of the house, which you could let for fifty more."

"Father! don't you see that is just the very thing that I object to, so much for nothing."

"You prefer nothing for nothing," said Mr. May, with a smile; "well, I suppose that is more fair, perhaps—to the public;—but how about me? A son of three-and-twenty depending upon me for everything, useless and bringing in nothing, does not suit me. You are all the same," he said, "all taking from me, with a thousand wants, education, clothes, amusement—"

"I am sure," said the irrepressible Janey, "it is not much clothes we get, and as for amusements—and education!"

"Hold your tongue," cried her father. "Here are six of you, one more helpless than another, and the eldest the most helpless of all. I did not force you into the Church. You might have gone out to James if you had liked—but you chose an academical career, and then there was nothing else for it. I gave you a title to orders. You are my curate just now—so called; but you know I can't pay a curate, and you know I can't afford to keep you. Providence—" said Mr. May, sitting up in his chair, with a certain solemnity, "Providence itself has stepped in to make your path clear. Here is better than a living, a provision for you. I don't bid you take it for life; take it for a year or two till you can hear of something better. Now what on earth is your objection to this?"

The girls had both turned their faces towards their brother. Janey, always the first in action, repeated almost unconsciously,

" Yes, what on earth, Reginald, can be your objection to this?"

Reginald stood in the middle of the room and looked help-lessly at them. Against his father alone he might have made a stand—but when the united family thus gazed at him with inquiring and reproachful looks, what was he to say?

" Objection!" he faltered, "you know very well what my objection is. It is not honest work—it is no work. It is a waste of money that might be better employed; it is a sinecure."

"And what do you call your nominal curateship," said his father, " is not that a sinecure too?"

"If it is," said Reginald, growing red, but feeling bolder, for here the family veered round, and placed itself on his side, "it is of a contrary kind. It is *sine* pay. My work may be bad, though I hope not, but my pay is nothing. I don't see any resemblance between the two."

"Your pay nothing!" cried the father, enraged ; "what do you call your living, your food that you are so fastidious about, your floods of beer and all the rest of it—not to speak of tailors' bills much heavier than mine?"

" Which are never paid."

"Whose fault is it that they are never paid? yours and the others who weigh me down to the ground, and never try to help or do anything for themselves. Never paid! how should I have gone on to this period and secured universal respect if they had never been paid? I have had to pay for all of you," said Mr. May, bitterly, "and all your vagaries ; education, till I have been nearly ruined ; dresses and ribbons, and a hundred fooleries for these girls, who are of no use, who will never give me back a farthing."

" Papa!" cried Ursula and Janey in one breath.

" Hold your tongues! useless impedimenta, not even able to scrub the floors, and make the beds, which is all you could ever be good for—and you must have a servant forsooth to do even that. But why should I speak of the girls?" he added, with a sarcastic smile, " they can do nothing better, poor creatures ; but you! who call yourself a man—a University man, save the mark—a fine fellow with the Oxford stamp upon you, twenty-three your next birthday. It is a fine thing that I should still have to support you."

Reginald began to walk up and down the room, stung beyond bearing—not that he had not heard it all before, but to get accustomed to such taunts is difficult, and it is still more diffi-cult for a young and susceptible mind to contradict all that is seemly and becoming in nature, and to put forth its own state-ment in return. Reginald knew that his education had in

reality cost his father very little, and that his father knew this.
He was aware, too, much more distinctly than Mr. May knew,
of James's remittances on his account ; but what could he say ?
It was his father who insulted him, and the young man's lips
were closed ; but the effort was a hard one. He could not
stand still there and face the man who had so little consideration for his feelings. All he could do was to keep his agitation
and irritation down by that hurried promenade about the room,
listening as little as he could, and answering not at all.

"Oh, papa! how can you ? " cried Janey, seizing the first
pause. Janey was not old enough to understand the delicacy
that closed Reginald's lips, and the impulse of self-defence was
stirring in her ; "how dare you talk to Ursula so ? I mayn't
be much use, but Ursula ! nice and comfortable you were when
she was away ! as if you didn't say so ten times in a morning ;
to be sure that was to make me feel uncomfortable. Scrub
floors ! " cried Janey, in the violence of her resentment. "I'll
go out and be a maid-of-all-work whenever you please. I am
sure it would be much happier than here."

"Hold your tongue," said Mr. May, "you scolding and
Ursula crying ; that's the beauty of the feminine element in a
house. I ought to be very thankful, oughtn't I, that I have
girls to furnish this agreeable variety ? But as for you, Reginald," his father added, "mark my words, if you determine to
reject this windfall that Providence has blown into your hands,
it must be done at once. No further play of I would and I
would not, if you please, here ; and if it does not suit you, you
will please to understand that I have no further need for a
curate that suits me still less. I want your room. If nothing
else can be done, I must try to take a pupil to add a little to
the income which has so many claims upon it ; and I don't
mean to go on keeping you—this is plain enough, I hope."

"Very plain, sir," said Reginald, who had grown as pale as
he was red before.

"I am glad to hear it ; you will write to the Corporation at
once, accepting or rejecting at your pleasure ; but this must
be done to-night. I must insist on its being done to-night ;
and if you find yourself sufficiently bold to reject an income,"
said Mr. May with emphasis, "and go off into the world without a penny in your pocket, I wash my hands of it ; it is
nothing to me."

Then there was a pause. The father of the family sat down
in his chair, and looked round him with the happy consciousness that he had made everybody miserable. The girls were
both crying, Reginald pale and desperate, coming and going

through the room. No one had escaped but Johnnie, who, happy in insignificance, lay all his length on the other side of the fire, and lifted his face from his book to watch the discomfiture of the others. Johnnie had no terrors on his own account. He had done nothing to call forth the paternal wrath. Mr. May could not resist this temptation.

"Is that a way to learn lessons as they ought to be learnt?" he cried suddenly, throwing one of his darts at the unthinking boy. "Get up this moment, and sit down to a table somewhere. Your own room, where there is nobody to disturb you, is better than amid the chit-chat here; do you hear me? get up, sir, and go."

Johnnie stumbled to his feet appalled; he was too much startled to say anything. He took his books across the room to the writing-table which Reginald had abandoned in a similar way. But by the time he reached that haven, he came to himself, and recovering his courage muttered something about the hardship to which he was thus exposed, as boys have a way of doing; upon which Mr. May got suddenly up, seized him by the shoulders and turned him out of the drawing-room. I said your own room, sir," cried this impartial father, distributing to all alike an equal share of his urbanities. When he had accomplished this, he stood for a moment and looked at the rest of his confused and uncomfortable family. "There is not much cheerful society to be had here this evening, I perceive," he said. "It is pleasant to come in from one's cares and find a reception like this, don't you think? Let some one bring me some coffee to my study. I am going to write."

"Whose fault is it that he gets such a reception?" burst forth Janey, the moment her father had closed the door. "Who does it all, I wonder? Who treats us like a set of wretches without any feeling? I can't hush, I won't hush! Oh, shouldn't I be glad to go out as a housemaid, to do anything!"

"Oh, Janey, hush! we can't help ourselves, we are obliged to put up with it," said Ursula; "but Reginald, he is not obliged, he can save himself when he likes, Oh, I know, I know papa is unreasonable; but, Reginald, aren't you a little bit unreasonable too?"

"Don't you begin to reproach me," cried the young man, "I have had enough for one day. Have I been such a charge upon him, Ursula? What has he spent upon me? Next to nothing. That tailor's bill he spoke of, he knew as well as I do that I paid it by the tutorship I had in the vacation. It is his bill that is not paid, not mine. And then James's money—"

" Oh, never mind that, never mind the past," cried Ursula,
"think of the present, that's what you ought to do. Oh,
Reginald, think ; if *I* had the chance of two hundred and fifty
pounds a year ! there is nothing I would not do for it. I
would scrub floors, as he said, I would do anything, the dirtiest
work. You will be independent, able to do what you please,
and never to ask papa for anything. Reginald, think ! Oh,
dear, dear, I wish I knew how to talk to you. To be independent, able to please yourself ! "

" I shall be independent anyhow after to-night," he said.
" Ursula, you will help me to pack my things, won't you ? It
is leaving you here, you girls, with nobody to stand up for you ;
it is that I feel most."

" Oh, Reginald, don't go and leave us," cried Janey, leaning
on the back of his chair; "what can we do without you ?
When he comes in, in a rage like to-night, as long as you are
here one can bear it. Oh, Reginald, can't you, can't you take
the chaplaincy ? Think what it would be for us."

" Yes, I will pack your things," said Ursula, " I will help
you to get out of it, though we must stay and put up with it
all, and never, never escape. But where will you go ? You
have no money, not enough scarcely to pay your railway fare.
You would have to take to teaching ; and where are you to
go ? "

" I have some friends left," cried Reginald, his lips quivering,
" some people care for me still and would hold out a hand. I
am—not—quite so badly off as he thinks ; I could go to town,
or to Oxford—or—"

" You don't know where ; and here is a nice old-fashioned
house all ready for you to step into, and an income," cried
Ursula, her tone deepening to mark the capital letter ; "an
Income, quite sure and ready—without any difficulty, without
any trouble, all if you say yes. Oh, only think what a comfort
for us all to be able to rush to you when we are in trouble !
Think of Johnnie and Robin ; and that delightful wainscoted
room for your study, with the bookcases all ready—and plenty
of money to buy books." This being the highest point to which
Ursula could reach, she dropped down after it into an insinu-
ating half whisper, " And plenty of work to do ; dear Reginald,
plenty of work in the parish, you may be sure, if you will only
help the Rector ; or here where you are working already, and
where you may be sure nobody will think of paying you. Oh,
Reginald, there is plenty, plenty of work."

The young man was already beginning to melt. " Do you
think so ? " he said.

"Think!" cried Janey, "I am sure you may do all papa's work for him and welcome, if that is all. For my part I think you are very silly, both Ursula and you. Work! Pay is far better if you weren't such a pair of simpletons. After all, he has a little reason to be angry. Good gracious! why shouldn't you take it? Some one else will, if you won't. I would in a minute, and so would Ursula if we could. And why should you be so much grander than anybody else? I think it is quite childish for my part."

"Reginald, never mind her, she is only a child and doesn't understand ('Child yourself,' cried Janey). I don't understand very well, but still I can see what you want. Oh, you might find such quantities of work, things nobody is ever found to do. What do the fellows do at Oxford that they get that money for? I have heard you say you would be very glad to get a fellowship—"

"That is different, that is a reward of scholarship."

"Well, and so is this too," said Ursula; "it is (I am sure) because the old men knew you were one that would be kind. You were always kind, Reginald, that is what it is for."

"The old men have nothing to do with it," he said, shaking his head, "it is the Corporation, and they are—"

"Very rich men, Reginald dear, a great many of them, very sensible! what does it matter about their education? And then you would be a really educated man, always ready to do anything that was wanted in Carlingford. Don't you see that was their meaning? They pay you for that which is not work, but they will find you plenty of work they don't pay for. That is what they mean; and oh, Reginald, to run over to you there in that pretty wainscoted room, and to have you coming in to us every day, and to know that you were there to stand by us!"

Here once more Ursula began to cry. As for Janey, she made a dash at the writing-table and brought him paper and pens and ink, "Say yes, say yes," she cried; "oh, Reginald, if it was only to spite papa!"

CHAPTER XVI.

THE NEW GENTLEMAN.

It seems difficult to imagine what connection there could be between Phœbe Beecham's appearance in Grange Lane and the interview which took place there between her and the "new gentleman," and Mr. May's sudden onslaught upon his family, which ended in Reginald's acceptance of the chaplaincy. But yet the connection was very distinct. Not even the Mays, in their excitement over the appearance of a stranger in Carlingford, could be more surprised than Phœbe was when her solitary walk was interrupted by the apparition across the street of a known person, a face familiar to her in other regions. "Mr. Northcote!" she cried, with a little start of surprise. As for the stranger, he made but two steps across Grange Lane in his delight at the sight of her. Not that he was Phœbe's lover, or possessed by any previous enthusiasm for the girl whom he had met about half-a-dozen times in his life, and of whom he knew little more than that she was the daughter of a "brother clergyman;" for both Mr. Beecham and he were in the habit of using that word, whether appropriate or inappropriate. This was the explanation of the white necktie and the formal dress which had puzzled Ursula.

Horace Northcote was not of Mr. Beecham's class. He was not well-to-do and genial, bent upon keeping up his congregation and his popularity, and trying to ignore as much as he could the social superiority of the Church without making himself in any way offensive to her. He was a political Nonconformist, a vigorous champion of the Dis-establishment Society, more successful on the platform than in the pulpit, and strenuously of opinion in his heart of hearts that the Church was the great drawback to all progress in England, an incubus of which the nation would gladly be rid. His dress was one of the signs of his character and meaning. Strong in a sense of his own clerical position, he believed in uniform as devoutly as any Ritualist, but he would not plagiarise the Anglican livery and walk about in a modified soutane and round hat like "our brethren in the Established Church," as Mr. Beecham kindly called them. To young Northcote they were not brethren, but enemies, and though he smiled superior

at the folly which stigmatised an M.B. waistcoat, yet he scorned
to copy. Accordingly his frock coat was not long, but of the
extremest solemnity of cut and hue, his white tie was of the
stiffest, his tall hat of the most uncompromising character. He
would not veil for a day in easier and more ordinary habili-
ments the distinct position he assumed as clerical, yet not of
the clergy; a teacher of men, though not a priest of the Anglican
inspiration. He could not help feeling that his appearance, as
he moved about the streets, was one which might well thrill
Anglican bosoms with a flutter of terror. He was the Church's
avowed enemy, and upon this he stood as his claim to the
honour of those who thought with him. This was very different
from the views held by the pastor of the Crescent Chapel, who
was very willing to be on the best terms with the Church, and
would have liked to glide into closer and closer amity, and perhaps finally to melt away altogether in her broad bosom, like a
fat raindrop contributing noiselessly to swell the sea. It was
not, however, any feeling of this difference which made Phœbe
draw herself back instinctively after the first start of recognition. Across her mind, even while she held out her hand to
the stranger, there flashed a sudden recollection of her grandmother and her grandfather, and all the homely belongings which
he, a minister of the connection, could not be kept in ignorance
of. It was but a momentary pang. Phœbe was not so foolish
as to shrink before the inevitable, or to attempt by foolish expedients to stave off such a danger. She shrank for a second,
then drew herself up and shook off all such ignoble cares. " I
am myself whatever happens," was her reflection; and she said
with something like security:

"I am so glad to meet you, Mr. Northcote; what an unexpected pleasure to see you here!"

"It is a most unexpected pleasure for me, I assure you," he
said, "and a very great one." He spoke with unaffected
honesty; for indeed his plunge into the society of Salem
Chapel had given him a shock not easily got over, and the appearance of a being of his own species, among all these excellent
poulterers and grocers, was a relief unspeakable; and then he
added, "May I walk with you, if you are going to walk?"

"Surely," said Phœbe with momentary hesitation, and it was
just at this moment that she perceived Ursula on the other
side of the road, and, glad of the diversion, waved her hand to
her, and said, "How do you do?"

"A friend of yours?" said Mr. Northcote, following her
gesture with his eyes, and feeling more and more glad that he
had met her. "I passed those young ladies just now, and

heard some of their conversation, which amused me. Do they belong to our people? If you will not be angry, Miss Beecham, I must say that I should be glad to meet somebody belonging to us, who is not—who is more like—the people one meets elsewhere."

"Well," said Phœbe, "we are always talking of wanting something original; I think on the whole I am of your opinion; still there is nothing very great or striking about most of the people one meets anywhere."

"Yes; society is flat enough," said the young man. "But —it is strange and rather painful, though perhaps it is wrong to say so—why, I wonder, are all our people of one class? Perhaps you have not seen much of them here? All of one class, and that—"

"Not an attractive class," said Phœbe, with a little sigh. "Yes, I know."

"Anything but an attractive class; not the so-called working men and such like. One can get on with them. It is very unpleasant to have to say it; buying and selling now as we have it in Manchester does not contract the mind. I suppose we all buy and sell more and less. How is it? When it is tea and sugar—"

"Or butter and cheese," said Phœbe with a laugh, which she could not quite keep from embarrassment. "I must be honest and tell you before you go any further. You don't know that I belong to the Tozers, Mr. Northcote, who are in that line of business. Don't look so dreadfully distressed. Perhaps I shouldn't have told you, had you not been sure to find out. Old Mr. Tozer is my grandfather, and I am staying there. It is quite simple. Papa came to Carlingford when he was a young clergyman, newly ordained. He was pastor at Salem Chapel, and married mamma, who was the daughter of one of the chief members. I did not know myself when I came to Carlingford that they actually kept a shop, and I did not like it. Don't apologize, please. It is a very difficult question," said Phœbe philosophically, partly to ease herself, partly to set him at his ease, "what is best to do in such a case. To be educated in another sphere and brought down to this, is hard. One cannot feel the same for one's relations; and yet one's poor little bit of education, one's petty manners, what are these to interfere with blood relationships? And to keep everybody down to the condition they were born, why, that is the old way—"

"Miss Beecham, I don't know what to say. I never meant —I could not tell. There are excellent, most excellent people in all classes."

"Exactly so," said Phœbe, with a laugh. "We all know that; one man is as good as another—if not better. . A butter-man is as good as a lord; but—" she added, with a little eleva-tion of her eyebrows and shrug of her shoulders, "not so pleasant to be connected with. And you don't say anything about my difficulty, Mr. Northcote. You don't realize it per-haps, as I do. Which is best: for everybody to continue in the position he was born in, or for an honest shopkeeper to educate his children and push them up higher until they come to feel themselves members of a different class, and to be ashamed of him? Either way, you know, it is hard."

Northcote was at his wit's end. He had no fellow-feeling for this difficulty. His friends were all much better off than he was as a poor minister. They were Manchester people, with two or three generations of wealth behind them, relations of whom nobody need be ashamed; and he was himself deeply humiliated and distressed to have said anything which could humiliate Phœbe, who rose immeasurably in his estimation in consequence of her bold avowal, though he himself would have sacrificed a great deal rather than put himself on the Tozer level. He did not know what to say.

"Miss Beecham, you know as well as I do, how falsely our opinions are formed in this respect, how conventional we are. What is position after all? To a grand Seigneur, for instance, the difference between his steward and his laquais seems no-thing, but to the steward it is a great gulf. I—I mean—the whole question is conventional—position, or station, or rank—"

Phœbe smiled. "I don't think that is quite the question," she said, "but never mind. I suppose you are here on some mission? You would not come to Carlingford for pleasure."

"Nay," said Northcote, with a reproachful tone. "I should have thought you must have heard of our Meeting. It is for to-night. I have come from the Disestablishment Society with some other friends; but it has been my fate to come on before to make the arrangements. The others come to-day."

"A hard fate, Mr. Northcote."

"I thought so this morning. I have not been much in the way of the country congregations. I was confounded; but, Miss Beecham, I no longer think my fate hard since I have met you. Your noble simplicity and frankness have taught me a lesson."

"It is not noble at all," said Phœbe; "if I had not been sure you must find out I should have said nothing about it. Now I fear I must turn back."

"But you will come to the Meeting," he said, turning with her. He felt it necessary to be obsequious to Phœbe, after the terrible mistake he had made."

"Not unless grandpapa insists. I should like to hear your speech," said Phœbe; "but I don't object to the Established Church as you do, neither does papa when you push him hard. I don't think England would be much nicer if we were all Dissenters. To be sure we might be more civil to each other."

"If there were no Dissenters, you mean."

"It comes to much the same thing; congregations are not pleasant masters, are they, Mr. Northcote? I know some people—one at least," said Phœbe, "who is often very insolent to papa; and we have to put up with it—for the sake of peace, papa says. I don't think in the Church that any leading member could be so insolent to a clergyman."

"That is perhaps rather—forgive me—a narrow, personal view."

"Wait till you get a charge, and have to please the congregation and the leading members!" cried Phœbe. "I know what you are thinking: it is just like a woman to look at a public question so. Very well; after all women are half the world, and their opinion is as good as another."

"I have the greatest respect for your opinion," said young Northcote; "but we must not think of individual grievances. The system, with all its wrongs, is what occupies me. I have heard something—even here—this very day— What is it, my good friend? I am busy now—another time; or if you want me, my lodgings are—"

A glance, half of pain, half of fun, came into Phœbe's eyes. "It is grandpapa!" she said.

"You shouldn't speak in that tone, sir, not to your elders, and maybe your betters," said Tozer, in his greasy old coat. "Ministers take a deal upon them; but an old member like me, and one as has stood by the connection through thick and thin, ain't the one to be called your good friend. Well, if you begs pardon, of course there ain't no more to be said; and if you know our Phœbe—Phœbe, junior, as I calls her. What of the meeting, Mr. Northcote? I hope you'll give it them Church folks 'ot and strong, sir. They do give themselves airs, to be sure, in Carlingford. Most of our folks is timid, seeing for one thing as their best customers belong to the Church. That don't touch me, not now-a-days," said Tozer, with a laugh, "not that I was ever one as concealed my convictions. I hope you'll give it 'em 'ot and strong."

"I shall say what I think," said the young man bewildered.

He was by no means broken into the ways of the connection, and his pride rebelled at the idea of being schooled by this old shopkeeper; but the sight of Phœbe standing by not only checked his rebellious sentiments, but filled him with a sympathetic thrill of feeling. What it must be for that girl to own this old man, to live with him, and feel herself shut into his society and friends of his choosing—to hear herself spoken of as Phœbe, junior! The idea made him shiver, and this caught old Tozer's always hospitable eye.

"You're chilly," he said, "and I don't wonder after the dreadful weather we've had. Few passes my door without a bite or a sup, specially at tea-time, Mr. Nor'cote, which is sociable time, as I always says. Come in and warm yourself and have a cup of tea. There is nothing as pleases my old woman so much as to get out her best tea-things for a minister; she 'as a great respect for ministers, has Mrs. Tozer, sir; and now she's got Phœbe to show off as well as the chiney. Come along, sir, I can't take no refusal. It's just our time for tea."

Northcote made an unavailing attempt to get away, but partly it appeared to him that to refuse the invitation might look to Phœbe like a pretence of superiority on his part, and partly he was interested in herself, and was very well aware he should get no company so good in Carlingford, even with the drawback of the old shop-people among whom she lived. How strange it was to see her in the dress of which Mrs. Sam Hurst had raved, and of which even the young Nonconformist vaguely divined the excellence, putting her daintily-gloved hand upon old Tozer's greasy sleeve, walking home with the shuffling old man, about whose social position no one could make the least mistake! He turned with them, with a sensation of thankfulness that it was in Grange Lane, Carlingford, where nobody knew him. As for Phœbe, no such comfort was in her mind; everybody knew her here, or rather, everybody knew old Tozer. No disguise was possible to her. The only way to redeem the position was to carry it with a high hand, as she did, holding her head erect, and playing her part so that all the world might see and wonder. "I think you had better come, Mr. Northcote, and have some tea," she said graciously, when the awestricken young man was floundering in efforts to excuse himself. Old Tozer chuckled and rubbed his hands.

"Take Phœbe's advice," he said, "Phœbe's the sensiblest girl I know; so was her mother before her, as married one of the most popular preachers in the connection, though I say it as shouldn't. My old woman always said as our Phœbe was cut out for a minister's wife. And Phœbe junior's just such another," cried the admiring grandfather. Heavens above! did this mean traps and snares for himself, or did the old shop-keeper think of him, Horace Northcote, as another possible victim? If he had but known with what sincere compassion-ate toleration Phœbe regarded him, as a young man whom she might be kind to, he might have been saved all alarm on this point. The idea that a small undistinguished Dissenting minister should think her capable of marrying him, was a humiliation which did not enter into Phœbe's head.

CHAPTER XVII.

A PUBLIC MEETING.

PHŒBE'S philosophy, however, was put to the test when, after the young pastor had taken tea and got himself away from the pressing hospitalities of the Tozers, her grandfather also disappeared to put on his best coat in order to attend the Meeting. Mrs. Tozer, left alone with her granddaughter, immediately proceeded to evolve her views as to what Phœbe was expected to do.

"I never see you out o' that brown thing, Phœbe," she said; "ain't you got a silk dress, child, or something that looks a bit younger-looking? I'd have thought your mother would have took more pride in you. Surely you've got a silk dress."

"Oh, yes, more than one," said Phœbe, "but this is con-sidered in better taste."

"Taste, whose taste?" cried the old lady; "my Phœbe didn't ought to care for them dingy things, for I'm sure she never got no such example from me. I've always liked what was bright-looking, if it was only a print. A nice blue silk now, or a bright green, is what you'd look pretty in with your complexion. Go now, there's a dear, and put on something very nice, something as will show a bit; you're going with your grandfather to this Meeting."

"To the Meeting? oh, I hope not," said Phœbe with fervour.

"And why should you hope not? isn't it natural as a young creature like you should get out a bit when she can, and see what's to be seen? I don't hold with girls moping in a house. Besides, it's very instructive, as I've always heard: and you as is clever, of course you'll understand every word. Mr. Northcote is a nicish-looking sort of young man. Ministers mayn't be much," said Mrs. Tozer, "though just see how your papa has got on, my dear. Nobody else as Phœbe could have married would have got up in the world like that; you may make a deal more money in trade, but it ain't so genteel, there's always that to be said. Now it's just as well as you should have your chance with the rest and let yourself be seen, Phœbe. Run, there's a darling, and put on something bright, and a nice lace collar. You can have mine if you like. I shouldn't grudge nothing, not a single thing I've got, to see you looking as nice as the best there; and so you will if you take a little pains. I'd do up my hair a bit higher if I was you; why, Phœbe, I declare! you haven't got a single pad. Now what is the use of neglecting yourself, and letting others get ahead of you like that?"

"Pads are going out of fashion, grandmamma," said Phœbe gravely, "so are bright colours for dresses. You can't think what funny shades we wear in town. But must I go to this Meeting? I should not like to leave you alone. It is so much nicer for me to be here."

"You *are* a good girl, you are," said Mrs. Tozer admiringly, "and me as was frightened for a fine lady from London! But Tozer would say as it was my doing. He would say as it wasn't natural for a young creature; and, bless you, they'll all be there in their best—that Pigeon and the others, and Mrs. Tom. I just wish I could go too, to see you outshine 'em all, which you'll do if you take pains. Take a little more pains with your hair, Phœbe, mount it up a bit higher, and if you want anything like a bit of lace or a brooch or that, just you come to me. I should like Mrs. Tom to see you with that brooch as she's always wanting for Minnie. Now why should I give my brooch to Minnie? I don't see no reason for it, for my part."

"Certainly not, grandmamma," said Phœbe, "you must wear your brooches yourself, that is what I like a great deal better than giving them either to Minnie or me."

"Ah, but there ain't a many like you, my sweet," cried the old woman, wiping her eyes. "You're my Phœbe's own daughter, but you're a touch above her, my darling, and us too, that's what you are. Run now and dress, or I don't know what Tozer will say to me. He's set his heart on showing you off to-night."

Thus adjured, Phœbe went away reluctantly. It is unnecessary to say that her disinterestedness about her grandmother's brooch was not perhaps so noble as it appeared on the outside.

The article in question was a kind of small warming-pan in a very fine solid gold mount, set with large pink topazes, and enclosing little wavy curls of hair, one from the head of each young Tozer of the last generation. It was a piece of jewelry very well known in Carlingford, and the panic which rose in Phœbe's bosom when it was offered for her own personal adornment is more easily imagined than described. She went upstairs feeling that she had escaped, and took out a black silk dress at which she looked lovingly.

"But grandmamma would think it was no better than this," she said to herself, and after much searchings of heart she chose a costume of Venetian blue, one soft tint dying into another like the lustre on a piece of old glass, which in her own opinion was a great deal too good for the occasion. "Some one will tread on it to a certainty, and the colours don't show in candle-light; but I must try to please grandmamma," she said heroically. When it was put on with puffings of lace such as Mrs. Tozer had never seen, and was entirely ignorant of the value of, at the throat and sleeves, Phœbe wrapt a shawl round her in something of the same dim gorgeous hue, covered with embroidery, an Indian rarity which somebody had bestowed upon Mrs. Beecham, and which no one had used or thought of till Phœbe's artistic eye fell upon it. It was a great deal too fine for Carlingford. An opera-cloak bought in Oxford Street for a pound or two would have much more impressed the assembly to which Phœbe was bound. Mrs. Tozer inspected her when she went downstairs, with awe, yet dissatisfaction.

"I dare say as it's all very fine, and it ain't like other folks, anybody can see; but I'd dress you different, my dear, if you was in my hands," said the old woman, walking round and round her. As for Tozer, he too showed less admiration than if he had known better.

"I got a fly, thinking as you'd have some fallal or other on you; but, bless my heart, you could have walked in that gown," he said. So that Phœbe's toilette, which would have been mightily admired in a London drawing-room, could not be said to be a success. She was somewhat discouraged by this, notwithstanding that she knew so very much better; and accordingly set out in the fly with her grandfather in his best coat, feeling, generally, in a depressed condition.

"It is clear that I must take to the pinks and blues to please them," she said to herself with a sigh. She could triumph over the slight that might be shown to herself in consequence of her relations; but those sneers at her dress went to Phœbe's heart.

The Music Hall was full of a miscellaneous crowd when Phœbe, following her grandfather, went in; and the seats allotted to these important people were on the platform, where, at least, Tozer's unacknowledged object of showing her off could be amply gratified. This arrangement did not, on the whole, displease Phœbe. Since she must be exhibited, it seemed better, on the whole, to be exhibited there, than in a less distinguished place; and all the speakers knew her, which was something. She sat down with some complaisance, and let her Indian scarf droop from her shoulders, and her pretty dress show itself.

"I declare if that isn't Phœbe, junior," said Mrs. Tom audibly, in the middle of the hall, "making a show of herself; but, Lord bless us, for all their grandeur, how she do dress, to be sure. A bit of a rag of an old shawl, and a hat on! the same as she wears every day. I've got more respect for them as comes to instruct us than that."

And, indeed, Mrs. Tom was resplendent in a red *sortie de bal*, with a brooch almost as big as that envied one of Mrs. Tozer's stuck into her gown, and a cap covered with flowers upon her head. This was the usual fashion of the Salem ladies on such rare occasions. The meeting of the Disestablishment Society was to them what a ball is to worldly-minded persons who frequent such vanities. The leading families came out *en masse* to see and to be seen. It would be wrong to say that they did not enter into all the arguments and recognise the intellectual feast set before them; no doubt they did this just as well as if they had come in their commonest attire; but still the seriousness of the occasion was, no doubt, modified by being thus made into a dissipation. The men were not so fine, perhaps, because it is more difficult for men to be fine—but they were all in their Sunday clothes; and the younger ones were in full bloom of coloured satin cravats and fine waistcoats. Some of them were almost as fine a sight as the ladies in their ribbons and flowers.

"I suppose by the look of them this must be an influential community—people of some pretensions," said an obese elderly minister, who had seated himself by Phœbe, and whose eyes were dazzled by the display. "I never expected all this dress in a quiet country place."

"Oh, yes! they are people of much pretension," said Phœbe gravely.

And then the proceedings began. Old Mr. Green, the grocer, whose son had married Maria Pigeon, and who had long been retired from business, occupying a house in the country and "driving his carriage," was in the chair; and the proceedings went on according to the routine of such assemblies, with differing degrees of earnestness on the part of the speakers. To most of these gentlemen it was the ordinary occupation of their lives; and they made their hearers laugh at well-known stories, and enjoyed their own wit, and elicited familiar cheers, and made hits such as they had made for years on the same subject, which was a comfortable *cheval de bataille*, not at all exciting to themselves, though they were quite willing to excite their audience, if that audience would allow itself to be excited. Things jogged on thus for the first hour very pleasantly! the Meeting was not excited, but it was amused and enjoyed itself. It was an intellectual treat, as Pigeon said to Brown, and if the younger people did not like it so well as they would have liked a ball, the elder people liked it a great deal better, and the hall rang with applause and with laughter as one speaker succeeded another. It was pleasant to know how unstable "the Church" was on her foundation; that aristocratical Church which looked down upon Dissent, and of which the poorest adherent gave himself airs much above Chapel folks; and how much loftier a position the Nonconformist held, who would have nothing to say to State support.

"For my part," said one of the speakers, "I would rather abandon my sacred calling to-morrow, or make tents as St. Paul did in its exercise, than put on the gilded fetters of the State, and pray or preach as an Archbishop told me; nay, as a Cabinet Council of godless worldlings directed. There are many good men among the clergy of the Church of England; but they are slaves, my friends, nothing but slaves, dragged at the chariot wheels of the State; ruled by a caste of hard-headed lawyers; or binding themselves in the rotten robes of tradition. It is we only who can dare to say that we are free!"

At this sentiment, the Meeting fairly shouted with applause and delight and self-complacency; and the speaker, delighted too, and tasting all the sweetness of success, gave place to the next, and came and sat down by Phœbe, to whose society the younger men were all very glad to escape.

"Miss Beecham, you are fashionably calm," whispered the orator, "you don't throw yourself, like the rest of us, into this great agitation."

"Have you a leading member?" whispered Phœbe back again; "and does he never drag you at his chariot wheels? Have you deacons that keep you up to the mark? Have you people you must drink tea with when they ask you, or else they throw up their sittings? I am thinking, of course, of papa."

"Have I deacons? Have I leading members? Miss Beecham, you are cruel—"

"Hush!" said Phœbe, settling herself in her chair. "Here is somebody who is in dreadful earnest. Don't talk, Mr. Northcote is going to speak."

Thus it will be seen that the Minister's daughter played her *rôle* of fine lady and *bel esprit* very fairly in an atmosphere so unlike the air that fine ladies breathe. Phœbe paid no more attention to the discomfited man at her elbow. She gathered up her shawl in her hand with a seeming careless movement, and let it drop lightly across her knee, where the gold threads in the embroidery caught the light; and she took off her hat, which she had thought proper to wear to show her sense that the Meeting was not an evening party; and prepared herself to listen. Her complexion and her hair, and the gold threads in the rich Indian work, thus blazed out together upon the startled audience. Many of them were as much struck by this as by the beginning of Mr. Northcote's speech, though it was very different from the other speeches. The others had been routine agitation, this was fiery conviction, crude, and jumping at conclusions, but still an enthusiasm in its way. Mr. North-cote approached his subject gradually, and his hearers, at first disappointed by the absence of their familiar watch-words, were dull, and bestowed their attention on Phœbe; but before he had been speaking ten minutes Phœbe was forgotten even by her uncle and aunt, the two people most interested in her. It would be dangerous to repeat to a reader, probably quite unin-terested in the controversy, Mr. Northcote's speech, in which he laid hold of some of those weak points which the Church, of course, has in common with every other institution in the world. Eloquence has a way of evaporating in print, even when the report is immediate. But his peroration was one which startled his hearers out of a calm abstract interest to all that keen personal feeling which accompanies the narrative of facts known to an audience, and affecting people within their own locality.

"I have only been in this place three days," said the speaker, "but in that short time I have heard of one of the most flagrant abuses which I have been indicating to you. There is in this town, as you all know, an institution called the College; what was its original object I do not know. Nests of idle pauper-ism, genteelly veiled under such a name, do exist, I know, over all the country; but it is at least probable that some educational purpose was in the mind of the pious founder who established it. The pious founder! how immense are the revenues, how incalculable the means of doing good, which have been locked up in uselessness, or worse than uselessness, by men who have purchased a pass into the kingdom of heaven at the last moment by such gifts, and become pious founders just before they ceased to be miserable sinners! Whatever may have been the original intention of the College, however, it is clear that it was meant for something more than the pitiful use it is put to now. This old foundation, ladies and gentlemen, which might provide half the poor children in Carlingford with a wholesome education, is devoted to the maintenance of six old men, need I say Churchmen?" (here the speaker was interrupted by mingled hisses and ironical " hear, hears ")—" and a chaplain to say their prayers for them. Six old men: and one able-bodied parson to say their prayers for them. What do you think of this, my friends? I understand that this heavy and onerous duty has been offered—not to some other mouldy old gentleman, some decayed clergyman who might have ministered in peace to the decayed old burghers without any interference on my part: for a refuge for the aged and destitute has something natural in it, even when it is a wrong appropriation of public money. No, this would have been some faint approach perhaps to justice, some right in wrong that would have closed our mouths. But no! it is given to a young gentleman, able-bodied, as I have said, who has appeared more than once in the cricket-field with your victorious Eleven, who is fresh from Oxford, and would no more condescend to consider himself on a footing of equality with the humble person who addresses you, than I would, having the use of my hands, accept a disgraceful sinecure! Yes, my friends, this is what the State Church does. She so cows the spirit and weakens the hearts of her followers that a young man at the very beginning of his career, able to teach, able to work, able to dig, educated and trained and cul-tured, can stoop to accept a good income in such a position as this. Think of it! Six old men, able surely, if they are good for anything, to mumble their prayers for themselves somehow; yet provided with an Oxford scholar, an able-bodied young man, to read the service for them daily! He thinks it very fine, no doubt, a good income and a good house for life, and nothing to do but to canter over morning and evening prayer at a swinging pace, as we have all heard it done: morning prayer, let us see, half an hour—or you may throw in ten minutes, in case the six should mumble their Amens slowly—

and twenty minutes for the evening, one hour a day. Here it is under your very eyes, people of Carlingford, a charming provision for the son of one of your most respected clergymen. Why, it is in your newspaper, where I read it! Can I give a more forcible instance of the way in which a State Church cuts honesty and honour out of men's hearts."

A great many people noticed that when Mr. Northcote ended this with a thundering voice, some one who had been listening near the door in an Inverness cape, and hat over his brows, gave himself a sudden impetuous shake which shook the crowd, and turning round made his way out, not caring whom he stumbled against. The whole assembly was in a hubbub when the orator ceased, and whispers ran freely round among all the groups in the front. "That's young May he means." "In course it's young May. Infernal job, as I've always said." "Oh hush, Pigeon, don't swear! but it do seem a black burning shame, don't it?" "Bravo, Mr. Nor'cote!" called out old Tozer, on the platform, "that's what I call giving forth no uncertain sound. That's laying it into them 'ot and 'ot."

This was the climax of the Meeting. Everything else was flat after such a decided appeal to personal knowledge. Phœbe alone gave a frigid reception to the hero of the evening.

"I dislike personalities," she said, pointedly. "They never do a cause any good; and it isn't gentlemanly; don't you think so, Mr. Sloely;" and she turned away from Northcote, who had come to speak to her, and devoted herself to the man at her elbow, whom she had snubbed a little while before. Mr. Northcote said to himself that this was untrue, and brought up a hundred very good reasons why he should have employed such an example, but the reproof stung him to the quick, for to be ungentlemanly was the reproach of all others most calculated to go to his heart.

But nobody knew how Mr. May went home in his Inverness cape, breathing fire and flame, nor of the execution he did thereupon.

CHAPTER XVIII.

MR. MAY'S AFFAIRS.

MR. MAY went into his study and closed the door. He poked the fire—he put himself into his easy-chair—he drew his writing-book towards him, and opened it at where a half-written sheet lay waiting. And then he paused, rubbed his hands softly together, and falling back again, laughed quietly to himself.

Yes; he who had stormed out of the drawing-room like a whirlwind, having discomfited everybody, leaving the girls in tears, and the boys in a white heat of passion, when he reached the profoundest depths of his own retirement, laughed. What did it mean? Of all the people in the world, his children would have been most entirely thunderstruck by this self-betrayal. They could not have understood it. They were acquainted with his passions, and with his moments of good temper. They knew when he was amiable, and when he was angry, by instinct, by the gleam of his eye, by the way in which he shut the door; but this was something totally unknown to them. The truth was that Mr. May, like many other people, having a naturally bad temper, which he indulged freely when he pleased, had attained the power of using it when it suited him to use it, without being suspected by anybody. A bad temper is a possession like another, and may be made skilful use of like other things which, perhaps, in themselves, are not desirable. He could work himself up into fury, and launch the doom he felt disposed to launch, like a burning and fizzing thunder-bolt from a hand which was, in reality, not at all excited; and like most other people who possess such an un-revealed power, it pleased him very much when he persuaded his surroundings that it was an impulse of rage which moved him. He had been at the Meeting at the Music Hall, "to hear what those fellows had to say for themselves." Contempt, unbounded but wrathful, was the feeling in his mind towards "those fellows;" but he felt that young Northcote's eloquence, reported in next day's papers, was quite enough to quash for ever all hopes of his son's acceptance of the chaplaincy. So he walked home as fast as his legs would carry him, and burst into his house, as we have seen, with a semblance of passion so perfect as to deceive his entire family and fill the place with anger and tears. Upon which, withdrawing from the scene of conflict, he threw himself down in his easy-chair and chuckled, recovering his composure by slow degrees.

When, however, this private indulgence was over, Mr. May's face grew dark enough. He pushed his writing away from him, and pulling out a drawer in his writing-table, which was full of papers of a very unliterary aspect, betook himself to the consideration of them, with anything but laughter in his looks, or in his mind. Letters upon blue paper in straight up and down handwriting—other papers, also blue, with ruled lines and numerals, for which Mr. May was more frightened than he would have been for a charge of cavalry. These were the very unattractive contents of this drawer. He brought two or three of them out in a bundle and read them over, one after another, with contracted brows. Debt is an idiosyncrasy like other things. Some people keep clear of it miraculously, some seem to drop into it without cause or meaning, and to spend all their lives afterwards in vain attempts to get out. Mr. May was one of these unfortunate men. He could not tell himself where his money went to. Poor man! it was not so much he had, and there was a large family to be fed and clothed, and schooled after a sort. But still other people on incomes as small as his had managed to maintain their families without dropping into this hopeless condition. He had been in debt since ever he could remember; and to be sure it was not the pain and trouble to him that it is to many people. So long as, by hook or by crook, he could manage to stave off the evil day, so long was he happy enough, and he had managed this by all sorts of semi-miraculous windfalls up to the present time. James's remittances had been like heavenly dew to him. It is true that these remittances had been intended to keep Reginald at Oxford, and perhaps something of the special hardness with which he regarded Reginald arose from the fact that he had done him wrong in this respect, and had appropriated what was intended for him. But after all, he had said to himself, the maintenance of the house in comfort, the keeping clean of the family name, and the staving off disagreeable revelations of the family's poverty, were more, for even Reginald's comfort, than a little more money in his pocket, which everybody knew was very dangerous for a young man.

Mr. May had always a bill coming due, which James's remittances arrived just in time to meet. Indeed, this was the normal condition of his life. He had always a bill coming due —a bill which some good-humoured banker had to be coaxed into renewing, or which was paid at the last moment by some skilful legerdemain in the way of pouring out of one vessel into another, transferring the debt from one quarter to another, so that there may have been said to be always a certain amount of quite fictitious and visionary money floating about Mr. May, money which existed only in the shape of symbol, and which, indeed, belonged to nobody—which was borrowed here to-day, and paid there to-morrow, to be re-borrowed and repaid in the same way, never really reaching anybody's pocket, or representing anything but that one thing which money is supposed to be able to extinguish—debt. When human affairs reach this very delicate point, and there is nothing at any moment, except a semi-miraculous windfall, to keep a man going, the crisis is very serious. And it was no wonder that Mr. May was anxious to drive his son into accepting any possible appointment, and that he occasionally railed unreasonably at his family. Unless a hundred pounds or so fell down from the skies within the next ten days, he saw nothing before him but ruin. This, it is needless to say, is very far from being a comfortable position. The *sourde* agitation, excitement, feverish hope and fear of the sufferer might well affect his temper. If he could not get a hundred pounds within ten days, he did not know what he was to do.

And nobody could say (he thought to himself) that he was an expensive man; he had no expensive habits. He liked good living, it is true, and a glass of good wine, but this amount of regard for the table does not ruin men. He liked books also, but he did not buy them, contenting himself with such as the library could afford, and those which he could obtain by the reviews he wrote for the Church Magazines. How then was it that he never could get rid of that rapidly maturing bill? He could not tell. Keeping out of debt is one thing, and getting rid of it when you have once taken its yoke upon your neck is another. His money, when he had any, "slipped through his fingers," as people say. When James's remittance or any other piece of good fortune gave him enough to pay that hundred pounds without borrowing elsewhere, he borrowed elsewhere all the same. It was a mysterious fatality, from which he seemed unable to escape. In such circumstances a crisis must come sooner or later, and it appeared to him that now at least, after many hairbreadth escapes, the crisis had come.

What was he to do? There was no chance, alas! of money from James, and even if Reginald accepted the chaplaincy, and was willing at once to come to his father's aid, there was no hope that he would have anything for some time—for chaplains incomes are not, any more than other people's, generally paid in advance. He leaned back in his chair and went over again, for the hundredth time, the list of all the people he could borrow from, or who would "back" a bill for him, and he was still employed in this melancholy and hopeless enumeration, when a low knock came to the door, and a maid-of-all-work, pushing it open, thrust in a homely little man in a dusty-brown coat, who put up a hand to his forehead as he came in with a salutation which was half charity school-boy, half awkward recruit. Beyond this there was no ceremony about his entrance, no leave asked or question made. Betsy knew very well that he was to come in when he pleased, and that her master did not deny himself to Cotsdean. Mr. May received him with a familiar nod, and pointed hastily to a chair. He did not even take the trouble to put away those blue papers, which he would have done if any other individual, even if one of his children had come into the room.

"Good evening, Cotsdean," he said, in a friendly tone. "Well, what news?"

"Nothing as is pleasant, sir," said the man, sitting down on a corner of his chair. "I've been to the bank, and it's no use my explaining, or begging ever so hard. They won't hear of it. 'We've done it times and times,' they says to me, 'and we won't do it no more. That's flat,' and so indeed it is flat, sir, as you may say downright Dunstable; but that ain't no advantage to you and me."

"Yes, it is, Cotsdean," said the clergyman, "it is a decided advantage, for it shows there is nothing to be hoped from that quarter, and that is always good—even though it's bad bad, as bad as can be—"

"You may say so, sir," said Cotsdean. "I don't know what's to be done no more than the babe unborn, and it's wearing me to death, that's what it's doing. When I looks round on my small family, it's all I can do not to cry out loud. What's to become of my children, Mr. May? Yours, sir, they'll never want friends, and a hundred or so here or there, that don't ruin gentlefolks; but without selling up the business, how am I ever to get a hundred pounds? It ain't equal, sir, I swear it ain't. You gets the money, and you takes it easy, and don't hold your head not a bit lower; but me as has no good of it (except in the way o' a bit of custom that is a deal more in looks than anything else), and has to go round to all the folks, to Mr. Brownlow, at the bank, and I don't know who, as if it was for me! I suffers in my credit, sir, and I suffers in my spirits, and I suffers in my health; and when the smash comes, what's to become of my poor children? It's enough to put a man beside himself, that's what it is."

Here the poor man's eyes grew bloodshot, partly with rubbing them, partly with tears. He rubbed them with the sleeve of his rough coat, and the tears were very real, though few in number. Cotsdean's despair was indeed tragical enough, but its outside had in it a dash of comedy, which, though he was in no mirthful mood, caught the quick eye of Mr. May. He was himself very painfully affected, to tell the truth, but yet it cost him an effort not to smile.

"Cotsdean," he said, "have I ever failed you yet? You have done a good deal for me, I don't deny it—you have had all the trouble, but beyond that what have you suffered except in imagination? If you choose to exaggerate dangers, it is not my fault. Your children are as safe as—as safe as the Bank of England. Now, have I ever failed you? answer me that."

"I can't say as you have, sir," said Cotsdean, "but it's dreadful work playing with a man's ruin, off and on like this, and nobody knowing what might happen, or what a day or an hour might bring forth."

"That is very true," said Mr. May. "I might die, that is what you mean; very true, though not quite so kind as I might have expected from an old friend—a very old friend."

"I am sure, Sir, I beg your pardon," cried the poor man, "it wasn't that; but only just as I'm driven out o' my seven senses with thinking and thinking."

"My dear Cotsdean, don't think; there could not be a more unnecessary exercise; what good does your thinking do, but to make you unhappy? leave that to me. We have been driven into a corner before now, but nothing has ever happened to us. You will see something will turn up this time. I ask you again, have I ever failed you? you know best."

"No, sir," said Cotsdean, somewhat doubtfully. "No, I didn't say as you had. It's only—I suppose I ain't so young as I once was—and a man's feelin's, sir, ain't always in his own control."

"You must take care that it is only to me that you make such an exhibition as this," said Mr. May. "Who is there? oh, my coffee! put it on the table. If you are seen coming here to me with red eyes and this agitated appearance," he went on, waiting pointedly till the door was closed, "it will be supposed there is some family reason for it—again—"

"Oh, lor', Sir! you know—"

"Yes, I know very well," said the clergyman. "I know that there couldn't be a better wife, and that bygones are bygones; but you must remember and take care; everybody doesn't know you—and her—so well as I do. When you come to see your clergyman in this agitated state, I put it to yourself, Cotsdean, I put it to your good sense, what is anybody to think? You must take great care not to betray yourself to anybody but me."

The man looked at him with a half-gasp of consternation, bewildered by the very boldness with which he was thus set down. Betray himself—he drew a long breath, as if he had received a *douche* of cold water in his face, which was indeed very much like the effect that this extraordinary address produced —betray himself! Poor Cotsdean's struggles and sufferings arose, at the present moment, entirely from the fact that he had allowed himself to be made use of for Mr. May's occasions, and both the men were perfectly aware of this. But though he gasped, Cotsdean was too much under the influence of his clergyman to do anything more. Had he been a Dissenter, he would have patronized young Northcote, who was as good a man as Mr. May (or far better if truth were told), with the frankest certainty of his own superior position, but being a humble churchman he yielded to his clergyman as to one of the powers that be. It is a curious difference. He sat still on the edge of his chair, while Mr. May walked across the room to the table by the door, where his *café noir* had been placed, and took his cup and drank it. He was not civil enough to ask his visitor to share it, indeed it never would have occurred to him, though he did not hesitate to use poor Cotsdean for his own purpose, to treat him otherwise than as men treat their servants and inferiors. When he had finished his coffee, he went leisurely back into his former place.

"You have nothing to suggest," he said, "nothing to advise? Well, I must try what I can do. It will be hard work, but still I must do it, you know." added Mr. May, in a gracious tone. "I have never concealed from you, Cotsdean, how much I appreciated your assistance; everything of this sort is so much worse in my position than in yours. You understand that? A gentleman—and a clergyman—has things expected from him which never would be thought of in your case. I have never omitted to acknowledge my obligations to you— and you also owe some obligations to me."

"I don't deny as you've been very kind, sir," said Cotsdean, half-grateful, half-sullen; then he wavered a little. "I never denied it, *her* and me could never have 'it it off but for you. I don't forget a favour—nobody can say that of me. I ain't forgot it in this case."

"I don't say that you have forgotten it. I have always put the utmost confidence in you; but, my good fellow, you must not come to me in this down-in-the-mouth way. Have I ever failed you? We've been hard pressed enough at times, but something has always turned up. Have not I told you a hundred times Providence will provide?"

"If you put it like that, sir—"

"I do put it like that. I have always been helped, you know, sometimes when it seemed the last moment. Leave it to me. I have no more doubt," said Mr. May, lifting up a countenance which was by no means so untroubled as could have been wished, "that when the time comes all will be well, than I have of the sun rising to-morrow—which it will," he added with some solemnity, "whether you and I live to see it or not. Leave it all, I say, to me."

Cotsdean did not make any reply. He was overawed by this solemnity of tone, and knew his place too well to set himself up against his clergyman; but still it cannot be denied that the decision was less satisfactory than one of much less exalted tone might have been. He had not the courage to say anything —he withdrew with his hat in his hand, and a cloud over his face. But as he left the house the doubt in his soul breathed itself forth. "If so be as neither me nor him see it rise, what good will that do to my family," said Cotsdean to himself, and went his way to his closed shop, through all the sacks of seeds and dry rustling grain, with a heavy heart. He was a cornfactor in a tolerable business, which, as most of the bankers of Carlingford knew, he had some difficulty in carrying along, being generally in want of money; but this was not so rare a circumstance that any special notice should be taken of it. Everybody who knew thought it was very kind of Mr. May to back him up as he did, and even to put his name to bills for poor Cotsdean, to whom, indeed, he was known to have been very kind in many ways. But nobody was aware how little of these said bills went to Cotsdean, and how much to Mr. May.

When he was gone, the clergyman threw himself back again into his chair with a pale face. Providence, which he treated like some sort of neutral deity, and was so very sure of having on his side when he spoke to Cotsdean, did not feel so near to him, or so much under his command, when Cotsdean was gone. There were still two days; but if before that he could not make some provision, what was to be done? He was not a cruel or bad man, and would have suffered keenly had anything happened to poor Cotsdean and his family on his account. But they must be sacrificed if it came to that, and the thought was very appalling. What was he to do? His friends were exhausted, and so were his expedients. There was no longer any one he could borrow from, or who would take even a share of his burden on their shoulders. What was he to do?

CHAPTER XIX.

THE NEW CHAPLAIN.

It cannot be denied that, reluctant as Reginald May had been to accept the chaplaincy of which so much had been said, he had no sooner fairly done so, and committed himself beyond remedy, than a certain sense of relief began to steal over the young man's mind. He had made the leap. Moved, at last, by arguments which, perhaps, were not worth very much logically, and which even while he yielded to them he saw the weakness of, he felt sure that when he woke in the morning, and realized what he had done, fearful feelings of remorse would seize him. But, curiously enough, this was not so; and his first sensation was relief that the conflict was over, and that he had no more angry remonstrances to meet with, or soft pleadings from Ursula, or assaults of rude abruptness from Janey. All that was over; and then a warm glow of independence and com. petency came over the young man. You may be sure he had no fire in his rooms to make him warm, and it was a chill January morning, with snow in the heavy sky, and fog in the yellow air; but, notwithstanding, there came a glow of comfort over him.

Independent! and with an income, without which independence is a mockery—free to go where he pleased, buy what he liked, spend his time as best seemed to him, with a "position" of his own; even a house of his own. He laughed softly to himself at this new idea. It did not somehow hurt him as he thought it would, this sinecure he had accepted. Could he not make it up, as Ursula said, "work for the town in other ways without pay, since the town had given him pay without work?" A genial feeling of toleration came over Reginald's mind. Why should he have made such a fuss about it? It was natural that his father should insist, and, now that it was done, he himself did not wish it undone, as he had expected to do. After all, if you judged matters with such rigidity, who was there without guilt? what public appointment was given and held according to abstract right, as, formally speaking, it ought to be? Those in the highest offices were appointed, not because of their personal excellence, but because of being some other man's son or brother; and yet, on the whole, public duty was well done, and the unjust ruler and hireling priest were exceptions. Even men whose entry into the fold was very precipitate, over the wall, violently, or by some rat-hole of private interest, made very good shepherds, once they were inside. Nothing was perfect in this world, and yet things were more good than evil; and if he himself made it his study to create for himself an ideal position, to become a doer of all kinds of volunteer work, what would it matter that his appointment was not an ideal appointment? It seemed very strange to him, and almost like an interposition of Providence in his favour, that he should feel in this way, for Reginald was not aware that such revulsions of feeling were very natural phenomena, and that the sensation, after any great decision, is almost invariably one of relief. To be sure it upset this manly state of mind a little when, coming down to breakfast, his father gave him a nod, and said briefly, "I am glad you have seen your duty at last."

This made him almost resolve to throw it up again; but the feeling was momentary. Why should he give it up? It had made him independent (already he thought of his independence as a thing accomplished), and he would make full amends to the Church and to Carlingford for taking two hundred and fifty pounds a year without working for it. Surely he could do that. He did not grudge work, but rather liked it, and would be ready to do anything, he did not care what, to make his sinecure into a volunteer's outpost for every good work. Yes, that was the way to look at it. And it was a glorious independence. Two hundred and fifty pounds a year!

"And the house," cried Ursula, when Mr. May had left the breakfast-table, and left them free to chatter. "The house— I don't think you are likely to find a tenant for it. The houses in Grange Lane are so cheap now; and some people object to the poor old men. I think you must keep the house. Furnishing will be an expense; but, of course, when you have a certain income, that makes such a difference; and you can come and see us every day."

"Why can't he live at home?" said Janey; "we are so poor; he ought to come and pay us something for his board, and help us to get on."

"What can you know about it, at your age?" said Ursula. "We have not got proper rooms for Reginald. He ought, at

least, to have a study of his own, as well as a bed-room, now
that he has an appointment. No, you must go to the College,
Reginald; and, perhaps, you might have one of the boys with
you, say Johnnie, which would be a great saving—for he has
an appetite; he eats more than two of the rest of us do. You
might take one of them with you—to save the bills a little—if
you like."

"Take me," said Janey, "I have a good appetite too; and
then I'm a girl, which is a great deal more useful. I could
keep your house. Oh, Reginald! mayn't we go out and see it?
I want to see it. I have never once been over the College—
not in all my life."

"We might as well go, don't you think, Ursula?" he said,
appealing to her with a delightful mixture of helplessness and
supremacy. Yesterday, he had not been able to assert any
exclusive claim to sixpence. Now he had a house—a house all
his own. It pleased him to think of taking the girls to it;
and as for having one of them, he was ready to have them all
to live with him. Ursula thought fit to accede graciously to
this suggestion, when she had looked after her numerous household duties. Janey, in the mean time, had been "practising"
in one of her periodical fits of diligence.

"For, you know, if Reginald did really want me to keep
house for him," said Janey, "(you have too much to do at
home; or, of course, he would like you best), it would be
dreadful if people found out how little I know."

"You ought to go to school," said Ursula, gravely. "It is
a dreadful thing for a girl never to have had any education.
Perhaps Reggie might spare a little money to send you to
school; or, perhaps, papa—"

"School yourself!" retorted Janey, indignant; but then she
thought better of it. "Perhaps just for a year to finish," she
added in a doubtful tone. They thought Reginald could do
anything on that wonderful two hundred and fifty pounds a
year.

The College was a picturesque old building at the other side
of Carlingford, standing in pretty grounds with some fine trees,
under which the old men sat and amused themselves in the
summer mornings. On this chilly wintry day none of them
were visible, except the cheerful old soul bent almost double,
but with a chirruppy little voice like a superannuated sparrow,
who acted as porter, and closed the big gates every night, and
fined the old men twopence if they were too late. He trotted
along the echoing passages, with his keys jingling, to show
them the chaplain's rooms.

"The old gentlemen is all as pleased as Punch," said Joe. "We was a feared as it might be somebody fureign—not a Carlingford gentleman; and some parsons is queer, saving your presence, Mr. May; but we knows where you comes from, and all about you, as one of the old gentlemen was just a-saying to me. Furnished, Miss? Lord bless you, yes! they're furnished. It's all furnished, is College. You'll think as the things look a bit queer; they wasn't made not this year, nor yet last year, I can tell you; and they ain't in the fashion. But if so be as you don't stand by fashion, there they is," said Joe, throwing open the door.

The young people went in softly, their excitement subdued into a kind of awe. An empty house, furnished, is more desolate, more overwhelming to the imagination, than a house which is bare. For whom was it waiting, all ready there, swept and garnished? Or were there already unseen inhabitants about, writing ghostly letters on the tables, seated on the chairs? Even Janey was hushed.

"I'd rather stay at home, after all," she whispered in Ursula's ear under her breath.

But after awhile they became familiar with the silent place, and awoke the echoes in it with their voices and new life. Nothing so young had been in the College for years. The last chaplain had been an old man and an old bachelor; and the pensioners were all solitary, living a sort of monastic life, each in his room, like workers in their cells. When Janey, surprised by some unexpected joke, burst into one of her peals of laughter, the old building echoed all through it, and more than one window was put up and head projected to know the cause of this profanation.

"Joe!" cried one portentous voice; "what's happened? what's the meaning of this?"

"It's only them a-laughing, sir," said Joe, delighting in the vagueness of his rejoinder. "They ain't used to it, that's the truth; but laugh away, Miss, it'll do you good," he added benignly. Joe was of a cheerful spirit, notwithstanding his infirmities, and he foresaw lightsome days.

Somewhat taken aback, however, by the commotion produced by Janey's laugh, the young party left the College, Ursula carrying with her sundry memoranda and measurements for curtains and carpets. "You must have curtains," she said, "and I think a carpet for the study. The other room will do; but the study is cold, it has not the sunshine. I wonder if we might go and look at some, all at once."

Here the three paused in the road, and looked at each other

somewhat overcome by the grandeur of the idea.   Even Reginald, notwithstanding his Oxford experience, held his breath a little at the thought of going right off without further consideration, and buying carpets and curtains.   As for Janey, she laughed again in pure excitement and delight.

"Fancy going into Holden's, walking right in, as if we had the Bank in our pockets, and ordering whatever we like," she cried.

"I suppose we must have them!" said Reginald, yielding slowly to the pleasure of acquisition.   Ursula was transformed by the instinct of business and management into the leader of the party.

"Of course you must have them," she said, with the air of a woman who had ordered curtains all her life, "otherwise you will catch cold, and that is not desirable," and she marched calmly towards Holden's, while Janey dropped behind to smother the laughter which expressed her amazed delight in this new situation.   It is doubtful whether Holden would have given them so good a reception had the Miss Mays gone to him to order curtains for the Parsonage—for the Carlingford tradesmen were very well aware of the difficulties, in point of payment, which attended Mr. May's purchases.   But Holden was all smiles at the idea of fitting up the rooms in the College.

"Carpets?   I have a Turkey carpet that would just suit one of those old rooms—old-fashioned rooms are so much thought of at present," said the man of furniture.

"Yes—I suppose that would do," said Reginald, with a side look at his sister, to know if he was right.   Ursula slew him with a glance of her brown eyes.   She was almost grand in superior knowledge and righteous indignation.

"Turkey! are you out of your senses?   Do you think we have the Bank in our pockets," she whispered to him angrily, "as Janey says?"

"How was I to know?   He said so," said the alarmed chaplain, cowed, notwithstanding his income.

"*He* said so!   that is just like you boys, taking whatever everyone tells you.   Why, a Turkey carpet costs a fortune.   Mr. Holden, I think, if you please, Brussels will do; or some of those new kinds, a jumble of colours without any decided pattern.   Not too expensive," said Ursula solemnly, the colour mounting to her face.   They were all rather brought down from their first delight and grandeur when this was said—for stipulating about expense made a difference all at once.   The delightful sensation of marching into Holden's as if the world belonged to them was over; but Janey was touched to see that

Holden still remained civil, and did not express, in his countenance, the contempt he must have felt.

When this was over, and Mr. Holden had kindly suggested the idea of sending various stuffs to the College, "that they might judge of the effect," the party went home, slightly subdued. The air was heavy and yellow, and prophesied snow; but a very red wintry sun had managed to make an opening temporarily in the clouds, and threw a ruddy ray down Grange Lane, bringing out the few passengers who were coming and going under the old garden walls. Ursula clasped her hands together, and came to a stop suddenly, when she turned her eyes that way.

"Oh!" she said, "here she is—she is coming! all by herself, and we can't help meeting her—the young lady in black!"

"Shall we speak to her?" said Janey with a little awe.

"Who is the young lady in black?" said Reginald, "this girl who is coming up? I never saw her before in Carlingford. Is she some one you have met with the Dorsets? She don't look much like Grange Lane."

"Oh, hush! here she is," said Ursula, losing all that importance of aspect which her position as leader of the expedition had given her. A pretty blush of expectation came over her face—her dimples revealed themselves as if by magic. You will think it strange, perhaps, that the sight of one girl should produce this effect upon another. But then Phœbe represented to Ursula the only glimpse she had ever had into a world which looked gay and splendid to the country girl—a world in which Phœbe had appeared to her as a princess reigning in glory and delight. Ursula forgot both her companions and her recent occupation. Would the young lady in black notice her; stop, perhaps, and talk to her—remember her? Her eyes began to glow and dance with excitement. She stumbled as she went on in her anxiety, fixing her eyes upon the approaching figure. Phœbe, for her part, was taking a constitutional walk up and down Grange Lane, and she too was a little moved, recognizing the girl, and wondering what it would be wisest to do—whether to speak to her, and break her lonely promenade with a little society, or remember her "place," and save herself from further mortification by passing the clergyman's daughter, who was a cousin of the Dorsets, with a bow.

"The Dorsets wouldn't recognise me, nor Miss May either," Phœbe said to herself, "*if they knew—*"

But Ursula looked so wistful as they approached each other that she had not the courage to keep to this wise resolution. Though she was only the granddaughter of Tozer, the butterman,

she was much more a woman of the world than this pretty
blushing girl who courted her notice. She put out her hand
instinctively when they met. "It can't harm anybody but
myself, after all," she thought.

"Oh, I am so glad you remember me," cried Ursula. "I
knew you in a moment. Have you come to stay here? This
is my brother, Reginald, and my little sister, Janey" (how
Janey scowled at that *little!* and with reason, for she was by
half an inch the taller of the two). "Are you taking a walk?
I do hope you like Carlingford. I do hope you are going to
stay. That is our house down at the end of the lane, close to
St. Roque's. Papa is the clergyman there. It will be so
delightful," said Ursula, repeating herself in her excitement,
"if you are going to stay."

"I am going to stay for some time," said Phœbe graciously,
"I don't quite know how long. I came here shortly after I
saw you in town. My grandfather lives here. Grange Lane
is very nice for a walk. Grandmamma is an invalid, so that I
don't leave her very often. It was great luck finding you just
as I had come out; for it is not cheerful walking alone."

Phœbe felt perfectly sure that through each of the three
heads turned towards her a hurried inquiry was going on as to
which of those enclosed houses contained the grandmother who
was an invalid; but no sort of enlightenment followed the
inquiry, and as for Ursula it terminated abruptly in her mind
with a rush of cordiality. She was not at an age when friendship pauses to make any inquiry into grandmothers.

"I am so glad! for if you are not going anywhere in particular, we may all walk together. Janey knows you quite
well. I have talked of you so often" (here Phœbe gave a
gracious bow and smile to Janey, who was not quite sure that
she liked to be thus patronized), "and so does my brother,"
said Ursula, more doubtfully. "Do you like Carlingford?
Have you seen many people? Oh! I do hope you will stay."

"I have not seen anybody," said Phœbe. "My people are
not much in society. When one is old and sick, I don't suppose one cares—"

"There is no society to speak of in Carlingford," said Reginald. "It is like most other country towns. If you like it we
shall be sure your liking is quite disinterested, for it has no
social charms—"

When had Reginald said so many words at a time to a young
lady before? The girls exchanged glances. "I think it is
pretty," said Phœbe, closing the subject. "It is going to snow,
don't you think? I suppose you skate like all the young ladies

now. It seems the first thing any one thinks of when the winter begins."

"Do you skate?" said Ursula, her eyes brighter and opener than ever.

"Oh, a little—as everybody does! Perhaps if there is no society," said Phœbe, turning to Reginald for the first time, "people are free here from the necessity of doing as everybody does. I don't think there is any such bondage in the world— dressing, living, working, amusing yourself—you have to do everything as other people do it. So I skate—I can't help myself; and a hundred foolish things beside."

"But I should think it *delightful*," cried Ursula, "I have always envied the boys. They look so warm when we are all shivering. Reginald, if it freezes will you teach us? I think I should like it better than anything in the world."

"Yes," said Reginald, "if Miss—if we can make up a party —if you," he added with a perfectly new inflection in his voice, "will come too."

"I see you don't know my name," said Phœbe, with a soft little laugh. "It is Beecham. One never catches names at a party. I remembered yours because of a family in a novel that I used to admire very much in my girlish days—"

"Oh! I know," cried Janey, "the Daisy Chain. We are not a set of prigs like those people. We are not goody, what- ever we are; we—"

"I don't suppose Miss Beecham cares for your opinion of the family character," said Reginald in a tone that made Janey furious. Thus discoursing they reached the gates of the Par- sonage, where Ursula was most eager that her friend should come in. And here Mr. May joined them, who was impressed, like everybody else, by Phœbe's appearance, and made himself so agreeable that Reginald felt eclipsed and driven into the background. Ursula had never been so satisfied with her father in her life; though there was a cloud on Mr. May's soul, it suited him to show a high good-humour with everybody in recompense for his son's satisfactory decision, and he was, in- deed, in a state of high complacence with himself for having managed matters so cleverly that the very thing which should have secured Reginald's final abandonment of the chaplaincy determined him, on the contrary, to accept it. And he admired Phœbe, and was dazzled by her self-possession and knowledge of the world. He supported Ursula's invitation warmly; but the stranger freed herself with graceful excuses. She had her patient to attend to.

"That is a very lady-like young woman," said Mr. May,

when they had gone in, after watching regretfully their new
acquaintance's progress through Grange Lane. "You met her
in town, did you? A friend of the Dorsets? Where is she
living, I wonder; and whom does she belong to? One does
not often see that style of thing her."

"I never saw any one like her before," said Ursula fervently; and they were still all uniting in admiration of Phœbe
—when—

But such an interruption demands another page.

CHAPTER XX.

THAT TOZER GIRL!

"WELL, who is she?" cried Mrs. Sam Hurst, too curious to
think of the ordinary decorums. She had no bonnet on, but a
light "cloud" of white wool over her cap, and her whole aspect
was full of eagerness and excitement. "Why didn't you tell
me you knew her? Who is she? I am dying to know."

"Who is—who?" said Ursula, rather glad of the opportunity of being politely rude to Mrs. Sam Hurst before papa.
"How is any one to find out from the way you speak? She?
who is she?"

"That is just what I want you to tell me," said Mrs. Sam
Hurst, with imperturbable good-humour. "You, Mr. May,
you are always good to me, though Ursula has her little
tempers—the girl you were talking to at the door. I stood
and watched from the window, and I scarcely could contain
myself sufficiently not to bounce out in the middle of the talk.
Now do tell, as the Americans say. Who is that Tozer girl?"

"That Tozer girl!" Ursula gave a little shriek, and grew
first red and then pale with horror and dismay.

"Yes; I told you about her; so well dressed and looking so
nice. That was she; with the very same dress, such a charming dress! so much style about it. Who is she, Ursula? Mr.
May, tell me who is she? You can't imagine how much I want
to know."

Ursula dropped into a chair, looking like a little ghost, faint
and rigid. She said afterwards to Janey that she felt in the
depths of her heart that it must be true. She could have cried
with pain and disappointment, but she would not give Mrs.
Sam Hurst the pleasure of making her cry.

"There must be some mistake," said Reginald, interposing. "This is a lady—my sister met her in town with the Dorsets."

"Oh, does she know the Dorsets too?" said the inquirer. "That makes it still more interesting. Yes, that is the girl that is with the Tozers; there can be no mistake about it. She is the granddaughter. She was at the Meeting last night. I had it from the best authority—on the platform with old Tozer. And, indeed, Mr. May, how any one that had been there could dare to look you in the face!—"

"I was there myself," said Mr. May. "It amused me very much. Tell me now about this young person. Is she an impostor, taking people in, or what is it all about? Ursula looks as if she was in the trick herself, and had been found out."

"I am *sure* she is not an impostor," said Ursula. "An impostor! If you had seen her as I saw her, at a great, beautiful, splendid ball. I never saw anything like it. I was nobody there—nobody—and neither were Cousin Anne and Cousin Sophy—but Miss Beecham! It is a mistake, I suppose," the girl said, raising herself up with great dignity; "when people are always trying for news, they get the wrong news sometimes, I don't doubt. You may be sure it is a mistake."

"That's me," said Mrs. Sam Hurst, with a laugh; "that is one of Ursula's assaults upon poor me. Yes, I confess it, I am fond of news; and I never said she was an impostor. Poor girl, I am dreadfully sorry for her. I think she is a good girl, trying to do her duty to her relations. She didn't choose her own grandfather. I dare say, if she'd had any say in it, she would have made a very different choice. But whether your papa may think her a proper friend for you—being Tozer's granddaughter, Miss Ursula, that's quite a different business, I am bound to say."

Again Ursula felt herself kept from crying by sheer pride, and nothing else. She bit her lips tight; she would not give in. Mrs. Hurst to triumph over her, and to give her opinion as to what papa might think proper! Ursula turned her back upon Mrs. Hurst, which was not civil, fearing every moment some denunciation from papa. But nothing of the kind came. He asked quite quietly after a while, "Where did you meet this young lady?" without any perceptible inflection of anger in his tone.

"Why, papa," cried Janey, distressed to be kept so long silent, "everybody knows where Ursula met her; no one has heard of anything else since she came home. She met her of course at the ball. You know; Reginald, *you* know! The ball where she went with Cousin Anne."

"Never mind Cousin Anne; I want the name of the people at whose house it was."

"Copperhead, papa," said Ursula, rousing herself. "If Cousin Anne does not know a lady from a common person, who does, I wonder? It was Cousin Anne who introduced me to her (I think). Their name was Copperhead, and they lived in a great, big, beautiful house, in the street where ambassadors and quantities of great people live. I forget the name of it; but I know there was an ambassador lived there, and Cousin Anne said——"

"Copperhead! I thought so," said Mr. May. "When Ursula has been set agoing on the subject of Cousin Anne, there is nothing rational to be got from her after that for an hour or two. You take an interest in this young lady," he said shortly, turning to Mrs. Sam Hurst, who stood by smiling, rather enjoying the commotion she had caused.

"Who, I? I take an interest in anybody that makes a stir, and gives us something to talk about," said Mrs. Hurst, frankly. "You know my weakness. Ursula despises me for it, but you know human nature. If I did not take an interest in my neighbours what would become of me—a poor lone elderly woman, without either chick or child?"

She rounded off this forlorn description of herself with a hearty laugh, in which Janey, who had a secret kindness for their merry neighbour, though she feared her "for papa," joined furtively. Mr. May, however, did not enter into the joke with the sympathy which he usually showed to Mrs. Hurst. He smiled, but there was something *distrait* and preoccupied in his air.

"How sorry we all are for you," he said; "your position is truly melancholy. I am glad, for your sake, that old Tozer has a pretty granddaughter to beguile you now and then out of recollection of your cares."

There was a sharp tone in this which caught Mrs. Hurst's ear, and she was not disposed to accept any sharpness from Mr. May. She turned the tables upon him promptly.

"What a disgraceful business that Meeting was! Of course, you have seen the paper. There ought to be some way of punishing those agitators that go about the country, taking away people's characters. Could not you bring him up for libel, or Reginald? I never knew anything so shocking. To come to your own town, your own neighbourhood, and to strike you through your son! It is the nastiest, most underhanded, unprincipled attack I ever heard of."

"What is that?" asked Reginald.

He was not easily roused by Carlingford gossip, but there was clearly more in this than met the eye.

"An Anti-State Church Meeting," said Mr. May, "with special compliments in it to you and me. It is not worth our while to think of it. Your agitators, my dear Mrs. Hurst, are not worth powder and shot. Now, pardon me, but I must go to work. Will you go and see the sick people in Back Grove Street, Reginald? I don't think I can go to-day."

"I should like to know what was in the paper," said the young man, with an obstinacy that filled the girls with alarm. They had been in hopes that everything between father and son was to be happy and friendly, now that Reginald was about to do what his father wished.

"Oh, you shall see it," said Mrs. Hurst, half alarmed too; "but it is not anything, as your father says; only we women are sensitive. We are always thinking of things which, perhaps, were never intended to harm us. Ursula, you take my advice, and don't go and mix yourself up with Dissenters and that kind of people. The Tozer girl may be very nice, but she is still Tozer's granddaughter, after all."

Reginald followed the visitor out of the room, leaving his sisters very ill at ease within, and his father not without anxieties which were so powerful, indeed, that he relieved his mind by talking of them to his daughters—a most unusual proceeding.

"That woman will set Reginald off at the nail again," he cried; "after he had begun to see things in a common-sense light. There was an attack made upon him last night on account of that blessed chaplaincy, which has been more trouble to me than it is worth. I suppose he'll throw it up now. But I wash my hands of the matter. I wonder how you girls can encourage that chattering woman to come here."

"Papa!" cried Janey, ever on the defensive, "we *hate* her! It is you who encourage her to come here."

"Oh, hush!" cried Ursula, with a warning glance; it was balm to her soul to hear her father call Mrs. Hurst *that woman*. "We have been to see the house," she said; "it was very nice. I think Reginald liked it, papa."

"Ah, well," said Mr. May, "girls and boys are queer articles. I dare say the house, if he likes it, will weigh more with him than justice or common sense. So Copperhead was the people's name? What would be wanted, do you think, Ursula, to make Reginald's room into a comfortable room for a pupil? Comfortable, recollect; not merely what would do; and one that has been used, I suppose, to luxury. You can look over it and let me know."

"Are we going to take a pupil, papa?" cried Janey, with widening eyes.

"I don't know what you could teach him," he said. "Manners, perhaps? Let me know, Ursula. The room is not a bad room; it would want a new carpet, curtains, perhaps—various things. Make me out a list. The Copperheads have a son, I believe. Did you see him at that fine ball of yours?"

"Oh! papa, he danced with me twice; he was very kind," said Ursula, with a blush; "and he danced all the night with Miss Beecham. It must be a falsehood about her being old Tozer's granddaughter. Mr. Clarence Copperhead was always by her side. I think Mrs. Hurst must have made it all up out of her own head."

Mr. May gave a little short laugh.

"Poor Mrs. Hurst!" he said, recovering his temper; "how bitter you all are against her. So he danced with you twice? You must try to make him comfortable, Ursula, if he comes here."

"Is Mr. Clarence Copperhead coming here?"

"Ursula was struck dumb by this piece of news. The grand house in Portland Place, and all Sophy Dorset's questions and warnings, came suddenly back to her mind. She blushed fiery red; she could not tell why. Coming here! How strange it would be, how extraordinary, to have to order dinner for him, and get his room in order, and have him in the drawing-room in the evenings! How should she know what to say to him? or would papa keep him always at work, reading Greek or something downstairs? All this flashed through her mind with the rapidity of lightning. Mr. May made no reply. He was walking up and down the room with his hands behind him, as was his habit when he was "busy." Being busy was separated from being angry by the merest visionary line in Mr. May's case; his children never ventured on addressing him at such moments, and it is impossible to describe how glad they were when he withdrew to his own room before Reginald's return; but not a minute too soon. The young man came back, looking black as night. He threw himself into a chair, and then he got up again, and began also to walk about the room like his father. At first he would make no reply to the questions of the girls.

"It is exactly what I expected," he said; "just what I looked for. I knew it from the first moment."

It was Janey, naturally, who had least patience with this unsatisfactory utterance.

"If it was just what you expected, and you looked for it all the time, why should you make such a fuss now ? " she cried. " I declare, for all you are young, and we are fond of you, you are almost as bad as papa."

Reginald did not take any notice of this address ; he went on repeating the same words at intervals.

" A child might have known it. Of course, from the beginning one knew how it must be." Then he suddenly faced round upon Ursula, who was nearly crying in excitement and surprise. " But if they think I am to be driven out of a resolution I have made by what they say—if they think that I will be bullied into giving up because of their claptrap," he cried, looking sternly at her, " then you will find you are mistaken. You will find I am not such a weak idiot as you suppose. Give up ! because some demagogue from a Dissenting Committee takes upon him to criticise my conduct. If you think I have so little self-respect, so little stamina," he said, fiercely, " you will find you have made a very great mistake."

" Oh, Reginald, *me ?* " cried Ursula, with tears in her eyes ; " did I ever think anything unkind of you ? did I ever ask you to do anything that was disagreeable ? You should not look as if it was me."

Then he threw himself down again on the old sofa, which creaked and tottered under the shock.

" Poor little Ursula ! " he cried, with a short laugh. " Did you think I meant you ? But if they thought they would master me by these means," said Reginald with pale fury, " they never made a greater mistake, I can tell you. A parcel of trumpery agitators, speechifiers, little petty demagogues, whom nobody ever heard of before. A fine thing, indeed, to have all the shopkeepers of Carlingford sitting in committee on one's conduct, isn't it—telling one what one ought to do ? By Jupiter ! It's enough to make a man swear ! "

" I declare ! " cried Janey loudly, " how like Reginald is to papa ! I never saw it before. When he looks wicked like that, and sets his teeth—but I am not going to be pushed, not by my brother or any one ! " said the girl, growing red, and making a step out of his reach. " I won't stand it. I am not a child any more than you."

Janey's wrath was appeased, however, when Reginald produced the paper and read Northcote's speech aloud. In her interest she drew nearer and nearer, and read the obnoxious column over his shoulder, joining in Ursula's cries of indignation. By the time the three had thus got through it, Reginald's own agitation subsided into that fierce amusement which is the frequent refuge of the assaulted.

"Old Green in the chair! and old Tozer and the rest have all been sitting upon me," he said, with that laugh which is proverbially described as from the wrong side of the mouth, whatever that may be. Ursula said nothing in reply, but in her heart she felt yet another stab. Tozer! This was another complication. She had taken so great a romantic interest in the heroine of that ball, which was the most entrancing moment of Ursula's life, that it seemed a kind of disloyalty to her dreams to give up thus completely, and dethrone the young lady in black; but what could the poor girl do? In the excitement of this question the personality of Reginald's special assailant was lost altogether: the girls did not even remember his name.

CHAPTER XXI.

A NEW FRIEND.

AFTER this there followed an exciting interval for the family at the Parsonage. Reginald, with the impatience of anger, insisted upon transporting himself to the College at once, and entering upon "his duties," such as they were, in defiance of all public comment. And Mr. May, delighted with the headstrong resentment which served his purpose so well, promoted it by all the means in his power, goading his son on, if he showed any signs of relaxing, by references to public opinion, and what the Liberation Society would say. Before those curtains were ready, which the girls had ordered with so much pride, or the carpet laid down, he had taken possession, and his room in the Parsonage was already turned upside down preparing for a new inmate. Many and strange were the thoughts in Ursula's mind about this new inmate. She remembered Clarence Copperhead as a full-grown man, beyond, it seemed to her, the age at which pupilage was possible. What was he coming to Carlingford for? What was he coming to the Parsonage for? What could papa do with a pupil quite as old as Reginald, who, in his own person, had often taken pupils? Ursula had read as many novels as were natural at her age, and can it be supposed that she did not ask herself whether there was any other meaning in it? Could he be coming to Carlingford on account of Miss Beecham; or, on account of—any one else? Ursula never whispered, even to her own imagination, on account of *me*. But it is not to be supposed that the unbidden inarticulate thought did not steal in, fluttering her girlish soul. Everybody knows that in fiction, at least, such things occur continually, and are the most natural things in the world; and to Ursula, beyond her own little common-place world, which she somewhat despised, and the strange world undeciphered and wonderful to which the Dorsets had introduced her for those ten brief days in London, the world of fiction was the only sphere she knew; and in that sphere there could be no such natural method of accounting for a young man's actions as that of supposing him to be "in love." The question remained, was it with Miss Beecham, or was it with— anybody else? Such an inquiry could not but flutter her youthful bosom. She made his room ready for him, and settled how he was to be disposed of, with the strangest sense of something beneath, which her father would never suspect, but which, perhaps, she alone might know.

Clarence Copperhead was a more imposing figure to Ursula than he was in reality. She had seen him only twice, and he was a big and full-grown "gentleman," while Ursula only realised herself as a little girl. She was not even aware that she had any intelligence to speak of, or that she would be a fit person to judge of "a gentleman." To be sure she had to do many things which wanted thought and sense; but she was too unthoughtful of herself to have decided this as yet, or to have created any private tribunal at which to judge a newcomer of Clarence Copperhead's dimensions. A much greater personage than she was, an individual whose comings and goings could not be without observation, whose notice would be something exciting and strange, was what she took him to be. And Ursula *was* excited. Did Mrs. Copperhead, that kind little woman, know why he was coming—was she in his confidence? And how was Ursula to entertain him, to talk to him—a gentleman accustomed to so much better society? She did not say anything to Janey on this subject, though Janey was not without her curiosities too, and openly indulged in conjectures as to the new pupil.

"I wonder if he will be fine. I wonder if he will be very good," said Janey. "I wonder if he will fall in love with Ursula. Pupils, in books, always do; and then there is a dreadful fuss and bother, and the girl is sent away. It is hard for the girl; it is always supposed to be her fault. I would not allow papa to take any pupils if it was me."

"And much your papa would care for your permission," said Mrs. Sam Hurst. "But so far I agree with you, Janey, that before he has pupils, or anything of that sort, there ought to be a lady in the house. He should marry—"

"Marry! we don't want a lady in the house," cried Janey, "we are ladies ourselves, I hope. Marry! if he does, I, for one, will do all I can to make his life miserable," said the girl with energy. "What should he want to marry for when he has daughters grown up? There are enough of us already, I should think."

"Too many," said Mrs. Sam Hurst with a sigh. It gave her the greatest secret delight to play upon the girl's fears.

Besides this, however, Ursula had another preoccupation. In that cordial meeting with the young lady who had turned out to be a person in such an embarrassing position, there had been a great deal said about future meetings, walks, and expeditions together, and Ursula had been very desirous that Phœbe should fix some time for their first encounter. She thought of this now with blushes that seemed to burn her cheeks. She was afraid to go out, lest she should meet the girl she had been so anxious to make a friend of. Not that, on her own account, after the first shock, Ursula would have been hard-hearted enough to deny her acquaintance to Tozer's granddaughter. In the seclusion of her chamber, she had cried over the downfall of her ideal friend very bitterly, and felt the humiliation for Phœbe more cruelly than that young lady felt it for herself; but Ursula, however much it might have cost her, would have stood fast to her friendship had she been free to do as she pleased.

"I did not like her for her grandfather," she said to Janey, of whom, in this case, she was less unwilling to make a confidant. "I never thought of the grandfather. What does it matter to me if he were a sweep instead of old Tozer?"

"Old Tozer is just as bad as if he were a sweep," said Janey; "if you had ever thought of her grandfather, and known he was old Tozer, you would have felt it would not do."

"What is there about a grandfather? I don't know if we ever had any," said Ursula. "Mamma had, for the Dorsets are her relations—but papa. Mr. Griffiths's grandfather was a candle-maker; I have heard papa say so—and they go everywhere."

"But he is dead," said Janey, with great shrewdness, "and he was rich."

"You little nasty calculating thing! Oh, how I hate rich people; how I hate this horrid world, that loves money and loves fine names, and does not care for people's selves whether they are bad or good! I shall never dare to walk up Grange Lane again," said Ursula, with tears. "Fancy changing to her, after being so glad to see her! fancy never saying another word about the skating, or the walk to the old mill! How she will despise me for being such a miserable creature! and she will think it is all my own fault."

At this moment Mr. May, from the door of his study, called "Ursula!" repeating the call with some impatience when she paused to dry her eyes. She ran down to him quickly, throwing down her work in her haste. He was standing at the door, and somehow for the first time the worn look about his eyes struck Ursula with a touch of pity. She had never noticed it before: a look of suppressed pain and anxiety, which remained about his eyes though the mouth smiled. It had never occurred to her to be sorry for her father before, and the idea struck her as very strange now.

"Come in," he said, "I want to speak to you. I have been thinking about the young woman—this friend of yours. We are all among the Dissenters now-a-days, whatever Mrs. Sam Hurst may say. You seem to have taken a fancy to this Tozer girl?"

"Don't call her so, papa, please. She is a lady in herself, as good a lady as any one."

"Well! I don't say anything against her, do I? So you hold by your fancy? You are not afraid of Grange Lane and Mrs. Sam Hurst."

"I have not seen her again," said Ursula, cast down. "I have not been out at all. I could not bear to be so friendly one day, and then to pass as if one did not know her the next. I cannot do it," cried the girl, in tears; "if I see her, I must just be the same as usual to her, whatever you say."

"Very well, *be* the same as usual," said Mr. May; "that is why I called you. I have my reasons. Notwithstanding Tozer, be civil to the girl. I have my reasons for what I say."

"Do you mean it, papa!" said Ursula, delighted. "Oh, how good of you! You don't mind—you really don't mind? Oh! I can't tell you how thankful I am; for to pretend to want to be friends, and then to break off all in a moment because of a girl's grandfather——"

"Don't make a principle of it, Ursula. It is quite necessary, in an ordinary way, to think of a girl's grandfather—and a boy's too, for that matter. No shopkeeping friends for me; but in this individual case I am willing to make an exception. For the moment, you see, Dissenters are in the ascendant. Young Copperhead is coming next week. Now, go."

Ursula marched delighted upstairs. "Janey, run and get your hat," she said; "I am going out. I am not afraid of any one now. Papa is a great deal nicer than he ever was before. He says I may see Miss Beecham as much as I like. He says we need not mind Mrs. Sam Hurst. I am so glad! I shall never be afraid of that woman any more."

Janey was taken altogether by surprise. "I hope he is not going to fall in love with Miss Beecham," she said suspiciously. "I have heard Betsy say that old gentlemen often do."

"He is not so foolish as to fall in love with anybody," said Ursula, with dignity. "Indeed, Janey, you ought to have much more respect for papa. I wish you could be sent to school and learn more sense. You give your opinion as if you were —twenty—more than that. I am sure I never should have ventured to say such things when I was a child like you."

"Child yourself!" said Janey indignant; which was her last resource when she had nothing more to say; but Ursula was too busy putting aside her work and preparing for her walk to pay any attention. In proportion as she had been subdued and downcast heretofore, she was gay now. She forgot all about old Tozer; about the Dissenters' meeting, and the man who had made an attack upon poor Reginald. She flew to her room for her hat and jacket, and ran downstairs, singing to herself. Janey only overtook her, out of breath, as she emerged into the road from the Parsonage door.

"What a dreadful hurry you are in," said Janey. "I always get ready so much quicker than you do. Is it all about this girl, because she is new? I never knew you were so fond of new people before."

But that day they went up and down Grange Lane fruitlessly, without seeing anything of Phœbe, and Ursula returned home disconsolate. In the evening Reginald intimated carelessly that he had met Miss Beecham. "She is much better worth talking to than most of the girls one meets with, whoever her grandfather may be," he said, evidently with an instant readiness to stand on the defensive.

"Oh, did you talk to her," said Ursula, "without knowing? Reginald, papa has no objections. He says we may even have her here, if we please."

"Well, of course I suppose he must guide you in that respect," said Reginald, "but it does not matter particularly to me. Of course I talked to her. Even my father could not expect that his permission was needed for me."

At which piece of self-assertion the girls looked at him with admiring eyes. Already they felt there was a difference. Reginald at home, nominal curate, without pay or position, was a different thing from Reginald with an appointment, a house of his own, and two hundred and fifty pounds a year. The girls looked at him admiringly, but felt that this was never likely to be their fate. In everything the boys had so much the best of it; and yet it was almost a comfort to think that they had seen Reginald himself trembling before papa. Reginald had a great deal to tell them about the college, about the old men who made a hundred daily claims on his attention, and the charities which he had to administer, doles of this and that, and several charity schools of a humble class.

"As for my time, it is not likely to hang on my hands as I thought. I can't be a parish Quixote, as we planned, Ursula, knocking down windmills for other people," he said, adjusting his round edge of collar. He was changed; he was important, a personage in his own sight, no longer to be spoken of as Mr. May's son. Janey ventured on a little laugh when he went away, but Ursula did not like the change.

"Never mind," cried Janey; "I hope Copperhead will be nice. We shall have him to talk to, when he comes."

"Oh!" cried Ursula, in a kind of despair, "who taught you to call gentlemen like that by their name? There is nothing so vulgar. Why, Cousin Anne says—"

"Oh, Cousin Anne!" cried Janey, shaking her head, and dancing away. After that she was aware there was nothing for it but flight.

Next day, however, they were more successful. Phœbe, though very little older than Ursula, was kind to the country girls, and talked to them both, and drew them out. She smiled when she heard of Clarence Copperhead, and told them that he was not very clever, but she did not think there was any harm in him.

"It is his father who is disagreeable," said Phœbe; "didn't you think so? You know, papa is a minister, Miss May," (she did not say clergyman when she spoke to a churchwoman, for what was the use of exciting any one's prejudices?) "and Mr. Copperhead comes to our church. You may be very thankful, in that respect, that you are not a dissenter. But it will be very strange to see Clarence Copperhead in Carlingford. I have known him since I was no bigger than your little sister. To tell the truth," said Phœbe, frankly, "I think I am rather sorry he is coming here."

"Why?" cried bold Janey, who was always inquisitive.

Miss Phœbe only smiled and shook her head; she made no distinct reply.

"Poor fellow, I suppose he has been 'plucked,' as the

gentlemen call it, or 'ploughed,' does your brother say? University slang is very droll. He has not taken his degree, I suppose, and they want him to work before going up again. I am sorry for your father, too, for I don't think it will be very easy to get anything into Clarence Copperhead's mind. But there is no harm at all in him, and he used to be very nice to his mother. Mamma and I liked him for that; he was always very nice to his mother."

"Will you come in and have some tea?" said Ursula. "Do, please. I hope, now that I have met you again, you will not refuse me. I was afraid you had gone away, or something—"

Ursula, however, could not help looking guilty as she spoke, and Phœbe perceived at once that there had been some reason for the two or three days' disappearance of the girls from Grange Lane.

"You must tell me first," she said, with a smile, "whether you know who I am. If you ask me after that, I shall come. I am old Mr. Tozer's granddaughter, who had a shop in the High Street. My uncle has a shop there now. I do not like it my-self," said Phœbe, with the masterly candour that distinguished her, "and no one else can be expected to like it. If you did not know—"

"Oh, we heard directly," cried Janey; "Mrs. Sam Hurst told us. She came shrieking, 'Who is she?' before your back was turned that day; for she wondered to see you with old Tozer—"

"Janey!" cried Ursula, with horror. "Of course we know; and please will you come? Every new person in Carlingford gets talked over, and if an angel were to walk about, Mrs. Sam Hurst would never rest till she had found out where he came from."

"And, perhaps, whether he had a broken feather in his wing," said Phœbe. "I am very glad you don't mind. It will be very pleasant to come. I will run in and tell them, and then I will join you. Grandmamma is an invalid, and would like to know where I am."

And the news made a considerable flutter in the dim room where Mrs. Tozer sat between the fire and the window, looking out upon the crocuses and regretting the High Street.

"But run and put on another dress, dear. What will they think of you in that everlasting brown frock as you're so fond of? I'd like them to see as my grandchild could dress as nice as any lady in the land."

"She'll not see much finery there," said Tozer; "they're as poor as church mice, are them Mays, and never a penny to pay a bill when it's wanted. I don't think as Phœbe need mind her dressing to go there."

"And you'll send for me if you want me, grandmamma; you will be sure to send?"

But for the brown frock, Mrs. Tozer's satisfaction would have been unalloyed as she watched her granddaughter walking across the garden.

"She's at home among the quality, she is," said the old woman; "maybe more so than she is with you and me; but there ain't a better girl in all England, and that I'll say for her, though if she would think a little more about her clothes, as is nat'ral at her age, it would be more pleasing to me."

"The worst dress as Phœbe has is better than anything belonging to them Mays," said Tozer.

He did not care for the parson at St. Roque; though he was pleased that his child should be among "the quality." But it was on that evening that poor old Mrs. Tozer had one of her attacks, and Phœbe had to be summoned back at an early hour. The servant went down with an umbrella and a note, to bring her home; and that trifling incident had its influence upon after affairs, as the reader shall shortly see.

CHAPTER XXII.

A DESPERATE EXPEDIENT.

It was something of a comfort to Phœbe to find that the "tea" to which Ursula asked her was a family meal, such as Mr. and Mrs. Tozer indulged in, in Grange Lane, with no idea of dinner to follow, as in more refined circles. This, she said to herself benignly, must be "country fashion," and she was naturally as bland and gracious at the Parsonage tea-table as anybody from town, knowing better, but desiring to make herself thoroughly agreeable, could be. She amused Mr. May very much, who felt the serene young princess, accepting her vulgar relations with gentle resignation, and supported by a feeling of her own innate dignity, to be something quite new to him. Phœbe had no objection to talk upon the subject, for, clever as she was, she was not so clever as to see through Mr. May's amused show of interest in her trials, but believed ingenuously that he understood and felt for her, and was, perhaps, at last, the one noble, impartial, and generous Churchman who could see the difficulties of cultivated Dissenters, and enter into them sympathetically. Why Mr. May took the trouble to draw her out on this point it is more difficult to explain. Poor man, he was in a state of semi-distraction over Cotsdean's bill. The ten days had shortened into three, and he was no nearer finding that hundred pounds than ever. Even while he smiled and talked to Phœbe, he was repeating over and over to himself the terrible fact which could not now be ignored. " 17th, 18th, 19th, and Friday will be the 20th," he was saying to himself. If that 20th came without any help, Cotsdean would be virtually made a bankrupt; for of course all his creditors would make a rush upon him, and all his affairs would be thrown open to the remorseless public gaze, if the bill, which had been so often renewed, had to be dishonoured at last. Mr. May had a conscience, though he was not careful of his money, and the fear of ruin to Cotsdean was a very terrible and real oppression to him. The recollection was upon him like a vulture in classic story, tearing and gnawing, as he sat there and smiled over the cup of tea Ursula gave him, feeling amused all the same at Phœbe's talk. He could scarcely have told why he had permitted his daughter to pursue her acquaintance with Tozer's granddaughter. Partly it was because of Clarence Copperhead; out of curiosity, as, being about to be brought in contact with some South Sea Islander or Fijian, one would naturally wish to see another who was thrown in one's way by accident, and thus prepare one's self for the permanent acquaintance. And she amused him. Her cleverness, her ease, her conversational powers, her woman of the world aspect, did not so much impress him, perhaps, as they did others; but the complacency and innocent confidence of youth that were in her, and her own enjoyment of the situation, notwithstanding the mortifications incurred—all this amused Mr. May. He listened to her talk, sometimes feeling himself almost unable to bear it, for the misery of those words, which kept themselves ringing in a dismal chorus in his own mind, and yet deriving a kind of amusement and distraction from it all the same.

" One of your friends was very hard upon my son—and myself—at your Meeting the other night, Miss Beecham."

" He was very injudicious," said Phœbe, shaking her head. " Indeed I did not approve. Personalities never advance any cause. I said so to him. Don't you think the Church has herself to blame for those political Dissenters, Mr. May? You sneer at us, and look down upon us—"

" I? I don't sneer at anybody."

" I don't mean you individually; but Churchmen do. They

treat us as if we were some strange kind of creatures, from the heart of Africa perhaps. They don't think we are just like themselves : as well educated; meaning as well ; with as much right to our own ideas."

Mr. May could scarcely restrain a laugh. "Just like themselves." The idea of a Dissenter setting up to be as well educated, and as capable of forming an opinion, as a cultivated Anglican, an Oxford man, and a beneficed clergyman, was too novel and too foolish not to be somewhat startling as well. Mr. May was aware that human nature is strangely blind to its own deficiencies, but was it possible that any delusion could go so far as this? He did laugh a little—just the ghost of a laugh—at the idea. But what is the use of making any serious opposition to such a statement? The very fact of contesting the assumption seemed to give it a certain weight.

"Whenever this is done," said Phœbe, with serene philosophy, "I think you may expect a revulsion of feeling. The class to which papa belongs is very friendly to the Established Church, and wishes to do her every honour."

"Is it indeed? We ought to be much gratified," said Mr. May.

Phœbe gave him a quick glance, but he composed his face and met her look meekly. It actually diverted him from his preoccupation, and that is a great deal to say.

"We would willingly do her any honour ; we would willingly be friends, even look up to her, if that would please her," added Phœbe, very gravely, conscious of the importance of what she was saying; "but when we see clergymen, and common persons also, who have never had one rational thought on the subject, always setting us down as ignorant and uncultured, because we are Dissenters——"

"But no one does that," said Ursula, soothingly, eager to save her new friend's feelings. She paused in the act of pouring out the children's second cup of tea, and looked up at her with eyes full of caressing and flattering meaning. "No one, at least, I am sure," she added, faltering, remembering suddenly things she had heard said of Dissenters, "who knows *you.*"

"It is not I that ought to be thought of, it is the general question. Then can you wonder that a young man like the gentleman we were talking of, clever and energetic, and an excellent scholar (and very good in philosophy, too—he was at Jena for two or three years), should be made bitter when he feels himself thrust back upon a community of small shopkeepers ? "

Mr. May could not restrain another short laugh.

"We must not join in the vulgar abuse of shopkeepers," he said.

Phœbe's colour rose. She raised her head a little, then perceiving the superiority of her former position, smiled.

"I have no right to do so. My people, I suppose, were all shopkeepers to begin with; but this gives me ways of knowing. Grandpapa is very kind and nice—really nice, Mr. May; but he has not at all a wide way of looking at things. I feel it, though they are so kind to me. I have been brought up to think in such a different way; and if I feel it, who am fond of them, think how that young minister must feel it, who was brought up in a totally different class?"

"What kind of class was this one brought up in?" said Mr. May, with a laugh. "He need not have assaulted Reginald, if he had been born a prince. We had done him no harm."

"That is making it entirely a private question," said Phœbe, suavely, "which I did not mean to do. When such a man finds out abuses—what he takes to be abuses—in the Church, which treats him like a roadside ranter, may not he feel a right to be indignant? Oh, I am not so. I think such an office as that chaplaincy is very good, one here and there for the reward of merit; and I think he was very right to take it; but still it would not do, would it, to have many of them? It would not answer any good purpose," she said, administering a little sting scientifically, "if all clergymen held sinecures."

These words were overheard by Reginald, who just then came in, and to whom it was startling to find Phœbe serenely seated at tea with his family. The hated word sinecure did not seem to affect him from her lips as it would have done from any one else's. He came in quite good-humouredly, and said with a smile—

"You are discussing me. What about me? Miss Beecham, I hope you take my side."

"I take everybody's side," said Phœbe; "for I try to trace people's motives. I can sympathise both with you and those who assailed you."

"Oh, that Dissenting fellow. I beg your pardon, Miss Beecham, if you are a Dissenter; but I cannot help it. We never go out of our way to attack them and their chapels and coteries, and why should they spring at our throats on every occasion? I think it is hard, and I can't say I have any charity to spare for this individual. What had we done to him? Ursula, give me some tea."

"Miss Beecham, I leave the cause of the Church in younger and, I hope, abler hands," said Mr. May, getting up.

Partly it was that Reginald's onslaught made him see for the first time certain weak points in the situation; partly it was that his private care became too clamorous, and he could not keep on further. He went away quite abruptly, and went downstairs to his study, and shut himself in there; and the moment he had closed the door, all this amusement floated away, and the vulture gripped at him, beak and talons digging into his very soul. Good God! what was he to do? He covered his face with his hands, and turned round and round mentally in that darkness to see if anywhere there might be a gleam of light; but none was visible east or west. A hundred pounds, only a hundred pounds; a bagatelle, a thing that to many men was as small an affair as a stray sixpence; and here was this man, as good, so to speak, as any—well educated, full of gifts and accomplishments, well born, well connected, not a prodigal nor open sinner, losing himself in the very blackness of darkness, feeling that a kind of moral extinction was the only prospect before him, for want of this little sum. It seemed incredible even to himself, as he sat and brooded over it. Somehow, surely, there must be a way of deliverance. He looked piteously about him in his solitude, appealing to the very blank walls to save him. What could they do? His few books, his faded old furniture, would scarcely realize a hundred pounds if they were sold to-morrow. All his friends had been wearied out, all natural resources had failed. James might any day have sent the money, but he had not done so—just this special time, when it was so hard to get it, James, too, had failed; and the hours of this night were stealing away like thieves, so swift and so noiseless, to be followed by the others; and Cotsdean, poor soul, his faithful retainer, would be broken and ruined. To do Mr. May justice, if it had been only himself who could be ruined, he would have felt it less; but it went to his very heart to think of poor Cotsdean, who had trusted in him so entirely, and to whom, indeed, he had been very kind in his day. Strife and discord had been in the poor man's house, and perpetual wretchedness, and Mr. May had managed, he himself could scarcely tell how, to set it right. He had frightened and subdued the passionate wife, and quenched the growing tendencies to evil, which made her temper worse than it was by nature, and had won her back to soberness and some kind of peace, changing the unhappy house into one of comparative comfort and cheerfulness. Most people like those best

to whom they have been kind, whom they have served or bene-
fited, and in this way Mr. May was fond of Cotsdean, who in
his turn had been a very good friend to his clergyman, serving
him as none of his own class could have done, going in the face
of all his own prejudices and the timorousness of nature, on
his account. And the result was to be ruin—ruin unmitigated
to the small man who was in business, and equally disastrous,
though in a less creditable way, to his employer. It was with
a suppressed anguish which is indescribable that he sat there,
with his face covered, looking this approaching misery in the
face. How long he had been there, he could scarcely himself
tell, when he heard a little commotion in the hall, the sounds
of running up and down stairs, and opening of doors. He was
in a feverish and restless condition, and every stir roused him.
Partly because of that impatience in his mind, and partly because
every new thing seemed to have some possibility of hope in it,
he got up and went to the door. Before he returned to his
seat, something might have occurred to him, something might
have happened—who could tell? It might be the postman
with a letter containing that remittance from James, which still
would set all right. It might be—he rose suddenly, and opening the door, held it ajar and looked out; the front door was
open, and the night air blowing chilly into the house, and on
the stairs, coming down, he heard the voices of Ursula and
Phœbe. Ursula was pinning a shawl round her new friend,
and consoling her.

"I hope you will find it is nothing. I am so sorry," she said.

"Oh, I am not very much afraid," said Phœbe. "She is ill,
but not very bad, I hope; and it is not dangerous. Thank you
so much for letting me come."

"You will come again?" said Ursula, kissing her; "promise
that you will come again."

Mr. May listened with a certain surface of amusement in his
mind. How easy and facile these girlish loves and fancies
were! Ursula knew nothing of this stranger, and yet so free
were the girl's thoughts, so open her heart to receive impressions,
that on so short knowledge she had received the other into it
with undoubting confidence and trust. He did not come forward himself to say good-bye, but he perceived that Reginald
followed downstairs, and took his hat from the table, to accompany Phœbe home. As they closed the outer door behind
them, the last gust thus forcibly shut in made a rush through
the narrow hall, and carried a scrap of paper to Mr. May's
feet. He picked it up almost mechanically, and carried it with
him to the light, and looked at it without thought. There was

not much in it to interest any one. It was the little note which Tozer had sent to his granddaughter by the maid, not prettily folded, to begin with, and soiled and crumpled by the bearer.

"Your grandmother is took bad with one of her attacks. Come back directly. She wants you badly.
"SAML. TOZER."

This was all that was in it. Mr. May opened it out on his table with a half-smile of that same superficial amusement which the entire incident had caused him—the contact, even momentary, of his own household with that of Tozer, the old Dissenting butterman, was so droll an event. Then he sank down on his chair again with a sigh, the amusement dying out all at once, purely superficial as it was. Amusement! how strange that even the idea of amusement should enter his head in the midst of his despair. His mind renewed that horrible mechanical wandering through the dismal circle of might-be's which still survived amid the chaos of his thoughts. Once or twice there seemed to gleam upon him a stray glimmer of light through a loophole, but only to throw him back again into the darkness. Now and then he roused himself with a look of real terror in his face, when there came a noise outside. What he was afraid of was poor Cotsdean coming in with his hand to his forehead, and his apologetic "Beg your pardon, sir." If he came, what could he say to him? Two days—only two days more! If Mr. May had been less sensible and less courageous, he would most likely have ended the matter by a pistol or a dose of laudanum; but fortunately he was too rational to deliver himself by this desperate expedient, which, of course, would only have made the burden more terrible upon the survivors. If Cotsdean was to be ruined, and there was no remedy, Mr. May was man enough to feel that it was his business to stand by him, not to escape in any dastardly way; but in the mean time to face Cotsdean, and tell him that he had done and could do nothing, seemed more than the man who had caused his ruin could bear. He moved about uneasily in his chair in the anguish of his mind. As he did so, he pushed off some of his papers from the table with his elbow. It was some sort of break in his feverish musings to pick them up again in a bundle, without noticing what they were. He threw them down in a little heap before him. On the top, as it chanced, came the little dirty scrap of paper, which ought to have been tossed into the fire or the waste-paper basket. Saml. Tozer!

What was Saml. Tozer to him that his name should stare him
in the face in this obtrusive way ?   Tozer, the old butterman!
a mean and ignorant person, as far beneath Mr. May's level as
it is possible to imagine, whose handwriting it was very strange
to see on anything but a bill.   He fixed his eyes upon it mechanically ; he had come, as it were, to the end of all things in
those feverish musings ; he had searched through his whole
known world for help, and found there nothing and nobody to
help him.   Those whom he had once relied on were exhausted
long ago ; his friends had all dropped off from him, as far, at
least, as money was concerned.   Some of them might put out
a hand to keep him and his children from starvation even now,
but to pay Cotsdean's bill, never.   There was no help anywhere,
nor any hope.   Natural ways and means were all exhausted,
and though he was a clergyman, he had no such faith in the
supernatural as to hope much for the succour of Heaven.
Heaven! what could Heaven do for him ?   Bank-notes did not
drop down out of the skies.   There had been a time when he
had felt full faith in " Providence ; " but he seemed to have
nothing to expect now from that quarter more than from any
other.   Samuel Tozer! why did that name always come uppermost, staring into his very eyes ?   It was a curious signature,
the handwriting very rude and unrefined, with odd, illiterate
dashes, and yet with a kind of rough character in it, easy to
identify, not difficult to copy—

What was it that brought beads of moisture all at once to
Mr. May's forehead ?   He started up suddenly, pushing his
chair with a hoarse exclamation, and walked up and down the
room quickly, as if trying to escape from something.   His heart
jumped up in his breast, like a thing possessed of separate life,
and thumped against his side, and beat with loud pulsations
in his ears.   When he caught sight of himself in the mirror
over the mantelpiece, he started as if he had seen a ghost.
Some one else seemed to see him ; seemed to pounce upon
and seize him out of that glass.   He retreated from the reach
of it, almost staggering ; then he returned to his table.   What
thought was it that had struck him so wildly, like a sudden
squall upon a boat ?   He sat down, and covered his face with
his hands ; then putting out one finger, stealthily drew the
paper towards him, and studied it closely from under the shadow
of the unmoved hand, which half-supported, half-covered his
face.   Well ! after all, what would be the harm ?   A gain of
three months' time, during which every sort of arrangement
could be made so nicely ; supplies got anywhere, everywhere ;
the whole machinery of being set easily in motion again, and

no harm done to any one: this was the real force of the idea—
no harm done to any one! Long before the three months were
out, that hundred pounds—a paltry business, a nothing, when
a man had time before him—could be got, one night make
sure; and where was the harm? *He* would never know it.
Poor Cotsdean need never have the slightest burden upon his
conscience. Here, in the stillness of his own room, it could
all be done as easily as possible, without a soul being taken
into confidence, except that bloodless wretch in the glass with
his staring face, Mr. May said to himself, only dimly sensible
that this wretch was himself. No, it would harm no one, that
was clear; it never need be known to any one. It was a mere
act of borrowing, and borrowing was never accounted a crime;
borrowing not money even, only a name, and for so short a time.
No harm; it could do no one in the world any harm.

While these reasonings went on in his mind, his heart dropped
down again into its right place; his pulse ceased to beat like
the pistons of a steam-engine; he came gradually to himself.
After all, what was it? Not such a great matter; a loan of
something which would neither enrich him who took, nor im-
poverish him who, without being aware of it, should give—a
nothing! Why people should entertain the prejudices they did
on the subject, it was difficult to see, though, perhaps, he
allowed candidly to himself, it might be dangerous for any
ignorant man to follow the same strain of thinking; but in the
hands of a man who was not ignorant, who knew, as he himself did, exactly how far to go, and what might be *innocently*
done; *innocently* done—in his own mind he put a great stress
on this—why, what was it? a thing which might be of use in
an emergency, and which was absolutely no harm.

Mr. May was late in leaving his room that night. It was
understood in the family that he "was writing," and all was
kept very quiet in the house; yet not sufficiently quiet, for
Janey, when she brought in the coffee, placing it on the table
close to the door, was startled by the fierceness of the exclamation with which her father greeted her entrance.

"What do you want prying here?" he said, dropping his
hand over the writing.

"Prying himself!" said Janey, furiously, when she was up
again in the cheerful light of the drawing-room; "a great deal
there is to pry into in that dreadful old study."

"Hush! he never likes to be disturbed in his writing," said
Ursula, soothingly.

And he sat at his "writing" to a much later hour than
usual, and he stumbled upstairs to his bedroom in the dead of

the night, with the same scared pale face which he had seen in
the glass.   Such a look as that when it once comes upon a
man's face takes a long time to glide away ; but his heart beat
more tranquilly, and the blood flowed even in his veins.   After
all, where was the harm ?

CHAPTER XXIII.

TIDED OVER.

NEXT morning, Cotsdean was mournfully turning over his
ledger in the High Street, wondering whether he should go
back to Mr. May on another forlorn expedition, or whether he
should betray his overwhelming anxiety to his wife, who knew
nothing about the state of affairs.   The shop was what is called
a cornfactor's shop, full of sacks of grain, with knots of wheat-
ears done up ornamentally in the window, a stock not very
valuable, but sufficient, and showing a good, if not a very important, business.   A young man behind, attended to what
little business was going on ; for the master himself was too
much preoccupied to think of bushels of seed.   He was as uneasy as Mr. May had been on the previous night, and in some
respects even more unhappy ; for he had no resource except a
sort of dumb faith in his principle, a feeling that he must be
able to find out some way of escape—chequered by clouds of
despondency, sometimes approaching despair.   For Cotsdean,
too, felt vaguely that things were approaching a crisis—that a
great many resources had been exhausted—that the pitcher
which had gone so often to the well must, at last, be broken,
and that it was as likely the catastrophe was coming now as at
any other time.   He said to himself that never in his previous
experience had things seemed so blank as at present ; never
had the moment of fate approached so nearly without any appearance of deliverance.   He had not even the round of possibilities before him which were in Mr. May's mind, however
hopeless, at this particular moment, he might find them.

Cotsdean, for his part, had nothing to think of but Mr. May.
Would he find some way out of it still, he who was always so
clever, and must, in his position, have always " good friends ? "
How the poor man wished that he had never been led into this
fatal course—that he had insisted, long ago, on the settlement
which must come some time, and which did not get any easier

by putting it off; but then, who was he to stand against
his clergyman? He did not feel able now to make any
stand against him. If he had to be ruined—he must be
ruined: what could he do? The man who had brought
him to this, held him in such subjection that he could not
denounce or accuse him even now. He was so much better,
higher, abler, stronger than himself, that Cotsdean's harshest
sentiment was a dumb feeling of injury; a feeling much
more likely to lead him to miserable tears than to resistance. His clergyman — how was he to stand against his
clergyman? This was the burden of his thoughts. And still,
perhaps, there might be salvation and safety in the resources,
the power, and cleverness, and superior strength of the man
for whom, in his humility, he had risked everything. Poor Cotsdean's eyes were red with sleeplessness and thinking, and the
constant rubbings he administered with the sleeve of his rough
coat. He hung helpless, in suspense, waiting to see what his
chief would say to him; if he would send for him—if he would
come. And in the intervals of these anxious thoughts, he
asked himself should he tell poor Sally—should he prepare her
for her fate? She and her children might be turned out of
house and home, very probably would be, he said to himself,
leaping to the extreme point, as men in his condition are apt
to do. They might take everything from him; they might
bring all his creditors on him in a heap; they might sell him
up; his shop by which he made his daily bread, and everything
he had, and turn his children out into the streets. Once more
he rubbed his sleeve over his eyes, which were smarting with
sleeplessness and easily-coming tears. He turned over the
pages of the ledger mechanically. There was no help in it—
no large debts owing to him that could be called in; no means
of getting any money; and nothing could he do but contemplate
the miseries that might be coming, and wait, wait, wondering
dully whether Mr. May was doing anything to avert this ruin,
and whether, at any moment, he might walk in, bringing safety
in the very look of his bold eyes. Cotsdean was not bold; he
was small and weakly, and nervous, and trembled at a sharp
voice. He was not a man adapted for vigorous struggling with
the world. Mr. May could do it, in whose hands was the final
issue. He was a man who was afraid of no one; and whose
powers nobody could deny. Surely now, even at the last
moment, he would find help somehow. It seemed profane to
entertain a doubt that he would be able to do it even at the
very last.

But Cotsdean had a miserable morning; he could do nothing.

Minute by minute, hour by hour, he waited to be called to the Parsonage; now and then he went out to the door of his shop and looked out wistfully down the street where it ended in the distance of Grange Lane. Was that the maid from the Parsonage coming up across the road? Were these the young ladies, who, though they knew nothing about the matter at issue, very frequently brought a note, or message, from their father to Cotsdean? But he was deceived in these guesses as well as in so many others. All the world seemed out of doors that morning, but nobody came. The ruddy sunshine shone full down the street, glorifying it with rays of warm gold, and tinting the mists and clouds which lurked in the corners. It had been heavy and overcast in the morning, but at noon the clouds had cleared away, and that big red globe of fire had risen majestically out of the mists, and everybody was out. But no one, except humble people in the ordinary way of business, came to Cotsdean. Bushels of grain for chickens, pennyworths of canary seed—oh! did any one think he could pay a hundred pounds out of these?—a hundred pounds, the spending of which had not been his, poor man; which was indeed spent long ago, and represented luxuries past and over, luxuries which were not Cotsdean's. Strange that a mere lump of money should live like this, long after it was, to all intents and purposes, dead, and spent and gone!

Then came the hour of dinner, when his Sally called him to the room behind the shop, from which an odour of bacon and fine big beans—beans which were represented in his shop in many a sackful. He went in unwillingly in obedience to her command, but feeling unable to eat, soon left the table, sending the young man to fill his place, with whose appetite no obstacle of care or thought interfered. Poor Cotsdean felt that the smell of the dinner made him sick—though he would have liked to eat had he been able—the smell of the bacon which he loved, and the sight of the small children whom he loved still better, and poor Sally, his wife, still red in the face from dishing it up. Sally was anxious about her husband's want of appetite.

"What ails you, John?" she said, pathetically; "it wasn't as if you were out last night, nor nothing o' that sort. A man as is sober like you don't ought to turn at his dinner."

She was half sorry, and half aggrieved, poor woman, feeling as if some blame of her cookery must be involved.

"It's the bile," said poor Cotsdean, with that simplicity of statement which is common in his class. "Don't you take on, Sally, I'll be a deal better by supper-time——or worse," he added to himself. Yes, he would make an effort to eat at supper-time; perhaps it might be the last meal he should eat in his own comfortable home.

He had been out at the shop door, gazing despairingly down the road; he had come in and sold some birdseed, wondering —oh, what good would that penny do him?—he who wanted a hundred pounds? and was standing listening with a sad heart to the sound of the knives and forks and chatter of the children, when suddenly all at once Mr. May walked into the shop, changing dismay into hope. What a thing it was to be a gentleman and a clergyman, Cotsdean could not but think! The very sight of Mr. May inspired him with courage; even though probably he had no money in his pocket, it was a supporting thing only to see him, and hear the sound of his free unrestrained step. He came in with a friendly nod to his humble helper; then he glanced round the shop, to see that no one was present, and then he said, "All right, Cotsdean," in a voice that was as music to the little corn-factor's ears. His heart, which had been beating so low, jumped up in his bosom; his appetite came back with a leap; he asked himself would the bacon be cold? and cried, "God be praised, sir," in a breath.

Mr. May winced slightly; but why should it be wrong to be grateful to God in any circumstances? he asked himself, having become already somewhat composed in his ideas on this particular point.

"Are we quite alone?" he said. "Nobody within hearing? I have not brought you the money, but a piece of paper that is as good as the money. Take it: you will have no difficulty in discounting this; the man is as well known as the Carlingford Bank, and as safe, though I dare say you will be surprised at the name."

Cotsdean opened out the new bill with trembling hands. "Tozer!" he said faintly, between relief and dismay.

"Yes. You must know that I am taking a pupil—one who belongs to a very rich Dissenting family in London. Tozer knows something about him, from his connection with the body, and through this young man I have got to know something of *him*. He does it upon the admirable security of the fees I am to receive with this youth; so you see, after all, there is no mystery about it. Better not wait for to-morrow, Cotsdean. Go at once, and get it settled. You see," said Mr. May, ingratiatingly, "it is a little larger than the other—one hundred and fifty, indeed—but that does not matter with such an excellent name."

"Tozer!" said Cotsdean, once more bewildered. He handled

the piece of paper nervously, and turned it upside down, and round about, with a sense that it might melt in his hold. He did not like the additional fifty added. Why should another fifty be added? but so it was, and there seemed nothing for him but to take the immediate relief and be thankful.

"I'd rather, sir, as Tozer hadn't known nothing about it; and why should he back a bill for me as ain't one of my friends, nor don't know nothing about me? and fifty more added on," said Cotsdean. It was the nearest he had gone to standing up against his clergyman; he did not like it. To be Mr. May's sole standby and agent, even at periodical risk of ruin, was possible to him; but a pang of jealousy, alarm, and pain came into his mind when he saw the new name. This even obliterated the immediate sense of relief that was in his mind.

"Come three months it'll have to be paid," said Cotsdean, "and Tozer ain't a man to stand it if he's left to pay; he'd sell us up, Mr. May. He ain't one of the patient ones, like—some other folks; and there's fifty pounds put on. I don't see my way to it. I'd rather it was just the clear hundred, if it was the same to you."

"It is not the same to me," said Mr. May, calmly. "Come, there is no cause to make any fuss. There it is, and if you don't like to make use of it, you must find some better way. Bring the fifty pounds, less the expenses, to me to-night. It is a good bit of paper, and it delivers us out of a mess which I hope we shall not fall into again."

"So you said before, sir," said the corn-factor sullenly.

"Cotsdean, you forget yourself; but I can make allowance for your anxiety. Take it, and get it settled before the bank closes; pay in the money to meet the other bill, and bring me the balance. You will find no difficulty with Tozer's name; and what so likely as that one respectable tradesman should help another? By the way, the affair is a private one between us, and it is unnecessary to say anything to him about it; the arrangement, you understand, is between him and me."

"Beg your pardon, sir," said Cotsdean, with a deprecatory movement of his hand to his forehead; "but it is me as will be come upon first if anything happens, and that fifty pounds—"

"Have you ever found me to fail you, Cotsdean? If you knew the anxiety I have gone through, that you might be kept from harm, the sleepless nights, the schemes, the exertions! You may suppose it was no ordinary effort to ask a man like Tozer."

Cotsdean was moved by the touching tone in which his partner in trouble spoke; but terror gave him a certain power. He grumbled still, not altogether vanquished.

"I don't say nothing against that, sir," he said, not meeting Mr. May's eye; "but when it comes to be paid, sir, I'm the first in it, and where is that other fifty to come from? That's what I'm a thinking for—for I'm the first as they'd haul up after all."

"You!" said Mr. May, "what could they get from you? You are not worth powder and shot. Don't be ridiculous, my good fellow. I never avoid my responsibilities, as you know. I am as good, I hope, for that fifty as for all that went before. Have you ever known me leave you or any one in the lurch?"

"No, sir, I can't say as—I don't suppose I have. I've always put my trust in you like in Providence itself," he cried, hastily, holding his breath.

"Then do as I tell you," said Mr. May, waving his hand with careless superiority; and though his heart was aching with a hundred anxious fears, he left the shop with just that mixture of partial offence and indifference which overawed completely his humble retainer. Cotsdean trembled at his own guilty folly and temerity. He did not dare to call his patron back again, to ask his pardon. He did not venture to go back to the table and snatch a bit of cold bacon. He was afraid he had offended his clergyman, what matter that he was hungry for his dinner? He called the young man from the bacon, which was now cold and all but eaten up, and snatched at his hat and went out to the bank. It was all he could do.

CHAPTER XXIV.

A VISIT.

"DEAR MAY,

"Young Copperhead, the young fellow whom you have undertaken to coach, is coming to the Hall for a few days before he enters upon his studies, and Anne wishes me to ask you to come over on Tuesday to dine and sleep, and to make acquaintance with him. You can carry him back with you if it suits you. In my private opinion, he is a cub of the most disagreeable kind; but the girls like his mother, who is a kind of cousin, as you know. It is not only because he has failed to take his degree (you know how I hate the hideous slang in which this fact is generally stated), but that his father, who is one of the rich persons who abound in the lower circles of society, is ambitious, and would like to see him in Parliament, and that sort of thing—a position which cannot be held credit-ably without some sort of education : at least, so I am myself disposed to think. Therefore, your pleasing duty will be to get him up in a little history and geography, so that he may not get quite hopelessly wrong in any of the modern modifica-tions of territory, for instance ; and in so much Horace as may furnish him with a few stock quotations, in case he should be called upon, in the absence of any more hopeful neophyte, to move the Address. He is a great hulking fellow, not very brilliant, you may suppose, but not so badly mannered as he might be, considering his parentage. I don't think he'll give you much trouble in the house ; but he will most probably bore you to death, and in that case your family ought to have a claim, I should think, for compensation. Anyhow, come and see him, and us, before you begin your hard task.

" Very truly yours,

"R. DORSET."

" Anne makes me open my letter to say that Ursula must come too. We will send a carriage to meet you at the station."

This letter caused considerable excitement in the Parsonage. It was the first invitation to dinner which Ursula had ever received. The dinner-parties in Carlingford were little fre-quented by young ladies. The male population was not large enough to afford a balance for the young women of the place, who came together in the evening, and took all the trouble of putting on their pretty white frocks, only to sit in rows in the drawing-room, waiting till the old gentlemen came in from the dining-room, after which everybody went away. There were no young gentlemen to speak of in Carlingford, so that when any one was bold enough to attempt a dancing-party, or any-thing of an equally amusing description, friends were sent out in all directions, as the beaters are sent into the woods to bring together the unfortunate birds for a *battue*, to find men. These circumstances will explain the flutter in Ursula's inno-cent bosom when her father read her that postscript. Mr. May was singularly amiable that day, a thing which happened at periodical intervals, usually after he had been specially "cross." On this occasion there was no black mark against him in the family reckoning, and yet he was more kind than any one had ever known him. Instead of making any objections, he decided at once that Ursula must go, and told her to put on her prettiest frock, and make herself look very nice.

"You must let Anne Dorset see that you care to please her," he said. "Anne is a very good woman, and her approval is worth having."

"Oh, papa!" cried Janey, "when you are always calling her an old maid!"

"L'un n'empêche pas l'autre," he said, which puzzled Janey, whose French was very deficient. Even Ursula, supposed to be the best French scholar in the family, was not quite sure what it meant; but it was evidently something in favour of Cousin Anne, which was sweet to the grateful girl.

Janey, though suffering bitterly under the miserable consciousness of being only fourteen, and not asked anywhere, helped with disinterested zeal to get her sister ready, and consoled herself by orders for unlimited muffins and cake for tea.

"There will only be the children," she said, resignedly, and felt herself *incomprise;* but indeed, the attractions of a good romp afterwards, no one being in the house to restrain the spirits of the youthful party, made even Janey amends.

As for Reginald, who was not asked, he was, it must be allowed, rather sulky too, and he could not solace himself either with muffins or romps. His rooms at the College were very pleasant rooms, but he was used to home; and though the home at the Parsonage was but faded, and not in such perfect order as it might have been, the young man felt even his wainscoted study dull without the familiar voices, the laughter and foolish family jokes, and even the little quarrels which kept life always astir. He walked with Ursula to the station, whither her little box with her evening dress had gone before her, in a half-affronted state of mind.

"What does he want with a pupil?" Reginald was saying, as he had said before. "A fellow no one knows, coming and taking possession of the house as if it belonged to him. There is plenty to do in the parish without pupils, and if I were not on the spot he would get into trouble, I can tell you. A man that has been ploughed, 'a big hulking fellow' (Sir Robert says so, not I). Mind, I'll have no flirting, Ursula; that is what always happens with a pupil in the house."

"Reginald, how dare you—"

"Oh, yes, I dare; my courage is quite equal to facing you, even if you do shoot thunderbolts out of your eyes. Mind you, I won't have it. There is a set of fellows who try it regularly, and if you were above them, would go in for Janey; and it would be great fun and great promotion for Janey; she

would feel herself a woman directly; so you must mind her as
well as yourself. I don't like it at all," Reginald went on.
"Probably he will complain of the dinners you give him, as
if he were in an inn. Confound him! What my father
means by it, I can't tell."

"Reginald, you ought not to swear," said Ursula. "It is
dreadfully wicked in a clergyman. Poor papa meant making a
little more money. What else could he mean? And I think
it is very good of him, for it will bother him most. Mr. Copperhead is very nice, Reginald. I saw him in London, you
know. I thought he was very——".

"Ah! oh!" said Reginald, "I forgot that. You met him in
London? To be sure, and it was there you met Miss
Beecham. I begin to see. Is he coming here after her, I
should like to know? She doesn't look the sort of girl to
encourage that sort of thing."

"The sort of girl to encourage that sort of thing! How
strangely you talk when you get excited: isn't that rather
vulgar? I don't know if he is coming after Miss Beecham or
not," said Ursula, who thought the suggestion uncalled for,
"but in a very short time you can judge for yourself."

"Ah—indignation!" said the big brother, who like most
big brothers laughed at Ursula's exhibition of offended dignity;
"and, by the way, Miss Beecham—you have not seen her since
that night when she was sent for. Will not she think it
strange that you never sent to inquire?"

"I sent Betsey—"

"But if Miss Beecham had been somebody else, you would
have gone yourself," he said, being in a humour for finding
fault. "If poor old Mrs. Tozer had been what you call a
lady—"

"I thought you were much more strong than I am against
the Dissenters?" said Ursula, "ever since that man's speech;
and, indeed, always, as long as I can recollect."

"She is not a mere Dissenter," said Reginald. "I think I
shall call as I go home. She is the cleverest girl I ever met;
not like one of you bread-and-butter girls, though she is not
much older than you. A man finds a girl like that worth talking to," said the young clergyman, holding himself erect.
Certainly Reginald had not improved; he had grown ever so
much more self-important since he got a living of his own.

"And if I was to say, 'Mind, I won't have it, Reginald?'"
cried Ursula, half-laughing, half-angry. "I think that is a
great deal worse than a pupil. But Miss Beecham is very
dignified, and you may be sure she will not think much of a

call from you. Heaven be praised! that is one thing you can't get into your hands; we girls are always good for something there. Men may think themselves as grand as they please," said Ursula, "but their visits are of no consequence; it is ladies of the family who must *call!*" After this little outbreak, she came down at once to her usual calm. "I will ask Cousin Anne what I ought to do; I don't think Miss Beecham wanted me to go then—"

"I shall go," said Reginald, and he left Ursula in her father's keeping, who met them at the station, and went off at once, with a pleasant sense of having piqued her curiosity, to Grange Lane.

It was still early, for the trains which stopped at the little country station next to the Hall were very few and inconvenient, and the sun, though setting, was still shining red from over St. Roque's upon Grange Lane. The old red walls grew redder still in the frosty night, and the sky began to bloom into great blazing patches of colour upon the wintry clearness of the blue. There was going to be a beautiful sunset, and such a thing was always to be seen from Grange Lane better than anywhere else in Carlingford. Reginald went down the road slowly, looking at it, and already almost forgetting his idea of calling on Miss Beecham. To call on Miss Beecham would be to call on old Tozer, the butterman, to whom alone the visit would be naturally paid; and this made him laugh within himself. So he would have passed, no doubt, without the least attempt at intruding on the privacy of the Tozers, had not the garden-door opened before he got so far, and Phœbe herself came out, with her hands in her muff, to take a little walk up and down as she did daily. She did not take her hand out of its warm enclosure to give it to him; but nodded with friendly ease in return to his salutation.

"I have come out to see the sunset," said Phœbe; "I like a little air before the day is over, and grandmamma, when she is poorly, likes her room to be very warm."

"I hope Mrs. Tozer is better. I hope you have not been anxious."

"Oh, no! it is chronic; there is no danger. But she requires a great deal of attendance; and I like to come out when I can. Oh, how fine it is! what colour! I think, Mr. May, you must have a *spécialité* for sunsets at Carlingford. I never saw them so beautiful anywhere else."

"I am glad there is something you like in Carlingford."

"Something! there is a very great deal; and that I don't like too," she said with a smile. "I don't care for the people

I am living among, which is dreadful. I don't suppose you
have ever had such an experience, though you must know a great
deal more in other ways than I. All the people that come to
inquire about grandmamma are very kind; they are as good as
possible; I respect them, and all that, but—— Well, it must
be my own fault, or education. It is education, no doubt, that
gives us those absurd ideas."

" Don't call them absurd," said Reginald, " indeed I can enter
into them perfectly well. I don't *know* them, perhaps, in my own
person; but I can perfectly understand the repugnance, the
distress—"

"The words are too strong," said Phœbe, "not so much as
that; the—annoyance, perhaps, the nasty disagreeable struggle
with one's self and one's pride; as if one were better than
other people. I dislike myself, and despise myself for it; but
I can't help it. We have so little power over ourselves."

" I hope you will let my sister do what she can to deliver
you," said Reginald; " Ursula is not like you; but she is a good
little thing, and she is able to appreciate you. I was to tell you
she had been called suddenly off to the Dorsets', with whom my
father and she have gone to pass the night—to meet, I believe,
a person you know."

" Oh, Clarence Copperhead; he is come then? How odd it
will be to see him here. His mother is nice, but his father is
——Oh, Mr. May! if you only knew the things people have
to put up with. When I think of Mr. Copperhead, and his
great, ugly, staring wealth, I feel disposed to hate money—
especially among Dissenters. It would be better if we were all
poor."

Reginald said nothing; he thought so too. In that case
there would be a few disagreeable things out of a poor clergyman's way, and assaults like that of Northcote upon himself
would be impossible; but he could scarcely utter these virtuous sentiments.

"Poverty is the desire of ascetics, and this is not an ascetic age,"
he said at length, with a half-laugh at himself for his stiff speech.

" You may say it is not an ascetic age; but yet I suppose
the Ritualists——. Perhaps you are a Ritualist yourself, Mr.
May? I know as little personally about the church here, as
you do about Salem Chapel. I like the service—so does papa
—and I like above all things the independent standing of a
clergyman; the feeling he must have that he is free to do his
duty. That is why I like the church; for other things of course
I like our own body best."

"I don't suppose such things can be argued about, Miss

Beecham. I wish I knew something of my father's new pupil. I don't like having a stranger in the house; my father is fond of having his own way."

"It is astonishing how often parents are so," said Phœbe, demurely ; "and the way they talk of their experience ! as if each new generation did not know more than the one that preceded it."

"You are pleased to laugh, but I am quite in earnest. A pupil is a nuisance. For instance, no man who has a family should ever take one. I know what things are said."

"You mean about the daughters ? That is true enough, there are always difficulties in the way ; but you need not be afraid of Clarence Copperhead. He is not the fascinating pupil of a church-novel. There's nothing the least like the Heir of Redclyffe about him."

"You are very well up in Miss Yonge's novels, Miss Beecham."

"Yes," said Phœbe ; "one reads Scott for Scotland (and a few other things), and one reads Miss Yonge for the church. Mr. Trollope is good for that too, but not so good. All that I know of clergymen's families I have got from her. I can recognize you quite well, and your sister, but the younger ones puzzle me ; they are not in Miss Yonge ; they are too much like other children, too naughty. I don't mean anything disagreeable. The babies in Miss Yonge are often very naughty too, but not the same. As for you, Mr. May——"

"Yes. As for me ? "

"Oh, I know everything about you. You are a fine scholar, but you don't like the drudgery of teaching. You have a fine mind, but it interferes with you continually. You have had a few doubts—just enough to give a piquancy ; and now you have a great ideal, and mean to do many things that common clergymen don't think of. That was why you hesitated about the chaplaincy ? See how much I have got out of Miss Yonge. I know you as well as if I had known you all my life ; a great deal better than I know Clarence Copperhead ; but then, no person of genius has taken any trouble about him."

"I did not know I had been a hero of fiction," said Reginald, who had a great mind to be angry. All this time they were walking briskly backward and forward before Tozer's open door, the Anglican, in his long black coat, following the lively movements of Tozer's granddaughter, only because he could not help himself. He was irritated, yet he was pleased. A young man is pleased to be thought of, even when the notice is but barely complimentary. Phœbe must have thought of him a good deal before she found him out in this way; but he was irritated all the same.

"You are, however," she answered lightly. "Look at that blaze of crimson, Mr. May; and the blue which is so clear and so unfathomable. Winter is grander than summer, and even warmer—to look at; with its orange, and purple, and gold. What poor little dirty, dingy things we are down here, to have all this exhibited every evening for our delight!"

"That is true," he said; and as he gazed, something woke in the young man's heart—a little thrill of fancy, if not of love. It is hard to look at a beautiful sunset, and then see it reflected in a girl's face, and not to feel something—which may be nothing, perhaps. His heart gave a small jump, not much to speak of. Phœbe did not talk like the other young ladies in Grange Lane.

"Mr. May, Mr. May!" she cried suddenly, "please go away! I foresee a disastrous encounter which alarms me. You can't fight, but there is no saying what you might do to each other. Please go away!"

"What is the matter?" he said. "I don't understand any encounter being disastrous here. Why should I go away?"

She laughed, but there was a certain fright in her tone. "Please!" she said, "I see Mr. Northcote coming this way. He will stop to speak to me. It is the gentleman who attacked you in the Meeting. Mr. May," she added entreatingly, between laughter and fright, "do go, please."

"I shall do nothing of the kind," said Reginald, roused; "I am not afraid. Let him come on. This wall shall fly from its firm base as soon as I."

Phœbe clasped her hands in dismay, which was partially real. "The typical churchman," she said, with a glance at Reginald's figure, which was not displeasing to him, "and the typical Dissenter! and what am I to do between them? Oh, I wish you would go away."

"Not an inch," said the young champion. Phœbe was frightened, but she was delighted. "I shall introduce him to you," she said threatening.

"I don't mind," he replied; "nothing on earth should induce me to fly."

CHAPTER XXV.

TEA.

Now here was a business! The typical Anglican and the typical Dissenter, as Phœbe said, with only that clever young woman to keep them from flying at each other's throats; the one obstinately holding his place by her side (and Phœbe began to have a slight consciousness that, being without any chaperon, she ought not to have kept Reginald May at her side; but in the Tozer world, who knew anything of chaperons?), the other advancing steadily, coming up the Lane out of the glow of the sunset, showing square against it in his frock-coat and high hat, formal and demagogical, not like his rival. The situation pleased Phœbe, who liked to " manage ; " but it slightly frightened her as well, though the open door behind, and the long garden with its clouds of crocuses, was a city of refuge always within reach.

" Is it really you, Mr. Northcote ? " she said. " You look as if you had dropped out of that lovely sunset I have been watching so long—and I thought you were at the other end of the world."

" I have been at the other end of England, which comes to the same thing," said Northcote, in a voice which was harsh by nature, and somewhat rough with cold; " and now they have sent me back to Salem Chapel, to take Mr. Thorpe's place for three months. They asked for me, I believe; but that you must know better than I do."

It was not in the nature of man not to be a little proud in the circumstances, and it is quite possible that he considered Phœbe to have something to do with the flattering request.

" No, I have not heard ; but I am glad," said Phœbe ; " and if it is not wicked to say so, I am glad Mr. Thorpe is to be away. Let us hope it will do him good. I am sure it will do the rest of us good, at all events."

Northcote made no answer ; but he looked at the other, and several questions began to tremble on his lips. That this was a Churchman did not immediately occur to him ; for, indeed, various young pastors of his own body put on the livery which he himself abjured, and the sight of it as a servile copy filled him with a certain contempt.

" Mr. May has been stopped in his way by the beauty of the skies," said Phœbe, rather enjoying the position as she got used to it. " Mr. Northcote—Mr. May. It is not easy to pass such an exhibition as that, is it ?—and given to us all for love, and nothing for reward," she added; for she was a well read young woman, and did not hesitate to suffer this to appear.

And then there was a momentary pause. Northcote was confused, it must be allowed, by thus coming face to face, without previous warning, with the man whom he had so violently assailed. Reginald had the best of it in every way, for he was the man injured, and had it in his power to be magnanimous ; and he had the advantage of full warning, and had prepared himself. Besides, was not he the superior by every social rule ? And that consciousness is always sweet.

" If Mr. Northcote is new to Carlingford, he will probably not know what a fine point of view we have here. That, like so many other things," said Reginald, pointedly, " wants a little personal experience to find it out."

" For that matter, to see it once is as good as seeing it a hundred times," said Northcote, somewhat sharply ; for to give in was the very last thing he thought of. A little glow of anger came over him. He thought Phœbe had prepared this ordeal for him, and he was vexed, not only because she had done it, but because his sense of discomfiture might afford a kind of triumph to that party in the connection which was disposed, as he expressed it, to " toady the Church."

" Pardon me, I don't think you can judge of anything at a first view."

" And, pardon me, I think you see everything most sharply and clearly at a first view," said the Nonconformist, who was the loudest ; " certainly in all matters of principle. After a while, you are persuaded against your will to modify this opinion and that, to pare off a little here, and tolerate a little there. Your first view is the most correct."

" Well," said Phœbe, throwing herself into the breach, " I am glad you don't agree, for the argument is interesting. Will you come in and fight it out ? You shall have some tea, which will be pleasant, for it shall be hot. I really cannot stay out any longer ; it is freezing here."

The new-comer prepared to follow ; but Reginald hesitated. Pride whispered that to go into the house of Tozer, the butter-man, was something monstrous ; but then it might be amusing. This " Dissenting fellow," no doubt, was a drawback ; but a kind of angry antagonism and disdain half-attracted him even to the Dissenting fellow. It might be well, on the whole, to

see what kind of being such a person was. All curious
phenomena are attractive to a student. " The proper study of
mankind is man," Reginald said to himself. Before he had
got through this little argument with himself, Phœbe had gone
in, and Northcote, whose disgust at the interposition of an adversary had no such softening of curiosity, followed her abruptly,
without any of those graces which are current in society.
This rudeness offended the other, who was about to walk on
indignant, when Phœbe turned back, and looked out at him
from the open door

" Are not you coming, Mr. May ? " she said softly, looking
at him with the least little shrug of her shoulders.

Reginald yielded without further resistance. But he felt
fully that to see him, the chaplain of the old College, walking
down through Tozer's garden, between the two rows of closed-
up crocuses which glimmered ghostly by the side of the path,
was one of the strangest sights in the world.

Phœbe, to tell the truth, was a little confused as to where to
convey her captive, out of whom she meant to get a little amusement for the long winter afternoon. For a girl of her active
mind, it may easily be imagined that a succession of long days
with Mrs. Tozer was somewhat monotonous, She did her duty
like a hero, and never complained ; but still, if a little amusement was possible, it was worth having. She carried in her two
young men as naughty boys carry stag-beetles, or other such
small deer. If they would fight it would be fun ; and if they
would not fight, why, it might be fun still, and more amusing
than grandmamma. She hesitated between the chilly drawing-
room, where a fire was lighted, but where there was no evidence
of human living, and the cozy parlour, where Mrs. Tozer sat
in her best cap, still wheezy, but convalescent, waiting for her
tea, and not indisposed to receive such deputations of the community as might come to ask for her. Finally, Phœbe opened
the door of that sanctuary, which was dazzling with bright fire-
light after the gloom outside. It was a very comfortable
interior, arranged by Phœbe to suit her own ideas rather than
those of grandmamma, though grandmamma's comfort had been
her chief object. The tea-things were sparkling upon the table,
the kettle singing by the fire, and Mrs. Tozer half-dozing in
the tranquillity and warmth.

" Grandmamma, I have brought Mr. May and Mr. Northcote
to see you," she said.

The poor old lady almost sprang from her chair in amazement.

" Lord bless us, Phœbe, Mr. May ! "

" Don't disturb yourself, grandmamma ; they will find seats.

Yes, we were all looking at the sunset, and as I knew tea must
be ready—I know you want it, dear granny—I asked them to
have some. Here it is, as I told you, quite hot, and very
fragrant this cold night. How cold it is outside! I think it
will freeze, and that skating may come off at last, Mr. May,
that you were talking of, you remember? You were to teach
your sisters to skate."

"Yes, with the advantage of your example."

Reginald had put himself in a corner, as far away as possible
from the old woman in the chair. His voice, he felt, had caught
a formal tone. As for the other, his antagonist, he had assumed
the front of the battle—even, in Tozer's absence, he had ventured
to assume the front of the fire. He was not the sort of man
Reginald had expected, almost hoped to see—a fleshy man,
loosely put together, according to the nature, so far as he knew
it, of Dissenters; but a firmly knit, clean-limbed young man,
with crisp hair curling about his head, and a gleam of energy
and spirit in his eye. The gentler Anglican felt by no means
sure of a speedy victory, even of an intellectual kind. The
young man before him did not look a slight antagonist. They
glared at each other, measuring their strength; they did not
know, indeed, that they had been brought in here to this warmth
and light, like the stag-beetles, to make a little amusement for
Phœbe; but they were quite ready to fight all the same.

"Mr. Northcote, sir, I'm glad to see you. Now this is
friendly; this is what I calls as it should be, when a young
pastor comes in and makes free, without waiting for an invitation," said Tozer kindly, bustling in; "that speech of yours,
sir, was a rouser: that 'it 'em off, that did, and you can see as
the connection ain't ungrateful. What's that you say, Phœbe?
what? I'm a little hard of hearing. Mr.—May!"

"Mr. May was good enough to come in with me, grandpapa.
We met at the door. We have mutual friends, and you know
how kind Miss May has been," said Phœbe, trembling with
sudden fright, while Reginald, pale with rage and embarrassment, stood up in his corner. Tozer was embarrassed too.
He cleared his throat and rubbed his hands, with a terrible
inclination to raise one of them to his forehead. It was all
that he could do to get over this class instinct. Young May,
though he had been delighted to hear him assailed in the
Meeting, was a totally different visitor from the clever young
pastor whom he received with a certain consciousness of patron-
age. Tozer did not know that the Northcotes were infinitely
richer, and quite as well-born and well-bred in their ways as
the Mays, and that his young Dissenting brother was a more

costly production, as well as a more wealthy man, than the young chaplain in his long coat; but if he had known this it would have made no difference. His relation to the one was semi-servile, to the other condescending and superior. In Reginald May's presence, he was but a butterman who supplied the family; but to Horace Northcote he was an influential member of society, with power over a Minister's individual fate.

"I assure you, sir, as I'm proud to see you in my house," he said, with a duck of his head, and an ingratiating but uncomfortable smile. "Your father, I hope, as he's well, sir, and all the family? We are a kind of neighbours now; not as we'd think of taking anything upon us on account of living in Grange Lane. But Phœbe here—Phœbe, junior, as we call's her—she's a cut above us, and I'm proud to see any of her friends in my 'umble 'ouse. My good lady, sir," added Tozer, with another duck, indicating with a wave of his hand his wife, who had already once risen, wheezy, but knowing her manners, to make a kind of half-bow, half-curtsey from her chair.

"You are very kind," said Reginald, feeling himself blush furiously, and not knowing what to say. The other young man stood with his back to the fire, and a sneer, which he intended to look like a smile, on his face.

And as for Phœbe, it must be allowed that, notwithstanding all her resources, even she was exquisitely uncomfortable for a minute or two. The young people all felt this, but to Tozer it seemed that he had managed everything beautifully, and a sense of elation stole over him. To be visited in this manner by the gentry, "making free," and "quite in a friendly way," was an honour he had never looked for. He turned to Northcote with great affability and friendliness.

"Well," he said, "Mr. Northcote, sir, it can't be denied as this is a strange meeting; you and Mr. May, as mightn't be, perhaps, just the best of friends, to meet quite comfortable over a cup of tea. But ain't it the very best thing that could happen? Men has their public opinions, sir, as every one should speak up bold for, and stick to; that's my way of thinking. But I wouldn't bring it no farther; not, as might be said, into the domestic circle. I'm clean against that. You say your say in public, whatever you may think on a subject, but you don't bear no malice; it ain't a personal question; them's my sentiments. And I don't know nothing more elevatin', nothing more consolin', than for two public opponents, as you may say, to meet like this quite cozy and comfortable over a cup o' tea."

"It is a pleasure, I assure you, which I appreciate highly," said Reginald, finding his voice.

"And which fills me with delight and satisfaction," said Northcote. Those stag-beetles which Phœbe, so to speak, had carried in in her handkerchief, were only too ready to fight.

"You had better have some tea first," she said breathless, "before you talk so much of its good effects. Sit down, grand-papa, and have your muffin while it is hot; I know that is what you like. Do you care about china, Mr. May? but every one cares for china now-a-days. Look at that cup, and fancy grandmamma having this old service in use without knowing how valuable it is. Cream Wedgwood! You may fancy how I stared when I saw it; and in everyday use! most people put it up on brackets, when they are so lucky as to possess any. Tell Mr. May, grandmamma, how you picked it up. Mr. Northcote, there is an article in this review that I want you to look at. Papa sent it to me. It is too metaphysical for me, but I know you are great in metaphysics—"

"I am greater in china; may not I look at the Wedgwood first?"

"Perhaps you will turn over the literature to me," said Reginald, "reviews are more in my way than teacups, though I say it with confusion. I know how much I am behind my age."

"And I too," whispered Phœbe, behind the book which she had taken up. "Don't tell any one. It is rare, I know; and everybody likes to have something that is rare; but I don't really care for it the least in the world. I have seen some bits of Italian *faience* indeed—but English pottery is not like Italian, any more than English skies."

"You have the advantage of me, Miss Beecham, both as regards the pottery and the skies."

"Ah, if it is an advantage; bringing poetry down to prose is not always an advantage, is it? Italy is such a dream—so long as one has never been there."

"Yes, it is a dream," said Reginald, with enthusiasm, "to everybody, I think; but when one has little money and much work all one's life—poverty stands in the way of all kinds of enjoyment."

"Poverty is a nice friendly sort of thing; a ground we can all meet on," said Phœbe. "But don't let us say that to grandpapa. How odd people are! he knows you are not Crœsus, but still he has a sort of feeling that you are a young prince, and do him the greatest honour in coming to his house; and yet, all the same, he thinks that money is the very grandest thing in existence. See what prejudice is! He would not allow that he had any class-reverence, and yet he can no more get rid of it—"

"Miss Beecham, it is very difficult for me to say anything on such a subject."

"Very difficult, and you show your delicacy by not saying anything. But you know, apart from this, which is not gratifying, I am rather proud of grandpapa's way of looking at some things. About saying out your opinions in public, and yet bearing no malice, for instance. Now, Mr. Northcote is the very Antipodes to you; therefore you ought to know him and find out what he means. It would be better for you both. That is what I call enlarging the mind," said Phœbe with a smile; which was, to tell the truth, a very pretty smile, and filled with a soft lustre the blue eyes with which she looked at him. Whether it was this, or the cogency of her argument, that moved the young Anglican, it would be hard to say.

"If you are to be the promoter of this new science, I don't object to studying under you," he said with a great deal of meaning in his voice.

Phœbe gave him another smile, though she shook her head; and then she turned to the hero on the other side.

"Is it genuine, Mr. Northcote? is it as fine as I thought? There now, I told you, grandmamma! Have you been telling Mr. Northcote how you picked it up? I am sure you will present him with a cup and saucer for his collection in return for his praises."

"Not for the world," said Northcote, with profound seriousness; "break a set of cream Wedgwood! what do you take me for, Miss Beecham? I don't mean to say that I would not give my ears to have it—all; but to break the set—"

"Oh, I beg your pardon! I was not prepared for such delicacy of feeling—such conscientiousness—"

"Ah!" said Northcote, with a long-drawn breath, "I don't think you can understand the feelings of an enthusiast. A set of fine China is like a poem—every individual bit is necessary to the perfection of the whole. I allow that this is not the usual way of looking at it; but my pleasure lies in seeing it entire, making the tea-table into a kind of lyric, elevating the family life by the application of the principles of abstract beauty to its homeliest details. Pardon, Miss Beecham, but Mrs. Tozer is right, and you are wrong. The idea of carrying off a few lines of a poem in one's pocket for one's collection—"

"Now that's what I call speaking up," said Mrs. Tozer, the first time she had opened her lips, "that's just what I like. Mr. Northcote has a deal more sense than the like of you. He

knows what's what. Old things like this as might have been
my granny's, they're good enough for every day, they're very
nice for common use; but they ain't no more fit to be put away
in cupboards and hoarded up like fine china, no more than I
am. Mr. Northcote should see our best—that's worth the looking at; and if I'd known as the gentleman was coming—but you
can't put an old head on young shoulders. Phœbe's as good as
gold, and the trouble she takes with an old woman like me is
wonderful; but she can't be expected to think of everything,
can she now, at her age?"

The two young men laughed—it was the first point of approach between them, and Phœbe restrained a smile, giving them
a look from one to another. She gave Reginald his cup of tea
very graciously.

"Mr. Northcote prefers the Wedgwood, and Mr. May
doesn't mind, grandmamma," she said sweetly. "So it is as
well to have the best china in the cupboard. Grandpapa,
another muffin—it is quite hot; and I know that is what you
like best."

"Well, I'll say that for Phœbe," said Tozer, with his mouth
full, "that whether she understands china or not I can't tell,
but she knows what a man likes, which is more to the purpose
for a young woman. That's what she does; and looks after
folk's comforts as I never yet saw her match. She's a girl in a
thousand, is Phœbe, junior. There be them as is more for dress,"
he added, fond and greasy, looking at her seated modestly in
that gown, which had filled with awe and admiration the experienced mind of Mrs. Sam Hurst; "and plays the pianny, and
that sort of style of girl; but for one as minds the comforts of
them about her——" Tozer turned back to the table, and made
a gulp of his last piece of muffin. Eloquence could have no
more striking climax; the proof of all his enthusiasm, was it
not there?

"Don't you play, Miss Beecham?" said Reginald, half-amused,
half-angry.

"A little," said Phœbe, with a laugh. She had brought down
a small cottage piano out of the drawing-room, where nobody
ever touched it, into a dark corner out of reach of the lamp.
It was the only accomplishment upon which she prided herself.
She got up from the table, when she had poured out another
cup of tea for her grandfather, and without saying a word went
to the little piano. It was not much of an instrument, and
Reginald May was very little of a *connoisseur*. Northcote,
who knew her gifts, gave himself up to listening, but the Tozers
looked on, shaking their heads, and it was only after some time

had passed, that Reginald began to understand that he was listening to something which he had never heard before. Ursula's school-girl tunes had never interested him very much ; he did not know what this was which seemed to creep into his heart by his ears. He got up by and by, and stole towards the piano bewildered.

"It'll soon be over, sir," said Tozer, encouragingly. "Don't you run away, Mr. May. Them are queer tunes, I allow, but they don't last long, and your company's an honour. As for the playing, it'll soon be over; you needn't run away.

CHAPTER XXVI.

THE HALL.

IT is unnecessary to say that the dinner party in the Hall bore very little resemblance to those simple amusements in No. 6, Grange Lane. There were three or four people to meet Mr. May, who, as an orator and literary man, had greater reputation even such a little way from home than he had in his own town. He was a very good preacher, and those articles of his were much admired as "thoughtful" papers, searching into many mental depths, and fathoming the religious soul with wonderful insight. Ladies especially admired them ; the ladies who were intellectual, and found pleasure in the feeling of being more advanced than their neighbours. The Rector's wife of the parish in which the Dorsets lived applied herself with great vigour to the art of drawing him out. She asked him questions with that air of delightful submission to an intellectual authority which some ladies love to assume, and which it pleases many men to accept. His daughters were not at all reverential of Mr. May, and it soothed him to get marks of devotion and literary submission out of doors. Even Sophy Dorset had gone through the phase of admiration for her cousin. This had been dissipated, it is true, long ago ; but yet she did not laugh, as she usually did, at the believers in him. She listened to Mrs. Rector plying him with eager questions, asking his advice on that point and the other, and smiled, but was charitable. As for Cousin Anne, she was charitable by nature, and all the world got the advantage of it. Little Ursula was one of her prime favourites—a motherless girl, who was the eldest, and who had to work for the family, was of all others the thing which moved her sympathies most. The little Indian children had long ere this yielded to the charms of Aunt Anne. They followed her wherever she went like little spaniels, hanging on by her dress. She had to go up to the nursery to hear them say their prayers before she dressed for dinner.

"You see, this is a proof that with children one should never be discouraged," she said; "for they did not take to me at first;" and she turned her mild countenance, beaming with soft light, upon Ursula. To be hampered by these babies clinging about her, to have them claiming imperiously her attention and her time, however she might be engaged; to give up to them the moments of leisure in which otherwise she might have had a little quiet and repose, this was what Anne Dorset considered as her recompense.

"Oh, I wish I could be as good to Amy and Robin! But I feel as if I should like to shake them often," cried Ursula, "even though I love them with all my heart. Oh! Cousin Anne, I don't think there is any one like you."

"Yes, that is what she thinks her reward," said Sophy. "I should like something better, if it was I. Don't copy her, Ursula. It is better to have children of your own, and get other people to nurse them. Anne, you see, likes it. I want you to marry, and get all the good things in this life. Let us leave the self-denials to her; she likes them, you perceive."

"I don't know why you should always talk of marrying to me, Cousin Sophy," said Ursula with gentle reproach. "I hope I am not a girl to think of such things."

"And why not? Is it not the first duty of woman, you little simpleton?" said Sophy Dorset, with a laugh.

But Ursula could not imagine that it was only in this general way that her cousin spoke. She could not but feel that this big Clarence Copperhead, with the diamond buttons, and that huge expanse of shirt-front, had something to do with Sophy's talk. There was six feet of him, which is a thing that goes a long way with a girl; and he was not bad-looking. And why did he come to Carlingford, having nothing in the world to do with the place? and coming to Carlingford, why was papa sought out, of all people, to be his tutor? Certainly the circumstances were such as invited conjecture, especially when added on to Sophy's allusions. He took Ursula in to dinner, which fluttered her somewhat; and though he was much intent upon the dinner itself, and studied the *menu* with a devotion which would have made her tremble for her housekeeping, had she been sufficiently disengaged to notice it, he yet found time to talk a little between the courses.

"I did not expect, when I saw you in London, that we were

to meet again so soon, Miss May," was the perfectly innocent remark with which he opened the conversation.

Ursula would have said it herself had he not said it, and all she could do was to answer, "No, indeed," with a smile.

"And I am coming to your father to be coached," continued the young man. "It is a funny coincidence, don't you think so? I am glad you came to that ball, Miss May. It makes me feel that I know you. I don't like starting off afresh, all at once, among people I don't know."

"No," said Ursula; "I should not like it either, But there are other people you know in Carlingford. There is the lady who was at the ball—the young lady in black, I used to call her—Miss Beecham; you must know her better than you know me."

"Who? Phœbe? really!" he said, elevating his eyebrows. "Phœbe in Carlingford! By Jove! how the governor will laugh! I should like to know," with a conscious smile on his countenance, "what *she* is doing there."

"Her grandmamma is ill, and she is nursing her," said Ursula simply, at which young Copperhead laughed again.

"Oh, that is how it is! Very good of her, don't you think? Shouldn't suppose she would be amusing, the old granny, and Phœbe likes to be amused. I must go to see her as soon as I can get there. You know, we are Dissenters at home, Miss May. Good joke, isn't it? The governor will not hear a word against them. As a matter of fact, nobody does go to chapel in our rank of life; but the governor sometimes is as obstinate as an old pig."

"I suppose he likes it best," said Ursula, gently; and here a new course came round, and for the moment Clarence had something else to do. He resumed after the *entrées*, which were poor, as he made a mental note.

"Is there anything to do at Carlingford, Miss May? I hope you skate. I am not much in the hunting way; nor your father, I suppose? for, to be sure, a hunting parson would never do. I am too heavy a weight for most horses, and the good of galloping over the country all day, after a poor brute of a fox!—but we must not say that before Sir Robert. I suppose it *is* dull?" he said, somewhat pathetically, looking in her face.

"We don't think it dull, Mr. Copperhead. It may be, perhaps, for a gentleman."

"That's it," said Clarence. "I don't know if it's because women have more resources, or because they want less; but you always get on better than we do, somehow; very lucky for you. You don't expect so much. I believe that's what it is."

"Then that shows we are the most sensible," said Ursula, roused, and a little indignant.

He paused, to make his choice between the inevitable turkey and the inevitable beef.

"I hope it's braised," he said, in a devout undertone. "You don't expect so much, Miss May, that's what it is; you're always in the house. You don't care for exercise. Bless you, if I didn't take exercise, I should be fifteen stone before you could turn round. How much are you? about eight, perhaps; not much more. That makes a deal of difference: you don't require to keep yourself down."

Ursula did not make any answer. She was prepared to look upon him very favourably, and accept what he said as full of originality and force; but the tone the conversation had taken was not entirely to her mind. Phœbe could have managed it; but Ursula was not Phœbe. She was more disposed to take offence at the young man's tone than to guide it into better ways.

"I hope your mother is well," she said at last, falteringly, after a long pause. Ursula thought her companion would remark this pause, and think her displeased. She might have saved herself the trouble, for it was the braised turkey which kept Clarence quiet, not offence.

"Oh, quite well, I thank you. Not so well as when I am at home; she don't like parting with me," he said, "but, of course, I can't be always at my mother's apron-strings. Women forget that."

"She was very kind when I was in London."

"Yes, that just pleases her; she is never so happy as when she is buying things for somebody," he replied, betraying an acquaintance with the exact manner of the kindness which somewhat disturbed poor Ursula: "that is exactly her way. I dare say she'll come and see the Dorsets while I'm here."

Then there was again a pause, and Clarence turned to speak to some one at his other side.

"No, I don't hunt much," he said; "I have come into the country to be coached. My father's a modern sort of man, and wants a fellow to be up in history, and that sort of thing. Bore—yes; and I dare say Carlingford is very dull. Oh, yes, I will go out with the hounds now and then, if there is not a frost. I should rather like a frost for my part."

It was a hunting lady who had started this new conversation, into which the stranger had drifted away, leaving Ursula stranded. She was slightly piqued, it must be allowed, and when Sophy asked her after dinner how she liked her companion, made a dignified reply.

"I have no doubt he is very nice," she said; "I don't know much of gentlemen. He talks of papa as if he were a schoolmaster, and thinks Carlingford will be dull."

"So it is, Ursula. I have often heard you say so."

"Yes, perhaps; but a stranger ought to be civil," said the girl, offended; and she went and entrenched herself by the side of Cousin Anne, where the new pupil could not come near her. Indeed he did not seem very anxious to do so, as Ursula soon saw. She blushed very hotly all by herself, under Cousin Anne's shadow: that she could have been so absurd as ever to think— But his size, and the weight over which he had lamented, and his abundant whiskers and large shirt front, made it quite impossible for Ursula to think of him as a person to be educated. It must be Miss Beecham, she said to herself.

No thoughts of this kind crossed Mr. Clarence Copperhead's mind, as he stretched his big limbs before the drawing-room fire after dinner, and said "Brava!" when the ladies sang. He knew "Brava" was the right thing to say. He liked to be at the Hall, which he had never visited before, and to know that it was undeniable gentry which surrounded him, and which at the piano was endeavouring to gain his approbation. He was so much his father's son that he had a sense of pleasure and triumph in being thus elevated; and he had a feeling, more or less, of contempt for the clergyman, "only a parson," who was to be his coach. He felt the power and the beauty of money almost as much as his father did. What was there he could not buy with it? the services of the most learned pundit in existence, for what was learning? or the prettiest woman going to be his wife, if that was what he wanted. It may be supposed then that he had very little attention indeed to bestow upon a girl like Ursula, who was only the daughter of his coach—nobody at all in particular—and that her foolish fancies on the subject might have been spared. He aired himself on the hearth-rug with great satisfaction, giving now and then a shake to one of his long limbs, and a furtive glance to see that all was perfect in the *sit* of the garment that clothed it. He had been ploughed it is true, but that did not interfere much with his mental satisfaction; for, after all, scholarship was a thing cultivated chiefly by dons and prigs, and poor men; and no doubt this other poor man, the parson, would be able to put all into his head that was necessary, just as much as would pay, and no more—a process the mere thought of which made Clarence yawn, yet which he had wound up his noble mind to submit to.

"Mind you, I don't say I am going to work," he had said to his mother; "but if you think he can put it into me, he may try," and he repeated much the same sentiment, with a difference, to Sophy Dorset, who by way of civility, while the Rector's wife paid court to Mr. May, talked to Clarence a little, from the corner of the ottoman close to the fire.

"Work! well, I suppose so, after a sort. I don't mean to make myself ill with midnight oil and that sort of thing," he said (he was not at all clear in his mind as to how the midnight oil was applied), "but if Mr. May can get it into me, I'll give him leave; for one thing, I suppose there will be nothing else to do."

"Not much in Carlingford; there are neither pictures, nor museums, nor fine buildings, nor anything of the sort; and very little society; a few tea-parties, and one ball in the season."

Mr. Clarence Copperhead shrugged his large shoulders.

"I shan't go to the tea-parties, that's certain," he said; "a fellow must hunt a little, I suppose, as the place is so destitute. As for pictures and museums, that don't trouble me. The worst of going abroad is that you've always got to look at things of that sort. To have to do it at home would be beyond a joke."

"Have you seen the box of curious things John sent me with the children?" said Sophy. "They are on the table at the end of the room,—yataghans, and I don't know what other names they have, all sorts of Indian weapons. I should think you would be interested in them."

"Thanks, Cousin Sophy, I am very well where I am," he said. He looked at her in such a way that she might have appropriated this remark as a compliment, had she pleased; but Sophy laughed, and it is to be feared did not feel the compliment, for she turned right round to somebody else, and took no more notice of Clarence. He was so fully satisfied with himself that he had not any strong sense of neglect, though he had but little conversation with the company. He was quite satisfied to exhibit himself and his shirt-front before the fire.

Next day he accompanied the Mays back to Carlingford. Mr. May had enjoyed his visit. His mind was free for the moment; he had staved off the evil day, and he had a little money in his pocket, the remains of that extra fifty pounds which he had put on to Tozer's bill. With some of it he had paid some urgent debts, and he had presented five pounds to Cotsdean to buy his wife a gown, and he had a little money in his pockets. So that in every way he was comfortable and more at ease than usual. The reckoning was four months off, which was like an eternity to him in his present mood of mind, and of course he would get the money before that time. There was so much time, indeed, that to begin to think of the ways and means of paying it at this early period seemed absurd. He was to have three hundred pounds for the year of Copperhead's residence with him, if he stayed so long, and that would do, if nothing else. Therefore Mr. May was quite easy in his mind, not in the least feeling the possibility of trouble in store for him. And the visit had been pleasant. He had enlarged his acquaintance, and that among the very sort of people he cared to know. He had been very well received by all the Dorsets, and introduced by Sir Robert as a relation, and he had received some personal incense about his works and his gifts which was sweet to him. Therefore he was in very good spirits, and exceedingly amiable. He conversed with his future pupil urbanely, though he had not concealed his entire concurrence in Sir Robert's opinion that he was "a cub."

"What have you been reading lately?" he asked, when they had been transferred from the Dorsets' carriage, to the admiration and by the obsequious cares of all the attendant officials, into the railway carriage. Mr. May liked the fuss and liked the idea of that superiority which attended the Dorsets' guests. He had just been explaining to his companions that Sir Robert was the Lord of the Manor, and that all the homage done to him was perfectly natural; and he was in great good-humour even with this cub.

"Well, I've not been reading very much," said Clarence, candidly. "What was the good? The governor did not want me to be a parson, or a lawyer, or anything of that sort, and a fellow wants some sort of a motive to read. I've loafed a good deal, I'm afraid. I got into a very good set, you know, first chop—Lord Southdown, and the Beauchamps, and that lot; and —well, I suppose we were idle, and that's the truth."

"I see," said Mr. May; "a good deal of smoke and billiards, and so forth, and very little work."

"That's about it," said the young man, settling himself and his trousers, which were the objects of a great deal of affectionate care on his part. He gave them furtive pulls at the knees, and stroked them down towards the ankle, as he got himself comfortably into his seat.

Mr. May looked at him with scientific observation, and Ursula with half-affronted curiosity; his self-occupation was an offence to the girl, but it was only amusing to her father. "An unmitigated cub," Mr. May pronounced to himself; but

there where he sat he represented three hundred a-year, and
that, at least, was not to be despised. Ursula was not so
charitable as her father; she was not amused by him in the
slightest degree. Had he come down to Carlingford in humble
worship of her pretty eyes, and with a romantic intention of
making himself agreeable to her, the captivating flattery would
have prepossessed Ursula, and prepared her to see him in a very
pleasant light, and put the best interpretation upon all he did
and said. But this pretty delusion being dissipated, Ursula
was angry with herself for having been so foolish, and naturally
angry with Clarence for having led her into it, though he was
quite without blame in the matter. She looked at him in his
corner—he had taken the best corner, without consulting her
inclinations—and thought him a vulgar coxcomb, which perhaps
he was. But she would not have been so indignant except for
that little bit of injured feeling, for which really, after all, he
was not justly to blame.

CHAPTER XXVII.

A PAIR OF NATURAL ENEMIES.

AFTER the evening at Grange Lane which has been described,
Reginald May met Northcote in the street several times, as was
unavoidable, considering the size of the place, and the concen-
tration of all business in Carlingford within the restricted
length of the High Street. The two young men bowed stiffly
to each other at first; then by dint of seeing each other fre-
quently, got to inclinations a little more friendly, until at length
one day when Northcote was passing by the College, as Reginald stood in the old doorway, the young chaplain feeling magnanimous on his own ground, and somewhat amused by the idea
which suddenly presented itself to him, asked his Dissenting
assailant if he would not come in and see the place. Reginald
had the best of it in every way. It was he who was the
superior, holding out a hand of favour and kindness to one who
here at least, was beneath him in social consideration; and it
was he who was the assailed, and, so to speak, injured party, and
who nevertheless extended to his assailant a polite recognition,
which, perhaps, no one else occupying the same position would
have given. He was amused by his own magnanimity, and

enjoyed it, and the pleasure of heaping coals of fire upon his adversary's head was entirely delightful to him.

"I know you do not approve of the place or me," he said, forgetting in that moment of triumph all his own objections to it, and the ground upon which these objections were founded. "Come in and see it, will you? The chapel and the rooms are worth seeing. They are fair memorials of the past, however little the foundation may be to your mind."

He laughed as he spoke, but without ill-humour; for it is easy to be good-humoured when one feels one's self on the gaining, not the losing side. As for Northcote, pride kept him from any demonstration of unwillingness to look at what the other had to show. He would not for worlds have betrayed himself. It was expedient for him, if he did not mean to acknowledge himself worsted, to put on a good face and accept the politeness cheerfully. So that it was on the very strength of the conflict which made them first aware of each other's existence, that they thus came together. The Dissenter declared his entire delight in being taken to see the place, and with secret satisfaction, not easily put into words, the Churchman led the way. They went to all the rooms where the old men sat, some dozing by the fire, some reading, some busy about small businesses; one had a turning-lathe, another was illuminating texts, a third had a collection of curiosities of a heterogeneous kind, which he was cleaning and arranging, writing neat little labels in the neatest little hand for each article.

"The charity of our ancestors might have been worse employed," said Reginald. "A home for the old and poor is surely as fine a kind of benevolence as one could think of—if benevolence is to be tolerated at all."

"Ye-es," said Northcote. "I don't pretend to disapprove of benevolence. Perhaps the young who have a future before them, who can be of use to their country, are better objects still."

"Because they will pay," said Reginald; "because we can get something out of them in return; while we have already got all that is to be had out of the old people? A very modern doctrine, but not so lovely as the old-fashioned way."

"I did not mean that," said the other, colouring. "Certainly it ought to pay; everything, I suppose, is meant to pay one way or other. The life and progress of the young, or the gratified sentiment of the benefactor, who feels that he has provided for the old—which is the noblest kind of payment? I think the first, for my part."

"For that matter, there is a large and most flourishing school, which you will come across without fail if you work among the poor. Do you work among the poor? Pardon my curiosity; I don't know."

"It depends upon what you call the poor," said the other, who did not like to acknowledge the absence of this element in Salem Chapel; "if you mean the destitute classes, the lowest level, no; but if you mean the respectable, comfortable—"

"Persons of small income?" said Reginald. "I mean people with no incomes at all; people without trades, or anything to earn a comfortable living by; labouring people, here to-day and away to-morrow; women who take in washing, and men who go about hunting for a day's work. These are the kind of people the Church is weighted with."

"I don't see any trace of them," said the Nonconformist. "Smooth lawns, fine trees, rooms that countesses might live in. I can't see any trace of them here."

"There is no harm in a bit of grass and a few trees, and the rooms are cheaper in their long continuance than any flimsy new rubbish that could be built."

"I know I am making an unfortunate quotation," said Northcote; "but there is reason in it. It might be sold for so much, and given to the poor."

"Cheating the poor, in the first place," said Reginald, warmly concerned for what he felt to be his own; "just as the paddock an old horse dies in might bear a crop instead, and pay the owner; but what would become of the old horse?"

"Half—quarter of this space would do quite as well for your pensioners, and they might do without—"

"A chaplain!" said Reginald, laughing in spite of himself. "I know you think so. It is a sinecure."

"Well, I think they may say their prayers for themselves; a young man like you, full of talent, full of capability—I beg your pardon," said Northcote, "you must excuse me, I grudge the waste. There are so many things more worthy of you that you might do."

"What, for example?"

"Anything almost," cried the other; "digging, ploughing, building—anything! And for me too."

This he said in an undertone; but Reginald heard, and did not carry his magnanimity so far as not to reply.

"Yes," he said; "if I am wasted reading prayers for my old men, what are you, who come to agitate for my abolition? *I* think, too, almost anything would be better than to encourage the ignorant to make themselves judges of public institutions, which the wisest even find too delicate to meddle with. The digging and the ploughing might be a good thing for more than me."

"I don't say otherwise," said the young Dissenter, following into the old fifteenth-century chapel, small but perfect, the young priest of the place. They stood together for a moment under the vaulted roof, both young, in the glory of their days, both with vague noble meanings in them, which they knew so poorly how to carry out. They meant everything that was fine and great, these two young men, standing upon the threshold of their life, knowing little more than that they were fiercely opposed to each other, and meant to reform the world each in his own way; one by careful services and visitings of the poor, the other by the Liberation Society and overthrow of the State Church; both foolish, wrong and right, to the utmost bounds of human possibility. How different they felt themselves standing there, and yet how much at one they were without knowing it! Northcote had sufficient knowledge to admire the perfect old building. He followed his guide with a certain humility through the details, which Reginald had already learned by heart.

"There is nothing so perfect, so beautiful, so real now-a-days," said the young Churchman, with a natural expansion of mind over the beauty to which he had fallen heir. It seemed to him, as he looked up at the tall windows with their graceful tracery, that he was the representative of all who had worked out their belief in God within these beautiful walls, and of all the perpetual worshippers who had knelt among the old brasses of the early founders upon the worn floor. The other stood beside him with a half envy in his mind. The Dissenter did not feel himself the heir of those centuries in the same unhesitating way. He tried to feel that he was the heir of something better and more spiritual, yet felt a not ungenerous grudge that he could not share the other kinship too.

"It is very beautiful and noble," he said. "I should like to feel for it as you do; but what I should like still better would be to have the same clear certainty of faith, the same conviction that what they were doing was the only right thing to do which made both building and prayer so unfaltering in those days. We can't be so sure even of the span of an arch now."

"No—nor can you be content with the old span, even though it is clearly the best by all rules," said Reginald. The other smiled; he was the most speculative of the two, being perhaps the most thoughtful; and he had no fifteenth-century chapel to charm, nor old foundation to give him an anchor. He smiled, but there was a little envy in his mind. Even to have one's life set out before one within clear lines like this, would not that be something? If it had but been possible, no doubt saying prayers for the world, even with no better than the old men of the College to say amen, had something more beautiful in it than tours of agitation for the Liberation Society; but Northcote knew that for him it was not possible, any more than was the tonsure of Reginald's predecessor, who had said mass when first those pinnacles were reared towards heaven. After he had smiled he sighed, for the old faith was more lovely than all the new agitations; he felt a little ashamed of the Liberation Society, so long as he stood under that groined and glorious roof.

"May!" said some one, coming in suddenly. "I want you to go to the hospital for me. I am obliged to go off to town on urgent business—convocation work; and I must get a lawyer's opinion about the reredos question; there is not a moment to lose. Go and see the people in the pulmonary ward, there's a good fellow; and there are two or three bad accidents; and that old woman who is ill in Brown's cottage, you saw her the other day; and the Simmonds in Back Grove Street. I should have had a day's work well cut out, if I had not had this summons to town; but the reredos question is of the first importance, you know."

"I'll go," said Reginald. There is nothing more effectual in showing us the weakness of any habitual fallacy or assumption than to hear it sympathetically, through the ears, as it were, of a sceptic. Reginald, seeing Northcote's keen eyes gleam at the sound of the Rector's voice, instinctively fell into sympathy with him, and heard the speech through him; and though he himself felt the importance of the reredos, yet he saw in a moment how such a question would take shape in the opinion of the young Dissenter, in whom he clearly saw certain resemblances to himself. Therefore he assented very briefly, taking out his note-book to put down the special cases of which the Rector told him. They had a confidential conversation in a corner, during which the new-comer contemplated the figure of Northcote in his strange semi-clerical garments with some amaze. "Who is your friend?" he said abruptly, for he was a rapid man, losing no time about anything.

"It is not my friend at all; it is my enemy who denounced me at the Dissenters' meeting."

"Pah!" cried the Rector, curling up his nostrils, as if some disagreeable smell had reached him. "A Dissenter here! I should not have expected it from you, May."

"Nor I either," said Reginald; but his colour rose. He was

not disposed to be rebuked by any rector in Carlingford or the world.

"Are you his curate," said Northcote, "that he orders you about as if you were bound to do his bidding ? I hope, for your own sake, it is not so."

Now it was Reginald's turn to smile. He was young, and liked a bit of grandiloquence as well as another.

"Since I have been here," he said, "in this sinecure, as you call it—and such it almost is—I have been everybody's curate. If the others have too much work, and I too little, my duty is clear, don't you think ? "

Northcote made no reply. Had he known what was about to be said to him, he might have stirred up his faculties to say something; but he had not an idea that Reginald would answer him like this, and it took him aback. He was too honest himself not to be worsted by such a speech. He bowed his head with genuine respect. The apology of the Churchman whom he had assaulted, filled him with a kind of reverential confusion; he could make no reply in words. And need it be said that Reginald's heart too melted altogether when he saw how he had confounded his adversary ? That silent assent more than made up for the noisy onslaught. That he should have thus overcome Northcote made Northcote appear his friend. He was pleased and satisfied beyond the reach of words.

"Will you come to the hospital with me ? " he said; and they walked out together, the young Dissenter saying very little, doing what he could to arrange those new lights which had suddenly flashed upon his favourite subject, and feeling that he had lost his landmarks, and was confused in his path. When the logic is taken out of all that a man is doing, what is to become of him ? This was what he felt; an ideal person in Reginald's place could not have made a better answer. Suddenly somehow, by a strange law of association, there came into his mind the innocent talk he had overheard between the two girls who were, he was aware, May's sisters. A certain romantic curiosity about the family came into his mind. Certainly they could not be an ordinary family like others. There must be something in their constitution to account for this sudden downfall, which he had encountered in the midst of all his theories. The Mays must be people of a different strain from others ; a peculiar race, to whom great thoughts were familiar; he could not believe that there was anything common or ordinary in their blood. He went out in silence, with the holder of the sinecure which he had so denounced, but which now seemed to him to be held after a divine fashion, in a way which common men had no idea of. Very little could he say, and that of the most commonplace kind. He walked quite respectfully by the young clergyman's side along the crowded High Street, though without any intention of going to the hospital, or of actually witnessing the kind of work undertaken by his new friend. Northcote himself had no turn that way. To go and minister at a sick-bed had never been his custom; he did not understand how to do it; and though he had a kind of sense that it was the right thing to do, and that if any one demanded such a service of him he would be obliged to render it, he was all in the dark as to how he could get through so painful an office; whereas May went to it without fear, thinking of it only as the most natural thing in the world. Perhaps, it is possible, Northcote's ministrations, had he been fully roused, would have been, in mere consequence of the reluctance of his mind to undertake them, more real and impressive than those which Reginald went to discharge as a daily though serious duty; but in any case it was the Churchman whose mode was the more practical, the more useful. They had not gone far together, when they met the Rector hurrying to the railway; he cast a frowning, dissatisfied look at Northcote, and caught Reginald by the arm, drawing him aside.

"Don't be seen walking about with that fellow," he said; "it will injure you in people's minds. What have you to do with a Dissenter—a demagogue? Your father would not like it any more than I do. Get rid of him, May."

"I am sorry to displease either you or my father," said Reginald stiffly; "but, pardon me, in this respect I must judge for myself."

"Don't be pig-headed," said the spiritual ruler of Carlingford; but he had to rush off for his train, and had no time to say more. He left Reginald hot and angry, doubly disposed, as was natural, to march Northcote over all the town, and show his intimacy with him. Get rid of an acquaintance whom he chose to extend his countenance to, to please the Rector! For a man so young as Reginald May, and so lately made independent, such an act of subserviency was impossible indeed.

Before they entered the hospital, however, another encounter happened of a very different character. Strolling along in the centre of the pavement, endeavouring after the almost impossible combination of a yawn and a cigar, they perceived a large figure in a very long great-coat, and with an aspect of languor and *ennui* which was unmistakable a hundred yards off. This apparition called a sudden exclamation from Northcote.

" If it was possible," he said, " I should imagine I knew that man. Are there two like him ? but I can't fancy what he can be doing here."

" *That* fellow ! " said Reginald. " It's a pity if there are two like him. I can't tell you what a nuisance he is to me. His name is Copperhead ; he's my father's pupil."

" Then it *is* Copperhead ! I thought there could not be another. He gives a sort of odd familiar aspect to the place all at once."

" Then you are a friend of his ! " said Reginald, with a groan. " Pardon the natural feelings of a man whose father has suddenly chosen to become a coach. I hate it, and my dislike to the thing is reflected on the person of the pupil. I suppose that's what my antipathy means."

" He does not merit antipathy. He is a bore, but there is no harm in him. Ah ! he is quickening his pace ; I am afraid he has seen us ; and anybody he knows will be a godsend to him, I suppose."

" I am off," said Reginald ; " you will come again ? that is," he added, with winning politeness, " I shall come and seek you out. We are each the moral Antipodes of the other, Miss Beecham says—from which she argues that we should be acquainted and learn the meaning of our differences."

" I am much obliged to Miss Beecham."

" Why, Northcote ! " said Clarence Copperhead, bearing down upon them in his big grey Ulster, like a ship in full sail. " Morning, May ; who'd have thought to see you here. Oh, don't turn on my account ! I'm only taking a walk ; it don't matter which way I go."

" I am very much hurried. I was just about to hasten off to an appointment. Good-bye, Northcote," said Reginald. " We shall meet again soon, I hope."

" By Jove ! this is a surprise," said Clarence ; " to see you here, where I should as soon have thought of looking for St. Paul's ; and to find you walking about cheek by jowl with that muff, young May, who couldn't be civil, I think, if he were to try. What is the meaning of it ? I suppose you're just as much startled to see me. I'm with a coach ; clever, and a good scholar and a good family, and all that ; father to that young sprig : so there ain't any mystery about me. What's brought you here ? "

" Work," said Northcote, curtly, He did not feel disposed to enter into any kind of explanation.

" Oh, work ! Now I do wonder that a fellow like you, with plenty of money in your pocket, should go in for work as you do. What's the good of it ? and in the Dissenting parson line

of all things in the world! When a fellow has nothing, you
can understand it; he must get his grub somehow. That's
what people think of you, of course. Me, I don't do anything,
and everybody knows I'm a catch, and all that sort of thing.
Now I don't say (for I don't know) if your governor has as
much to leave behind him as mine— But halt a bit! You walk
as if we were going in for athletics, and doing a two mile."

"I'm sorry to see you so easily blown," said Northcote, not
displeased in his turn to say something unpleasant. "What is
it? or are you only out of training?"

"That's it," said Clarence, with a gasp. "I'm awfully out of
training, and that's the fact. We do, perhaps, live too well in
Portland Place; but look here—about what we were saying—"

"Do you live with the Mays?"

"Worse luck! It's what you call plain cooking; and bless
us all, dinner in the middle of the day, and the children at
table. But I've put a stop to that; and old May ain't a bad
old fellow—don't bother me with work more than I like, and
none of your high mightiness, like that fellow. I'll tell you
what, Northcote, you must come and see me. I haven't got a
sitting-room of my own, which is a shame, but I have the use
of their rooms as much as I like. The sisters go flying away
like a flock of pigeons. I'll tell you what, I'll have you asked
to dinner. Capital fun it will be. A High Church parson
cheek by jowl with a red-hot Dissenter, and compelled to be
civil. By Jove! won't it be a joke?"

"It is not a joke that either of us will enjoy."

"Never mind, *I'll* enjoy it, by Jove!" said Copperhead.
"He daren't say no. I'd give sixpence just to see you together,
and the Bashaw of two tails—the young fellow. They shall
have a party; leave it all to me."

CHAPTER XXVIII.

THE NEW PUPIL.

MR. MAY, since the bargain was fairly concluded with the
Copperheads, had thought a great deal about the three hundred a-year he was to get for his pupil. It almost doubled his
income in a moment, and that has a great effect upon the
imagination. It was true he would have another person to
maintain on this additional income, but still that additional
person would simply fill Reginald's place, and it did not at first

occur to him that what was good enough for himself, Mr. May, of St. Roque's, was not good enough for any *parvenu* on the face of the earth. Therefore the additional income represented a great deal of additional comfort, and that general expansion of expenditure, not going into any special extravagances, but representing a universal ease and enlargement which was congenial to him, and which was one of the great charms of money in his eyes. To be sure, when he reflected on the matter, he felt that the first half-year of Clarence's payment ought to be appropriated to that bill, which for the present had brought him so much relief; but this would be so entirely to lose the benefit of the money so far as he was himself concerned, that it was only in moments of reflection that this appeared urgent. The bill to which Tozer's signature had been appended did not oppress his conscience. After all, what was it? Not a very large sum, a sum which when put to it, and with time before him, he could so easily supply; and as for any other consideration, it was really, when you came to think of it, a quite justifiable expedient, not to be condemned except by squeamish persons, and which being never known, could do no harm in the world. He had not harmed anybody by what he had done. Tozer, who was quite able to pay it over and over again, would never know of it; and in what respect, he asked himself, was it worse to have done this than to have a bill really signed by a man of straw, whose "value received" meant nothing in the world but a simple fiction? Cotsdean was no more than a man of straw; if left to himself, he could not pay anything, nor had he anything really to do with the business for which his name stood sponsor; and Tozer's name was merely placed there in the same fictitious way, without any trouble to Tozer, or burden of responsibility. What was the difference, except that it saved trouble and anxiety to everybody except the principal in the affair—he who ought to bear the brunt? Mr. May recognised this without doubt. It was he who had reaped the advantage; and whether Cotsdean was the instrument who knew all about it, or Tozer, who did not know anything about it, it was he, Mr. May, whose natural duty it was to meet the claim and pay the money. He was an honest man; if he was occasionally a little slow in his payments, no one could throw any doubt upon his character. But, of course, should any unforeseen emergency arise, the pupil at once made that straight. Mr. May felt that he had only to go to the bank, which generally did not encourage his visits, and tell them of his pupil, to have the money at once. Nobody could reject such unmistakeable security. So that really there was no further occasion for so much as thinking of Tozer; that was provided for; with the freest conscience in the world he might put it out of his mind. But how he could feel this so strongly, and at the same time revel in the consciousness of a fuller purse, more to enjoy, and more to spend, is a mystery which it would be difficult to solve. He did so, and many others have done so besides him, eating their cake, yet believing that they had their cake with the fullest confidence. He was a sensible man, rather priding himself on his knowledge of business, with much experience in human nature, and a thoughtful sense (fully evidenced in his writings) of all the strange inconsistencies and self-deceits of mankind; but he dropped into this strain of self-delusion with the calmest satisfaction of mind, and was as sure of his own good sense and kindness as if he had never in all his life taken a step out of the rigidest of the narrow ways of uprightness.

Some part of this illusion, however, was sharply dispelled at a very early date. Clarence Copperhead, who was not likely to err by means of too much consideration for the feelings of others, grumbled frankly at the mid-day meal.

"I don't understand a two o'clock dinner," he said; "it's lunch, that's what I call it; and I won't be disagreeable about the kids, but I must have my dinner. Bless you! a man can't live without his dinner. What is he to do? It is the sort of thing you can look forward to, whatever happens. If it's a wet day, or anything of that sort, there's always dinner; and after it's over, if there's music or a rubber, why that's all very well; or if a man feels a bit sleepy, it doesn't matter. Why, dinner's your stand-by, wherever you are. I'd as soon do without my head, for my part."

Ursula hastened to tell her father this with dismay in her looks.

"I've always heard that late dinners were so expensive; you require twice as many dishes. At two, one has only what is necessary; but at seven, you require to have fish, and soup, and *entrées*, and all sorts of things, besides the joint. It was disgraceful of him to say it!" cried Ursula; "and I think he ought to be made to follow our plan, whatever it is, and not do everything he likes here."

"That is all very true," said Mr. May; "but he is right about the dinner; it is a great deal more agreeable."

"And expensive, papa."

"Well, perhaps it is a great deal to expect at your age; but if you read your cookery-book, as I have often said, when you were reading those novels, and learned how to toss up little dishes out of nothing, and make *entrées*, and so forth, at next to no expense—"

The tears came into Ursula's eyes at this unjust assault.

"Papa," she said, "you ought to know better at your age. One forgives the boys for saying such silly things. How can I toss up little dishes out of nothing? If you only knew the price of butter, not to talk of anything else. Made dishes are the most expensive things! A leg of mutton, for instance; there it is, and when one weighs it, one knows what it costs; but there is not one of those *entrées* but costs *shillings* for herbs and truffles and gravy and forcemeat, and a glass of white wine here, and a half pint of claret there. It is all very well to talk of dishes made out of nothing. The meat may not be very much—and men never think of the other things, I suppose."

"It is management that is wanted," said Mr. May, "to throw nothing away, to make use of everything, to employ all your scraps. If you once have a good sauce—which is as easy as daylight when you take the trouble—you can make all sorts of things out of a cold joint; but women never will take the trouble, and that is the secret of poor dinners. Not one in fifty will do it. If you wanted really to help us, and improve my position, you might, Ursula. I can't afford to fall out with Copperhead, he is very important to me just at this moment; and perhaps it is better that I should give in to him at once about the late dinner."

"You may say it is not my business," said Ursula, "but we have already another maid, and now two dinners—for it is just the same as two dinners. He will not be any advantage to you like that, and why should he be so much harder to please than we are? Reginald never grumbled, who was much better bred and better educated than Mr. Copperhead."

"And with so much money to keep up his dignity," said her father mockingly. "No, it is not your business, the cookery-book is your business, and how to make the best of everything; otherwise I don't want any advice from you."

"What did he say?" cried Janey, rushing in as soon as her father had left the room. Ursula, a very general consequence of such interviews, was sitting by the fire, very red and excited, with tears glistening in her eyes.

"Of course I knew what he would say; he says it is not my business, and there are to be late dinners, and everything that man chooses to ask for. Oh, it is so hard to put up with it!" cried Ursula, her eyes flashing through her tears. "I am to read up the cookery-book and learn to make *entrées* for them; but to say we can't afford it is not my business. I wonder whose business it is? It is I who have to go to the tradespeople and to bear it all if they grumble; and now this horrible man, who dares to tell me the coffee is not strong enough, as if I was a barmaid—"

"Barmaids don't have to do with coffee, have they?" said matter-of-fact Janey; "but the fact is *he is not a gentleman;* why should you mind? What does it matter what a person like that says or does? You said so yourself, he is not a bit a gentleman. I wonder what Cousin Anne and Cousin Sophy could mean."

"It is not their fault; they think of his mother, who is nice, who sent those things; but Mr. Copperhead knew about the things, which was not so nice of her, was it? But never mind, we must try to make the best of it. Get the cookery-book, Janey; perhaps if you were to read it out loud, and we were both to try to fix our mind upon it—for something must be done," said Ursula gravely. "Papa will never find it out till all the money is spent, but we shall be poorer than we were before we had the pupil. Who is that, Janey, at the door?"

It was Phœbe, who came in blooming from the cold, in a furred jacket, at which the girls looked with unfeigned admiration. "The skating will soon come on in earnest now," she said; "grandmamma is better, and I thought I might come and see you. I had a long talk with your brother the other day, did he tell you? and I made him know Mr. Northcote, one of our people. I know you will turn up your pretty nose, Ursula, at a Dissenter."

"I should think so," cried Janey; "we have nothing to do with such people, being gentlefolks, have we, Ursula? Oh, I forgot! I beg your pardon, I didn't mean to say—"

Phœbe smiled upon her serenely. "I am not angry," she said, "I understand all that; and in Carlingford I have no right, I suppose, to stand upon being a lady, though I always thought I was one. I am only a young woman here, and not so bad either for that, if you will promise, Janey, not to call me a young person—"

"Oh, Miss Beecham!"

"Mr. Copperhead is a Dissenter," said Ursula, somewhat sullenly, "we put up with him because he is rich. Oh, it is all very disagreeable! I don't want to know any new people whatever they are; I find the old ones bad enough. Reginald hates him too, a big lazy useless being that treats one as if one were a chambermaid!"

"Is it Clarence? It is not quite his fault. His mother is a lady, but his father is a brute," said Phœbe, "thinking of nothing but his horrible money. Clarence is not so bad. It is because he has no imagination, and does not understand other people's feelings; he does not mean it, poor fellow; he goes trampling about with his big feet upon everybody's toes, and never is a bit the wiser. Here he is—he is coming in with your father. I suppose there must be a great deal in race," she added with a soft little sigh, "Clarence looks a clown, and your father such a gentleman. I suppose I show just the same when I stand beside you."

Now Phœbe was well aware that this was not the case, and Ursula's indignant disclaimer made her rather laugh, because it was so unnecessary, than be pleased by its vehemence. There was an old convex mirror opposite which reflected the girls in miniature, making a pretty picture of them as they sat together, Ursula with her dark locks, and Phœbe in her golden hair, and the tall sharp school-girl, Janey, all elbows and angles, short petticoats and grey stockings. Janey was the only one in whom there could have been suspected any inferiority of race; but her awkwardness was that of youth, and her disordered hair and dress belonged also to her age, for she was at that troublesome period when frocks are constantly getting too short, and sleeves too scanty. Janey was shuffling slowly round the visitor, admiring her at every point; her garments were not made as dresses were made in Carlingford. Their fit and their texture were alike too perfect for anything that ever came out of High Street. The furred jacket had not been seen in Grange Lane before. Perhaps it was because the cold had become more severe, an ordinary and simple reason—or because Clarence Copperhead, who knew her, and in whose eyes it was important to bate no jot of her social pretensions, was here; and the furred jacket was beyond comparison with anything that had been seen for ages in Carlingford. The deep border of fur round the velvet, the warm waddings and paddings, the close fit up to the throat, were excellencies which warranted Janey's tour of inspection. Phœbe perceived it very well, but did not confuse the girl by taking any notice, and in her heart she was herself slightly pre-occupied, wondering (as Ursula had done) what the man had come here for, and what he would say when he saw her. Both of these young women had a secret belief that something romantic, something more than the mere prose of reading in the first tutor's house that happened to have been suggested to him, had brought young Copperhead to such an unlikely place as Carlingford. Ursula had by this time

learned to reject this hypothesis with much indignation at
herself for having entertained it, but Phœbe still felt slightly
fluttered by this possibility, and was eager for the entrance of
Clarence. She would know at once what had brought him, she
said to herself, the moment she caught his eye.

And though Mr. May had reconciled himself so completely
to the Tozer business, the appearance of Tozer's granddaughter
gave him a momentary shock. What did you do with my
grandfather's letter ? he thought her eyes said, and the meeting
confused and disturbed him. This, however, was only for a moment. He was a man to whom it was always possible to make
himself agreeable to women, and though he felt so easy in his
mind about Tozer, still it was evident that to conciliate Tozer's
relation, and that so influential a relation, was on the whole a
good thing to do. He was going up to her accordingly with
outstretched hands, and the most amiable inquiries about her
grandmother's health, when, to his surprise, he was frustrated
by Clarence who had come in before him—his large person
swelling out, as it always seemed to do when he presented
himself upon a new scene, with importance and grandeur.

"Miss Beecham!" he said, "really, who would have thought
it ? Now look here, I came to Carlingford thinking there was
not a soul I knew in the place ; and here have you turned up
all at once, and Northcote (you know Northcote ?). It is very
queer."

"It is odd, isn't it ?" said Phœbe quickly. "I was astonished
to see Mr. Northcote, and though I heard you were coming I
am not less surprised to see you." "He has not come for me,"
she said rapidly to herself, "nor for Ursula either; then who
is it ?" Phœbe demanded in the depths of her own bosom; that
he should have come for nobody at all, but simply for his own
purposes, to get a little information put into his head, seemed
incredible to both the girls. Ursula, for her part, had been
angry when she discovered his want of meaning, though why
she would have found it hard to say. But Phœbe, for her part,
was not angry. She took this like other things of the kind,
with great and most philosophical calm, but she could not outgrow it all at once. For whom was it ? His cousins, those
Miss Dorsets ? But they were much older, and not the kind
of women for whom such an act was likely. Her mind wandered forth lively and curious in search of the necessary clue.
She could not consent to the fact that no clue was necessary
where no mystery was.

"I am glad to see that you venture out in this wintry weather,"
said Mr. May; "you set us all a good example. I am always

telling my girls that cold weather is no sufficient reason for staying indoors. I wish Ursula would do as you do."

"Papa, how can you talk so?" said Janey, indignant, "when you know very well it is not the cold that keeps Ursula in, but because she has so much to do."

"Oh, yes, one knows the sort of things young ladies have to do," said Clarence, with a laugh; "read stories, and look up pretty dresses for their parties, eh, Miss Janey? and consult the fashion-books. Oh, of course you will deny it; but my mother makes me her confidant, and I know that's what you all do."

"To be sure," said Phœbe, "we are not so clever as you are, and can't do so many things. We know no Latin or Greek to keep our minds instructed; we acknowledge our infirmity; and we couldn't play football to save our lives. Football is what you do in this season, when you don't hunt, and before the ice is bearing? We are poor creatures; we can't parcel out our lives, according as it is time for football or cricket. You must not be so severe upon girls for being so inferior to you."

("Oh, don't be too hard upon him,") whispered Ursula, in a parenthesis, afraid that this irony should drive the pupil to desperation. ("Hard upon him! he will never find it out,") Phœbe whispered back in the same tone.

"Oh, hang it all, I don't mean to be severe upon girls," said Clarence, pulling his moustache with much complacency; "I am sorry for them, I can tell you. It ain't their fault; I know heaps of nice girls who feel it horribly. What can they do? they can't go in for cricket and football. There ought to be something invented for them. To be sure there is lawn-tennis, but that's only for summer. I should go mad, I think, if I had nothing to do."

"But you have more brain and more strength, you see, than we have; and besides, we are used to it," said Phœbe. "I am afraid, Ursula, grandmamma will want me, and I must go."

Here Mr. May said something to his daughter which filled Ursula with excitement, mingled of pleasure and displeasure.

"Papa says, will you come to dinner to-morrow at seven? It appears there is some one you know coming—a Mr. Northcote. I don't know who he is, but it will be very kind if you will come on my account," the girl concluded, whispering in her ear, "for how shall I ever get through a dinner-party? We never gave one in my life before."

"Of course I will come," said Phœbe. "Dinner-parties are not so common here that I should neglect the chance. I must thank Mr. May. But I hope you know who Mr. Northcote is," she added, laughing. "I gave an account of myself loyally, before I permitted you to ask me; but Mr. Northcote—Oh, no! he does not belong to——the lower classes; but he is a fiery red-hot——"

"What?" cried eager Janey, pressing to the front. "Radical? I am a radical too; and Reginald used to be once, and so was Ursula. Oh, I wish it was to-night!" said Janey, clasping her hands.

"Not a radical, but a Dissenter; and you who are a clergyman, Mr. May! I like you, oh, so much for it. But I wonder what the people will say."

"My dear Miss Beecham," said the suave Churchman, quite ready to seize the chance of making a point for himself, "in the Church, fortunately, what the people say has not to be studied, as your unfortunate pastors, I am informed, have to do. While Mr. Copperhead is under my roof, I make his friends welcome—for his sake first, probably afterwards for their own."

"Yes, I asked Northcote," said Clarence; "I never thought they would have any objection. He's not a common Dissenter, like the most of those fellows that have nothing but their salaries. He's well off; he don't require, bless you, to keep people in good temper, and toady to 'em, like most do. He's as independent as I am; I don't say that he's quite as well off; but money always finds its level. I shouldn't have thought of asking May to receive a common Dissenting fellow, like the rest."

Phœbe laughed. It did not occur to the accomplished scion of the house of Copperhead, nor to the two girls, who were not experienced enough to think of such things, what was the meaning expressed in Phœbe's laugh, which was not cheerful. Mr. May himself had the advantage of more discrimination.

"I hope you will find that, Dissenter or not, I know what is my duty to my friends," he said. "What my guests may possess, or the exact nature of their opinions on all points, are not subjects to be discussed by me."

"Oh, there is nothing to find fault with in *you*," said Phœbe, with less than her usual universal courtesy, "you are always kind, Mr. May:" and then she laughed again. "Some people are very clever in finding out the vulnerable places," she said.

"She is changed," said Clarence, when she was gone. "She is not the jolly girl she used to be. She was always a very jolly girl; ready to help a fellow out of a scrape, you know. But Northcote's a fearfully clever fellow. You should just hear him talk. He and May will go at it hammer and tongs, as sure as fate."

CHAPTER XXIX.

URSULA'S ENTRÉES.

IT would be difficult to describe the anxiety with which that first "late dinner" was regarded by Ursula. Janey, too, had thrown herself into it heart and soul, until she received the crushing intimation from her father, that her company was not expected at this stately meal; a discovery which altogether extinguished poor Janey, accustomed to be always in the front whatever occurred, and to whom suggestions of things that could not be done by a girl who was not "out," had never presented themselves. She retired to her own room dissolved in tears when this fearful mandate went forth, and for the rest of the morning was good for nothing, her eyes being converted into a sort of red pulp, her rough hair doubly dishevelled, her whole being run into tears. She was of no more use now to go errands between the kitchen and the drawing-room, or to read the cookery-book out loud, which was a process upon which Ursula depended very much, to fix in her mind the exact ingredients and painful method of preparation of the *entrées* at which she was toiling. Betsy, the former maid-of-all-work, now promoted under the title of cook, could be trusted to roast the saddle of mutton, which, on consideration that it was "a party," had been thought preferable to a leg, and she could boil the fish, after a sort, and make good honest family soup, and the rice-pudding or apple-tart, which was the nearest approach to luxury indulged in at the Parsonage; but as for *entrées*, Betsy did not know what they were. She had heard of made dishes indeed, and respectfully afar off had seen them when she was kitchen-maid at Lady Weston's—the golden age of her youthful inexperience. But this was so long ago, that her recollections were rather confusing than useful to Ursula, when she went downstairs to make her first heroic effort.

"La, Miss, that ain't how cook used to do 'em at Lady Weston's," Betsy said, looking on with unbelieving eyes. She was sure of this negative, but she was not sure of anything else, and utterly failed to give any active assistance, after driving the girl desperate with her criticisms. Altogether it was a confused and unpleasant day. When Reginald came in in the morning, his sister had no time to speak to him, so anxious was

she and preoccupied, and the drawing-room was being turned
upside down, to make it look more modern, more elegant, more
like the Dorsets' drawing-room, which was the only one
Ursula knew. The comfortable round table in the middle,
round which the family had grouped themselves for so long, had
been pushed aside into a corner, leaving one fresh patch of carpet, quite inappropriate, and unconnected with anything else;
and instead of the work and the school-books which so often
intruded there, all that was gaudy and uninteresting in the May
library had been produced to decorate the table; and even a
case of wax flowers, a production of thirty years since, which
had been respectfully transferred to a china closet by Ursula's
better taste, but which in the dearth of ornament she had
brought back again. Reginald carried off the wax flowers and
replaced the table with his own hands, while Ursula scorched
her cheeks over the *entrées* downstairs.

"All this for Northcote," he said, when she ran up for a
moment, done up in a big white apron, her face crimson with
the fire and anxiety combined : "for Miss Beecham has been
here before, and you made no fuss about her then."

"She came to tea," said Ursula. "And I got a cake, which
was all any one could do; but a dinner is a very different thing."
Indeed she had by this time come to share her father's opinion,
that dinner was the right and dignified thing in all cases, and
that they had been hitherto living in a very higgledy-piggledy
way. The dinner had gone to her head.

"Then it is for Northcote, as I say," said Reginald. "Do
you know who he is ? "

"A Dissenter," said Ursula, with a certain languor; "but
so, you know, is Mr. Copperhead, and he is the chief person
here now-a-days. Papa thinks there is nobody like him. And
so is Phœbe."

"Oh, have you come so far as that ? " said Reginald, with a
little tinge of colour in his face. He laughed, but the name
moved him. "It is a pretty fresh sort of country name, not
quite like such an accomplished person."

"Oh, that is just like you men, with your injustice ! Because
she is clever you take it amiss; you are all jealous of her. Look
at her pretty colour and her beautiful hair; if that is not fresh
I should like to know what is. She might be Hebe instead of
Phœbe," said Ursula, who had picked up scraps of classical
knowledge in spite of herself.

"You are a little goose," said Reginald, pinching her ear, but
he liked his sister for her generous partizanship. "Mind you
don't come to dinner with cheeks like that," he said. "I like my

sister to be herself, not a cook-maid, and I don't believe in *entrées*;" but he went away smiling, and with a certain warmth in his breast. He had gone up and down Grange Lane many times at the hour of sunset, hoping to meet Phœbe again, but that sensible young woman had no mind to be talked of, and never appeared except when she was certain the road was clear. This had tantalized Reginald more than he chose to avow, even to himself. Pride prevented him from knocking at the closed door. The old Tozers were fearful people to encounter, people whom to visit would be to damn himself in Carlingford; but then the Miss Griffiths were very insipid by the side of Phœbe, and the variety of her talk, though he had seen so little of her, seemed to have created a new want in his life. He thought of a hundred things which he should like to discuss with her—things which did not interest Ursula, and which the people about him did not understand much. Society at that time, as may be presumed, was in a poor way in Carlingford. The Wentworths and Wodehouses were gone, and many other nice people; the houses in Grange Lane were getting deserted, or falling into inferior hands, as was apparent by the fact that the Tozers—old Tozer, the butterman—had got one of them. The other people were mostly relics of a bygone state of things: retired old couples, old ladies, spinsters, and widows—excellent people, but not lively to talk to—and the Griffiths, above mentioned, put up with in consideration of tolerable good looks and "fun," became tiresome when anything better was to be had. The mere apparition of Phœbe upon the horizon had been enough to show Reginald that there were other kinds of human beings in the world. It had not occurred to him that he was in love with her, and the idea of the social suicide implied in marrying old Tozer's granddaughter, had not so much as once entered his imagination. Had he thought of it, he would have pulled that imagination up tight, like an unruly horse, the thing being too impossible to bear thinking of. But this had never entered his mind. He wanted to see Phœbe to talk to her, to be near her, as something very new, captivating and full of interest—that was all. No one else within his sphere could talk so well. The Rector was very great indeed on the reredos question, and the necessity of reviving the disused "Church" customs; but Reginald could not go so far as he did as to the importance of the reredos, and was quite in doubt whether it was not as well for most people to "direct" themselves by their own consciences as to be directed by the spiritual head of the parish, who was not over wise in his own concerns. His father, Reginald knew, could be very agreeable among strangers, but he seldom chose to be so in his own house. All this made the advent of Phœbe appear to him like a sudden revelation out of a different world. He was an Oxford man, with the best of education, but he was a simpleton all the same. He thought he saw in her an evidence of what life was like in those intellectual professional circles which a man may hope to get into only in London. It was not the world of fashion he was aware, but he thought in his simplicity that it was the still higher world of culture and knowledge, in which genius, and wit, and intellect stood instead of rank or riches. How Tozer's granddaughter had got admission there, he did not ask himself, but this was what he thought, and to talk to her was a new sensation. He was quite unconscious of anything more.

Nobody knew when Ursula took her place at the head of the table in her pretty white dress, which she had worn at the Dorsets', how much toil and anxiety the preparations had given her. At the last moment, when her mind was so far clear of the *entrées*, &c.—as clear as the mind of an inexperienced dinner-giver can be, until the blessed moment when they are eaten and done with—she had to take Sarah in hand, who was not very clear about the waiting, and to instruct her according to her own very imperfect knowledge how to fulfil her duties.

"Think it is not a dinner-party at all, but only just our ordinary luncheon, and don't get fluttered; and when I look at you like *this* come quite close, and I will whisper what you are to do. And oh, Sarah, like a good creature, don't break anything!" said Ursula almost with tears.

These were all the directions she could give, and they, it must be allowed, were somewhat vague. The excitement was becoming to her. She sat down with a dreadful flutter in her heart, but with her eyes shining and sparkling. Clarence Copperhead, who extended an arm very carelessly to take her downstairs, absolutely certain of being a more important person than his guest Northcote, was roused for the first time to the consciousness that she was very pretty, which he had not found out before. "But no style," he said to himself. Phœbe was the one who had style. She sat between Mr. May and the stranger, but devoted herself to her host chiefly, displaying a gentle contempt of the younger men in his presence. No anxiety was in her mind about the dinner. She did not follow the fate of those *entrées* round the table with terrible palpitations, as poor Ursula did; and, alas, the *entrées* were not good, and Ursula had the mortification to see the dishes she had taken so much trouble with, rejected by one and another.

Reginald ate some, for which she blessed him, and so did Phœbe, but Mr. May sent his plate away with polite execrations.

"Tell your cook she shall go if she sends up such uneatable stuff again, Ursula," her father cried from the other end of the table.

Two big tears dashed up hot and scalding into Ursula's eyes. Oh, how she wished she could be dismissed like Betsy! She turned those two little oceans of trouble piteously, without knowing it, upon Northcote, who had said something to her, without being able to reply to him. And Northcote, who was but a young man, though he was a fiery political Dissenter, and who had come to the Parsonage with a curious mixture of pleasure and reluctance, immediately threw down any arms that nature might have provided him with, and fell in love with her there and then on the spot! to his own absolute consternation. This was how it happened. The moment was not romantic, the situation was not sublime. A little motherless housekeeper crying because her father scolded her in public for a piece of bad cookery. There is nothing in this to make an idyll out of; but such as it was, it proved enough for Horace Northcote; he yielded himself on the spot. Not a word was said, for Ursula felt that if she tried to talk she must cry, and anything further from her troubled thoughts than love it would be impossible to imagine; but then and there, so far as the young man was concerned, the story began. He talked very little for the rest of the meal, and Ursula did not exert herself, though she recovered slightly when the mutton turned out to be very good, and was commended; but what was the mutton in comparison with her *entrées*, which she had made with her own hands, and which were a failure? She was reduced to silence, and she thought that the stranger at her left hand was nice, because he did not bother her, and was content with a very little talk.

"Oh, Phœbe, did you hear papa about those *entrées*?" she cried, when they reached the drawing-room; and sitting down on the stool by the fire which Janey usually appropriated, she cried, poor child, with undisguised passion. "I had made them myself; I had been busy about them all day; I read the cookery-book till my head ached, and took such pains! and you heard what he said."

"Yes, dear, I heard him; but he did not think what he was saying, it never occurred to him that it was you. Don't shake your little head, I am sure of it; you know, Ursula, your papa is very agreeable and very clever."

"Yes, I know he is clever; and he can be nice when he likes—"

"Did you like it?" cried Janey, bursting in, red-eyed and dishevelled in her morning frock. "Oh, no, I am not dressed, I don't mean to, to let him get the better of me, and think I care. Only just for a moment to see you two. Oh, isn't Phœbe grand in that dress? She is like a picture; you are nothing beside her, Ursula. Tell me, is it nice to have dinner instead of tea? Did it go off very well, did you enjoy yourselves? Or were you all unhappy, sitting round the table, eating beef and mutton," cried Janey with all the scorn of ignorance, "at that ridiculous hour!"

"I was as miserable as I could be," cried Ursula, "I was not happy at all. Enjoy myself! with the *entrées* on my mind, and after what papa said. Oh, run away, Janey, and dress, or else go to bed. Papa will be so angry if he comes up and finds you here."

"I should like to make him frantic," cried Janey with vindictive force, "I should just like to drive him out of his senses! Never mind, yes, I am angry; haven't I a right to be angry? I am as tall as Ursula—I hope I know how to behave myself—and when there were people coming, and a real dinner—"

"Oh, I hear them," cried Ursula in alarm, and Janey flew off, her hair streaming behind her. Phœbe put her arm round Ursula, and raised her from the stool. She was not perhaps a perfect young woman, but had her own ends to serve like other people; yet she had a friendly soul. She gave her friend a kiss to preface her admonition, as girls have a way of doing.

"I would not let Janey talk so," she said, "I think you should not talk so yourself, Ursula, if you will forgive me, of your papa; he is very nice, and so clever. I should try all I could to please him, and I should not let any one be disrespectful to him if it was I."

"Oh, Phœbe, if you only knew—"

"Yes, I know, gentlemen don't understand often; but we must do our duty. He is nice, and clever, and handsome, and you ought to be proud of him. Dry your eyes, here they are really, coming upstairs. You must be good-humoured and talk. He is ever so much nicer than the young men," said Phœbe, almost loud enough to be heard, as Clarence Copperhead, sauntering in advance of the others with his large shirt-front fully displayed, came into the room. He came in half whistling in serene indifference. Phœbe had "style," it was true; but she was only a Dissenting parson's daughter, and what were two such girls to Clarence Copperhead? He came in whistling an opera air, which he let drop only after he was well inside the door.

"Miss Beecham, let us have some music. I know you can play," he said.

"If Miss May likes," said Phœbe, covering his rudeness; and then she laughed, and added, "if you will accompany me."

"Does Mr. Copperhead play too?"

"Oh beautifully. Has he not let you see his music? Won't you bring it here and let us look over it? I dare say there are some things we can play together."

"You can play everything," said the young man. "And I'll bring my violin, if you like."

He was delighted; he quickened his steps almost into a run as he went away.

"You should not laugh at Mr. Copperhead," Ursula retorted on her friend. "You should be good-humoured, too. You are better than I am, but you are not quite good, after all."

"Violin!" said Mr. May. "Heaven and earth! is there going to be any fiddling? Miss Beecham, I did not expect you to bring such a horror upon me. I thought I had nothing but good to expect from you."

"Wait till you hear him, sir," said Phœbe.

Mr. May retired to the far corner of the room. He called young Northcote to him, who was standing beside Ursula, eager to talk, but not knowing how to begin. It was bad enough to be thus withdrawn from his chance of making himself agreeable; but the reader may imagine what was the Dissenter's feelings when Mr. May, with a smile, turned upon him. Having given him a (tolerably) good dinner, and lulled him into a belief that his sins against the family were unknown, he looked at him, smiling, and began.

"Mr. Northcote, the first time I saw you, you were discoursing at an Anti-Establishment Meeting in the Town Hall."

Northcote started. He blushed fiery red. "It is quite true. I wished to have told you; not to come here on false pretences; but Copperhead—and your son has been very kind—"

"Then I suppose your views are modified. Clergymen no longer appear to you the demons in human shape you thought them then; and my son, in particular, has lost his horns and hoofs?"

"Mr. May, you are very severe; but I own there is reason—"

"It was you who were severe. I was not quite sure of you till Copperhead brought you in. Nay," said the clergyman, rubbing his hands; "do you think that I object to the utterance of a real opinion? Certainly not. As for Reginald, it was the thing that decided him; I leave you to find out how; so that we are positively in your debt. But I hope you don't fiddle too. If you like to come with me to my study—"

Northcote gave a longing look round the room, which had become all at once so interesting to him. Mr. May was too clear-sighted not to see it. He thought, quite impartially, that perhaps it was an excusable weakness, even though it was his own society that was the counter attraction. They were two nice-looking girls. This was how he put it, being no longer young, and father to one of them; naturally, the two young men would have described the attraction of Phœbe and Ursula more warmly. Clarence Copperhead, who had come in with an armful of music and his fiddle, was not thinking of the girls, nor of anything but the sweet sounds he was about to make— and himself. When he began to tune his violin, Mr. May got up in dismay.

"This is more than mortal can stand," he said, making as though he would have gone away. Then he changed his mind, for, after all, he was the chaperon of his motherless girl. "Get me the paper, Ursula," he said. It would be hard to tell with what feelings Northcote contemplated him. He was the father of Ursula, yet he dared to order her about, to bring the tears to her eyes. Northcote darted the same way as she was going, and caught at the paper on a side-table, and brought it hastily. But alas, that was last week's paper! he did not save her the trouble, but he brought upon himself a gleam of mischief from her father's eyes. "Mr. Northcote thinks me a tyrant to send you for the paper," he said, as he took it out of her hands. "Thank him for his consideration. But he was not always so careful of your peace of mind," he added, with a laugh.

Ursula looked at him with a wondering question in her eyes; but those tears were no longer there which had gone to Northcote's heart.

"I don't know what papa means," she said, softly; and then, "I want to beg your pardon, please. I was very silly. Will you try to forget it, and not tell any one, Mr. Northcote? The truth was, I thought I had done them nicely, and I was vexed. It was very childish," she said, shaking her head with something of the same moisture floating back over the lustre in her pretty eyes.

" I will never tell any one, you may be sure," said the young man ; but Ursula did not notice that he declined to give the other pledge, for Reginald came up just then with wrath in his eyes.

"Is that idiot going to fiddle all night ? " he cried (poor Clarence had scarcely begun) ; " as if anybody wanted to hear him and his tweedle-dees. Miss Beecham plays like St. Cecilia, Ursula ; and I want to speak to her about something. Can't you get that brute beguiled away ? "

Clarence was the one who was *de trop* in the little party ; but he fiddled beatifically, with his eyes fixed on the ceiling, without the slightest suspicion of the fact, while Phœbe accompanied him, with little smiles at her friends, and shrugs of her shoulders. Reginald felt very strongly, though for the first time, that she was over doing the Scriptural maxim of being all things to all men.

CHAPTER XXX.

SOCIETY AT THE PARSONAGE.

AFTER this dinner-party, such as it was, the Parsonage became gradually the centre of a little society, such as sometimes forms in the most accidental way in a house where there are young men and young women, and of which no one can say what momentous results may arise. They came together fortuitously, blown to one centre by the merest winds of circumstance, out of circles totally different and unlike. Why it was that Mr. May, so good a Churchman, permitted two people so entirely out of his sphere to become his habitual guests and the companions of his children was very perplexing to the outside world, who half in mere surprise, and a little in despite, wondered and commented till they were tired, or till they had become so familiar with the strange spectacle that it ceased to strike them. A rich pupil might be forgiven for being a Dissenter, indeed in Carlingford as elsewhere money made up for most deficiencies ; but even natural complacency towards the rich pupil scarcely accounted for the reception of the others. The neighbours could never be quite sure whether the family at the Parsonage knew or did not know that their new friend

Northcote was not only acting as Minister of Salem Chapel, but was the assailant of Reginald May at the Anti-Establishment Meeting, and various persons in Grange Lane held themselves for a long time on the tip-toe of preparation, ready to breathe to Mr. May the painful intelligence, in case he was unaware of it. But he never gave them the opportunity. Honestly, he had forgotten the speaker's name at first, and only recognized him when he was introduced by young Copperhead; and then the situation was piquant and amused him, especially the evident confusion and consternation of the culprit when found out.

"I don't know what he thinks he has done to you," said Clarence, "I could scarcely make him come in. He says he is sure you can't wish to see him."

This was two days after the dinner, when Horace Northcote came to leave a respectful card, hoping that he might see Ursula at a door or window. Clarence had seized upon him and dragged him in, in spite of himself.

"On the contrary, I am very glad to see him," said Mr. May, with a smile. He looked at the young Dissenter with a jeer in his eyes. He liked to punish him, having suddenly perceived that this jeer was much more potent than any serious penalty. "If he will promise not to slay me, I shan't quarrel with him." Mr. May was in such good spirits at this moment that he could afford to joke; his own magnanimity, and the other's confused looks of guilt, overcame his gravity. "Come back again," he said, holding out his hand; and though Horace retired for the moment utterly confounded, yet the attractions of the cheerful house overcame, after a while, his sense of humiliation and inappropriateness. If the injured family had condoned his offence, why should he mind? and the pleasant girlish friendliness, without any *arrière pensée*, of Ursula, was enough to have set any man at his ease; the facts of the case being that Mrs. Hurst was away upon a long visit, and that, having no other gossip within the range of her acquaintance, Ursula did not know. Reginald, who did, had the same sense of magnanimity as his father had, and began to like the society of the congenial yet different spirit which it was so strange to him to find under a guise so unlike his own. And Northcote, on his side, finding no house to which he could betake himself among those whom Phœbe called "our own people," found a refuge, which gradually became dearer and dearer to him, at the Parsonage, and in his profound sense of the generosity of the people who had thus received him, felt his own partizanship wax feebler and feebler every day. He seemed to see the ground cut from under his feet, as he watched the young chaplain at his work. Mr. May, to be sure, was no example of pastoral diligence, but he was a pleasant companion, and had put himself from the first in that position of moral superiority which naturally belongs to an injured person who can forgive heartily and without prejudice. And Ursula! He did not venture to call her Ursula, even in the secret depths of his heart. There a pronoun was enough, as, indeed, incipient Love generally finds it. She spoke to him, smiled at him in the street; and immediately life became a *Vita Nuova* to him. The young Dissenter was as Dante, and simple Ursula, with her housekeeping books in her hand, became another Beatrice. It is not every one who has the capacity for this perfect and absorbing sentiment; but Horace Northcote had, and for a long time Ursula was as unconscious of it as heart could desire.

Phœbe's admission to the house had been more simple still. A girlish fancy on Ursula's part, a fit of good-nature on her father's, and then that secret thread of connection with Tozer which no one knew of, and the coming of Clarence Copperhead, to please whom Mr. May permitted himself to be persuaded to do much; and in addition to all this, her good looks, her pretty manners, her cleverness and the deference she had always shown in the proper quarter. Mr. May did not enter into the lists with his son, or think of offering himself as a suitor to Phœbe; but he liked to talk to her, and to watch what he called " her little ways," and to hear her play when Clarence and his violin were otherwise disposed of. He was an experienced man, priding himself on a knowledge of human nature, and Phœbe's "little ways" amused him greatly. What did she mean ?—to "catch" Clarence Copperhead, who would be a great match, or to fascinate Northcote? Oddly enough Mr. May never thought of Reginald, though that young man showed an eagerness to talk to Phœbe which was more than equal with his own, and had always subjects laid up ready to discuss with her, when he could find the opportunity. Sometimes he would go up to her in the midst of the little party and broach one of these topics straight on end, without preface or introduction, as which was her favourite play of Shakespeare, and what did she think of the character of King Lear? It was not very wise, not any wiser than his neighbour was, who made pretty little Ursula into the ideal lady, the most gentle and stately figure in poetry; and yet no doubt there was something in both follies that was a great deal better than wisdom. The society formed by these two young pairs, with Clarence Copperhead as a heavy floating balance, and Mr. May and

Janey—one philosophical, wise and mistaken; the other sharp-
sighted and seeing everything—as spectators, was very pleasant
to the close little coterie themselves, and nobody else got within
the charmed circle.   They grew more and more intimate daily,
and had a whole vocabulary of domestic jokes and allusions which
no one else could understand.   It must be allowed, however,
that the outside world was not pleased with this arrangement
on either side of the question.   The Church people were
shocked with the Mays for harbouring Dissenters under any
circumstances whatever, and there had not been a Minister at
Salem Chapel for a long time so unpopular as Horace Northcote, who was always "engaged" when any of the connection
asked him to tea, and preached sermons which went over their
heads, and did not remember them when he met them in the
street.   Tozer was about the only one of the congregation who
stood up for the young man.   The others thanked Heaven that
"he was but tempory," and on the whole they were right, for
certainly he was out of place in his present post.

As for Clarence Copperhead, he led an agreeable life enough
among all these undercurrents of feeling, which he did not
recognise with any distinctness.   He was comfortable enough,
pleased with his own importance, and too obtuse to perceive
that he bored his companions; and then he considered himself
to be slightly "sweet upon" both the girls.   Ursula was his
favourite in the morning, when he embarrassed her much by
persistently seeking her company whenever liberated by her
father; but Phœbe was the queen of the evening, when he
would get his fiddle with an unfailing complacency which drove
Reginald frantic.   Whether it was mere good-nature or any
warmer impulse, Phœbe was strangely tolerant of these fiddlings,
and would go on playing for hours with serene composure,
never tired and never impatient.   Yet poor Clarence was not
an accompanyist to be coveted.   He was weak in the ear and
defective in science, but full of a cheerful confidence which was
as good as genius.

"Never mind, Miss Phœbe," he would say cheerfully, when
he had broken down for the twentieth time, "play on and I'll
catch you up."   He had thus a series of trysting places in
every page or two, which might have been very laughable to an
indifferent spectator, but which aggravated the Mays, father
and son, to an intolerable extent.   They were the two who
suffered.   As for Horace Northcote, who was not a great talker,
it was a not disagreeable shield for his silent contemplation of
Ursula, and the little things which from time to time he
ventured to say to her.   For conversation he had not the

thirst which animated Reginald, and Ursula's talk, though lively and natural, was not like Phœbe's; but while the music went on he could sit by her in a state of silent beatitude, now and then saying something to which Ursula replied if she was disposed, or if she was not disposed put aside by a little shake of her head, and smiling glance at the piano. Sometimes it was simple wilfulness that made her silent; but Northcote set it down to an angelical sweetness which would not wound even the worst of performances by inattention. They were happy enough sitting there under the shelter of the piano, the young man absorbed in the dreams of a young love, the girl just beginning to realize the adoration which she was receiving, with a timid perception of it—half-frightened, half-grateful. She was in spite of herself amused by the idea only half understood, and which she could scarcely believe, that this big grown man, so much more important than herself in everybody's eyes, should show so much respect to a little girl whom her father scolded, whom Reginald sent trotting about on all sorts of errands, and whom Cousin Anne and Cousin Sophy considered a child. It was very strange, a thing to call forth inextinguishable laughter, and yet with a strange touch of sweetness in it, which almost made her cry in wondering gratitude. What she thought of him, Ursula did not ask herself; that he should think *like this* of her was the bewildering, extraordinary, ridiculous fact that at present filled her girlish head.

But if they were sweet to Northcote, these evenings were the crown of Clarence Copperhead's content and conscious success; he was supremely happy, caressing his fiddle between his cheek and his shoulder, and raising his pale eyes to the ceiling in an ecstasy. The music, and the audience, and the accompanyist all together were delightful to him. He could have gone on he felt not only till midnight, but till morning, and so on to midnight again, with short intervals for refreshment. Every ten minutes or so there occurred a break in the continuity of the strain, and a little dialogue between the performers.

"Ah, yes, I have missed a line; never mind; go on, Miss Phœbe, I will make up to you," he said.

"It is those accidentals that have been your ruin," said Phœbe laughing; "it is a very hard passage, let us turn back and begin again," and then the audience would laugh, not very sweetly, and (some of them) make acrid observations; but the pianist was good-nature itself, and went back and counted and kept time with her head, and with her hand when she could take it from the piano, until she had triumphantly tided him

over the bad passage, or they had come to the point of ship-
wreck again. During these labours, Phœbe, who was really a
good musician, ought to have suffered horribly; but either she
did not, or her good-nature was stronger than her good taste,
for she went on serenely, sometimes for hours together, while
her old and her young admirers sat secretly cursing (in such
ways as are becoming to a clergyman) each in his corner.
Perhaps she had a slight degree of pleasure in the evident
power she had over father and son; but it was difficult fully to
understand her views at this somewhat bewildering period of
her life, in which she was left entirely to her own resources.
She was herself groping a little through paths of uncertain
footing, enjoying herself a great deal, but not seeing clearly
where it led to, and having no definite purpose, or chart of
those unknown countries in her mind.

"How you can go on," said Reginald, on one of these
occasions, having at length managed to seize upon and get her
into a corner, "for hours, having your ears sacrificed and your
patience tried by these fearful discords, and smile through it, is
a mystery which I cannot fathom! If it was only consideration for your audience, that might be enough to move any one
—but yourself—"

"I don't seem to feel it so very much myself."

"And yet you are a musician!"

"Don't be too hard upon me, Mr May. I only play—a
little. I am not like my cousins in the High Street, who are
supposed to be very clever at music; and then poor Mr.
Copperhead is a very old friend."

"Poor Mr. Copperhead! poor us, you mean, who have to
listen—and you, who choose to play."

"You are very vindictive," she said, with a piteous look.
"Why should you be so vindictive? I do what I can to
please my friends, and—there is no doubt about what poor
Clarence likes best; if you were to show me as plainly what
you would like—*quite* plainly, as he does——"

"Don't you know?" said Reginald, with glowing eyes.
"Ah, well! if I may show you plainly—quite plainly, with the
same results, you may be sure not to be left long in doubt.
Talk to me! it is easier, and not so fatiguing. Here," said the
young man, placing a chair for her; "he has had your patient
services for two hours. Do only half as much for me."

"Ah! but talking is a different thing, and more—difficult—
and more—personal. Well!" said Phœbe, with a laugh and
a blush, taking the chair, "I will try, but you must begin;
and I cannot promise, you know, for a whole hour."

"After you have given that fellow two! and such a fellow! If it was Northcote, I might be equally jea—displeased, but I could understand it, for he is not a fool."

"I think," said Phœbe, looking towards the other end of the room, where Northcote was occupied as usual close to Ursula's work-basket, "that Mr. Northcote manages to amuse himself very well without any help of mine."

"Ah!" cried Reginald, startled; for of course it is needless to say that the idea of any special devotion to his little sister had never entered his mind. He felt disposed to laugh at first when the idea was suggested to him, but he gave a second look, and fellow-feeling threw a certain enlightenment upon the subject. "That would never do," he said gravely; "I wonder I never thought of it before."

"Why would it not do? She is very nice, and he is clever and a rising man; and he is very well off; and you said just now he was not a fool."

"Nevertheless it would never do," said Reginald, opposing her pointedly, as he had never opposed her before; and he remained silent for a whole minute, looking across the room, during which long interval Phœbe sat demurely on the chair where he had placed her, looking at him with a smile on her face.

"Well?" she said at length, softly, "it was talk you said you wanted, Mr. May; but you are not so ready to tune up your violin as Mr. Copperhead, though I wait with my fingers on the piano, so to speak."

"I beg your pardon!" he cried, and then their eyes met, and both laughed, though, as far as Reginald was concerned, in an embarrassed way.

"You perceive," said Phœbe, rising, "that it is not nearly so easy to please you, and that you don't know half so exactly what you want, as Clarence Copperhead does, though you abuse him, poor fellow. I have got something to say to Ursula! though, perhaps, she does not want me any more than you do."

"Don't give me up for one moment's distraction; and it was your fault, not mine, for suggesting such a startling idea."

Phœbe shook her head, and waved her hand as a parting salutation, and then went across the room to where Ursula was sitting, where Horace Northcote at least found her very much in his way. She began at once to talk low and earnestly on some subject so interesting that it absorbed both the girls in a way which was very surprising and unpleasant to the young men, neither of whom had been able to interest the one whose attention he was specially anxious to secure half so effectually.

Northcote, from the other side of the table, and Reginald from
the other end of the room, gazed and gloomed with discomfited
curiosity, wondering what it could be; while Clarence strutted
uneasily about the piano, taking up his fiddle now and then,
striking a note, and screwing up his strings into concord, with
many impatient glances. But still the girls talked. Was it
about their dresses or some nonsense, or was it a more serious
subject, which could thus be discussed without masculine help?
but this matter they never fathomed, nor have they found out
till this hour.

CHAPTER XXXI.

SOCIETY.

NOTWITHSTANDING such little social crosses, however, the
society at the Parsonage, as thus constituted, was very agreeable. Mr. May, though he had his faults, was careful of his
daughter. He sat in the drawing-room every evening till she
retired, on the nights their visitors came, and even when it
was Clarence only who remained, an inmate of the house, and
free to go and come as he pleased. Ursula, he felt, must not
be left alone, and though it is uncertain whether she fully appreciated the care he took of her, this point in his character is
worth noting. When the young party went out together, to
skate, for instance, as they did, for several merry days, Reginald
and Janey were, he considered, sufficient guardians for their
sister. Phœbe had no chaperon—" Unless you will take that
serious office upon you, Ursula," she said, shrugging her
shoulders prettily; but she only went once or twice, so well
was she able, even when the temptation was strongest, to
exercise self-denial, and show her perfect power of self-guidance.
As for old Tozer and his wife, the idea of a chaperon never
entered their homely head. Such articles are unnecessary in
the lower levels of society. They were anxious that their child
should enjoy herself, and could not understand the reason of
her staying at home on a bright frosty day, when the Mays
came to the door in a body to fetch her.

" No, if they'd have gone down on their knees, nor if I had
gone down on mine, would that girl have left me," cried the old
lady, with tears in her eyes. " She do behave beautiful to her old

granny. If so be as I haven't a good night, no power on earth would make that child go pleasuring. It's 'most too much at her age."

But Phœbe confided to Ursula that it was not altogether anxiety about her grandmother.

"I have nobody of my own to go with. If I took grandpapa with me, I don't think it would mend matters. Once or twice it was possible, but not every day. Go and enjoy yourself, dear," she said, kissing her friend.

Ursula was disposed to cry rather than to enjoy herself, and appealed to Reginald, who was deeply touched by Phœbe's fine feeling. He took his sister to the ice, but that day he went so far as to go back himself to No. 6, actually into the house, to make a humble protest, yet to insinuate his admiration. He was much impressed by, and approved highly of this reticence, having a very high standard of minor morals for ladies, in his mind, like most young men.

"She is not one of the girls who rush about everywhere, and whom one is sick of seeing," he said.

"I think it is very silly," cried Janey. "Who cares for a chaperon! and why shouldn't Phœbe have her fun, like the rest, instead of shutting herself up in a stuffy room with that dreadful old Mrs. Tozer?"

Her brother reproved her so sharply for this speech that Janey withdrew in tears, still asking "Why?" as she rushed to her room. Clarence Copperhead, for his part, stroked his moustache and said it was a bore.

"For she is the best skater of all the ladies here," he said. "I beg your pardon, Miss Ursula. She's got so much go in her, and keeps it up like fun. She's the best I know for keeping a fellow from getting tired; but as it's Thursday, I suppose she'll be there in the evening."

Clarence never called them anything but Miss Ursula and Miss Phœbe, dropping the prefix in his thoughts. He felt that he was "a little sweet upon" them both; and, indeed, it had gleamed dully across his mind that a man who could marry them both need never be bored, but was likely always to find something "to do." Choice, however, being necessary, he did not see his way so clearly as to which he would choose. "The mountain sheep are sweeter, but the valley sheep are fatter," he said to himself, if not in these immortal words, yet with full appreciation of the sentiment. Ursula began to understand dinners with a judicious intelligence, which he felt was partly created by his own instructions and remarks; but in the evening it was Phœbe who reigned supreme. She was

so sensible that most likely she could invent a *menu* all out of
her own head, he thought, feeling that the girl who got him
through the "Wedding March" with but six mistakes, was
capable of any intellectual feat. He had not the slightest
doubt that it was in his power to marry either of the girls as
soon as he chose to intimate his choice; and in the mean time
he found it very agreeable to maintain a kind of mental possibility of future proprietorship of them both.

And thus the pleasant life ran on in the most agreeable
absorption and abstraction from the world outside. "Don't
ask any one else; why should we have any one else?" they
all said, except Janey, who had condescended to appear in the
evening in her best frock, though she was not admitted at dinner, and who thought a few additional guests, and a round
game now and then, would be delightful variations upon the
ordinary programme; but the others did not agree with her.
They became more and more intimate, mingling the brother
and sister relationship with a something unnamed, unexpressed,
which gave a subtle flavour to their talks and flirtations. In
that incipient stage of love-making this process is very pleasant
even to the spectators, full of little excitements and surprises,
and sharp stings of momentary quarrel, and great revolutions,
done with a single look, which are infinitely amusing to the
lookers-on. The house became a real domestic centre, thought
of by each and all with tender sentiment, such as made its
owners somewhat proud of it, they could scarcely tell why.
Even Mr. May felt a certain complacence in the fact that the
young men were so fond of the Parsonage, and when he heard
complaints of the coldness and dullness of domestic intercourse,
smiled, and said that he did not feel it so, with that pleasant
sense of something superior in himself to cause this difference,
which is sweet to the greatest Stoic; for he was not as yet enlightened as to the entire indifference of the little circle to any
charm in him, and would have been utterly confounded had
any one told him that to the grave and reflective Northcote,
whom he had treated with such magnanimous charity, binding
him (evidently) by bonds of gratitude to himself for ever, it
was little Ursula, and not her father, who was the magnet of
attraction. Mr. May was a clever man, and yet it had not
occurred to him that any comparison between his own society
and that of Ursula was possible. Ursula! a child! He would
have laughed aloud at the thought.

But all this pleasant society, though father and daughter
both agreed that it cost nothing, for what is a cake and a cup
of tea? and the late dinners and the extra maid, and the ad-

ditional fires, and general enlargement of expenditure made immense inroads, it must be allowed, into the additional income brought by Clarence Copperhead. The first quarter's payment was spent, and more than spent, before it came. The money that was to be laid up for that bill of Tozer's—perhaps—had now no saving peradventure left in it; for the second half would not be due till two months after the Tozer bill, and would but be half, even if procurable at once. Mr. May felt a slight shock while this gleamed across his mind, but only for a moment. There was still a month, and a month is a long time, and in the mean time James was almost certain to send something, and his Easter offerings might, probably would, this year be something worth having. Why they should be better than usual this year Mr. May did not explain to himself; his head was a little turned it must be supposed by the momentary chance of having more money in his hands than he used to have. Already he had got into the habit of ordering what he wanted somewhat recklessly, without asking himself how the things he ordered were to be paid for, and, as so often happened, followed up that first tampering with the rules of right and wrong by a general recklessness of the most dangerous kind. He was not so much alone as he had been; his house, in which he was infinitely more amiable than of old, had become more pleasant to him; he liked his life better. His son was independent with an income of his own, and therefore he felt much more respect for him, and treated him as a companion. His daughter had developed, if not in the way of *entrées*, a talent for dinners which raised her very much in his eyes; and naturally the regard shown to her by the visitors reacted upon Mr. May, though it had not crossed his mind as yet that any one could be in love with Ursula. All this made him happier in spite of himself. When you begin to esteem and be proud of your children your life is naturally happier than when you scoff and jeer at them, and treat them as creatures of inferior mould to yourself. Mr. May found out all at once that Reginald was a fine young fellow, that Ursula was pretty and pleasant, and that droll Janey, with her elf-locks and angles, was amusing at least, if no more. As for the little ones, they were considerably thrust into a corner when the elder youth forced itself into the front. They learned their lessons in corners, and had their tea by themselves, and were much humbled and subdued from the moment in which their school-books and toys had meandered over the whole house, and their looks and likings had been just as important as anything else. When there is no mother to protect them, the elder sister's first lover marks a terribly critical period for the children of the house. They were banished from the drawing-room, except on special occasions, when they came *en grande tenue*, in their best things, and were jeered at by Mr. Copper-head. He called them "the kids," both Amy and Robin were aware, and they resented it unspeakably. Thus the inward happiness of the Mays confined itself to the upper regions of the family. Even Betsy regretted the days when, if she had more to do, she had at least "her kitchen to herself," and nobody to share the credit. There was more fuss and more worry, if a trifle less labour, and the increase in consequence which resulted from being called cook, instead of maid-of-all-work, was scarcely so sweet in possession as had seemed in prospect.

"Them late dinners" were the object of her perpetual rail-ings; "oh, how much more comfortable it was, if gentry would but think so, to have your dinner at two, and get done with your washing up before you was cleaned, or had any occasion to bother yourself about your cap!" When little Amy cried over the loneliness of "the children's tea," which they fre-quently had to pour out for themselves, Betty gave her a cake and a kiss, and felt disposed to cry too.

"And she don't know, poor child, not the half," said Betty, which was a kind of oracular sentence difficult for Betty her-self to understand. The children had nothing to do with the late dinner; they were sent to bed earlier than they used to be, and scolded if any distant sounds of romps made itself audible at seven o'clock when their elders were dining; and then when the little ones went injured to bed, and Johnnie, indignant, worked at his lessons by himself in a corner of the old nursery, deeply aware that his schoolboy boots and jacket were quite unfit for the drawing-room, the grown-up young people ran lightly upstairs, all smiles and pleasure, and those delightful evenings began.

The children sometimes could not get to sleep for the piano and the raspings of the fiddle, which sounds of mirth suggested nothing but the wildest enjoyment to them; and when the door opened now and then, bursts of laughter and mingling voices would come out like the sounds the Peri heard at the gates of Paradise. The elder ones were happy; their little atoms of individual life had all united for the moment into one sunshiny and broad foundation, on which everything seemed to rest with that strange sense of stability and continuance, which such a moment of happiness, though it carries every element of change in it, almost invariably brings. It felt as if it might go on for ever, and yet the very sentiment that inspired it made separation and convulsion inevitable—one of those strange paradoxes which occur every day.

Thus the year crept round, and winter melted away with all its amusements, and spring began. Mr. Northcote's time at Salem Chapel was more than half over, a fact on which the congregation congratulated itself much.

"If so be as he had a settled charge of his own, I shouldn't be sorry to see him gone to-morrow," said one of the recent members.

"Settled charge! You take my word," said Mrs. Pigeon, who was getting old, but always continued a woman of spirit, "he'll never have a settled charge in our connection. He carries on here, 'cause he can't help hisself, but he ain't cut out for a pastor, and he's a deal too thick with them Church folks. A parson, too! I'd 'a thought he had more pride."

"Nay, now, but I don't wish him no harm," said the first speaker; "he's a civil spoken gentleman if he ain't so free and so pleasant as a body looks for."

"Civil spoken!" said the other; "one of our own ministers in our own connection! Bless you! they're our servants, that's what they are. I'd like to see one on 'em as 'ud take upon him to be civil spoken to me."

"Well, I wouldn't go as far as that," cried Mrs. Brown; "we pays 'em their salary, and we 'as a right to a civil word: but a minister's a minister, and I'll show him respect as long as he deserves it. I ain't one for being too hard upon ministers, especially when they're young men, as has their temptations like, we all know."

"I don't know what you call temptations," said Mrs. Pigeon; "licking the dust under the feet of a Church parson! and after speaking up so bold against young May and them old cheats at the College. I wish he was gone from here, that's what I wish, and our old pastor (if we can't get none better) back again. He was one as knew his place, and wouldn't have set his foot inside one of them Parsonages. Parsonages, indeed! kept up with our money. If ever there was an iniquity on this earth it's a State Church, and all the argufying in the world won't put that out of me."

It happened that Northcote was in the poulterer's shop, talking to the poulterer himself at this moment, and he heard the conclusion of this speech delivered with much unction and force. Such sentiments would have charmed him three months ago, and probably he would have thought this uneducated but strenuous partisan an extremely intelligent woman. He hurried away now with an uncomfortable smile. If an opinion is the

right opinion, why should it have an air of absurdity thrown
upon it by being thus uttered in ungrammatical language by a
poulterer's wife?   Truth is the same by whomsoever stated;
but yet, was not dogmatism on any subject the sign of an inexperienced and uncultivated, or a rude and untutored mind?
What did this woman know of the Parsonage, which she
supposed she helped to pay for?   What had he himself known
three months ago of Reginald May, whom he had assaulted so
savagely?   This Church family, which Mrs. Pigeon knew no
better than to abuse, with what divine charity it had received
himself, notwithstanding his public sin against it.   When he
thought of that public sin, Northcote's countenance glowed
with shame, and it continued to glow with a more agreeable
warmth when he escaped into thought of the goodness which
the Mays had shown him.   Had there ever been such goodness?
Was there ever so sweet a home of the heart as that faded,
homely drawing-room?   His heart beat high, his steps quickened; they carried him down Grange Lane in a path so often
trod that he felt there must be a special track of his own under
the garden walls, going Parsonage way.

CHAPTER XXXII.

LOVE-MAKING.

MRS. SAM HURST had been a long time out of Carlingford;
she had been paying visits among her friends, with whom,
though the young Mays would never believe it, she was very
popular, for she was not ill-natured in her gossip, and she was
often amusing in the fulness of her interest in other people.
It was April when she came back, and the early warmth and
softness of the spring were beginning to be felt in Grange
Lane; the doors of the houses began to be left open, and the
girls at the Parsonage had taken to running out and in without
their hats, gleaming through the little shrubbery in front, and
round to the back garden.   One evening it was so mild that
they all (which comprehensive term, sometimes extended to
"the whole party," began to be commonly used among them
with that complacence in the exclusiveness of their little coterie,
which every "set" more or less feels) came downstairs in a
body, and wandered about among the laurel-bushes in the
spring moonlight.   There was Ursula and Mr. Northcote,

Phœbe and Reginald, and Clarence Copperhead, with Janey behind, who followed where they went, but did not enjoy the ceremony. It was bad enough in the drawing-room ; but moonlight, who cared about moonlight ? Janey said to herself indignantly. She was the only one who looked up to Mrs. Hurst's window, where there was a faint light, and when the voices became audible Janey perceived some one come behind the curtain and look out. The girl was divided between her faithful family feud against Mrs. Hurst, and a vague sense of satisfaction in her presence as a Marplot, who one way or other would infallibly interfere.

"She will say something to papa," said Janey, her heart involuntarily rising at the thought, though at the same time she shivered to think of the treachery involved to all the tenets of the family. Janey sat on the steps and listened to the others talking. No one pointed out the stars to her, or followed her about as Reginald followed Phœbe. As for Mr. Copperhead, Janey thought he was almost as lonely as she was. He had lighted his cigar, and was strolling up and down, interrupting both of the other pairs occasionally, breaking into the midst of Northcote's astronomical lecture abruptly, and stopping Phœbe herself in the middle of a sentence. Janey, watching sharply from the steps, noticed, as a spectator has it in her power to do, that whereas Northcote was extremely impatient of the interruption, and discovered immediately that the stars could be seen better from another spot, Phœbe took it quite sweetly, and addressed herself to him as she went on, which Reginald did not like, Janey was sure. Were they in love with each other ? the girl asked herself—was this how it was managed ? When the moon went under a cloud for a moment Clarence Copperhead's vast shirt-front made a kind of substitute down below. Janey lost the other two among the bushes, but she always beheld that orb of white moving backward and forward with two dark figures near. She felt sure Reginald did not want to have him in such close neighbourhood ; but Phœbe's voice went on talking to both alike. Janey was half-pleased, and half-indignant. She had a jealous dislike, such as most girls have, to see her brother engrossed by any one, but no more did she like to see another man preferred to Reginald ; she was jealous both ways. As she sat and watched, a slight little creak came to her sharp ears, and looking up she saw Mrs. Hurst's drawing-room window opened the very least little bit in the world. Ah ! Janey said, with a long breath. There was nothing she would not have given to have talked it all over with Mrs. Hurst, and to hear what she

would say, if she had not been the traditional adversary against
whom all the family steeled their hearts.

That was a very pleasant evening; they all remembered it
afterwards. It was the moment when Ursula discovered all
in the darkness, when the moon was under that cloud, *what
Mr. Northcote meant*. It flashed upon her like a sudden light,
though they were standing in the shade of a great laurel. He
did not make any declaration, nor say a word that she could
remember. And yet all at once, by some magic which is not
explainable, she found out that *that* was what he was meaning.
This is not an admirable sentence; but it is difficult to know
how to put it better. It was quite a strange discovery. It set her
heart beating, thumping against her breast. She herself meant
nothing whatever, and she never thought of any response,
or of the time when he might ask her to make a response.
The sensation of the moment was quite enough for Ursula.
She was greatly startled, surprised, yet not surprised, touched
and full of a wondering respect and sympathy, awe and half-
amusement. Could it be possible, was *that* what it was?
Though he was not conscious of betraying himself in any way,
Northcote thought he had done something to offend her. Her
shy silence and withdrawal from him went to his heart; never
had her society been so sweet, never had he had her so completely to himself. What had he done to alarm or offend her?
He went home with his head full of this, able to think of
nothing else.

And Phœbe went home too, escorted by Reginald and Clarence together, to her grandfather's door, with her head buzzing
with many thoughts. It was not her heart that was in a commotion, like little Ursula's. She was more experienced, though
she was not much older, and had gone through such discoveries
before now. But a much more perplexing accident had
befallen her. Reginald May had fallen in love with her, and
Clarence Copperhead, after considerable resistance and hanging
off, was making up his mind to propose. · Yes. Phœbe felt
with unerring instinct that this was the state of affairs. He
was making up his mind to propose. So much of her and so little
of her had at length made an end of all the prudent hesitations
that lay under the crisp pie-crust of that starched and dazzling
shirt front. That he should never be able to speak a word to
her without that May! that fellow! "the son of my coach!"
poking himself in, was a thing which at length had fired his
cool blood to fever heat. Nobody else could play his accom-
paniments like that, or pull him through the "Wedding
March" like that; and who would look better at the head of a

table, or show better at a ball, or get on better in society? No one he knew, certainly. It was true she was only a Minister's daughter, and without a penny; for the little fortune Mr. and Mrs. Beecham had carefully gathered together and preserved for their daughter, what was that to the Copperheads?—nothing, not a penny. But, on the other hand, Clarence felt that he himself, or rather his father, was rich enough to be able to afford a wife without money. There was no reason why he should marry money; and a wife like Phœbe, what a relief that would be, in the way of education! No need of any more coaching. She was clever, and fond of reading, and so forth. She would get everything up for him, if he went into parliament, or that sort of thing; why, she'd keep him posted up. "There ain't many girls that could do that," he said to himself. She would save him worlds of trouble; save his money even, for coaches and that sort of thing cost money; and then that fellow May would be out of it; his nose would be put out of joint. These are not eloquent sentiments, but so it was that Clarence's natural feelings expressed themselves. He had intimated that he would see Miss Phœbe home, but May had stalked out side by side with him—had not left them for a moment; and Clarence determined that he would not stand it any longer. If there was no other way of shaking this fellow off, why, then he would make up his mind to it, and propose.

Phœbe somehow saw all this written in his fine countenance, and she saw at the same time that poor Reginald, who was (she thought) young and simple, and just the sort of poor boy to yield to such folly, was in love with her; and her head was buzzing with the double discovery. The first was (of course) the most important. She had no time to indulge her thoughts while she walked up between them, keeping them in play each with a word, talking all the way to fill up the somewhat sulky silence between them; but when she got safely within the garden door, and heard it shut behind her, and found herself in the quiet of the little green enclosure, with the budding trees and the lilac bushes for her only companions, the relief was very grateful to her. She could not go in all at once to make conversation for grandpapa and grandmamma, and give them the account they liked to hear, of how she had "enjoyed herself." She took off her hat to be cooler, and walked slowly down under the moonlight, her head all throbbing and rustling with thought. The paths were bordered with primroses, which made a pale glimmer in the moon, and shed a soft fragrance about. Phœbe had nothing to appeal to Heaven about, or to seek counsel from Nature upon, as sentimental people might do. She took counsel with herself, the person most interested. What was the thing she ought to do? Clarence Copperhead was going to propose to her. She did not even take the trouble of saying to herself that he loved her; it was Reginald who did that, a totally different person, but yet the other was more urgent. What was Phœbe to do? She did not dislike Clarence Copperhead, and it was no horror to her to think of marrying him. She had felt for years that this might be on the cards, and there were a great many things in it which demanded consideration. He was not very wise, nor a man to be enthusiastic about, but he would be a career to Phœbe. She did not think of it humbly like this, but with a big capital —a Career. Yes; she could put him into parliament, and keep him there. She could thrust him forward (she believed) to the front of affairs. He would be as good as a profession, a position, a great work to Phœbe. He meant wealth (which she dismissed in its superficial aspect as something meaningless and vulgar, but accepted in its higher aspect as an almost necessary condition of influence), and he meant all the possibilities of future power. Who can say that she was not as romantic as any girl of twenty could be? only her romance took an unusual form. It was her head that was full of throbbings and pulses, not her heart. No doubt there would be difficulties and disagreeables. His father would oppose it, and Phœbe felt with a slight shiver that his father's opposition was nothing to be laughed at, and that Mr. Copperhead had it in him to crush rebellion with a ferocious hand. And would Clarence have strength of mind or spirit to hold out? This was a very serious question, and one which included all the rest. If she accepted his proposal, would he have the heart to stand to it against his father? or would her consent simply involve her in a humiliating struggle which would end in defeat? That was the great question. If this should be the case, what use would there be in any sacrifice that Phœbe might make? A struggle with Mr. Copperhead would affect her father's position as much or more than her own, and she knew that a great many of the congregation would infallibly side with Mr. Copperhead, feeling it a most dangerous precedent that a pastor's daughter should be encouraged to think herself eligible for promotion so great, and thus interfere with the more suitable matrimonial prospects of wealthy young men who might happen to attend her father's chapel. Such a thing the conscript fathers of the connection would feel ought to be put a stop to with a high hand. So it may be supposed that Phœbe

had enough to think of, as she strolled about in the moonlight
alone, between the two borders of primroses. Tozer thought
she had gone upstairs to take off her "things," and it was
natural that when a girl got before a looking-glass she should
forget the progress of time; so that he merely wondered at
her non-appearance until the little chill of air stole in from
the open door, and made Mrs. Tozer cough.

"If it ain't our Phœbe a-walking about in the moonlight
like a play-actor!" said Tozer, in consternation, drawing aside
the curtain to look out. "I'll tell you what, old woman, the
girl's in love; and that's what it is." He thought this was a
capital joke, and followed his witticism with a laugh.

"Not much wonder, neither, with all them young fellows
about," said the old lady. "You may laugh; but, Tozer, I ain't
so easy in my mind as you. If it's him as they call Northcote,
that don't matter; but if it's that big gabby of a Copperhead,
there's troubles a-coming; though he's as rich, they do say, as
Creases, whoever Creases might be, and it would be a credit to
have the girl make a match like that out of our house."

Whereat Tozer again laughed loud and long.

"Well," he said, "if Mister Creases himself was here, I
wouldn't say as he was a bit too good for our Phœbe. Don't
you trouble your head, old woman; Copperhead or t'other one,
let her make her choice. Phœbe junior's the girl as'll be their
match, and you may take my word for that. Phœbe's the one
as will keep them in their right place, whoever they may be."

Phœbe heard this laugh echo out into the quiet of the night.
Of course, she did not know the cause of it, but it disturbed
her in her thoughts. Poor, kind, excellent grandpapa, she said
to herself, how would he get on with Mr. Copperhead? He
would touch his forelock to so rich a man. He would go down
metaphorically upon his knees before so much wealth; and
what a fool Clarence would be thought on every side for wanting to marry her! Even his mother, who was a romantic
woman, would not see any romance in it if it was she, Phœbe,
who was the poor girl whom he wanted to marry. Ursula
might have been different, who was a clergyman's daughter, and
consequently a lady by prescriptive right. But herself, Tozer's
granddaughter, Tom Tozer's niece, fresh from the butter-shop,
as it were, and redolent of that petty trade which big trade
ignores, as much as the greatest aristocrat does! Phœbe was
too sensible by far to vex or distress herself on this point, but
she recognised it without any hesitation, and the question remained—was it for her advantage to enter upon this struggle,
about which there could be no mistake, or was it not? And

this question was very difficult. She did not dislike Clarence, but then she was not in love with him. He would be a Career, but he was not a Passion, she said to herself with a smile ; and if the struggle should not turn out successful on her part, it would involve a kind of ruin, not to herself only, but to all concerned. What, then, was she to do ? The only thing Phœbe decided upon was that, if she did enter upon that struggle, it *must* be successful. Of this alone there could be no manner of doubt.

CHAPTER XXXIII.

A DISCLOSURE.

" WELL, young ladies ! " said Mrs. Sam Hurst, " I left you very quiet, but there seems to be plenty going on now-a-days. What a beautiful moon there was last night ! I put up my window to look at it, and all at once I found there was a party going on below. Quite a *fête champêtre*. I have newly come from abroad, you know, and it seemed quite congenial. I actually rubbed my eyes, and said to myself, ' I can't have come home. It's Boulogne still, it isn't Carlingford ! ' "

" There was no company," said Ursula with dignity ; " there was only our own party. A friend of Reginald's and a friend of mine join us often in the evening, and there is papa's pupil —if you call that a party. We are just as quiet as when you went away. We never invite strangers. We are as much by ourselves as ever."

" With a friend of Reginald's, and a friend of yours, and papa's pupil ! " said Mrs. Hurst, laughing ; " double your own number, Ursula ! and I don't suppose Janey counts yet. Why, there is a young man too many. How dare you waste the gifts of Providence, you prodigal child ? And now let me hear who they are."

" You may say Janey doesn't count," cried that young woman in person. " Oh, Mrs. Hurst, what a bore they are ! If that's society, I don't care for society. One always following Ursula about whenever she moves, so that you can't say a word to her; and the others pulling poor Phœbe to pieces, who hates them, I am sure. Phœbe was so jolly at first. She would talk to you, or she would play for you ! Why, she taught Johnnie and me a part-song to sing with her, and said he had a delightful voice; but she never has any time to look at us now," said Janey, stopping in this breathless enumeration of wrongs. "She is always taken up with those horrible men."

"I suppose you call Reginald a horrible man?" said Ursula, with rising colour. "If that was my opinion of my own brother, I should take care not to say it, at least."

"Oh, Reginald isn't the worst! There's your Mr. Northcote, and there's that Copperhead—Woodenhead, we call him in the nursery. Oh, how papa can put up with him, I can't tell! he never had any patience with us. You can't think how dull he is, Mrs. Hurst! I suppose girls don't mind when a man *goes on*, whether he's stupid or not. I never heard Mr. Northcote say much that was interesting either; but he looks clever, and that is always something."

"So Mr. Northcote is Ursula's one," said Mrs. Hurst, laughing. "You are a perfect jewel, Janey, and I don't know how I should ever find out anything that's going on, but for you. Northcote! it is a new name in. Carlingford. I wonder I have not heard of him already; or have you kept him entirely to yourself, and let nobody know that there was a new man in the place?"

There was a little pause here. The girls knew nothing about Northcote, except the one fact that he was a Dissenter; but as Mrs. Hurst was an excellent Churchwoman, much better than they were, who had, perhaps, been brought up too completely under the shadow of the Church to believe in it implicitly, they hesitated before pronouncing before her that unfortunate name.

"I don't know whether you are aware," Ursula said at last, with some slowness and reluctance, "that papa's pupil is of a Dissenting family. He is related, through his mother, to our cousins, the Dorsets." (This fact Ursula put forth with a little triumph, as refuting triumphantly any ready conclusion as to the social standing of Dissenters.) "I think Mr. Northcote came first to the house with Mr. Copperhead. He is a Dissenter too."

"Why, Ursula," cried Mrs. Hurst, "not the man who attacked Reginald in the Meeting? It was all in the papers. He made a frightful violent speech about the College and the sinecure, and what a disgraceful thing it was that your brother, a young man, could accept it. You don't mean him?"

Ursula was struck dumb. She looked up at her questioner with her lips falling apart a little, with a look of mingled consternation and fear.

"Of course it can't be," said the gossip, who was not ill-natured. "You never read the papers, but your papa does, and so does Reginald. Oh, you may be sure it is some other Northcote, though I don't know the name."

"Ursula doesn't like to tell you," said Janey; "but he's the Dissenting Minister, I know he is. Well! I don't care! He is just as good as anybody else. I don't go in for your illiberal ways of thinking, as if no one was worth talking to except in the Church. Mr. Northcote is very nice. I don't mind what you say. Do you mean to tell me that all those curates and people who used to plague our lives out were nicer? Mr. Saunders, for instance; he is a real good Churchman, I have always heard people say—"

"Hold your tongue, Janey; you don't know anything about it," said Mrs. Hurst, whom this wonderful disclosure elevated into authority. "A Dissenting Minister! Ah, me! what a thing it is for you poor girls to have no mother. I did not think your papa would have had so little consideration as to expose you to society like that. But men are so thoughtless."

"I don't know what right you have to speak of exposing us to society like that," cried Ursula, quivering all over with sudden excitement.

She felt as if some one had dug a knife into her, and turned it round in the wound.

"Men have so little consideration," repeated Mrs. Hurst, "especially when a girl is concerned. Though how your papa could have received a man who made such an assault upon him —even if he had passed over the attack upon Reginald, he was attacked himself."

"It must be a mistake," said Ursula, growing pale. Her hands came together half-unconsciously, and clasped in a mute gesture of appeal. "It is not possible; it cannot be true."

"Well, it is very odd that your papa should show such charity, I allow. I don't think it is in human nature. And Reginald, what does Reginald say? If it is that man, it will be the strangest thing I ever heard of. But there could not be two Northcotes, Dissenting Ministers in Carlingford, could there? It is very strange. I can't think what your papa can have had in his head. He is a man who would do a thing for a deep reason, whether he liked it or not. How did this Mr. Northcote come first here?"

"Oh, it was through Mr. Copperhead," said Janey. "It was the first dinner-party we had. You should have seen the fright Ursula was in! And papa would not let me come to dinner, which was a horrid shame. I am sure I am big enough, bigger than Ursula."

"If he came with the pupil, that makes it all quite plain. I suppose your papa did not want to quarrel with his pupil. What a predicament for him, if that was the case! Poor Mr. May! Of course, he did not want to be uncivil. Why, it was in the 'Gazette,' and the 'Express,' and all the papers; an account of the Meeting, and that speech, and then a leading article upon it. I always file the 'Express,' so you can see it if you like. But what an embarrassment for your poor papa, Ursula, that you should have taken this man up! And Reginald, how could he put up with it, a touchy young man, always ready to take offence? You see now the drawback of not paying a little attention to what is going on round you. How uncomfortable you must have made them! It might be very well to look over an offence, not to be unpleasant to the stranger; but that you should have thoughtlessly led this man on into the position of an intimate—"

"I did nothing of the sort," cried Ursula, growing red and growing pale, starting up from her work with a sense of the intolerable which she could not restrain. "What have I done to be spoken of so? I never led him on, or any one. What you say is cruel, very cruel! and it is not true."

"Isn't it true that he was here last night, following you about, as Janey says? Oh, I know how these sort of things go on. But you ought to think of your papa's position, and you ought to think of Reginald. If it was to come to the Bishop's ears that St. Roque's Parsonage was a refuge for Dissenters! For I know who *your* friend is, Ursula! That Tozer girl, another of them! Indeed, I assure you, it makes me feel very uncomfortable. And Reginald, just at the very beginning of his career."

Ursula did not make any reply. She bent her head down over her work, so low that her flushed cheeks could scarcely be seen, and went on stitching with energy and passion such as needles and thread are seldom the instruments of; and yet how much passion is continually worked away through needles and thread! Mrs. Hurst sat still for some time, looking at her, very little satisfied to keep silence, but feeling that she had discharged an efficient missile, and biting her lips not to say more to weaken its effect. When some time had passed in this way, and it was apparent that Ursula had no intention of breaking the silence, her visitor got up and shook out her skirts with a little flutter of indignation.

"You are offended," she said, "though I must say it is very ill on your part to be offended. What motive can I have but your good, and regard for your poor dear papa? It is he that is always the victim, poor man, whether it is your vagaries he has to pay for, or Reginald's high-flying. Oh, yes; you may be as angry as you like, Ursula; but you will find out the difference if your encouragement of this Dissenter interferes with something better—a li.ing for Reginald, perhaps, or better preferment for your poor papa."

"Oh!" cried Janey, awe-stricken; "but after all, it was not Ursula; it was papa himself. I think he must have done it to please Mr. Copperhead; for, Mrs. Hurst, you know Mr. Copperhead is very important. We have all to give in to him. He pays papa three hundred a-year."

"Three thousand wouldn't make up for it if it spoilt all your career," cried the indignant woman, and she swept away without saying any more to Ursula, who kept quite still over her work without budging. Janey went downstairs meekly after her to open the door, whispering an entreaty that she would not be angry.

"No, no, I am not angry," said Mrs. Hurst, "but I shall keep it up for a day or two. It is the best thing for her. I think she was struck with what I said."

Janey stole upstairs again, feeling rather guilty; but Ursula took little notice of her. The dinner was ordered and everything settled for the day. She was busy with her week's mending and darning, with the stockings and other things in a big basket beside her. When she came to some articles belonging to Janey, she threw them out with great impatience.

"You may surely mend your things yourself, you are big enough. You can talk for yourself and me too," cried Ursula with sudden impetuosity; and then she sat and worked, her needle flying through the meshes of her darning, though it is hard to darn stockings in that impassioned way. They were socks of Johnnie's, however, with holes in the heels that you could put your fist through, and the way in which the big spans filled themselves up under this influence was wonderful to see. Janey, who was not fond of mending, set to work quite humbly under the influence of this example, and made two or three attempts to begin a conversation but without avail.

The girls were seated thus in a disturbed and restless silence, working as if for their lives, when the usual little jar of the gate and sound of the bell downstairs announced a visitor. On ordinary occasions, they were both in the habit of rushing to the window when the gate was opened to see who was coming, and Janey had thrown aside her work to do so when a look from Ursula stopped her. High-spirited as Janey was, she did not dare to disobey that look. By right of the passion that had got possession of her, Ursula took the absolute command of the situation in a way she had never done before, and some sudden intuition made her aware who it was who was coming. The girls both sat there still and breathless, waiting for his appearance. He never came in the day, never had been seen in the Parsonage at that hour before, and yet Ursula was as certain who it was as if she had seen him a mile off. He came into the room, himself looking a little breathless and disturbed, and gave a quick impatient look at Janey as he went up to her sister. Ursula saw it and understood well enough. Janey was in his way; he had come this morning with a special purpose. Her heart sank down to her very shoes, and then rose again with a feverish and unreal leap. Was it not her duty to take the initiative, to cut away the very ground from beneath his feet? He took a seat, not far from where she was sitting, and made an effort to begin a little ordinary conversation, throwing frequent glances at Janey. He said it was a fine day, which was self-evident; that he almost feared they would be out; that he had come to—to tell her something he had forgotten last night, about—yes, about—Cassiopeia's chair, to correct what he said about Orion—yes, that was it; and again he looked at Janey, who saw his looks, and wondered much what she ought to do—go away, as he evidently wished her, or stay and listen, which was the eager desire of her mind. When Ursula lifted her head from her darning, and looked at him with cheeks alternately white and crimson, Janey felt herself grow hot and breathless with kindred excitement, and knew that the moment had come.

"Mr. Northcote," said Ursula, looking at him fixedly, so fixedly that a nervous trembling ran over him, "I have a question to ask you. You have been coming to us very often, and perhaps papa may know, but I don't. Is it true that you made a speech about Reginald when you first came here?"

Janey, looking eagerly on, saw Northcote grow pale, nay, grey in the fresh daylight. The colour seemed to ebb out of him. He started very slightly, as if waking up, when she began to speak, and then sat looking at her, growing greyer and greyer. A moment elapsed before he made any reply.

"Yes, I did," he said, with a half-groan of pain in his voice.

"You did! really you did! Oh!" cried Ursula, the hot tears falling suddenly out of her eyes, while she still looked at him, "I was hoping that it was all some horrible mistake, that you would have laughed. I hoped you would laugh and say no."

Northcote cleared his throat; they were waiting for him to defend himself. Janey, holding herself on the leash, as it were, keeping herself back from springing upon him like a hound. Ursula gazed at him with great blazing reproachful eyes; and all he could do was to give that sign of embarrassment, of guilt, and confusion. He could not utter a word. By the time he had got himself wound up to the point of speech, Ursula, impatient, had taken the words out of his mouth.

"Reginald is my brother," she said. "Whatever is against him is against us all; we have never had any separate interests. Didn't you think it strange, Mr. Northcote, to come to this house, among us all, when you had been so unkind to him?"

"Miss May—"

He made a broken sort of outcry and motion of his head, and then cleared his throat nervously once more.

"Did you think how your own brothers and sisters would have stood up for you? that it would have been an offence to them if anybody had come to the house who was not a friend to you? that they would have had a right—"

"Miss May," said the culprit; "all this I have felt to the bottom of my heart; that I was here on false pretences—that I had no right to be here. But this painful feeling was all quenched and extinguished, and turned into gratitude by the goodness of your father and brother. I did not even know that you had not been told. I thought you were aware from the beginning. You were colder than they were, and I thought it was natural, quite natural, for it is easier to forgive for one's self than for those one loves; and then I thought you melted and grew kinder to me, that you saw how all my ideas were changed, all my feelings—my mind itself; changed by the great charity, the wonderful goodness I have found here!"

"Mr. Northcote!" Ursula had been struggling to break in all the time; but while he spoke her words dispersed, her feelings softened, and at the end she found nothing but that startled repetition of his name with which to answer him. No doubt if he had given her time the eloquence would have come back; but he was too much in earnest to be guilty of such a mistake.

"What can I say about it?" cried the young man. "It has filled me with shame and with happiness. I have been taken in my own trap—those whom I attacked as you say— went out of my way to attack, and abused like a fool because I knew nothing about them—have shown me what the Bible means. Your father and brother knew what I had done, they met me separately, quite independent of each other, and both of them held out their hands to me; why, except that I had offended them, I cannot tell. A stranger, belonging to an obscure class, I had no claim upon them except that I had done what ought to have closed their house against me. And you know how they have interpreted that. They have shown me what the Bible means."

The two girls sat listening, both with their heads bent towards him, and their eyes fixed upon his face. When he stopped, Janey got up with her work in her lap, and coming a little nearer to Ursula, addressed her in a wondering voice.

"Is it *papa* he is talking of like that?" she said, under her breath.

"Yes," he said, fervently, turning to her. "It is your father. He has made charity and kindness real things to me."

"Poor papa!" said Ursula, whose tears were arrested in her eyes by the same surprised sensation, half-pleasure, half-pain, which hushed even Janey's voice. They were "struck," as Mrs. Hurst had said, but by such a strange mingling of feelings that neither knew what to make of them. Northcote did not understand what they meant; their words conveyed a slight shock of surprise, but no distinct idea to him; and when Janey, too much impressed to settle down again, went away after a while musingly, carrying her work in the upper skirt of her gown, held like a market-woman's apron by her elbow against her side; and he found himself to have attained in the very confusion of his intentions to what he wished, *i.e.*, an interview with Ursula by herself, he was almost too much agitated to take advantage of it. As for Ursula, she had floated a hundred miles away from that sensation of last night which, had no stronger feeling come in to bewilder her, would have made his errand very plain to her mind. She had ceased to think about him, she was thinking with a certain tenderness, and wondering, half-awed, half-amused, self-questioning, about her father. Was he so good as this? had he done this Christian action? were they all perhaps doing papa injustice? She was recalled to herself by Northcote's next proceeding. He went to the door and closed it after Janey, who had left it open, of course, and then he came to the back of the chair on which stood the great basket of darning. His voice was tremulous, his eyes liquid and shining with emotion.

"Will you forgive me, since they have forgiven me? and may I ask *you* something?" he said.

CHAPTER XXXIV.

AN EXTRAVAGANCE.

MR. MAY did not take any particular notice of what was going on around him among the young people. Nobody could have been more startled than he, had he been told of the purpose with which Horace Northcote, the Dissenting minister, had paid his early morning visit; and though he had a half-scornful, half-amused glimmer of insight into the feelings of his son, and saw that Clarence Copperhead was heavily veering the same way, it did not occur to him that any crisis was approaching. He was enjoying himself in his way, and he had not done that for a long time. He dearly liked the better way of living, the more liberal strain of housekeeping and expenditure; he liked the social meetings in the evening, the talk after dinner with the three young men, the half-fatherly flirtation with Phœbe, which she too enjoyed much, avowedly preferring him, with pretty coquetry, to the others. All this was very pleasant to him; and the additional money in his pocket was very pleasant, and when the post came in, one of these April mornings, and brought a letter from James, enclosing a draft for fifty pounds, his satisfaction was intense. The sight of the money brought an itching to his fingers, a restlessness about him generally. And yet it was not all that might have been desired, only fifty pounds! he had been buoying himself up by vain thoughts of how James this time, having been so long writing, would send a larger sum, which would at once tide him over the Tozer business, and on this account had been giving himself no trouble about it. Never before had he been so *insouciant*, although never before had the risk been so great. He had suffered so much about it last time, probably, that was why he took it so easily now; or was it because his trust in the chapter of accidents had grown greater since he was more dependent on it? or because of the generally expanded sense of living in him which made anxiety uncongenial anyhow? Whatever the cause was, this was the effect. A momentary disappointment when he saw how little James's draft was— then a sense of that semi-intoxication which comes upon a poor man when a sum of money falls into his hands—gradually invaded his soul. He tried to settle down to his writing, but

did not feel equal to the effort. It was too little for the purpose, he said to himself, for which he wanted it; but it was
enough to do a great many pleasant things with otherwise.
For the first time he had no urgent bills to swallow it up; the
very grocer, a long-suffering tradesman who made less fuss than
the others, and about whom Ursula made less fuss, had been
pacified by a payment on account of the Copperhead money,
and thus had his mouth stopped. Barring that bill, indeed,
things were in a more comfortable state than they had been for
a long time in the May household; and putting that out of
account, James's money would have been the nearest approach
to luxury—reckoning luxury in its most simple form as money
to spend without any absolutely forestalling claim upon it—
which Mr. May had known for years. It is so seldom that
poor people have this delicious sense of a little, ever so little
surplus! and it would be hard to say how he could entertain
the feeling that it was an overplus. There was something of
the fumes of desperation perhaps, and impending fate in the
lightness of heart which seized upon him. He could not keep
still over his writing. He got up at last, and put James's
draft into his pocket-book, and got his hat to go out. It was
a fine morning, full of that exhilaration which belongs only to
the spring. He went to the bank, and paid in the money, getting a small sum at the same time for his own immediate use;
but somehow his restlessness was scarcely satisfied by that very
legitimate piece of business, and he extended his walk into the
town, and strayed, half by chance, half by intention, to the old
furniture shop at the other end of the High Street, which was
a favourite resort of the higher classes in Carlingford, and
where periodically there was an auction, at which sometimes
great bargains were to be had. Mr. May went into this dangerous place boldly. The sale was going on; he walked into
the midst of temptation, forgetting the prayer against it, which
no doubt he had said that morning. And as evil fate would
have it, a carved book-case, the very thing he had been sighing
for, for years, was at that moment the object of the auctioneer's
praises. It was standing against the wall, a noble piece of furniture, in which books would show to an advantage impossible
otherwise, preserved from dust and damp by the fine old oak
and glass door. Mr. May's heart gave a little jump. Almost
everybody has wished for something unattainable, and this had
been the object of his desires for years. He gave a little start
when he saw it, and hurried forward. The bidding had actually
begun; there was no time to think and consider, if he wished
to have a chance, and it was going cheap, dead cheap. After

a minute or two of competition the blood rose to his cheeks, he got thoroughly excited. The effect of this excitement was two-fold—not only did it drive all thought of prudence out of his head, but it raised by several pounds the price of the book-case, which, had he gone about it coolly, he might have had at a much cheaper rate. When he suddenly woke up to find him-self the owner of it, a thrill of consternation ran over him—it was all so sudden; and it was perfectly innocent, if only he had any money; and to be sure he had James's money, which was not enough to do anything else—certainly not to do the thing he wanted it for. He tried to laugh at himself for the little thrill of alarm that ran through him; but it was too late to recede; and he gave his cheque for the money and his directions as to having it sent to the Parsonage, with a quake at his heart, yet a little flourish of satisfaction.

"Just what I have been wanting for years," he said, as he examined his new acquisition, and the people about looked at him with additional respect he felt, not being used to see Mr. May so prompt in payment, and so ready with his money. This pleased him also. He walked home with his head a little turned still, although there was a quake and flutter underneath. Well! he said to himself, who could call it an extravagance? a thing he had wanted for years—a thing which was a necessity, not for luxury, but every-day use—a thing which was not dear, and which was very handsome and substantial, and *really good;* how could any one say it was extravagant? Ursula might stare with her big eyes, but she was only a silly little girl, and women always were silly about expenses, alarmed by a big bold handsome purchase, though there was nobody better at the art of frittering away money in petty nothings. When he got home, he began at once nervously to clear the space where it should stand. What an improvement it would be! and his books were getting spoiled daily in those unsightly, open shelves, entirely spoiled. It was exciting to anticipate its arrival, and the admiration and commotion in the house. He called in Betsy and gave her orders about it; how, if it came when he was absent, it was to be put in that particular place, no other.

"And mind that great care is taken, for it is valuable, and a beautiful piece of furniture," he said.

"La, sir!" said Betsy, who was thunderstruck, though she knew it was not "her place" to show any feeling. He did not think it was necessary to appeal to Ursula on the same subject, but was rather glad to get out again, feeling the restlessness which had not been dissipated, but rather the reverse. He went and saw one or two poor people, to whom he was much more tolerant and kind than his wont, for in general Mr. May was not attracted towards the poor; and he gave them a shilling or two of the money he had drawn at the bank that morning—though somehow it had acquired a certain value in his eyes, and it was with a grudge that he took it out of his pocket. I must not spend this, he said to himself; but gave the shillings as a kind of tithe or propitiatory offering to Providence, that things might go well with him. Why should not things go well with him? He was not a bad man, he wronged nobody. He had done nothing to-day that a saint might not have done; he wanted the book-case, and he had the money, a sum not big enough for any more important purpose; but which was far better disposed of so than frittered away in nothings, as no doubt it would have otherwise been. By the afternoon, when the book-case arrived, he had convinced himself that it was not only quite reasonable, but a most lucky chance, a thing he could scarcely have hoped for, the opportunity and the money both coming in such exact accord with each other. When he returned from his walk the girls were looking at it, Ursula somewhat scared, Janey in open raptures.

"It is very nice indeed, papa," said the elder girl; "but it must have cost a deal of money."

"Be thankful that you haven't got to pay for it," he said, brusquely. He was not disposed to stand criticism. How it filled up his bare room, and made it, Mr. May thought, all at once into a library, though the old writing-table and shabby chairs looked rather worse perhaps than before, and suggested renewal in the most urgent way. To make it all of a piece, to put a soft Turkey carpet instead of the drugget, how pleasant it would be!—not extravagant, only a natural inclination towards the seemly, and a desire to have things around him becoming his position. No doubt such things were things which he ought to have in his position; a gentleman and a scholar, how humiliating it was that nothing but the barest elements of comfort should be within his reach. This was not how life ought to be; a poor creature like Clarence Copperhead, without birth, or breeding, or brains, or anything but money, was able to gratify every wish, while he—his senior, his superior! Instead of blaming himself, therefore, for his self-indulgence, Mr. May sympathized with himself, which is a much less safe thing to do; and accordingly, it soon began to appear to him that his self-denial all this time in not giving himself what he wanted had been extreme, and that what he had now done, in conceding himself so harmless a gratification, was what he ought to have done years ago. It was his own money sent to him by his dutiful son without conditions; and who had any right to interfere?

When he was at dinner, Betsy came behind his chair under pretence of serving him; Betsy, whose place was in the kitchen, who had no right to show in the dining-room at all, and whose confused toilette had caught Ursula's eye and filled her with horror. "Please, sir," she said, breathing hot on Mr. May's ear, till he shrank with sensitive horror. "Cotsdean's in the kitchen. He says as how he must see you; and I can't get him away."

"Ah, Cotsdean? tell him if he has anything to say to me, to write it down."

"Which he's done, sir," said Betsy, producing a little bit of paper rolled tightly together, "but I wasn't to give it till I'd asked you to see him. Oh, please see him, sir, like a dear good gentleman. He looks like a man as is going off his head."

"He is a fool," said Mr. May, taking the paper, but setting his teeth as he did so. Evidently he must get rid of this fellow—already beginning to trouble him, as if he was not the best person to know when and how far he could go.

"Tell him I'll attend to it, he need not trouble himself," he said, and put the paper into his pocket, and went on with his dinner. Cotsdean, indeed! surely there had been enough of him. What were his trumpery losses in comparison with what his principal would lose, and how dare that fellow turn up thus and press him continually for his own poor selfish safety? This was not how Mr. May had felt three months before; but everything changes, and he felt that he had a right to be angry at this selfish solicitude. Surely it was of as much consequence to him at least as to Cotsdean. The man was a fussy disagreeable fool, and nothing more.

And as it happened they sat late that night at dinner, without any particular reason, because of some discussion into which Clarence and Reginald fell, so that it was late before Mr. May got back to his room, where his books were lying in a heap waiting their transportation. They seemed to appeal to him also, and ask him reproachfully how they had got there, and he went to work arranging them all with all the enthusiasm natural to a lover of books. He was a book-lover, a man full of fine tastes and cultured elegant ways of thinking. If he had been extravagant (which he was not) it would have been in the most innocent, nay delightful and laudable way. To attach any notion of criminality, any suspicion of wrong-doing to such a virtuous indulgence, how unjust it would be! There was no company upstairs that evening. Copperhead had strolled out with Reginald to smoke his cigar, much against the will of the latter, and was boring him all the way to the College with accounts of his own lavish expenditure, and how much he had given for this and that; his cameos, his diamond studs, the magnificent dressing-case which was the wonder of the Parsonage. "Hang it all, what is the good of having money if you don't spend it?" said Clarence, and Reginald, who had not much money to spend, felt as near hating him as it was in his nature to do. Thus Mr. May was released from duty in the drawing-room, where Ursula, palpitating with many thoughts which were altogether new to her, sat doing her darning, and eluding as well as she could Janey's questions. Janey was determinedly conversational that night. She drove Ursula nearly out of her senses, and kept Johnnie—who had crept into the drawing-room in high delight at finding it for once free to him—from learning his lessons.

"Oh, how nice it is to be by ourselves," said Janey, "instead of all those new people. I don't mind Phœbe; but strange men in the house, what a nuisance they are, always getting in one's way—don't you think so, Ursula?"

Ursula made no reply, and after awhile even Janey sank into silence, and the drawing-room, usually so gay, got a cold and deserted look. The new life which had come in had left its mark, and to go back to what had once been so pleasant in the past was no longer possible. Johnnie and Janey might like it, having regained their former places, but to Ursula the solitude was horrible. She asked herself, with a great blush and quiver, what she would do if that temporary filling up of new interests and relationships was to fall away, as was likely, and leave her to the old life unbroken, to Janey's childish society and questions, and papa's imperious and unmodified sway. She grew pale and chill at the very thought.

But Mr. May, as we have said, was off duty. He forgot all about Cotsdean and the note in his pocket, and set to work with the most boyish simplicity of delight to arrange his books in his new shelves. How well they looked! never before had their setting done them justice. There were books in gorgeous bindings, college prizes which had never shown at all, and which now gleamed out in crimson and gold from behind the glass, and made their owner's heart beat with pleasure. Alas! to think how much innocent pleasure is denied us by the want of that small sum of money! and worse still, how an innocent pleasure becomes the reverse of innocent when it is purchased by the appropriation of something which should have been employed elsewhere. Perhaps, however, the sense of guilt which he kept under, added zest in Mr. May's mind to the pleasure of his acquisition; he was snatching a fearful joy, Heaven knows how soon the penalty might overwhelm him. In the mean time he was determined to take the good of it, and enjoy what he had gained.

When the books were all in he sat down at his table and surveyed it, rubbing his dusty hands. How much that is childish, how much that is fresh, and youthful, and innocent must be in the mind of a man (you would say) who could be thus excited about a bookcase! and yet this was not the kind of man whom you would call unsophisticated and youthful. It was probably the state of suppressed excitement in which he was, the unreality of his position, that helped him to that sense of elation as much as anything else; for emotion is a Proteus ready to take any form, and pain itself sometimes finds vent in the quick blazing up of fictitious delight, as much as in the moanings that seem more accordant with its own nature. He put his hand into his pocket for his pencil to make a note of the contents of the new shelves, and then he found Cotsdean's note, which he had not forgotten, but which he had felt no desire to remember. When he felt it between his fingers his countenance fell a little; but he took it out and read it with the smile still upon his face. It was a dirty little roll of paper, scribbled in pencil.

"Rev. Sir,

"I hope as you are not forgetting the 15th. Pleas excuse anxiety and bad writing, i am a poor nervous man I no, a word of answer just to say as it is all right will much oblidge.

"Rev. Sir,
"Your humble servant,
"T. Cotsdean."

Betsy knocked at the door as he read this, with a request for an answer to Mr. Cotsdean's note. "Little Bobby, sir, is waiting for it in the kitchen."

"Give Bobby some supper," said Mr. May, "tell him to tell his father it's all right, and I shan't forget. You understand? He is a troublesome little fool; but it's all right, and I shan't forget, and give the child some supper, Betsy. He ought not to be out so late."

"He is a delicate little thing, sir, thankye, sir," said Betsy, half-frightened by her master's amiability; and he smiled and repeated,

"Tell him it's all right."

Was it all right, the 15th? Cotsdean must have made a mistake. Mr. May's countenance paled, and the laugh went off; he opened a drawer in his writing-table and took out a book, and anxiously consulted an entry in it. It was the 18th certainly, as clear as possible. Something had been written on the opposite page, and had blotted slightly the one on which these entries were written; but there it stood, the 18th April. Mr. May prided himself on making no mistakes in business. He closed the book again with a look of relief, the smile coming back once more to his face. The 18th, it was three days additional, and in the time there was no doubt that he would find out what was the right thing to do.

CHAPTER XXXV.

THE MILLIONNAIRE.

When Mr. May woke next morning, it was not the book-case he thought of, but that date which had been the last thing in his mind on the previous night. Not the 15th,—the 18th. Certainly he was right, and Cotsdean was wrong. Cotsdean was a puzzle-headed being, making his calculations by the rule of thumb; but he had put down the date, and there could be no possible mistake about it. He got up disposed to smile at the poor man's ignorance and fussy restlessness of mind. "I have never left him in the lurch, he may trust to me surely in the future," Mr. May said to himself, and smiled with a kind of condescending pity for his poor agent's timidity; after all, perhaps, as Cotsdean had so little profit by it, it was not wonderful that he should be uneasy. After this, it might be well if they did anything further of the sort, to divide the money, so that Cotsdean too might feel that he had got something for the risk he ran; but then, to be sure, if he had not the money he had no trouble, except by his own foolish anxiety, for the payment, and always a five-pound note or two for his pains. But Mr. May said to himself that he would do no more in this way after the present bill was disposed of; no, he would make a stand, he would insist upon living within his income. He would not allow himself to be subject to these perpetual agitations any more. It would require an effort, but after the effort was made all would be easy. So he said to himself; and it was the 18th, not the 15th, three days more to make his arrangements in. It had come to be the 12th now, and up to this moment he had done nothing, having that vague faith in the Indian mail which had been realized, and yet had not been realized. But still he had nearly a week before him, which was enough certainly. Anything that he could do in six months, he said to himself, he could easily do in six days —the mere time was nothing; and he smiled as he dressed himself leisurely, thinking it all over. Somehow everything looked perfectly easy to him this time; last time he had been plunged into tragic despair; now, and he did not know why, he took it quite easily; he seemed to fear nothing. There were various ways of getting the money as natural as the daylight, and in the mean time why should he make himself unhappy? As soon as he was ready he went to his room and had another look at the book-case which, with his best books in it, all in order and ranged in unbroken lines, looked everything a book-case ought to look. It made him feel more of a man somehow, more like the gentleman and scholar he had meant to be when he started in life; he had not intended then to be a poor district incumbent all his life, with a family of eight children. His book-case somehow transported him back to the days when he had thought of better things for himself, and when life had held an ideal for him. Perhaps at the best of times it had never been a very high ideal; but when a man is over fifty and has given up doing anything but struggle through each day as it comes, and get out of his work as best he may, doing what he must, leaving undone what he can, any ideal almost seems something higher than himself; but the recollection of what he had meant to be, came back to him strongly when he looked at his carved oak. It had not been carried out; but still he felt rehabilitated and better in his own opinion as he stood beside this costly purchase he had made, and felt that it changed his room and all his surroundings. It might have been almost wicked to run into such an extravagance, but yet it did him good.

"My people came down to the Hall last night," Clarence Copperhead said to him at breakfast, "and the Governor is coming over along with Sir Robert. He'd like to see you, I am sure, and I suppose they'll be going in for sight-seeing, and that sort of thing. He is a dab at sight-seeing, is the Governor. I can't think how he can stand it for my part."

"Then you must remember that I put myself at his orders for the day," said Mr. May graciously. "Sir Robert is not a bad guide, but I am a better, though it sounds modest to say it; and, Ursula, of course Mr Copperhead will take luncheon with us."

"Don't think of that," said Clarence, "he's queer and likes his own way. Just as likely as not he'll think he ought to support the hotels of the place where he is—sort of local production, you know. I think it's nonsense, but that is how it is —that's the man."

"We shall look for him all the same," said Mr. May, with a nod at Ursula; and a sudden project sprang up in his mind, wild as projects so often are. This father whom his fancy, working upon what Clarence said, immediately invested with all the prodigal liberality of a typical rich man; this stranger to whom a hundred pounds was less then a penny was to himself, would give him the money he wanted. What so easy? He drew a long breath, and though he had not been aware that he was anxious, he was suddenly conscious of a sense of relief. Yes, to be sure, what so simple, what so likely? he would explain his monetary necessities lightly and with grace, and Mr. Copperhead would supply them. He was in the mildest state of desperation, the painless stage, as may be seen, when this strange idea entered into his head. He hugged it, though he was a man of the world and might have known better, and it produced a kind of elation which would have been a very strange spectacle to any looker-on who knew what it meant. The thing seemed done when he next thought of it ten minutes later, settled as if it had been so for years. Mr. Copperhead would make it all right for him, and after that he would undertake such risks no more.

Mr. Copperhead, however, did not come for two days, though Ursula spent all the morning and a great deal of trouble in arranging a luncheon for him; but on the second morning he came, driven by Sir Robert, who had changed horses on the road, and who was in a somewhat irritated and excited condition, very glad to get rid of his visitor.

"I hope you don't mind having your toes trodden on, May," he said, privately; "that fellow is never happy but when he's insulting some one." And indeed Mr. Copperhead began this favourite pastime at once by making very big eyes at the sight of Ursula. "A—ha!" he said, rubbing his hands, and elevating his eyebrows; and he gave a meaning laugh as he shook hands with her, and declared that he did not expect to find young ladies here. "I haven't a great deal of education myself, and I never knew it could be carried on so pleasantly," he said. "You're a lucky young dog, Clar, that's what you are;" and the son laughed with the father at this excellent joke, though the rest of the company looked on with great gravity. Ursula,

for her part, turned with wondering eyes from the new-comer
to her old friend, Sir Robert.

"What does he mean?" she asked, with an appealing look.

"He is the greatest brute I know," said poor Sir Robert,
under his breath; and he went off suddenly on the plea of
business, leaving his unpleasant visitor in Mr. May's hands,
who undertook the charge not unwillingly, being possessed by
his own plan. Mr. Copperhead went all over Carlingford. He
inspected the town-hall, the infirmary, and the church, with
the business-like air of a man who was doing his duty.

"Poor little place, but well enough for the country," he said.
"A country-town's a mistake in my opinion. If I had it in
my power I'd raze them all to the ground, and have one London and the rest green fields. That's your sort, Mr. May.
Now you don't produce anything here, what's the good of
you? All unproductive communities, sir, ought to be swept
off the face of the earth. I'd let Manchester and those sort of
places go on till they burst; but a bit of a little piggery like
this, where there's nothing doing, no trade, no productions of
any kind."

"We like it all the same," said Mr. May; "we small sort of
people who have no enterprise like you—"

"I dare say you like it! To be sure, you can moon about
here as much as you please, and make believe to do something,
and there's nobody to contradict you. In a great centre of
industry you couldn't live like that; you must work or you'll
get pushed aside altogether; unless, of course, you're a
millionnaire to start with," Mr. Copperhead added, with a noisy
laugh.

"Which I am not certainly—very much the reverse—in
short, a poor man with a large family, which I suppose is a
thing about as objectionable in a centre of industry as anything
can be."

"The large family ain't objectionable if you make 'em work,"
said Mr. Copperhead; "it all depends on that. There's always
objections, you know," he said, with a jocular grin, "to pretty
girls like that daughter of yours put straight in a young fellow's
way. You won't mind my saying it? They neither work
themselves nor let others work—that sort. I think we could
get on with a deal fewer women, I must allow. There's where
Providence is in a mistake. We don't want 'em in England;
it's a waste of raw material. They're bad for the men, and they
ain't much good for themselves, that I can see."

"You are a little hard upon the ladies, Mr. Copperhead."

"Not I—we can't do without 'em of course, and the surplus we ought to export as we export other surpluses; but I object to them in a young man's way, not meaning anything unpleasant to you. And perhaps if I had been put up to it sooner—but let's hope there's no mischief done. What is this now? some of your antiquities, I suppose. Oh yes, let's have a look at it; but I confess it's the present age I like best."

"This is the College," cried Mr. May, swallowing certain sensations which impaired his sense of friendliness; "but not an educational college, a foundation for old men—decayed citizens, as they are called—founded in the fifteenth century. My son is the chaplain, and will be very glad to show it you. There are twelve old men here at present, very comfortably looked after, thanks to the liberal arrangements of the founder. They attend chapel twice a day, where Reginald officiates. It is very agreeable to me to have him settled so near me."

"Cunning I call it," said Mr. Copperhead, with his hoarse laugh; "does you credit; a capital snug nest—nothing to do —and pay—pay good now? those old fellows generally managed that; as it was priests that had the doing of it, of course they did well for their own kind. Good Lord, what a waste of good money all this is!" he continued, as they went into the quadrangle, and saw the little park beyond with its few fine trees; "half-a-dozen nice villas might be built on this site, and it's just the sort of place I should fancy where villas would pay. Why don't the Corporation lay hands on it? And your son lives here? Too dull for me; I like a little movement going on, but I dare say he likes it; and with how much a year?"

"Two hundred and fifty; and some advantages beside—"

"Bravo!" said Mr. Copperhead, "now how many curates could you get for that two and a-half? I've got a great respect for you, Mr. May; you know what's what. That shows sense, that does. How do you do, sir? fine old place you've got here—capital snug appointment. I've just been saying to your father I admire his sense, looking out for you a nice fat easy appointment like this."

Reginald turned from red to white, and then to portentous blackness. The subject was of all others the one least likely to please him.

"It is not very fat," he said, with a look of offence, quite undeserved by the chief sufferer, towards his father, "nor very easy. But come in. It is rather an interesting old place. I suppose you would like to see the Chapel, and the old captain's rooms; they are very fine in their way."

"Thank you; we've been seeing a deal already, and I feel tired. I think I'll let you off the chapel. Hallo! here's another old friend—Northcote, by George! and what are *you* doing here I should like to know, a blazing young screamer of the Liberation Society, in a high and dry parson's rooms? This is as good as a play."

"I suppose one is not required to stay at exactly the same point of opinion all one's life," said Northcote, with a half-smile.

"By George! but you are though, when you're a public man; especially when you're on a crusade. Haven't I heard you call it a crusade? I can tell you that changing your opinion is just the very last thing the public will permit you to do. But I shan't tell for my part—make yourself easy. Clarence, don't you let it out; your mother, fortunately, is out of the way. The world shall never know through me that young Northcote, the anti-state Churchman, was discovered hob-nobbing with a snug chaplain in a sinecure appointment. Ha, ha! had you there."

"To do Northcote justice," said Mr. May; "he began life in Carlingford by pointing out this fact to the neighbourhood; that it was a sinecure, and that my son and I—"

"Would it not be more to the point to inspect the chapel?" said Reginald, who had been standing by impatiently playing with a big key; upon which Mr. Copperhead laughed more loudly than before.

"We'll not trouble the chapel," he said, "railway stations are more in my way; you are all a great deal finer than I am, and know a deal more, I suppose; but my roughness has served its purpose on the whole, better perhaps for some things —yes, for some things, Clar, and you may thank your stars, old boy. If you had been a parson's son, by George! there would have been no fat appointment waiting for you."

"After all, my son's appointment is not so very fat," said Mr. May, forcing a laugh. "It is not so much as many a boy at school gets from his father."

"Ah, you mean my boy at school! he's an extravagant dog. His mother and he, sir, are made of different clay from me; they are porcelain and I am delft. They want fine velvet cupboards to stand themselves in, while I'm for the kitchen dresser. That's the difference. But I can afford it, thank Heaven. I tell Clarence that he may thank his stars that I can afford it, and that he isn't born a poor man's son. He has been plucked at Oxford, you know," he said, with a big laugh, thrusting forth his chest as Clarence thrust forth his shirt-front, with an apparent complacency over the very plucking. My son can afford to be plucked, he seemed to say. He got up as he spoke, and approaching the fireplace turned his back to it, and gathered up his coat-tails under his arm. He was no taller than Mr. May, and very little taller than Reginald; but they both shrank into insignificance beside the big self-assertive figure. He looked about the room as if he was thinking of "buying up" the whole contents of it, and thought very little of them. A glance of contempt, a shrug more implied than actual, testified his low opinion of everything around. When he withdrew his eyes from the furniture he shook out his leg, as Clarence had done his, and gave a pull to his trousers that they might sit properly. He had the word "Rich" painted in big letters all over him, and he seemed to feel it his vocation to show this sense of superiority. Clarence by his side, the living copy of the great man's appearance and manners, strutted and put himself forward like his father, as a big calf might place itself beside the parent cow. Mr. Copperhead did not look upon his offspring, however, with the cow's motherly complacency. He laughed at him openly, with cynical amusement. He was clever in his way, and Clarence was stupid; and besides he was the proprietor, and Clarence, for all he was porcelain, was his goods and chattels. When he looked at him, a wicked leer of derision awoke in his eye.

"Yes, my boy," he said, "thank your stars; you would not make much of it if you were a poor man. You're an ornament that costs dear; but I can afford you. So, Northcote, you're changing your opinions—going over to the Church, eh? Extremes meet, they say; I shouldn't have thought it—"

"I am doing nothing of the kind," said Northcote stoutly. He was not in a mood to be taken to task by this Mammon of unrighteousness, and indeed had at all times been a great deal too independent and unwilling to submit to leading members of the connection. Mr. Copperhead, however, showed no resentment. Northcote too, like Clarence, had a father before him, and stood on quite a different footing from the ordinary young pastor, whose business it was to be humble and accept all that his betters might portion out.

"Well," he said, "you can afford to please yourself, and that's always something. By the way, isn't it time to have something to eat? If there is a good hotel near—"

"Luncheon will be waiting at my house," said Mr. May, who was still doing his best to please the man upon whom he had built such wild hopes, "and Ursula will be waiting."

"Ah, ah, the young lady! so she will. I wouldn't miss that for something; but I don't like putting you to so much expense.

My son here has an excellent appetite, as you must have found out by this time, and for my part so have I. I think it a thousand pities to put you to this trouble—and expense."

"Pray don't think of that," said Mr. May with courtesy, which belied his feelings, for he would have liked nothing so well as to have knocked down his complacent patron. He led the way out, almost with eagerness, feeling Mr. Copperhead to be less offensive out of doors than within four walls. Was this the sort of man to be appealed to for help as he had thought? Probably his very arrogance would make him more disposed towards liberality. Probably it would flatter his sense of consequence, to have such a request made to him. Mr. May was very much at sea, letting I dare not wait upon I would; afraid to speak lest he should shut this door of help by so doing, and afraid to lose the chance of any succour by not speaking. He tried hard, in spite of all his difficulties, to be smooth and agreeable to a man who had so much in his power; but it was harder work than he could have thought.

CHAPTER XXXVI.

FATHER AND SON.

URSULA had prepared a very careful luncheon for the stranger. She thought him disagreeable, but she had not looked at him much, for, indeed, Ursula's mind was much unsettled. Horace Northcote had spoken to her that morning, after Mrs. Hurst's visit and her retaliation upon him, as no man yet had ever spoken to her before. He had told her a long story, though it was briefly done, and could have been expressed in three words. He was not of her species of humanity; his ways of thinking, his prejudices, his traditions, were all different from hers, and yet that had happened to him which happens all over the world in every kind of circumstances—without knowing how it was, he had got to love her. Yes, he knew very well how it was, or rather, he knew when it was, which is all that is to be expected from a lover. It was on the evening of the *entrées*, the first dinner-party, and he had gone on ever since, deeper and deeper, hearing her say many things which he did not agree in, and tracing her life through a score of little habits which were not congenial to his, yet loving her more and more for all that was new to him, and even for the things which were

uncongenial. He had told her all this, and Ursula had listened
with a kind of awe, wondering at the ardour in the young
man's eyes, and the warmth with which he spoke; wondering
and trembling a little. She had guessed what he meant the
night before, as has been said, and this had touched her
with a little thrill of awakened feeling; but the innocent girl
knew no more about passion than a child, and when she saw it,
glowing and ardent, appealing to her, she was half-alarmed,
half-overawed by the strange sight. What answer could she
make to him? She did not know what to say. To reject
him altogether was not in Ursula's heart; but she could not
respond to that strange, new, overwhelming sentiment, which
put a light in his eyes which she dared not meet; which dazzled
her when she ventured a glance at him. "Was he to go away?"
he asked, his voice, too, sounding musical and full of touching
chords. Ursula could not tell him to go away either. What
she did say to him, she never quite knew; but at least, whatever it was, it left him hopeful, if unsatisfied.

And since that time her mind had been in a strange confusion,
a confusion strange but sweet. Gratified vanity is not a pretty
title to give to any feeling, and yet that mixture of gratification
and gratitude, and penetrating pleasure in the fact of being
elevated from an often-scolded and imperfect child to an admired and worshipped woman is, perhaps, of all the sensations
that feminine youth is conscious of, the most poignant in its
sweetness. It went through her whole life; sometimes it made
her laugh when she was all alone, and there was nothing of a
laughter-producing nature in her way; and sometimes it made
her cry, both the crying and the laughter being one. It was
strange, very strange, and yet sweet. Under the influence of
this, and of the secret homage which Northcote paid her whenever they met, and which she now understood as she had never
understood it before, the girl's whole nature expanded, though
she did not know. She was becoming sweet to the children, to
puzzled Janey, to every one around her. Her little petulances
were all subdued. She was more sympathetic than she had
ever been before. And yet she was not in love with her lover.
It was only that the sunshine of young life had caught her, that
the highest gratification of youth had fallen to her share unawares. All this might have been, and yet some one else come
in to secure Ursula's real love; but in the mean time she was all
the happier, all the better for the love which she did not return.

This is a digression from our immediate subject, which was
the luncheon prepared for Mr. Copperhead. Ursula sent up
an urgent message for Phœbe, who came to her in her prettiest

morning dress, very carefully arranged, but with a line of care upon her brow.

"I will come if you wish it, dear," she said; "but I don't want to meet Mr. Copperhead. I don't like him."

"Neither do I like him," cried Ursula. "He said something disagreeable the little moment he was here. Oh, I don't remember what it was, but something. Please stay. What am I to do with them all by myself? If you will help me, I may get through."

Phœbe kissed her with a tremulous kiss; perhaps she was not unwilling to see with her own eyes what the father of Clarence meant, and what brought him here. She sat down at the window, and was the first to see them coming along the street.

"What a gentleman your father looks beside them," cried Phœbe; "both of them, father and son; though Clarence, after all, is a great deal better than his father, less like a British snob."

Ursula came and stood by her, looking out.

"I don't think he is much better than his father," she said.

Phœbe took her hand suddenly and wrung it, then dropped it as if it had hurt her. What did it all mean? Ursula, though rays of enlightenment had come to her, was still perplexed, and did not understand.

Mr. Copperhead did not see her till he went to luncheon, when Phœbe appeared with little Amy May looking like a visitor, newly arrived. She had run upstairs after that first sight of him from the window, declaring herself unable to be civil to him except at table. The great man's face almost grew pale at the sight of her. He looked at Ursula, and then at Clarence, and laughed.

"'Wheresoever the carcase is the eagles are gathered together,'" he said. "That's Scripture, ain't it, Miss Ursula? I am not good at giving chapter and verse."

"What does it mean?" asked Ursula.

She was quite indifferent to Mr. Copperhead, and perfectly unconscious of his observation. As for Phœbe, on the contrary, she was slightly agitated, her placid surface ruffled a little, and she looked her best in her agitation. Mr. Copperhead looked straight at her across the table, and laughed in his insolent way.

"So you are here too, Miss Phœbe!" he said. "I might think myself in the Crescent if I didn't know better. I met young Northcote just now, and now you. What may you be doing here, might one ask ? It is what you call a curious coincidence, ain't it, Clarence and you both here ? "

"I said so when Mr. Clarence came," said Phœbe. "*I* came to take care of my grandmother, who is ill; and it was a very lucky thing for me that I had met Miss May at your ball, Mr. Copperhead."

" By Jove, wasn't it!" said Clarence, roused to some dull sense of what was going on. "We owe all the fun we have had here to that, so we do. Odd, when one thinks of it; and thought so little of it then, didn't we? It's a very queer world."

" So you've been having fun here ? " said his father. "I thought you came here to work ; that's how we old fellows get taken in. Work ! with young ladies dangling about, and putting things into your head ! I ought to have known better, don't you think so, Miss Ursula ? *You* could have taught me a thing or two."

" I ? " said Ursula, startled. "I don't know what I could teach any one. I think Mr. Clarence Copperhead has kept to his hours very steadily. Papa is rather severe ; he never would take any excuse from any of us when we were working with him."

" He is not so severe now, I'll be bound," said Mr. Copperhead. "Lets you have your fun a little, as Clarence tells me ; don't you, May ? Girls will be girls, and boys, boys, whatever we do ; and I am sure, Miss Phœbe, you have been very entertaining, as you always were."

" I have done my best," said Phœbe, looking him in the face. "I should have had a dull life but for the Parsonage, and I have tried to be grateful. I have accompanied your son on the violin a great many evenings, and I hope our friends have liked it. Mr. Clarence is a promising player, though I should like him to trust less to his ear ; but we always pulled through."

" Thanks to you," said Clarence, in the middle of his cutlet

He did not quite see why she should flourish this music in his father's face ; but still he was loyal in a dull fashion, and he was obstinate, and did not mean to be "sat upon," to use his own words. As for Phœbe, her quick mind caught at once the best line of policy. She determined to deliver Ursula, and she determined at the same time to let her future father-in-law (if he was to be her father-in-law) see what sort of a person he had to deal with. As soon as she made up her mind, her agitation disappeared. It was only the uncertainty that had cowed her ; now she saw what to do.

" So ! " said Mr. Copperhead, "musical evenings ! I hope

you have not turned poor Clar's head among you, young ladies. It's not a very strong head; and two is more than a match for one. I dare say he has had no chance between you."

"Make yourself quite easy," said Phœbe, with her sweetest smile; "he was only one of a party. Mr. Reginald May and Mr. Northcote are both very pleasant companions. Your son is bored sometimes, but the rest of us are never bored. You see, he has been accustomed to more brilliant society; but as for us, we have no particular pretensions. We have been very happy. And if there has been two to one, it has been the other way."

"I think I must let your people know of your gaieties, Miss Phœbe. If your mother sent you here, I don't doubt it was for a purpose, eh? She knows what she's about, and she won't like it if she knows you are fritting away your chances and your attentions. She has an eye for business, has Mrs. Beecham," said the leading member, with a laugh.

"You cannot tell mamma more about me than she knows already," said Phœbe, with rising colour.

And by this time every one else at table was uncomfortable. Even Clarence, who had a dull appreciation of his father's jokes when they were not levelled at himself, and who was by no means indisposed to believe that "girls," generally, were "after him," and that even in this particular case Phœbe herself might have come to Carlingford on purpose to complete his conquest, even Clarence was moved.

"I don't know what you mean by brilliant society," he said. "I know I'm the dull one among you clever people. I don't say much, but I know it all the same; and it's awfully good of you to pull me through all that music. I don't begrudge you your laugh after. Is my mother coming over, sir, to see the place?"

"To see what? There is not much in the place," said Mr. Copperhead. "You're coming back with me, my boy. I hope it won't inconvenience you, May. I've other views for him. Circumstances alter cases, you know. I've been turning it over in my head, and I think I can see my way to another arrangement."

"That, of course, is entirely in your own hands," said Mr. May, with a cheerfulness he did not feel. His heart sank, but every rule of good society made it incumbent upon him to show no failure at such a moment. "Copperhead, see that your father has some wine. Well, I suppose our poor little Carlingford is not much of a place; no trade, no movement, no manufactures—"

" The sort of place that should be cleared off the face of the earth," said the millionnaire; "meaning no offence, of course. That's my opinion in respect to country towns. What's the good of them? Nests of gossip, places where people waste their time, and don't even amuse themselves. Give me green fields and London, that is my sort. I don't care if there was not another blessed brick in the country. There is always something that will grow in a field, corn or fat beasts—not that we couldn't get all that cheaper from over the water if it was managed as it ought to be. But a place like this, what's the good of it? Almshouses and chaplains, and that kind of rubbish, and old women; there's old women by the score."

" They must be somewhere, I suppose," said Mr. May. " We cannot kill them off, if they are inoffensive, and keep the laws. So that, after all, a country town is of use."

" Kill 'em off—no; it's against what you benevolent humbugs call the spirit of the time, and Christianity, and all that; but there's such a thing as carrying Christianity too far; that's my opinion. There's your almshouses now. What's the principle of them? I call it encouraging those old beggars to live," said Mr. Copperhead; "giving them permission to burden the community as long as they can manage it; a dead mistake, depend upon it, the greatest mistake in the world."

" I think there is a great deal to be said in favour of Euthanasia," said Phœbe, quietly stepping into the conversation; "but then it would have to be with the consent of the victims. When any one found himself useless, unnecessary to the world, or unhappy in it—"

" Humbug and nonsense," said Mr. Copperhead. "A likely thing for anybody to do. No, it is not a question for lawmaking. Let 'em die out naturally, that's my opinion. Don't do anything to hurry 'em—that is, I don't see my way to it; but let 'em go quiet, and don't bring 'em cordials and featherbeds, and all that middyeval nonsense, to keep 'em going as long as possible. It's wicked, that's what it is."

" At all events," said Mr. May, who, poor man, was bent on pleasing, "it is refreshing to hear opinions so bold and original. Something new is always a blessing. I cannot say I agree with you—"

" No parson would be bold enough for that. Christianity's been a capital thing for the world," said Mr. Copperhead, "I don't say a word against it; but in these go-ahead days, sir, we've had enough of it, that's to say when it's carried too far. All this fuss about the poor, all the row about dragging up a lot of poor little beggars to live that had far better die, and

your almshouses to keep the old ones going, past all nature!
Shovel the mould over them, that's the thing for the world;
let 'em die when they ought to die; and let them live who can
live—that's my way of thinking—and what's more, I'm right."

"What a fine thing for you, Mr. Clarence," cried Phœbe,
"who are going into Parliament! to take up your father's
idea and work it out. What a speech you could make on the
subject! I saw a hospital once in Paris that would make such
a wonderful illustration. I'll tell you about it if you like.
Poor old wretched people whose life was nothing but wretchedness kept going, kept living for years and years—why, no one
could tell; for I am sure it would have been better, far better
for them to die and be done with it. What a speech you
might make when you bring a bill into Parliament to abolish
almshouses and all sorts of charities!" she added with a
laugh, turning from Clarence, at whom she had been looking,
to his father, who was puzzled, and did not know how to understand the young woman's eyes.

"I'll never make much of a speech in Parliament," said
Clarence; "unless you make it for me," he added in an
undertone. But no one else was speaking, and the undertone
was quite audible. Meanwhile Phœbe had not ceased to look
at his father, and held him with a pair of eyes not like the
Ancient Mariner's. Mr. Copperhead was confused, his power
even of insolence was cowed for the moment. He obeyed
quite docilely the movement made to leave the table. Was it
possible that she defied him, this Minister's daughter, and
measured her strength against his? Mr. Copperhead felt
as if he could have shaken the impertinent girl, but dared not,
being where he was.

And lunch being over, Mr. May led his pupil's father into
his study. "I want to show you what your boy has been
doing," he said, pointing to a line of books which made the
millionnaire's soul shrink within him. "I have not bothered
him with classics; what was the use as he is not going back to
Oxford? but I have done my best for him in a practical way.
He has read history, largely as you see, and as much as I could
give him of political and constitutional—"

"Yes, yes," said Mr. Copperhead, reading the titles of some
of the books under his breath. They impressed him deeply,
and took away for a moment his self-confidence. It was his
habit to boast that he knew nothing about books; but in their
presence he shrank, feeling that they were greater than he,
which was, there is little doubt, a sign of grace.

" If you wish to remove Clarence," said Mr. May, "perhaps I had better make out a scheme of reading for him."

" Look here," cried the rich man, " I didn't want to remove him ; but there he is, the first I see of him, cheek for jowl with a good-looking girl. I don't mean to say a word against Miss May, I've no doubt she's charming ; but anyhow there she is side by side with Clar, who is no more able to resist that sort of thing—"

Mr. May laughed, and this time with unmitigated amusement. " Do you mean Ursula ? I think I can answer for it that she made no attempts upon him for which resistance would be necessary."

" That's all very well to say ; but bless you they do it, every one," said Mr. Copperhead, " without exception, when a young fellow's well off and well-looking; and as if one wasn't bad enough, you've got Phœbe Beecham. You won't tell me she doesn't mean anything ?—up to any mischief, a real minister's daughter. I don't mean anything uncivil to you or yours. I suppose a parson's different ; but we know what a minister's daughter is in our connection. Like the men themselves, in short, who are always pouncing on some girl with a fortune if her relations don't take care. And Clarence is as weak as a baby ; he takes after his mother—a poor bit of a feeble creature, though he's like me in exterior. That's how it is, you perceive ; I don't quite see my way to letting him go on."

" That is of course precisely as you please," said Mr. May, somewhat sharply. He would preserve his dignity even though his heart was sinking; but he could not keep that tone of sharpness out of his voice.

" Of course it is as I please. I'll pay up of course for the second three months, if you choose, fair and square. I meant him to stay, and I'll pay. But that's all. You've no further claim upon me that I know of ; and I must say that for a tutor, a regular coach, to keep girls in his house, daughters, or whatever you choose to call them, is something monstrous. It's a thing no fellow's friends would put up with. It's what I call dishonourable."

" Perhaps," said Mr. May, with all the self-possession he was master of, " you will let your son know at once that he must pack and go. I dare say, Sir Robert can take him, and we will send the portmanteaux. In such a case, it is better there should not be a moment's delay."

" Clarence ! " cried Mr. Copperhead, walking to the door and opening it. " Come along, look sharp, you're to go. I'll

take you with me, do you hear ?   And May will see to sending
you your boxes.   Quick, come along, there's no time to lose."

"Go !" said Clarence, coming in startled, with his eyebrows
rising almost into his hair.   "Go ?   What do you mean ?
Out of the Parsonage ?   The Governor's been having too much
sherry," he said, coming close to Mr. May's arm ; he had himself been taking too much of the sherry, for the good reason
that nobody had taken any notice of what he did, and that he
had foreseen the excitement that was coming.   "You don't
mean it, I know," he added aloud ; "I'll go over for the night
if Sir Robert will have me, and see my mother—"

"Ask May," said Mr. Copperhead, "you'll believe him, I
suppose ; he's as glad to get rid of you as I am to take you
away."

"Is this true ?" cried Clarence, roused and wondering,
"and if so, what's happened ?   I ain't a baby, you know, to
be bundled about from one to another.   The Governor forgets
that."

"Your father," said Mr. May, "chooses to remove you, and
that is all I choose to say."

"But, by George, I can say a deal more," said Mr. Copperhead.   "You simpleton, do you think I am going to leave
you here where there's man-traps about ?   None of such nonsense for me.   Put your things together, I tell you.   Phœbe
Beecham's bad enough at home ; but if she thinks she's to have
you here to pluck at her leisure, she and her friends—"

"W—hew !" said Clarence, with a long whistle.   "So
that's it.   I am very sorry, father, if these are your sentiments ;
but I may as well tell you at once I shan't go."

"You—must go."

"No," he said, squaring his shoulders and putting out his
shirt front ; he had never been roused into rebellion before,
and perhaps without these extra glasses of sherry he would not
have had the courage now.   But what with sherry, and what
with *amour propre*, and what with the thing he called love,
Clarence Copperhead mounted all at once upon a pedestal.
He had a certain dogged obstinacy in him, suspected by nobody
but his mother, who had little enough to say in the guidance
of her boy.   He set himself square like a pugilist, which was
his notion of resistance.   Mr. May looked on with a curious
mixture of feelings.   His own sudden and foolish hope was
over, and what did it matter to him whether the detestable
father or the coarse son should win ?   He turned away from
them with contempt, which was made sharp by their utter uselessness to himself.   Had it been possible that he might have

what he wanted from Mr. Copperhead, his patience would have held out against any trial; but the moment that hope was over, what further interest had he in the question? He went to his writing-table and sat down there, leaving them to fight it out as they would, by themselves. It was no affair of his.

CHAPTER XXXVII.

A PLEASANT EVENING.

THE result, however, was a compromise. Clarence Copperhead went off with his father and Sir Robert to the Hall for the night, but was to return next day, and Phœbe was left in a condition of some excitement behind them, not quite knowing what to think. She was as sure as ever that he had made up his mind to propose; but he had not done it, and what effect his father's visit, and perhaps his mother's entreaties, might have upon him, Phœbe could not tell. The crisis excited her beyond any excitement which she would have thought possible in respect to Clarence Copperhead. She was more like an applicant for office kept uncertain whether she was to have a desirable post or not, than a girl on the eve of a lover's declaration. This was her own conception of the circumstances. She did not dislike Clarence; quite the reverse. She had no sympathy with Ursula's impatience of his heavy vanity. Phœbe had been used to him all her life, and had never thought badly of the heavy boy whom she had been invited to amuse when she was six years old, and whom she had no particular objection to amuse still, let the others wonder at her as they might. Poor Reginald, contemplating bitterly her many little complacencies to his rival, set them down hastily to an appreciation of that rival's worldly advantages, which was not quite a just sentence. It was true, and yet it was not true; other feelings mingled in Phœbe's worldliness. She did, indeed, perceive and esteem highly the advantages which Clarence could give her; but she had not the objections to Clarence himself that the others had. She was willing, quite willing, to undertake the charge of him, to manage, and guide, and make a man of him. And yet, while it was not pure worldliness, much less was it actual love which moved her. It was a kind of habitual affection, as for the "poor thing, but mine own, sir," of the jester. He was but a poor creature, but Phœbe knew she

could make something of him, and she had no distaste to the
task.   When she began to perceive that Reginald, in so many
ways Clarence's superior, was at her disposal, a sense of gratification went through Phœbe's mind, and it certainly occurred
to her that the feeling he might inspire would be a warmer and
a more delightful one than that which would fall to Clarence
Copperhead ; but she was not tempted thereby to throw
Clarence off for the other.   No, she was pleased, and not unwilling to expend a little tender regret and gratitude upon
poor Reginald.   She was ready to be "kind" to him, though
every woman knows that is the last thing she ought to be to a
rejected lover ; and she was full of sympathy for the disappointment which, nevertheless, she fully intended was to be his lot.
This seems paradoxical, but it is no more paradoxical than
human creatures generally are.   On this particular evening
her heart beat very high on account of Clarence, to know if he
would have strength of mind to hold his own against his father,
and if he would come back to her and ask her, as she felt certain he meant to do, that one momentous question.   Her heart
would not have been broken had he not done so, but still she
would have been disappointed.   Notwithstanding when the
evening came, the absence of Clarence was a relief to Phœbe
as well as to the rest of the party, and she gave herself up to
the pleasures of a few hours of half-tender intercourse with
Reginald, with a sense of enjoyment such as she seldom felt.
This was very wrong, there is no denying it, but still so it was.
She was anxious that Clarence should come back to her, and
ask her to be his wife ; and yet she was pleased to be rid of
Clarence, and to give her whole attention and sympathy to
Reginald, trying her best to please him.   It was very wrong ;
and yet such things have happened before, and will again ;
and are as natural, perhaps, as the more absolute and unwaver-
ing passion which has no doubt of its object, passion like Northcote's, who had neither eyes nor ears for anything but Ursula.
The four were alone together that evening, and enjoyed it
thoroughly.   Clarence was away, who, to all but Phœbe, was
an interruption of their intercourse ; and Mr. May was away
in his study, too much absorbed to think of any duties that
ought to have devolved upon him as chaperon ; and even Janey
was out of the way, taking tea with Mrs. Hurst.   So the two
young pairs sat round the table and talked ; the girls, with a
mutual panic, which neither breathed to the other, keeping
together, avoiding separation into pairs.   Ursula out of very
shyness and fright alone, lest another chapter of the strange,
novel, too moving love-tale might be poured into her ears ;

but Phœbe with more settled purpose, to prevent any disclosure on the part of Reginald. The evening was mixed up of pleasure and pain to the two young men, each eager to find himself alone with the girl whom he loved; but it is to be feared the girls themselves had a furtive guilty enjoyment of it, which they ought not to have had. Open and outrageous love-making is not half so delicate a pastime as that in which nothing distinct dare be said, but all is implication, conveyed and understood without words. I know it is a dangerous thing to confess, but veracity requires the confession; you may say it was the playing of the cat with the mouse, if you wish to give a disagreeable version of it; but, however you choose to explain it, this was how it was.

It was with fear and trembling at last that Phœbe went to the piano, which was at the other end of the room, after making all the resistance which was possible.

"Thank Heaven, that idiot and his fiddle aren't here to-night to interfere!" cried Reginald.

Phœbe shook her head at him, but ventured on no words; and how she did exert herself on the piano, playing things which were a great deal too classical for Reginald, who would have preferred the simplest stock piece, under cover of which he might have talked to her hanging over her chair, and making belief to turn over the music! This was what he wanted, poor fellow. He had no heart nor ears for Beethoven, which Phœbe played to him with a tremor in her heart, and yet, the wicked little witch, with some enjoyment too.

"This is not the sort of thing you play when Copperhead is here," he said at last, driven to resistance.

"Oh, we play Mendelssohn," said Phœbe, with much show of innocence; and then she added, "You ought to feel the compliment if I play Beethoven to you."

"So I ought, I suppose," said Reginald. "The truth is, I don't care for music. Don't take your hands off the keys."

"Why, you have done nothing but worry me to play!"

"Not for the music," said Reginald, quite satisfied to have got his will. "Why will you not talk to me and play to me, as I wish?"

"Perhaps, if I knew what you wish—" Phœbe said, in spite of herself.

"Oh, how I should like to tell you! No, not Beethoven; a little, just a little music. Heavens!" cried Reginald, as she crashed into a fortissimo, "another sonata! Listen, I am not equal to sonatas. Nay, Miss Beecham, play me a little nothing—talk to me."

She shook her head at him with a laugh, and went on playing the hardest piece of music she could think of, complicating herself in difficult chords and sudden accidentals. If there had been anybody there to hear who could have understood, Phœbe's performance would, no doubt, have appeared a masterpiece of brilliant execution, as it was; but the two others were paying not the slightest attention, and as for Reginald, he was in a state of tantalized vexation, which half-amused himself, and filled the performer with an exhilarating sense of successful mischief. Northcote was trying to say — what was he not trying to say ?—to Ursula, under cover of the music, which was the best shield he could have had; and perhaps in reality, though Reginald was tantalized to the utmost degree of tantalization, even he had a certain enjoyment in the saucy self-defence which was more mischievous than cruel. He stood behind Phœbe's chair, now and then meeting her laughing glance with one of tender appeal and reproach, pleased to feel himself thus isolated with her, and held an arm's-length in so genial a way. He would have his opportunity after a while, when there would be no piano to give her a momentary refuge, and then he would say out all that was in his heart, with no possible shadow of a rival to interfere with him. Angry ? no ; as he stood behind her, watching her fingers fly over the keys, a delightful calm stole over Reginald. Now and then she would throw a half-mocking glance at him upward over her shoulder, as she swept over the resounding board. When the sonata was concluded, Phœbe sprang up from the piano, and went back to the table. She proposed that they should play a game at cards, to which Ursula agreed. The young men shrugged their shoulders and protested ; but, after all, what did it matter, so long as they were together ? They fell into their places quite naturally, the very cards assisting ; and so the moments flew by. There was not so much sound as usual in the old faded drawing-room, which had come to look so bright and homelike ; not so much sound of voices, perhaps less laughter—yet of all the evenings they had spent there together, that was the one they looked back upon, all four, with most tender recollection. They had been so happy, or, if not happy, so near (apparently) to happiness, which is better sometimes than happiness itself.

"Don't let Reginald come with me," Phœbe whispered, as she kissed her friend, and said good night, "or ask Mr. Northcote to come too."

"Why ? " said Ursula, with dreamy eyes ; her own young tide of life was rising, invading, for the moment, her perceptions, and dulling her sense of what was going on round her.

There was no time, however, for anything more to be said, for Reginald was close behind with his hat in his hand. Phœbe had to resign herself, and she knew what was coming. The only thing was, if possible, to stop the declaration on the way.

"This is the first chance I have had of seeing you home without that perpetual shadow of Copperhead—"

"Ah, poor Clarence!" said Phœbe. "I wonder how he is getting on away from us all to-night."

"Poor Clarence!" echoed Reginald aghast. "You don't mean to say that you—miss him, Miss Beecham? I never heard you speak of him in that tone before."

"Miss him! no, perhaps not exactly," said Phœbe, with a soft little sigh; "but still—I have known him all my life, Mr. May; when we were quite little I used to be sent for to his grand nursery, full of lovely toys and things—a great deal grander than mine."

"And for that reason—" said Reginald, becoming bitter, with a laugh.

"Nothing for that reason," said Phœbe; "but I noticed it at six as I should at twenty. I must have been a horrid little worldly-minded thing, don't you think? So you see there are the associations of a great many years to make me say Poor Clarence, when anything is the matter with him."

"He is lucky to rouse your sympathies so warmly," cried Reginald, thoroughly wretched; "but I did not know there was anything the matter."

"I think there will be if he has to leave our little society, where we have all been so happy," said Phœbe, softly. "How little one thought, coming here a stranger, how pleasant it was to be! I especially, to whom coming to Carlingford was rather—perhaps I might say a humiliation. I am very fond of grandpapa and grandmamma now, but the first introduction was something of a shock—I have never denied it; and if it had not been for sweet kind Ursula and you—all."

The little breathless fragmentary pause which Phœbe made between the *you* and the "all," giving just a ghost of emphasis to the pronoun, sounded to poor Reginald in his foolishness almost like a caress. How cleverly it was managed, with just so much natural feeling in it as gave it reality! They were approaching No. 6, and Martha, the maid, already was visible at the open door.

"Then you do give me some share—some little share," he cried, with a broken voice. "Ah, if you would only let me tell you what your coming has been to me. It has opened up my life; I feel everything different, the old earth itself; there is a new light upon the whole world—"

"Hush, here is Martha!" cried Phœbe, "she will not understand about new lights. Yes, it has been pleasant, very pleasant; when one begins to sigh and realize how pleasant a thing has been, I always fear it is going to be broken up."

"*Absit omen!*" cried Reginald, fervently, taking the hand she had put out to bid him good night, and holding it fast to detain her; and was there moisture in the eyes which she lifted to him, and which glistened, he thought, though there was only the distant light of a lamp to see them by?

"You must not keep me now," cried Phœbe, "here is grandpapa coming. Good night, Mr. May, good night."

Was Phœbe a mere coquette *pure et simple?* As soon as she had got safe within these walls, she stooped down over the primroses to get rid of Martha, and then in the darkness had a cry, all by herself, on one side of the wall, while the young lover, with his head full of her, checked, but not altogether discouraged, went slowly away on the other. She cried, and her heart contracted with a real pang. He was very tender in his reverential homage, very romantic, a true lover, not the kind of man who wants a wife or wants a clever companion to amuse him, and save him the expense of a coach, and be his to refer to in everything. That was an altogether different kind of thing. Phœbe went in with a sense in her mind that perhaps she had never touched so close upon a higher kind of existence, and perhaps never again might have the opportunity; but before she had crossed the garden, she had begun once more to question whether Clarence would have the fortitude to hold his own against everything that father or mother could do to change his mind. Would he have the fortitude? Would he come back to her, safe and determined, or would he yield to arguments in favour of some richer bride, and come back either estranged or at the least doubtful? This gave her a pang of profound anxiety at the bottom of her heart.

CHAPTER XXXVIII.

AN EXPEDITION.

MR. MAY did not come upstairs that evening. It was not that he was paralysed as he had been on the previous occasion, when he sat as now and heard Phœbe go away after her first visit, and when the wind blowing in from the open door playfully carried to his feet the scribbled note with Tozer's name. He was not stupefied as then, nor was he miserable. The threatened withdrawal of Clarence Copperhead was more to him than the impending ruin meant by that bill which was so nearly due. He was occupied by that to the exclusion of the other. It would be a most serious change to him in every way. He had calculated on the continuance of this additional income for at least a year, and short of the year it would have done him no good, but had simply plunged him into additional expense. It was this he was thinking of, and which kept him in his study after the young people had assembled. Cotsdean had come again while Mr. May was at dinner, which by some curious unconscious aggravation on his part was the time he epecially chose as most convenient for him; and he had again sent a dirty note by Bobby, imploring his principal to think of the impending fate, and not to desert him. Mr. May was angry at this perpetual appeal. "Why should I desert him, the idiot?" he said to himself; and moved by the man's persistence, he took out his pocket-book again, and made out beyond all chance of mistake, that it was the 18th. Why should the fool insist upon its being the 15th with such perpetual iteration? There were the figures as plain as possible, 18th April. Mr. May wrote a peremptory note announcing this fact to Cotsdean, and then returned to his own thoughts. Sir Robert had asked him to go over that morning and spend the day at the Hall with the Copperheads, not knowing of any breach between them. He thought he had better do this. If Clarence determined to stay, that would be a great thing in his favour, and he had seen that the young man's dull spirit was roused; and if that hope failed, there might still be advantage even in this sudden breaking of the bond. Part of the second quarter was gone, and the father had offered three months additional pay. These two payments would make up the hundred and fifty pounds at once, and settle the business. Thus, in either way, he should be safe, for if Clarence went away the money would be paid; and if he stayed, Mr. May himself had made up his mind to risk the bold step of going to the bank and asking an advance on this inalienable security. All these deliberations made his mind easy about the bill. It must come right one way or another; he might have chosen perhaps not to run it quite so close; but after all the 15th was only to-morrow, and there were still three days. While his mind was full of these things he did not care to go upstairs. He heard the voices of the young people, but he was too much engrossed with his own calculations to care to join them. It was a close thing, he said to himself, a very close thing; but still he felt that he could do it—surely he could do it. If Mr. Copperhead settled with him—and he was the sort of man, a man to whom money was nothing, to do so on the spot if he took it into his head—then all was right. And if Mr. Copperhead did not do so, the bank, though his past transactions with it had not been encouraging, would certainly make all right on account of these Copperhead payments, which were as certain as any payments could be. He went to bed early, being engrossed by these thoughts, not even saying good-night to Ursula, as was his wont; and he made up his mind to take an early breakfast, and start the first thing in the morning for the Hall. There was an early train which would suit admirably. He could not afford to drive, as Sir Robert had done, changing horses half way. He went upstairs to bed, somewhat heavily, but not discontented, seeing his way. After all, the great thing in life is to see your way. It does not matter so much whether that way is great or small, so long as you can see it plain before you. Mr. May breathed a sigh of anxiety as he ended the day. He had a great many things on his mind; but still he was not altogether heavy-hearted or discouraged beyond measure; things, he felt, would shape themselves better than he had hoped. He was not perhaps going to be so much better off than of old, as he thought possible when Clarence Copperhead came. Such delusive prospects do glimmer across a poor man's path when any apparent expansion of means occurs to him; but in the majority of cases he has to consent to see the fine fictitious glow die away. Mr. May was not ignorant of this experience already. A man who is over fifty is generally more or less prepared for anything that can happen to him in this kind; but he thought he could " get on; " and after all that is the sum of life to three parts of mankind.

He was silent at breakfast, but not disagreeable, and Ursula was too much taken up with her own concerns to pay much attention to him. Ursula's concerns were developing with a rapidity altogether extraordinary. In the mind of a girl of twenty, unforestalled by any previous experience, the process that goes on between the moment when the surprising, overwhelming discovery rushes upon her that some one loves her in the old way of romance, until the corresponding moment when she finds out that her own heart too has been invaded by this wonderful sentiment, which is like nothing that was ever known before, is of a very rapid description. It is like the bursting of a flower, which a day's sunshine brings to the blooming point like a miracle, though it is in reality the simplest result of nature. Already there began to glow a haze of brightness about those three months past in which everything had begun. When or how it began she could not now tell. The glow of it was in her eyes and dazzled her. She heard the voices of the others sounding vaguely through this bright mist in which she herself was isolated; when she was obliged to reply, she called herself back with an effort, and did so—but of her own will she seldom spoke. How Janey chattered, how the children maundered on about their little concerns, which were of consequence to nobody! Papa was the person whom Ursula really respected this morning, for he had more sense than to talk. How could people talk, as if there was pleasure in that? But papa had more sense, he had things to think of —too. So the girl approved her father, and thought more highly of him, and never inquired what it might be that occupied his mind, and kept him from noticing even when the children were unruly. And it would be giving the reader an unfair idea of the children, if we attempted to conceal that they did take advantage of their opportunities, and were as unruly as well-conditioned children in the circumstances were likely to be. Mr. May took no notice; he took his coffee hurriedly and went off to the station.

"If I don't return this evening you need not be alarmed. I shall come back at the latest to-morrow morning," he said.

The children all rushed to the window to see him go away; even Ursula looking out dreamily remarked him too, as she seldom did; and Mrs. Sam Hurst at her window, wondering where her neighbour could be going, heaved a deep sigh of admiration, which though she was not "in love," as the girls thought, with Mr. May, was a passing tribute to his good looks and training. He looked a gentleman every inch of him—an English gentleman, spotless in linen, speckless in broadcloth, though his dress was far from new; the freshness of sound

health and a clear conscience on his handsome face, though he
was no longer young. His abundant hair, steel-grey, slightly
crisped under his hat, not curling exactly, but with a becoming
twist in it—clerical, yet not too clerical, a man given to no
extremes, decorously churchmanlike, yet liberal and tolerant of
the world. Though she was too wise to compromise her own
comfort by marrying him, Mrs. Hurst felt that there was a
great pleasure in making his daughters anxious about her
"intentions," and that even to be said to be in love with such
a man was no shame, but rather the reverse.

He went away accordingly, taking a short cut to the railway,
and thus missing Cotsdean, who came breathless ten minutes
after he was gone, and followed him to the train; but too late.
"Well, well," Cotsdean said to himself, wiping his forehead,
"Old Tozer has plenty, it ain't nothing to him to pay. They
can settle it between 'em."

Cotsdean himself was easier in his mind than he had ever
been before on such an occasion. His clergyman, though personally an awful and respect-inspiring personage, was so far as
money went a man of straw, as he well knew, and his name on
a bill was very little worth; but Tozer was a man who could
pay his way. A hundred and fifty pounds, or even ten times
that, would not ruin the old shopkeeper. Cotsdean's sense of
commercial honour was not so very keen that the dishonour-
ing of his bill in the circumstances should give him a very
serious pang. He would not be sold up, or have an execution
put into his shop when the other party to the bill was so substantial a person. Of course Tozer, when he signed it, must
have been told all about it, and Cotsdean did not see how with
two such allies against ruin, anything very serious could befall
him. He was uneasy indeed, but his uneasiness had no such
force in it as before. He went back to his shop and his business prepared to take the matter as calmly as possible. He
was but passive in it. It could not harm him much in the eyes
of his banker, who knew his affairs too well to be much astonished at any such incident, and Tozer and Mr. May must settle
it between them. It was their affair.

Meanwhile Mr. May rattled along in the railway towards
the Hall. He got a dogcart at the little inn at the station to
take him over, though generally when he went to see the
Dorsets it was his custom to walk. "But what were a few
shillings?" he said to himself, the prodigality of desperation
having seized upon him. In any case he could pay that, and
if he was to be ruined, what did a few shillings more or less
matter? but the discomfort of walking over those muddy

roads, and arriving with dirty boots and a worn-out aspect, mattered a great deal. He reached the Hall at a propitious moment, when Mr. Copperhead was in the highest good-humour. He had been taken over the place, from one end to another, over the stables, the farm-buildings, the farm itself from end to end, the preserves, the shrubberies, the green-houses, everything; all of which details he examined with an unfailing curiosity which would have been highly flattering to the possessors if it had not been neutralized by a strain of comment which was much less satisfactory. When Mr. May went in, he found him in the dining-room, with Sir Robert and his daughters standing by, clapping his wings and crowing loudly over a picture which the Dorsets prized much. It represented a bit of vague Italian scenery, mellow and tranquil, and was a true " Wilson," bought by an uncle of Sir Robert's, who had been a connoisseur, from the Master himself, in the very country where it was painted; and all these details pleased the imagination of the family, who, though probably they would have been but mildly delighted had they possessed the acquaintance of the best of contemporary painters, were proud that Uncle Charles had known Italian Wilson, and had bought a picture out of his studio. A Hobbema or a Poussin would scarcely have pleased them as much, for the worst of an old Master is that your friends look suspiciously upon it as a copy ; whereas Wilson is scarcely old enough or precious enough to be copied. They were showing their picture and telling the story to the millionnaire with an agreeable sense that, though they were not so rich, they must, at least, have the advantage of him in this way.

" Ha !" said Mr. Copperhead, " you should see my Turner. Didn't I show you my Turner ? I don't venture to tell you, Sir Robert, what that picture cost me. It's a sin, it is, to keep that amount of capital hanging useless upon a bit of wall. The Wilson may be all very well. I ain't a judge of art, and I can't give my opinion on that point, though it's a common sort of a name, and there don't seem to be much in it ; but everybody knows what a Turner means. Here's May ; he'll be able to tell you as well as another. It means a few cool thousands, take my word for it. It means, I believe, that heaps of people would give you your own price. I don't call it a profitable investment, for it brings in no interest ; but they tell me it's a thing that grows in value every year. And there it is, Sir, hanging up useless on my wall in Portland Place, costing a fortune, and bringing in not a penny. But I like it; I like it, for I can afford it, by George ! Here's May ; he knows what that sort of thing is; he'll tell you that a Turner is worth its weight in gold."

"Thank you, I don't think I need any information on that subject," said Sir Robert. "Besides, I saw your Turner. It is a pretty picture—if it is authentic; but Wilson, you know—"

"Wasn't a big-enough swell not to be authentic, eh?" said Mr. Copperhead. "Common name enough, and I don't know that I ever heard of him in the way of painting; but I don't pretend to be a judge. Here's May; now, I dare say he knows all about it. Buying's one thing, knowing's another. Your knowing ones, when they've got any money, they have the advantage over us, Sir Robert; they can pick up a thing that's good, when it happens to come their way, dirt cheap; but fortunately for us, it isn't often they've got any money," he added, with a laugh, slapping Mr. May on the shoulder in a way which made him totter. But the clergyman's good-humour was equal even to this assault. It is wonderful how patient and tolerant we can all be when the motive is strong enough.

"That is true," he said; "but I fear I have not even the compensation of knowledge. I know enough, however, to feel that the possessor of a Turner is a public personage, and may be a public benefactor if he pleases."

"How that? If you think I am one to go lending my pictures about, or leaving them to the nation when I'm done for, that's not my sort. No, I keep them to myself. If I consent to have all that money useless, it is for myself, you may depend, and not for other people. And I'll leave it to my boy Clarence, if he behaves himself. He's a curiosity, too, and has a deal of money laid out on him that brings no interest, him and his mother. I'll leave it to Clar, if he doesn't make a low marriage, or any folly of that kind."

"You should make it an heir-loom," said Sir Robert, with sarcasm too fine for his antagonist; "leave it from father to son of your descendants, like our family diamonds and plate."

Anne and Sophy looked at each other and smiled, the one sadly, the other satirically. The Dorset family jewels were rose-diamonds of small value, and the plate was but moderate in quantity, and not very great in quality. Poor Sir Robert liked to blow his little trumpet too, but it was not so blatant as that of his visitor, whose rude senses did not even see the intended malice.

"By George! I think I will," he said. "I'm told it's as safe as the bank, and worth more and more every year, and if it don't bring in anything, it don't eat anything; eh, May? Look here; perhaps I was hasty the other day," he said, pushing the clergyman a little apart from the group with a large hand on his shoulder. "Clarence tells me you're the best coach he ever saw, and that he's getting on like a house on fire."

"He does make progress, I think," answered the tutor, thus gracefully complimented.

"But all the same, you know, I had a right to be annoyed. Now a man of your sense—for you seem a man of sense, though you're a parson, and know what side your bread's buttered on—ought to see that it's an aggravating thing when a young fellow has been sent to a coach for his instruction, and to keep him out of harm's way, to find him cheek by jowl with a nice-looking young woman. That's not what a father has a right to expect."

"You couldn't expect me to do away with my daughter because I happened to take a pupil?" said Mr. May, half-amused; "but I can assure you that she has no designs upon your son."

"So I hear, so I hear," said the other, with a mixture of pique and satisfaction. "Won't look at him, Clar tells me; got her eye on some one else, little fool! She'll never have such a chance again. As for having no designs, that's bosh, you know; all women have designs. I'm a deal easier in my mind when I'm told she's got other fish to fry."

"Other fish to fry?" said Mr. May; this time he was wholly amused, and laughed. "This is news to me. However, we don't want to discuss my little Ursula; about your son it will be well that I should know, for I might be forming other engagements. This moment is a time of pecuniary pressure with me," he added, with the ingratiating smile and half-pathetic frankness of the would-be borrower. "I have not taken pupils before, but I want money for the time. My son's settlement in life, you see, and—but the father of a large family can always find good reasons for wanting money."

"That's it," said Mr. Copperhead, seriously. "Why are you the father of a large family? That's what I ask our ministers. It's against all political economy, that is. According as you've no money to give 'em, you go and have children—when it should be just the other way."

"That may be very true; but there they are, and can't be done away with; and I do want money, as it happens, more now than I shall want it a year hence, or, perhaps, even six months hence."

"Most people do," said Mr. Copperhead, withdrawing his hand from his pocket, and placing his elbow tightly against the orifice of that very important part of him. "It's the com-

monest thing in the world. I want money myself, for that matter.
I've always got a large amount to make up by a certain date,
and a bill to pay. But about Clar, that's the important matter.
As he seems to have set his mind on it, and as you assure me
there's no danger—man-traps, or that sort of thing, eh ? "

The colour came to Mr. May's cheek ; but it was only for a
moment. To have his own daughter spoken of as a man-trap
gave him a momentary thrill of anger ; but, as he would have
applied the word quite composedly to any other man's daughter,
the resentment was evanescent. He did not trust himself to
answer, however, but nodded somewhat impatiently, which made
the millionnaire laugh the more.

"Don't like the man-trap ? " he said. " Bless you, they're all
alike, not yours more than the rest. But as I was saying, if
it's warranted safe I suppose he'll have to stay. But I don't
stand any nonsense, May ; and look here, your music and all
that ain't in the agreement. He can have a master for his
music, he's well enough able to pay for it ; but I won't have a
mistress, by George, to put folly into his head."

" I am to forbid him the drawing-room, I suppose, and take
his fiddle from him ! I have no objections. Between ourselves,
as I am not musical, it would be very agreeable to me ; but
perhaps he is rather over the age, don't you think, for treat-
ment of that kind ? "

Clarence had come in, and stood watching the conversation,
with a look Mr. Copperhead was not prepared for. Those
mild brown eyes, which were his mother's share in him, were
full a-stare with sullen resolution, and his heavy mouth shut
like that of a bull-dog. He lingered at the door, looking at
the conversation which was going on between his father and his
tutor, and they both noticed him at the same moment, and
drew the same conclusion. Mr. May was in possession of the
parole, as the French say, and he added instinctively in an
under-tone,

" Take care ; if I were you I would not try him too far."

Mr. Copperhead said nothing ; but he stared too, rather
aghast at this new revelation. What ! his porcelain, his Dresden figure of a son, his crowning curiosity, was *he* going to show
a will of his own ? The despot felt a thrill go over him. What
kind of a sentiment love was in his mind it would be hard to
tell ; but his pride was all set on this heavy boy. To see him
a man of note, in Parliament, his name in the papers, his
speeches printed in the "Times," was the very heaven of his
expectations. " Son of the famous Copperhead, the great contractor." He did not care about such distinction in his own

person; but this had been his dream ever since Clarence came into being. And now there he stood gloomy, obdurate. If he had made up his mind to make a low marriage, could his father hinder him—could anything hinder him? Mr. Copperhead looked at his son and quailed for the first time in his life.

" May," he said, hurriedly, " do the best you can ; he's got all his mother's d——d obstinacy, you can see, can't you ? but I've set my heart on making a man of him—do the best you can."

Mr. May thought to himself afterwards if he had only had the vigour to say, " Pay me six months in advance," the thing would have been done. But the lingering prejudices of breeding clung about him, and he could not do it. Mr. Copperhead, however, was very friendly all the rest of the day, and gave him private looks and words aside, to the great admiration of the Dorsets, to whom the alliance between them appeared remarkable enough.

CHAPTER. XXXIX.

A CATASTROPHE.

Mr. May left the Hall before dinner, notwithstanding the warm invitation which was given to him to stay. He was rather restless, and though it was hard to go out into the dark just as grateful odours began to steal through the house, it suited him better to do so than to spend the night away from home. Besides, he comforted himself that Sir Robert's cook was not first-rate, not good enough to make it a great temptation. It was a long walk to the station, for they had no horses at liberty to drive him, a fact at which he was slightly offended, though he was aware that Sir Robert's stable was but a poor one. He set out just as the dressing-bell began to ring, fortified with a glass of sherry and a biscuit. The night was mild and soft, the hedgerows all rustling with the new life of the spring, and the stars beginning to come out as he went on ; and on the whole the walk was pleasant, though the roads were somewhat muddy. As he went along, he felt himself fall into a curious dreamy state of mind, which was partly fatigue perhaps, but was not at all unpleasant. Sometimes he almost seemed to himself to be asleep as he trudged on, and woke up with a start, thinking that he saw indistinct figures, the skirt of a dress or the tail of a long coat, disappearing past him, just gone before he was fully awake to what it was. He knew there was no one on the lonely road, and that this was a dream or illusion, but still he kept seeing these vanishings of indistinct wayfarers, which did not frighten him in the least, but half-amused him in the curious state of his brain. He had got rid of his anxiety. It was all quite plain before him what to do,—to go to the Bank, to tell them what he had coming in, and to settle everything as easily as possible. The consciousness of having this to do acted upon him like a gentle opiate or dream-charm. When he got to the railway station, and got into a carriage, he seemed to be float-ing somehow in a prolonged vision of light and streaks of darkness, not quite aware how far he was going, or where he was going, across the country ; and even when he arrived at Carlingford he roused himself with difficulty, not quite certain that he had to get out; then he smiled at himself, seeing the gas-lights in a sort of vague glimmer about him, not uncomfortable, but misty and half-asleep. "If Sir Robert's sherry had been better, I should have blamed that," he said to himself; and in fact it was a kind of drowsy, amiable mental intoxication which affected him, he scarcely could tell how. When he got within sight of his own house, he paused a moment and looked up at the lights in the windows. There was music going on; Phœbe, no doubt, for Ursula could not play so well as that, and the house looked full and cheerful. He had a cheerful home, there was no doubt of that. Young Copperhead, though he was a dunce, felt it, and showed an appreciation of better things in his determination not to leave the house where he had been so happy. Mr. May felt an amiable friendliness stealing over him for Clarence too.

Upstairs in the drawing-room another idyllic evening had begun. Phœbe "had not intended to come," but was there notwithstanding, persuaded by Ursula, who, glad for once to escape from the anxieties of dinner, had celebrated tea with the children, to their great delight, though she was still too dreamy and pre-occupied to respond much to them. And Northcote had "not intended to come." Indeed, he had gone further than this, he had intended to keep away. But when he had eaten his solitary dinner, he, too, had strayed towards the centre of attraction, and walking up and down in forlorn con-templation of the lighted windows, had been spied by Regi-nald, and brought in after a faint resistance. So the four were together again, with only Janey to interpose an edge of general criticism and remark into the too personal strain of the con-versation. Janey did not quite realize the importance of the place she was occupying, but she was keenly interested in all that was going on, very eager to understand the relationships in which the others stood, and to see for herself what progress had been made last night while she was absent. Her sharp girlish face, in which the eyes seemed too big for the features, expressed a totally different phase of existence from that which softened and subdued the others. She was all eyes and ears, and watchful scrutiny. It was she who prevented the utterance of the half-dozen words trembling on Northcote's lips, to which Ursula had a soft response fluttering somewhere in her pretty throat, but which was not destined to be spoken tonight; and it was she who made Phœbe's music quite a simple performance, attended with little excitement and no danger. Phœbe was the only one who was grateful to her, and perhaps even Phœbe could have enjoyed the agitations of the evening better had Janey been away. As it was, these agitations were all suppressed and incipient; they could not come to anything; there were no hairbreadth escapes, no breathless moments, when the one pursued had to exercise her best skill, and only eluded the pursuer by a step or two. Janey, with all her senses about her, hearing everything, seeing everything, neutralized all effort on the part of the lovers, and reduced the condition of Ursula and Phœbe to one of absolute safety. They were all kept on the curb, in the leash, by the presence of this youthful observer; and the evening, though full of a certain excitement and mixture of happiness and misery, glided on but slowly, each of the young men outdoing the other in a savage eagerness for Janey's bed-time.

"Do you let her sit up till midnight every night?" said Reginald, with indignation.

"Let me sit up!" cried Janey, "as if I was obliged to do what she tells me!"

Ursula gave a little shrug to her pretty shoulders, and looked at the clock.

"It is not midnight yet; it is not nine o'clock," she said, with a sigh. "I should have thought papa would have come home before now. Can he be staying at the Hall all night?"

Just then, however, there was the well-known ring at the bell, and Ursula ran downstairs to see after her father's supper. Why couldn't Janey make herself useful and do that, the little company thought indignantly and with one accord, instead of staying here with her sharp eyes, putting everybody out? Mr. May's little dinner, or supper, served on a tray, was very comfortable, and he ate it with great satisfaction, telling Ursula that he had, on the whole, spent a pleasant day.

"The Dorsets were kind, as they always are, and Mr. Copperhead was a little less disagreeable than he always is; and you may look for Clarence back again in a day or two. He is not going to leave us. You must take care that he does not fall in love with you, Ursula. That is the chief thing they seem to be afraid of."

"Fall in love with *me!*" cried Ursula. "Oh, papa, where are your eyes? He has fallen in love, but not with me. Can't you see it? It is Phœbe he cares for."

Mr. May was startled. He raised his head with a curious smile in his eyes, which made Ursula wonder painfully whether her father had taken much wine at the Hall.

"Ah, ha! is that what they are frightened for?" he said, and then he shrugged his shoulders. "She will show bad taste, Ursula; she might do better; but I suppose a girl of her class has not the delicacy—So that is what they are frightened for! And what are the other fish *you* have to fry?"

"Papa!"

"Yes. He told me he was not alarmed about you; that you had other fish to fry, eh! Well, it's too late for explanations to-night. What's that? Very odd, I thought I saw some one going out at the door—just a whiff of the coat-tails. I think my digestion must be out of order. I'll go into the study and get my pills, and then I think I'll go to bed."

"Won't you come upstairs to the drawing-room?" said Ursula, faltering, for she was appalled by the idea of explanations. What had she to explain, as yet? Mr. May shook his head, with that smile still upon his face.

"No, you'll get on excellently well without me. I've had a long walk, and I think I'll go to bed."

"You don't look very well, papa."

"Oh, yes, I'm well enough; only confused in the head a little with fatigue and the things I've had to think about. Good-night. Don't keep those young fellows late, though one of them is your brother. You can say I'm tired. Good-night, my dear."

It was very seldom that he called her "my dear," or, indeed, said anything affectionate to his grown-up children. If Ursula had not been so eager to return to the drawing-room, and so sure that "they" would miss her, she would have been anxious about her father; but as it was, she ran upstairs lightly when he stopped speaking, and left him going into the study, where already his lamp was burning. Betsy passed her as she ran up the stairs, coming from the kitchen with a letter held between two folds of her apron. Poor papa! no doubt it was some tiresome parish business to bother him, when he was tired already. But Ursula did not stop for that. How she wanted to be there

again, among " them all," even though Janey still made one !
She went in breathless, and gave her father's message only half-
articulately. He was tired. " We are never to mind ; he says
so." They all took the intimation very easily. Mr. May being
tired, what did that matter ? He would, no doubt, be better
to-morrow; and in the mean time those sweet hours, though
so hampered by Janey, were very sweet.

Betsy went in, and put down the note before Mr. May on
his table. He was just taking out his medicine from the
drawer, and he made a wry face at the note and at the pills
together.

" Parish ? " he said, curtly.

" No, sir ; it's from Mr. Cotsdean. He came this morning,
after you'd gone, and he sent over little Bobby."

" That will do."

A presentiment of pain stole over him. He gave Betsy a
nod of dismissal, and went on with what he was doing. After
he had finished, he took up the little note from the table with
a look of disgust. It was badly scrawled, badly folded, and
dirty. Thank Heaven, Cotsdean's communications would soon
be over now.

Janey had proposed a round game upstairs. They were all
humble in their desire to conciliate that young despot. Reginald got the cards, and Northcote put chairs round the table.
He placed Ursula next to himself, which was a consolation, and
sat down by her, close to her, though not a word, except of the
most commonplace kind, could be said.

Just then—what was it ? an indescribable thrill through the
house, the sound of a heavy fall. They all started up from
their seats to hear what it was. Then Ursula, with a cry of
apprehension, rushed downstairs, and the others after her.
Betsy, alarmed, had come out of the kitchen, followed by her
assistant, and was standing frightened, but irresolute ; for Mr.
May was not a man to be disturbed with impunity. And this
might be nothing—the falling of a chair or a table, and nothing
more.

" What is it ? " cried Ursula, in an anxious whisper.

She was the leader in the emergency, for even Reginald held
back. Then, after a moment's pause, she opened the door, and
with a little cry rushed in. It was, as they feared, Mr. May
who had fallen ; but he had so far recovered himself as to be
able to make efforts to rise. His face was towards them.
It was very pale, of a livid colour, and covered with moisture,
great beads standing on his forehead. He smiled vaguely when
he saw the circle of faces.

"Nothing—nothing—a faintness," he faltered, making again an effort to rise.

"What is it, papa? Oh, what's the matter?" cried Janey, rushing at him and seizing him by the arm. "Get up! get up! what will people think? Oh, Ursula, how queer he looks, and he feels so heavy. Oh, please get up, papa!"

"Go away," said Mr. May, "go away. It is—a faintness. I am very well where I am—"

But he did not resist when Reginald and Northcote lifted him from the floor. He had a piece of paper tightly clasped in his hand. He gave them a strange suspicious look all round, and shrank when his eyes fell upon Phœbe. "Don't let her know," he said. "Take me away, take me away."

"Reginald will take you upstairs, papa—to your room—to bed; you ought to go to bed. It is the long walk that has worn you out. Oh, Reginald, don't contradict him, let him go where he pleases. Oh, papa, where *are* you going?" cried Ursula, "the other way; you want to go to bed."

"This way, take me—somewhere," said the sufferer; though he could not stand he made a step, staggering between them, and an effort to push towards the hall door, and when they directed him in the other direction to the staircase which led to his room, he struggled feebly yet violently with them. "No, no, no, not there!" he cried. The sudden confusion, dismay, and alarm into which the family was plunged, the strange sense of a catastrophe that came upon them, cannot be told. Ursula, calling out all the time that they were not to contradict him, insisted imperiously with words and gestures that he should be taken upstairs. Janey, altogether overcome, sat down on the lower steps of the staircase and cried. Reginald almost as pale as his father, and not saying a word, urged him towards the stairs. To get him up to his room, resisting as well as he could, and moaning inarticulate remonstrances all the way, was no easy business. As the procession toiled along Phœbe was left below, the only one in possession of her faculties. She sent the housemaid hurriedly off for the doctor, and despatched Betsy to the kitchen.

"Hot water is always wanted," said Phœbe; "see that you have enough in case he should require a bath."

Then with her usual decision she stepped back into the study. It was not vulgar curiosity which was in Phœbe's mind, nor did it occur to her that she had no right to investigate Mr. May's private affairs. If she could find what had done it, would not that be a great matter, something to tell the doctor, to throw light on so mysterious a seizure? Several bits of torn paper were lying on the floor; but only one of these was big enough to contain any information. It was torn in a kind of triangular shape, and contained a corner of a letter, a section of three lines,

> "must have mistaken the date
> presented to-day,
> paid by Tozer,"

was what she read. She could not believe her eyes. What transactions could there be between her grandfather and Mr. May? She secured the scrap of paper, furtively putting it into her pocket. It was better to say nothing either to the doctor, or any one else, of anything so utterly incomprehensible. It oppressed Phœbe with a sense of mystery and of personal connection with the mystery, which even her self-possession could scarcely bear up against. She went into the kitchen after Betsy, avowedly in anxious concern for the boiling of the kettle.

"Hot water is good for everything," said Phœbe; "mamma says a hot bath is the best of remedies. Did Mr. May have anything—to worry him, Betsy? I suppose it is only fatigue, and that he has taken too long a walk."

"I don't believe in the long walk, Miss," said Betsy, "it's that Cotsdean as is always a-tormenting with his dirty letters. When that man comes bothering here, master is always put out."

"Cotsdean? I don't know the name."

"Don't say nothing, Miss," said Betsy, sinking her voice, "but you take my word it's money. Money's at the bottom of everything. It's something, as sure as you're alive, as master has got to pay. I've been a deal with gentlefolks," added Betsy, "and ne'er a one of them can abide that."

CHAPTER XL.

THE SINNED-AGAINST.

PHŒBE'S mind was full of many and somewhat agitating thoughts. She went upstairs with a restless haste, which she would have been the first to condemn, to the room where the others were congregated, when they had laid Mr. May on his bed with no small difficulty, and were now consulting what to do. Ursula had fallen a little from the position of command

she had taken up. To get him to bed, to send for the doctor,
these were evident practical steps to take; but after having
done these she was bewildered and fell back upon her advisers.

"We can't do anything, we can only wait and watch him,"
Reginald was saying, as Phœbe, herself unseen, looked in at
the anxious party; and without asking any question she turned
and went downstairs again, and hastily putting on her shawl
and hat, went out, shutting the door softly, and ran home on
the shady side of Grange Lane, where nobody could see her.
It was a very quiet road, and she was not disturbed by any unreasonable alarms. It was still early when she got home,
earlier than usual, and her intention was not to stay there at
all, but to go back again and offer her assistance to Ursula,
for whom she had left a message to this effect. Phœbe was
full of genuine regard and friendliness towards the Mays.

She felt that she had obligations to all of them, to the
parson-father for submitting to her presence, nay, encouraging
it, and to Ursula for receiving her with that affectionate fervour of friendship which had completely changed the tenor of
Phœbe's life at Carlingford. She was obliged to them, and
she knew that she was obliged to them. How different these
three months would have been but for the Parsonage ; what a
heavy leaden-coloured existence without variety and without
interest she must have lived ; whereas it had gone by like a
summer day, full of real life, of multiplied interests, of everything that it was most desirable to have. Not at home and in
London could she have had the advantages she had enjoyed
here. Phœbe was sensible enough—or perhaps we might use
a less complimentary word—worldly enough, to count within
those manifest benefits the advantage of seeing more of Clarence
Copperhead, and of drawing him within the charmed circle of
her influence, and she was grateful to the Mays, for this was
their doing. And then, on the other hand, quite a different
thing, her heart was touched and softened with gratitude to
Reginald for loving her ; of all her gratitudes, perhaps this indeed was the most truly felt. They had given her unbounded
kindness, friendliness, everything that is most sweet to the
solitary ; and over and above, as if these were not enough, they
had made her the exquisite present of a heart, the best thing
that can be given or received by man. Phœbe felt herself
penetrated with gratitude for all this, and she resolved that, if
anything she could do could benefit the Mays, the effort on her
part should not be wanting. "Paid by Tozer." What had been
paid by Tozer ? What had her grandfather to do with it. Could
it be he who had lent money to Mr. May ? Then Phœbe re-

solved, with a glow on her face, he should forgive his debtors.
She went in with her mind fully made up, whatever might
happen, to be the champion of the sufferer, the saviour of the
family. This would show them that their kindness had been
appreciated. This would prove even to Reginald that, though
she would not sacrifice her own prospects by marrying him,
yet that she was grateful to him, to the bottom of her heart. Her
mind was full of generous ardour as she went in. She knew
her power; her grandfather had never yet refused her anything, never resisted her, and it did not seem likely that he
should begin now.

Mrs. Tozer was by herself in the parlour, dozing over the
fire. She woke up with a little start when Phœbe came in
and smiled at the sight of her.

"I didn't expect as you'd have come so soon," she said;
"you've broke up early to-night, darling. Couldn't you have
no music? I didn't look for you for an hour or more."

"You know, grandmamma, it is Mr. Copperhead who teases
me most for music, and he is not here."

"Yes, yes, *I* know," said the old lady, nodding her head
with many smiles. "I know a deal more about it than you
think for, Phœbe, and don't you think as I disapprove, for it's
quite the other way. But you won't tell me as there ain't
others as cares for music as well as young Copperhead. I've seen
one as couldn't take his eyes off of you while you were playing."

"Hush, grandmamma; the others like music for music's
sake, or perhaps for my sake; but Mr Copperhead likes it for
his own sake, and therefore he is the one who insists upon it.
But this is not the reason why I have come home so soon.
Mr. May has been taken suddenly ill."

"Lord bless us!" cried Mrs. Tozer, "deary, deary me!
I'm very sorry, poor gentleman, I hope it ain't anything
serious. Though he's a church parson, he's a very civil-
spoken man, and I see his children drag him into his own house
one day as me and Tozer was passing. I said to Tozer at the
time, you take my word, whatever folks say, a man as lets his
children pull him about like that ain't a bad one. And so he's
ill, poor man! Is there anything as we can do to help, my
dear? They ain't rich, and they've been as kind to you as if
you'd been one of their own."

"I thought that would be the first thing you would ask me,"
said Phœbe gratefully, giving her a kiss—"dear grandmamma,
it is like your kind heart—and I ran off to see that you were
quite well and comfortable, thinking perhaps if you did not want
me I might go back to poor Ursula for the night."

To hear her granddaughter call Miss May by her Christian name was in itself a pleasure to Mrs. Tozer. She gave Phœbe a hug. "So you shall, my darling, and as for a bottle of good wine or that, anything as is in the house, you know you're welcome to it. You go and talk to your grandfather; I'm as comfortable as I can be, and if you'd like to run back to that poor child—"

"Not before you are in bed," said Phœbe, "but if you please I'll go and talk to grandpapa as you said. There are things in which a man may be of use."

"To be sure," said Mrs. Tozer, doubtfully; "your grand-father ain't a man as is much good in sickness; but I won't say as there ain't some things—"

"Yes, grandmamma, I'll take your advice and run and talk to him; and by the time I come back you will be ready for bed."

"Do, my dear," said Mrs. Tozer. She was very comfortable, and did not care to move just then, and, as Phœbe went away, looked after her with dreamy satisfaction. "Bless her! there ain't her match in Carlingford, and the gentlefolks sees it," said Mrs. Tozer to herself. But she had no idea how Phœbe's heart was beating as she went along the dimly-lighted passage, which led to a small room fitted up by Tozer for himself. She heard voices in earnest talk as she approached, but this made her only the more eager to go in, and see for herself what was going on. There could be no doubt, she felt sure of it, that the discussion here had some connection with the calamity *there*. What it was she had not the slightest idea; but that somehow the two were connected she felt certain. The voices were loud as she approached the door.

"I'll find out who done it, and I'll punish him—as sure as that's my name, though I never put it on that there paper," Tozer was saying. Phœbe opened the door boldly, and went in. She had never seen her grandfather look so unlike himself. The knot of the big white neckerchief round his neck was pushed away, his eyes were red, giving out strange lights of passion. He was standing in front of the fireplace gesticulating wildly. Though it was now April and the weather very mild and genial, there were still fires in the Tozer sitting-rooms, and as the windows were carefully shut, Phœbe felt the atmosphere stifling. The other person in the room was a serious, large man, whom she had already seen more than once; one of the chief clerks in the bank where Tozer kept his account, who had an old acquaintance with the butterman, and who was in the habit of coming when the bank had anything to say to so sure a customer about rates of investment or the value of money. He was seated at one side of the fire, looking very grave and shaking his head as the other spoke.

"That is very true, and I don't say anything against it. But, Mr. Tozer, I can't help thinking there's some one else in it than Cotsdean."

"What one else? what is the good of coming here to me with a pack of nonsense? He's a poor needy creature as hasn't a penny to bless himself with, a lot of children, and a wife as drinks. Don't talk to me of some one else That's the sort of man as does all the mischief. What, Phœbe! run away to your grandmother, I don't want you here."

"I am very sorry to interrupt you, grandpapa. Mayn't I stay? I have something to say to you—"

Tozer turned round and looked at her eagerly. Partly his own fancy, and partly his wife's more enlightened observations, had made him aware that it was possible that Phœbe might one day have something very interesting to reveal. So her words roused him even in the midst of his pre-occupation. He looked at her for a second, then he waved his hand and said,

"I'm busy; go away, my dear, go away; I can't talk to you now."

Phœbe gave the visitor a look which perplexed him; but which meant, if he could but have read it, an earnest entreaty to him to go away. She said to herself, impatiently, that he would have understood had he been a woman; but as it was he only stared with lack-lustre eyes. What was she to do?

"Grandpapa," she said, decisively, "it is too late for business to-night. However urgent it may be, you can't do anything to-night. Why, it is nearly ten o'clock, and most people are going to bed. See Mr.——, I mean this gentleman—to-morrow morning the first thing; for you know, however anxious you may be, you can't do anything to-night."

"That is true enough," he said, looking with staring eyes from her to his visitor, "and more's the pity. What had to be done should ha' been done to-day. It should have been done to-day, sir, on the spot, not left over night like this, to give the villain time to get away. It's a crime, Phœbe, that's what it is—that's the fact. It's a crime."

"Well, grandpapa, I am very sorry; but it will not mend matters, will it, if sitting up like this, and agitating yourself like this, makes you ill? That will not do away with the crime. It is bed-time, and poor grandmamma is dozing, and wondering what has become of you. Grandpapa——"

"Phœbe, go away, it ain't none of your business; you're

only a bit of a girl, and how can you understand? If you think I'm going to sit down with it like an old fool, lose my money, and what is worse nor my money, let my very name be forged before my eyes—"

Phœbe gave so perceptible a start that Tozer stopped short, and even the banking-clerk looked at her with aroused curiosity. "Forged!" she cried, with a gasp of dismay; "is it so bad as that?" She had never been more near betraying herself, showing a personal interest more close than was natural. When she saw the risk she was running, she stopped short and summoned all her energies. "I thought some one had pilfered something," she said with an attempt at a laugh. "I beg your pardon, grandpapa; but anyhow what can you do to-night? You are keeping—this gentleman—and yourself out of bed. Please put it off till to-morrow."

"I think so too," said the banker's clerk. "I'll come to you in the morning as I go to the Bank. Perhaps I may have been wrong; but I think there's more in it than meets the eye. To-morrow we can have the man Cotsdean up and question him."

"After he's had time to take himself off," said Tozer, vehemently. "You take my word he ain't in Carlingford, not now, let alone to-morrow."

"Then that shows," said Phœbe, quietly, "that it is of no use making yourself ill to-night. Grandpapa, let this gentleman go—he wants to go; and I have something to say to you. You can do anything that is necessary to-morrow."

"I think so indeed," said Mr. Simpson, of the Bank, getting up at last, "the young lady is quite right. We can't act hastily in a thing like this. Cotsdean's a man of good character, Mr. Tozer; all that has to be taken into account—and he is not a beggar. If he has done it, we can recover something at least; but if he has been taken advantage of—I think the young lady is a good counsellor, and that it's much the best to wait till to-morrow."

Phœbe seized upon her grandfather's arm to restrain him, and held him back. "Good-night," she said; "grandpapa, stay with me, I have something to say to you. Listen; you don't think me very silly, do you, grandpapa dear?"

"Silly!" he said, listening to the steps of the departing visitor as they receded along the passage. "What has a chit like you to do with business? I tell you it'll kill me. Me a-signing of accommodation bills for a bit of a small shopkeeper like that Cotsdean! I tell you it'll make an end of me, that will, unless I gets my money and clears myself afore the world. And here you've been and sent away Simpson, and who's to manage for me? I ain't a lawyer to know what to do. Get away, get away, and leave me to myself, I can't be disturbed with women-folks when I've got real business in hand."

"I'll manage for you," said Phœbe; "you need not stare at me like that, grandpapa—"

"Go out o' the room this moment, Miss!" he cried furious; "you! here's a sort of thing for me to put up with. Sam Tozer wasn't born yesterday that a bit of an impudent girl should take upon her to do for him. Manage for me! go out o' my sight; I'm a fool, am I, and in my dotage to have a pack of women meddling in my affairs?"

Phœbe had never met with such an outburst of coarse anger in her life before, and it gave her a shock, as such assaults naturally do to people brought up softly, and used to nothing but kindness. For a moment she wavered, doubtful whether she should not proudly abandon him and his affairs altogether; but this was to abandon her friends too. She mastered herself accordingly, and the resentment which she could not help feeling—and stood pale but quiet opposite to the infuriated old man. His grey eyes seemed to give out sparks of fire. His hair bristled up on his head like the coat of a wild animal enraged. He went up and down on the hearth-rug like the same animal in a cage, shaking his fist at some imaginary culprit.

"Once I get him, see if I let him go," he cried, his voice thick with fast-coming words and the foam of fury. "Let the bank do as it likes; I'll have him, I will. I'll see justice on the man as has dared to make free with my name. It ain't nothing to you, my name; but I've kep' it honest, and out of folk's mouths, and see if I'll stand disgrace thrown on it now. A bill on me as never had such a thing, not when I was struggling to get on! Dash him! damn him!" cried the old man, transported with rage. When he had come to this unusual and terrible length, Tozer paused dismayed. He had lost his temper before in his life; but very seldom had he been betrayed into anything so desperate as this. He stopped aghast, and cast a half-frightened look at Phœbe, who stood there so quiet, subdued out of her usual force, pale and disapproving—his own grandchild, a pastor's daughter! and he had forgotten himself thus before her. He blushed hotly, though he was not used to blushing, and stopped all at once. After such frightful language, so unbecoming a deacon of Salem, so unlike a consistent member of the connection, what could he say?

"Grandpapa," said Phœbe softly, "it is not good to be so angry; you are made to say things you are sorry for. Will you listen to me now? Though you don't think it, and perhaps won't believe it, I have found out something quite by chance—"

He went up to her and clutched her by the arm. "Then what are you a-standing there for, like a figure in stone? Can't you out with it, and ease my mind? Out with it, I tell you! Do you want to drive me out of my senses?"

He was so much excited that he shook her in the hot paroxysm of returning rage. Phœbe was not frightened, but indignation made her pale. She stood without flinching, and looked at him, till poor old Tozer let go his hold, and dropping into a chair, covered his face with his hands. She was too generous to take advantage of him, but went on quietly, as if nothing had occurred.

"Grandpapa, as I tell you, I have found out something by chance that has to do with the thing that troubles you; but I don't know quite what it is. Tell me first, and then—is this the thing?" said Phœbe, curiously, taking up a slip of paper from the table, a stamped piece of paper, in a handwriting which seemed horribly familiar to her, and yet strange. Tozer nodded at her gloomily, holding his head between his hands, and Phœbe read over the first few words before her with an aching heart, and eyes that seemed to ache in sympathy. Only a few words, but what evidence of guilt, what pitiful misery in them! She did not even think so much of the name on the back, which was and was not her grandfather's name. The rest of the bill was written in a hand disguised and changed; but she had seen a great deal of similar writing lately, and she recognized it with a sickening at her heart. In the kind of fatherly flirtation which had been innocently carried on between Phœbe and her friend's father, various productions of his in manuscript had been given to her to read. She was said, in the pleasant social jokes of the party, to be more skilled in interpreting Mr. May's handwriting than any of his family. She stood and gazed at the paper, and her eyes filled with tears of pain and pity. The openness of this self-betrayal, veiled as it was with a shadow of disguise which could deceive no one who knew him, went to Phœbe's heart. What could he have done it for? Mere money, the foolish expenses of every day, or, what would be more respectable, some vague mysterious claim upon him, which might make desperate expedients necessary? She stood, temporarily stupefied, with her eyes full, looking at that pitiful, terrible, guilty bit of paper, stupefied by the sudden realization of her sudden guess at the truth—though, indeed, the truth was so much more guilty and appalling than any guess of hers.

" Well," said Tozer, "you've seen it, and now what do you think of it? That's my name, mind you, my name! I hope the Almighty will grant me patience. Stuck on to what they calls a kite, an accommodation bill. What do you think of that, Miss Phœbe? A-a-ah! if I had hold of him—if I had him under my fists—if I had him by the scruff of the neck!"

" Grandpapa, doesn't it say in the Bible we are to forgive when harm is done to us?"

Phœbe had begun to tremble all over; for the first time she doubted her own power.

He got up again, and began to prowl about the table, round and round, with the same wild look in his eyes.

" I am not one as would go again' Scripture," he said, gloomily; " but that's a spiritual meaning as you're too young to enter into. You don't suppose as Scripture would approve of crime, or let them escape as had wronged their fellow-creatures? There wouldn't be no business, no justice, no trade, on such a rule as that."

" But, grandpapa—"

" Don't you but me. You've seen me in good spirits and good temper, Phœbe, my girl; but you don't know old Sam Tozer when his spirit's up. D—— him!" cried the old man, striking his hand violently on the table; "and you may tell your father, as is a Minister, that I said so. The Bible's spiritual; but there's trade, and there's justice. A man ain't clear of what he's done because you forgive him. What's the law for else? Forgive! You may forgive him as fast as you like, but he's got to be punished all the same."

" But not by you."

" By the law!" cried Tozer. His inflamed eyes seemed to glare upon her, his rough grey hair bristled on his head, a hot redness spread across his face beneath his fiery eyes, which seemed to scorch the cheek with angry flames. " The law that ain't a individual. That's for our protection, whether we like it or not. What's that got to do with forgiving? Now, looking at it in a public way, I ain't got no right to forgive."

" Grandpapa, you have always been so kind, always so good to everybody. I have heard of so many things you have done—"

" That is all very well," said Tozer, not without a certain gloomy complacence, "so long as you don't touch me. But the moment as you touches me, I'm another man. That's what I can't bear, nor I won't. Them as tries their tricks upon me shan't be let off, neither for wife nor child; and don't you think, my girl, though you're Phœbe, junior, that you are a-going for to come over me."

Phœbe could not but shiver in her fright and agitation; but distressed and excited as she was, she found means to take a step which was important indeed, though at the moment she did not fully realize its importance, and did it by instinct only. She had a handkerchief in her hand, and almost without consciousness of what she was doing, she crushed up the miserable bit of paper, which was the cause of so much evil and misery, in its folds. He was far too impassioned and excited to observe such a simple proceeding. It was the suggestion of a moment, carried out in another moment like a flash of lightning. And as soon as she had done this, and perceived what she had done, fortitude and comfort came back to Phœbe's soul.

"You will not hear what I have found out, and now I do not choose to tell you, grandpapa," she said, with an air of offence. "Unless you wish to be ill, you will do much better to go to bed. It is your usual hour, and I am going to grandmamma. Say good-night, please. I am going out again to stay all night. Mr. May is ill, and I ought to help poor Ursula."

"You go a deal after them Mays," said Tozer, with a cloud over his face.

"Yes. I wonder whom else I should go after? Who has been kind to me in Carlingford except the Mays? Nobody. Who has asked me to go to their house, and share everything that is pleasant in it? None of your Salem people, grandpapa. I hope I am not ungrateful, and whatever happens, or whatever trouble they are in," cried Phœbe, fervently, "I shall stand up for them through thick and thin, wherever I go."

The old man looked at her with a startled look.

"You speak up bold," he said; "you won't get put upon for want of spirit; and I don't know as what you're saying ain't the right thing—though I don't hold with the Church, nor parsons' ways. I'd do a deal myself, though you think me so hard and cross, for folks as has been kind to you."

"I know you will, grandpapa," said Phœbe, with a slight emphasis which startled him, though he did not know why; and she kissed him before she went to her grandmother, which she did with a perfectly composed and tranquil mind. It was astonishing how the crackle of that bit of paper in her handkerchief calmed and soothed her. She recovered her breath, her colour, and her spirits. She ran up to her room and changed her dress, which was silk, for a soft merino one, which made no rustling; and then she folded the bill carefully, and put it into the safe keeping of the little purse which she always carried in her pocket. No one would think of searching for it there, and she would always have it at hand whatever happened. When she had made these needful arrangements, she went to old Mrs. Tozer, and took her comfortably upstairs. Never was there a more devoted nurse. The old lady chatted cheerfully, yet sympathetically, of the poor gentleman and his illness, with the half-satisfaction of an invalid in hearing of some one else who is ill.

"And be sure you take him some of the port wine as the doctor ordered, and Tozer paid that dear for. I don't care for it, not a bit, Phœbe. I'd sooner have it from the grocer's, at two shillings a bottle. That's what I've always been used to, when I did take a glass of wine now and again. But I dare say as Mr. May would like it, poor gentleman."

When Mrs. Tozer had laid her head, all nodding with white muslin frills, edged with cotton lace, upon her pillow, Phœbe, noiseless in her soft merino gown, went back, accompanied by Martha, to the Parsonage, where Ursula's careworn face lighted a little at sight of her. Ursula had left her father for the moment in Betsy's care, to get something that was wanted, and she stole into the dining-room on hearing of her friend's arrival, and talked a little in a whisper, though the sick man was on the upper floor, and could not possibly have heard anything. Northcote was still there, sitting with Reginald, too anxious and excited to go away; and they all conversed in whispers, the three of them talking together for the benefit of the new-comer.

"Not paralysis; at least, he does not think so; a great mental shock—but we can't tell a bit what it was—coming when he was dreadfully tired, and not able to bear it."

They all spoke together, each of them saying a few words, and kept close together in the centre of the room, a curious little half-frightened group, overawed and subdued by the sudden change and strange calamity dropt into their midst. Phœbe seemed to bring them new life and hope.

"If it is going to be an illness," she said, "you gentlemen had better go home and go to bed, to be able to help us when we want help. Anyhow, what good can they do, Ursula? They had much better go to bed."

Ursula looked at them with a certain regret; though they could not do much good, it was a relief to come and whisper a few words to them now and then, giving them news of the patient. But Phœbe was right, and there was nothing to be said against her decision. The two young women and the faithful Betsy were enough, and, indeed, more than enough to watch over Mr. May.

CHAPTER XLI.

A MORNING'S WORK.

"Go and lie down for an hour," whispered Phœbe. "I am not sleepy at all. I have sat up before, and never felt it. You never did, I can see it in your poor little white face; and besides, I am steadier, because I am not so anxious. Now go, Ursula, if you are really fond of me, as you say—"

"Oh, Phœbe! if you think he is a little better. Oh, how horrible it is to be sleepy, as if you were all body, and had no heart at all!"

"You have plenty of heart, but you have never been used to this nursing. Leave your door open, so that I may call you in a moment. I have sat up often. Now go, to please me," said Phœbe. She had another object than mere rest to her friend, who at last, very much ashamed and crying softly, yet so weary that nothing on this earth seemed so desirable to her as sleep, crept to her room, and lay down there as the pale morning began to dawn. Betsy slept heavily in an easy-chair outside the door of the sick-room. She was there at hand in case anything was wanted, but she was happily unconscious where she was, sleeping the sleep of hard work and a mind undisturbed. Phœbe had seen that the patient was stirring out of the dull doze in which his faculties had been entirely stilled and stupefied. He was rousing to uneasiness, if not to full consciousness. Two or three times he made a convulsive movement, as if to raise himself; once his eyes, which were half open, seemed to turn upon her with a vague glimmer of meaning. How strangely she felt towards him, as she sat there in the grey of the morning, sole guardian, sole confidant of this erring and miserable man! The thought ran through her with a strange thrill. He was nothing to her, and yet he was absolutely in her power, and in all heaven and earth there seemed no one who was capable of protecting him, or cared to do so, except herself only. She sat looking at him with a great pity in her mind, determined to be his true protector, to deliver him from what he himself had done. She had not realized at first what it was he had done, and indeed it was only now that its full enormity, or rather its full consequences (which were the things that affected her most urgently), made themselves apparent to her. Generalizations are unsafe things; and whether it was because she was a woman that Phœbe, passing over the crime, fixed her thoughts upon the punishment, I do not venture to say; but she did so. After all a few lines of writing on a bit of paper is not a crime which affects the imagination of the inexperienced. Had it been a malicious slander Phœbe would have realized the sin of it much more clearly; but the copy of her grandfather's signature did not wound her moral sense in the same way, though it was a much more serious offence. That Mr. May could have intended to rob him of the money appeared impossible to her; and no doubt the borrowing of the signature was wrong—very wrong. Yes, of course it was horribly, fatally wrong; but still it did not set her imagination aglow with indignant horror, as smaller affairs might have done. But the consequences— disgrace, ruin, the loss of his position, the shame of his profession, moral death indeed, almost as frightful as if he had been hanged for murder. She shivered as she sat by him, veiled by the curtain, and thought of her grandfather's vindictive fierceness ; only she stood between him and destruction, and Phœbe felt that it was by no legitimate means that she was doing so, not by her influence over her grandfather as she had hoped, but only by an unjustifiable expedient which in itself was a kind of crime. This, however, brought a slight smile on her face. She took out her little purse from her pocket, and looked at the bit of paper carefully folded in it. The faint perfume of the Russia leather had already communicated itself to the document, which had not been so pleasant in Tozer's hands. As she looked at it lying peacefully on her lap, her attention was suddenly called by the patient, who sat upright and looked furtively about him, with his hand upon the coverings ready to throw them off. His ghastly white face peered at her from behind the curtain with wild eagerness—then relaxed, when he met her eye, into a kind of idiot smile, a painful attempt to divert suspicion, and he fell back again with a groan. The trance that had stupefied him was over; he had recovered some kind of consciousness, how much or how little she could not tell. His mind now seemed to be set upon hiding himself, drawing his coverings over him, and concealing himself with the curtain, at which he grasped with an excess of force which neutralized itself.

"Mr. May," said Phœbe, softly. "Mr. May! do you know me ?"

She could not tell what answer he made, or if he made any answer. He crouched down under the bed-clothes, pulling them over his face, trying to hide himself from her; from which she divined that he did recognize her, confused though his faculties were. Then a hoarse murmuring sound seemed to come out of the pillow. It was some time before she could make out what it was.

" Where am I ? " he said.

With the lightning speed of sympathy and pity, Phœbe divined what his terror was. She said, almost whispering,

"At home, in your own bed—at home! and safe. Oh, don't you know me—I am Phœbe." Then after a pause, " Tozer's granddaughter; do you know me now ? "

The strange, scared, white-faced spectre shrank under his covering, till she could see no more of him except two wild eyes full of terror which was almost madness.

" Listen ! " she said eagerly, " try to understand ! Oh, Mr. May, try to understand ! I know about it—I know everything, and you are safe—quite safe; you need not have any fear ! "

He did not follow what she said, Phœbe perceived with pain and terror. Even the impression made by the first sight of her seemed to fade from his mind. His grasp relaxed upon the curtains and coverlet; and then the hoarse murmuring was resumed. Straining all her ears, she made out that he was not speaking to her or any one, but moaned to himself, saying the same words over and over again. It took her a long time to make out even what these words were. When at last she did make them out they filled the girl with an alarm beyond words.

" It used to be hanging," he said. " Hard labour; can I bear hard labour ? And the children—the children ! Hard labour—for life. Hanging—was soon over. The children ! I cannot bear it. I never was put to—hard labour—in all my life."

Phœbe was too sick at heart to listen to more. She drew a little apart, but near enough to be seen by him. If he chose to spring up, to fling himself from the window, as she had heard of men doing in delirium, who could restrain him ? Not she, a slight girl, nor Betsy, even if Betsy could be roused to the danger. She did not know how long the vigil which followed lasted, but it seemed like years to her; and when at last she was relieved by the joyful sound of Reginald's voice and footstep coming up the stairs, she felt disposed to run to the glass at once, and look if her hair had grown white, or her countenance permanently changed with the terror. Reginald, for his part, thought of his father in the second place only, as children are apt to do; he came up to her first, and with a thrill in his voice of surprise and emotion, addressed her hastily by her name.

"Phœbe! is it *you* who are watching—you, darling?"

"Hush! I sent Ursula to bed; she was so tired. Don't leave him. I am frightened," cried Phœbe. "He is wandering in his mind. Oh, don't leave him, Mr. May!"

"I will do exactly as you tell me," said Reginald, in a confused transport of feeling, the very anxiety in his mind helping to destroy his self-control. He stooped down and kissed her hands before she could divine what he was about to do. "Only you or an angel would have done it," he cried, with a tremulous voice.

Was it not natural that he should think that some thought of him had made Phœbe so careful of his father? His heart was swelling, too full to hold, with a sudden joy, which expanded the pain, and made that greater too.

"Oh, what does it matter about me? Mr. May, think what I am saying. Don't leave him for a moment. He might throw himself out of the window, he might do some harm to himself. Ah! again!" said Phœbe, trembling.

But this time it was only a convulsive start, nothing more. The patient dropped down again softly upon his pillows, and relapsed into his doze, if doze it could be called, in which his faculties were but half-dormant, and his open eyes contradicted all the appearances of natural sleep.

When she was relieved from the sick room—and now she had a double motive in getting away—Phœbe stole softly into the faded little place where Ursula lay, still fast asleep, though fully dressed, and bathed her face and strained eyes. "I wonder if my hair is grey underneath," she said to herself. "I wonder nothing has happened to me." But a great deal had happened to her. Such a night is rarely encountered by so young a creature, or such an alarming charge undertaken. And sudden hot kisses upon little, cold, agitated hands, worn by fatigue to nervous perception of every touch, are very exciting and strange to a girl. They had given her a kind of electric shock. She was not in love with Reginald, and therefore she felt it all the more, and her heart was still throbbing with the suddenness and excitement of the incident. And after she had made an effort to get over this, there remained upon her mind the disturbing burden of a knowledge which no one shared, and a responsibility which was very heavy and terrible, and too tremendous for her slight shoulders. After she had made that hasty toilette, she sat down for a moment at the foot of the bed on which Ursula lay sleeping, unconscious of all those mysteries, and tried to think.

It is not an easy process at any time, but after a long night's watching, terror, and agitation, it seemed more impossible to Phœbe than it had ever done before. And she had so much occasion for thought, so much need of the power of judging clearly. What was she to do?—not to-morrow, or next week, but now. She had taken the responsibility of the whole upon herself by the sudden step she had taken last night; but, bold as she had been, Phœbe was ignorant. She did not know whether her theft of the bill would really stop the whole proceedings, as had seemed so certain last night ; and what if she was found out, and compelled to return it, and all her labour lost ! A panic took possession of her as she sat there at the foot of Ursula's bed, and tried to think. But what is the use of trying to think ? The more you have need of them, the more all mental processes fail you. Phœbe could no more think than she could fly. She sat down very seriously, and she rose up in despair, and, thought being no longer among her possibilities, resolved to do something at once, without further delay, which would be a consolation to herself at least. How wonderful it was to go out in the fresh early morning, and see the people moving about their work, going up and down with indifferent faces, quite unconcerned about the day and all it might bring forth ! She went up Grange Lane with a curious uncertainty as to what she should do next, feeling her own extraordinary independence more than anything else. Phœbe felt like a man who has been out all night, who has his own future all in his hands, nobody having any right to explanation or information about what he may choose to do, or to expect from him anything beyond what he himself may please to give. Very few people are in this absolutely free position, but this was how Phœbe represented it to herself, having, like all other girls, unbounded belief in the independence and freedom possessed by men. Many times in her life she had regarded with envy this independence, which, with a sigh, she had felt to be impossible. But now that she had it, Phœbe did not like it. What she would have given to have gone to some one, almost any one, and told her dilemma, and put the burden a little off her shoulders! But she durst not say a word to any one. Very anxious and pre-occupied, she went up Grange Lane. Home? She did not know ; perhaps she would have thought of something before she reached the gate of No. 6. And accordingly, when she had lifted her hand to ring the bell, and made a step aside to enter, an inspiration came to Phœbe. She turned away from the door and went on up into the town, cautiously drawing her veil over her face, for already the apprentices were taking down the shutters from her uncle's shop, and she might be seen. Cotsdean's shop was late of opening that morning, and its master was very restless and unhappy. He had heard nothing more about the bill, but a conviction of something wrong had crept into his mind. It was an altogether different sensation from the anxiety he had hitherto felt. This was no anxiety to speak of, but a dull pain and aching conviction that all was not right. When he saw the young lady entering the shop, Cotsdean's spirits rose a little, for a new customer was pleasant, and though he thought he had seen her, he did not know who she was. She was pleasant to look upon, and it was not often that any one came so early. He came forward with anxious politeness; the boy (who was always late, and a useless creature, more expense than he was worth) had not appeared, and therefore Cotsdean was alone.

"I wanted to speak to you, please," said Phœbe. "Will you mind if I speak very plainly, without any ceremony? Mr. Cotsdean, I am Mr. Tozer's granddaughter, and live with him at No. 6 in the Lane. I dare say you have often seen me with Miss May."

"Yes—yes, Miss, certainly," he said, with a thrill of alarm and excitement running through him. He felt his knees knock together under cover of the counter, and yet he did not know what he feared.

"Will you please tell me frankly, in confidence, about—— the bill which was brought to my grandfather yesterday?" said Phœbe, bringing out the question with a rush.

Whether she was doing wrong, whether she might bring insult upon herself, whether it was an interference unwarrantable and unjustifiable, she could not tell. She was in as great a fright as Cotsdean, and more anxious still than he was; but fortunately her agitation did not show.

"What am I to tell you about it, Miss?" said the man, terrified. "Is it Mr. Tozer as has sent you? Lord help me! I know as he can sell me up if he has a mind; but he knows it ain't me."

"Don't speak so loud," said Phœbe, trembling too. "Nobody must hear; and remember, you are never, never to talk of this to any one else; but tell me plainly, that there may be no mistake. Is it—Mr. May?"

"Miss Tozer," said Cotsdean, who was shaking from head to foot, "if that's your name—I don't want to say a word against my clergyman. He's stood by me many a day as I wanted him, and wanted him bad; but as I'm a living man, that money was never for me; and now he's a-gone and left me in the lurch, and if your grandfather likes he can sell me up, and that's the truth. I've got seven children," said the poor man, with a sob breaking his voice, "and a missus; and nothing as isn't in the business, not a penny, except a pound or two in a savings' bank, as would never count. And I don't deny as he could sell me up; but oh! Miss, he knows very well it ain't for me."

"Mr. Cotsdean," said Phœbe, impressively, "you don't know, I suppose, that Mr. May had a fit when he received your note last night?"

"Lord help us! Oh! God forgive me, I've done him wrong, poor gentleman, if that's true."

"It is quite true; he is very, very ill; he can't give you any advice, or assist you in any way, should grandpapa be unkind. He could not even understand if you told him what has happened."

Once more Cotsdean's knees knocked against each other in the shadow of the counter. His very lips trembled as he stood regarding his strange visitor with scared and wondering eyes.

"Now listen, please," said Phœbe, earnestly; "if any one comes to you about the bill to-day, don't say anything about *him*. Say you got it—in the way of business—say anything you please, but don't mention *him*. If you will promise me this, I will see that you don't come to any harm. Yes, I will; you may say I am not the sort of person to know about business, and it is quite true. But whoever comes to you remember this—if you don't mention Mr. May, I will see you safely through it; do you understand?"

Phœbe leant across the counter in her earnestness. She was not the kind of person to talk about bills, or to be a satisfactory security for a man in business; but Cotsdean was a poor man, and he was ready to catch at a straw in the turbid ocean of debt and poverty which seemed closing round him. He gave the required promise with his heart in his mouth.

Then Phœbe returned down the street. Her fatigue began to tell upon her, but she knew that she dared not give in, or allow that she was fatigued. However heavy with sleep her eyes might be, she must keep awake and watchful. Nothing, if she could help it, must so much as turn the attention of the world in Mr. May's direction. By this time she was much too deeply interested to ask herself why she should do so much for Mr. May. He was her charge, her burden, as helpless in her hands as a child; and nobody but herself knew anything about it. It was characteristic of Phœbe's nature that she had no doubt as to being perfectly right in the matter, no qualm lest she should be making a mistake. She felt the weight upon her of the great thing she had undertaken to do, with a certain half-pleasing sense of the solemnity of the position and of its difficulties; but she was not afraid that she was going wrong or suffering her fancy to stray further than the facts justified; neither was she troubled by any idea of going beyond her sphere by interfering thus energetically in her friend's affairs. Phœbe did not easily take any such idea into her head. It seemed natural to her to do whatever might be wanted, and to act upon her own responsibility. Her self-confidence reached the heroic point. She knew that she was right, and she knew moreover that in this whole matter she alone was right. Therefore the necessity of keeping up, of keeping alert and vigilant, of holding in her hand the threads of all these varied complications was not disagreeable to her, though she fully felt its importance—nay, almost exaggerated it in her own mind if that could be. She felt the dangerous character of the circumstances around her, and her heart was sore with pity for the culprit, or as she called him to herself the chief sufferer; and yet all the same Phœbe felt a certain sense of satisfaction in the great *rôle* she herself was playing. She felt equal to it, though she scarcely knew what was the next step she ought to take. She was walking slowly, full of thought, to Tozer's door, pondering upon this, when the sound of rapid wheels behind roused her attention, and looking up, surprised, she suddenly saw leaping out of a dog-cart the imposing figure of Clarence Copperhead, of whom she had not been thinking at all. He came down with a heavy leap, leaving the light carriage swinging and quivering behind him with the shock of his withdrawal.

"Miss Phœbe!" he said, breathless; "here's luck! I came over to see you, and you are the first person I set eyes on—"

He was rather heavy to make such a jump, and it took away his breath.

"To see me?" she said, laughing, though her heart began to stir. "That is very odd. I thought you must have come to see poor Mr. May, who is so ill. You know—"

"May be hanged!" said the young man; "I mean—never mind—I don't mean him any harm, though, by Jove, if you make such a pet of him, I don't know what I shall think. Miss Phœbe, I've come over post-haste, as you may see; chiefly to see you; and to try a horse as well," he added, "which the governor has just bought. He's a very good 'un to go; and pleased the governor would be if he knew the use I had put him to," he concluded, with a half-laugh.

Phœbe knew as well as he did what that use was. He had brought his father's horse out for the first time, to carry him here to propose to her, in spite of his father. This was the delicate meaning which it amused him to think of. She understood it all, and it brought a glow of colour to her face; but it did not steel her heart against him. She knew her Clarence, and that his standard of fine feeling and mental elevation was not high.

"Look here," he said, "I wish I could speak to you, Miss Phœbe, somewhere better than in the street. Yes, in the garden—that will do. It ain't much of a place either to make a proposal in, for that's what I've come to do; but you don't want me to go down on my knees, or make a fuss, eh? I got up in the middle of the night to be here first thing and see you. I never had a great deal to say for myself," said Clarence, "you won't expect me to make you fine speeches; but I *am* fond of you—awfully fond of you, Phœbe, that's the truth. You suit me down to the ground, music and everything. There's no girl I ever met that has taken such a hold upon me as you."

Phœbe heard him very quietly, but her heart beat loud. She stood on the gravel between the flower-borders, where the primroses were beginning to wither, and glanced over her life of the past and that of the future, which were divided by this moment like the two beds of flowers; one homely, not very distinguished, simple enough—the other exalted by wealth to something quite above mediocrity. Her heart swelled, full as it was with so many emotions of a totally different kind. She had gained a great prize, though it might not be very much to look at; more or less, she was conscious this golden apple had been hanging before her eyes for years, and now it had dropped into her hand. A gentle glow of contentment diffused itself all over her, not transport, indeed, but satisfaction, which was better.

"Mr. Copperhead—" she said, softly.

"No, hang it all, call me Clarence, Phœbe, if you're going to have me!" he cried, putting out his big hands.

"Grandmamma is looking at us from the window," she said, hurriedly, withdrawing a little from him.

"Well, and what does that matter? The old lady won't say a word, depend upon it, when she knows. Look here, Phœbe, I'll have an answer. Yes or no?"

"Have you got your father's consent—Clarence?"

"Ah, it is yes then! I thought it would be yes," he cried, seizing her in his arms. "As for the governor," added Clarence, after an interval, snapping his fingers, "I don't care *that* for the governor. When I've set my mind on a thing, it ain't the governor, or twenty governors, that will stop me."

CHAPTER XLII.

" Have you any notion what was the cause ? "

" None," said Reginald. " Oh, no, none at all," said Ursula. They were all three standing at the door of the sick-room, in which already a great transformation had taken place. The doctor had sent a nurse to attend upon the patient. He had told them that their father was attacked by some mysterious affection of the brain, and that none of them were equal to the responsibility of nursing him. His children thus banished had set the door ajar, and were congregated round it watching what went on within. They did not know what to do. It was Northcote who was asking these questions ; it was he who was most active among them. The others stood half-stunned, wholly ignorant, not knowing what to do.

" I don't think papa is ill at all," said Janey. " Look how he glares about him, just as I've seen him do when he was writing a sermon, ready to pounce upon any one that made a noise. He is watching that woman. Why should he lie in bed like that, and be taken care of when he is just as well as I am ? You have made a mistake all the rest of you. I would go and speak to him, and tell him to get up and not make all this fuss, if it was me."

" Oh, Janey ! hold your tongue," said Ursula ; but she, too, looked half-scared at the bed, and then turned wistful inquiring eyes to Northcote. As for Reginald, he stood uncertain, bewildered, all the colour gone out of his face, and all the energy out of his heart. He knew nothing of his father's affairs, or of anything that might disturb his mind. His mind ; all that his son knew of this was, that whatsoever things disturbed other minds his father had always contemptuously scouted all such nonsense. " Take some medicine," Mr. May had been in the habit of saying. " Mind ! you mean digestion," was it nothing more than some complicated indigestion that affected him now ?

" Is it anything about—money ? " said Northcote.

They all turned and looked at him. The idea entered their minds for the first time. Yes, very likely it was money.

" We have always been poor," said Ursula, wistfully. Northcote took her hand into his ; none of them except Ursula herself paid any attention to this involuntary, almost unconscious caress, and even to her it seemed a thing of course, and quite natural that he should be one of them, taking his share in all that was going on.

"I—am not poor," he said, faltering. "You must not think me presumptuous, May. But the first thing to be done is to get him out of his difficulties, if he is in difficulties—and you must let me help to do it. I think you and I should go out and see about it at once."

"Go—where ? " Reginald, like most young people, had taken little notice of his father's proceedings. So long as things went smoothly, what had he to do with them ? When there was a pressure for money, he knew he should hear of it, at least in the shape of reproaches and sneers from his father at his useless life, and the expenses of the family. But even these reproaches had died away of late, since Reginald had possessed an income of his own, and since the revenues of the Parsonage had been increased by Clarence Copperhead. Reginald was more helpless than a stranger. He did not know where to turn. "Do you think we could ask him ? I am almost of Janey's opinion. I don't think he is so ill as he seems."

And then they all paused and looked again into the room. The nurse was moving softly about, putting everything in order, and Mr. May watched her from the bed with the keenest attention. His face was still livid and ghastly in colour ; but his eyes had never been so full of eager fire in all the experience of his children. He watched the woman with a close attention which was appalling; sometimes he would put his covering half aside as if with the intention of making a spring. He was like some imprisoned animal seeing a possibility of escape. They looked at him, and then at each other, with a miserable helplessness. What could they do ? He was their father, but they knew nothing about him, and just because he was their father they were more slow to understand, more dull in divining his secrets than if he had been a stranger. When there came at last a suggestion out of the silence, it was Northcote who spoke.

"I don't see how you can leave him, May. It is plain he wants watching. I will go if you will let me—if Ursula will say I may," said the young man with a little break in his voice. This roused them all to another question, quite different from the first one. Her brother and sister looked at Ursula, one with a keen pang of involuntary envy, the other with a sharp thrill of pleasurable excitement. Oddly enough they could all of them pass by their father and leave him out of the question, more easily, with less strain of mind, than strangers could. Ursula for her part did not say anything; but she looked at her lover with eyes in which two big tears were standing. She could scarcely see him through those oceans of moisture, bitter and salt, yet softened by the sense of trust in him, and rest upon him. When he stooped and kissed her on the forehead before them all, the girl did not blush. It was a solemn betrothal, sealed by pain, not by kisses.

"Yes, go," she said to him in words which were half sobs, and which he understood, but no one else.

"You perceive," he said, "it is not a stranger interfering in your affairs, May, but Ursula doing her natural work for her father through me—her representative. God bless her! I am Ursula now," he said with a broken laugh of joy; then grew suddenly grave again. "You trust me, May?"

Poor Reginald's heart swelled; this little scene so calmly transacted under his eyes, would it ever happen for him, or anything like it? No, his reason told him—and yet; still he was thinking but little of his father. He had his duty too, and this happened to be his duty; but no warmer impulse was in the poor young fellow's heart.

And thus the day went on. It was afternoon already, and soon the sky began to darken. When his children went into the room, Mr. May took no notice of them—not that he did not know them; but because his whole faculties were fixed upon that woman who was his nurse, and who had all her wits about her, and meant to keep him there, and to carry out the doctor's instructions should heaven and earth melt away around her. She too perceived well enough how he was watching her, and being familiar with all the ways, as she thought, of the "mentally afflicted," concluded in her mind that her new patient was further gone than the doctor thought.

"I hope as you'll stay within call, sir," she said significantly to Reginald; "when they're like that, as soon as they breaks out they're as strong as giants; but I hope he won't break out, not to-day."

Reginald withdrew, shivering, from the idea thus presented to him. He stole down to his father's study, notwithstanding the warning she had given him, and there with a sick heart set to work to endeavour to understand his father—nay, more than that, to try to find him out. The young man felt a thrill of nervous trembling come over him when he sat down in his father's chair and timidly opened some of the drawers. Mr. May was in many respects as young a man as his son, and Reginald and he had never been on those confidential terms which bring some fathers and sons so very close together. He felt that he had no business there spying upon his father's privacy. He could not look at the papers which lay before him. It seemed a wrong of the first magnitude, wrought treacherously, because of the helplessness of the creature most concerned. He could not do it. He thrust the papers back again into the drawer. In point of fact there were no secrets in the papers, nor much to be found out in Mr. May's private life. All its dark side might be inferred from, without being revealed in, the little book which lay innocently on the desk, and which Reginald looked over, thinking no harm. In it there were two or three entries which at length roused his curiosity. Cotsdean, October 10th. Cotsdean, January 12th. C. & T. April 18th. What did this mean? Reginald remembered to have seen Cotsdean paying furtive visits in the study. He recollected him as one of the few poor people for whom his father had a liking. But what could there be between them? He was puzzled, and as Betsy was passing the open door at the time, called her in. The evening was falling quickly, the day had changed from a beautiful bright morning to a rainy gusty afternoon, tearing the leaves and blossoms from the trees, and whirling now and then a shower of snowy petals, beautiful but ill-omened snow, across the dark window. Beyond that the firmament was dull; the clouds hung low, and the day was gone before it ought. When Betsy came in she closed the door, not fastening it, but still, Reginald felt, shutting him out too much from the sick-bed, to which he might be called at any moment. But he was not alarmed by this, though he remarked it. He questioned Betsy closely as to his father's possible connection with this man. In such a moment, confidential, half-whispered interviews are the rule of a house. Every one has so much to ask; so much to say in reply; so many particulars to comment upon which the rest may have forgotten. She would have liked to enter upon the whole story, to tell how the master was took, and how she herself had thought him looking bad when he came in; but even to talk about Cotsdean was pleasant.

"I told Miss Beecham," said Betsy, "and I told the other gentleman, Mr. Northcote, as was asking me all about it. It's months and months since that Cotsdean got coming here—years I may say; and whenever he came master looked bad.

If you'll believe me, Mr. Reginald, it's money as is at the bottom of it all."

"Money? hush, what was that? I thought I heard something upstairs."

"Only the nurse, sir, as is having her tea. I'm ready to take my oath as it's money. I've been in service since I was nine years old," said Betsy, "I've had a deal of experience of gentlefolks, and it's always money as is the thing as sets them off their head. That's what it is. If that Cotsdean didn't come here something about money, never you believe me no more."

"Cotsdean! a poor shopkeeper! what could he have to do with my father's affairs?" Reginald was not speaking to the woman, but drearily to himself. If this was the only clue to the mystery, what a poor clue it was!

"I dunno, sir," said Betsy, "it ain't for me to tell; but one thing I'm sure of—Lord bless us, what's that?"

Reginald rushed to the door, nearly knocking her down as he pushed her aside with his hand. When they got outside, it was only the hat-stand in the hall that had fallen, something having been torn off from it apparently in mad haste, and the door had opened and shut. Reginald rushed upstairs, where the nurse was sitting quietly at her tea, the bed-curtains being drawn.

"All right, sir; he's in a nice sleep," said that functionary; "I didn't light no candles, not to disturb him, poor gentleman."

Reginald tore the curtains aside, then turned and dashed downstairs, and out into the windy twilight. In that moment of stillness and darkness the patient had escaped. He could see a strange figure walking rapidly, already half way up Grange Lane, and rushed on in pursuit without taking thought of anything. The sick man had seized upon a long coat which had been hanging in the hall, and which reached to his heels. Reginald flew on, going as softly as he could, not to alarm him. Where could he be going, utterly unclothed except in this big coat? Was it simply madness that had seized him, nothing more or less? He followed, with his heart beating loudly. There seemed nobody about, no one to whom he could make an appeal to help him, even if he could overtake the rapidly progressing fugitive. But even while this thought crossed his mind, Reginald saw another figure, broad and tall, developing in the distance, coming towards them, which stopped short, and put out an arm to stop the flight. Even that moment gave him the advantage, and brought him near enough to make out that it was Mr. Copperhead.

"The very man I want," he heard him say with his loud voice, putting his arm within that of Mr. May, who resisted, but not enough to attract the attention of the new comer, as Reginald came up breathless and placed himself on his father's other side. The darkness prevented any revelation of the strange appearance of the fugitive, and Mr. Copperhead was not lively of perception in respect to people unconnected with himself.

"You, too," he cried, nodding at Reginald, "come along. I've come to save that boy of mine from a little artful—Come, both of you. The sight of a young fellow like himself will shame him more than anything; and you, May, you're the very man I want—"

"Not there, not there, for God's sake!" said Mr. May, with a hoarse cry, "not there, my God! Reginald! it used to be hanging. Do you mean to give me up?"

"Hold him fast," Reginald whispered in desperation, "hold him fast! It is madness."

"Lord bless us!" said Mr. Copperhead, but he was a man who was proud of his strength, and not given to timidity. He held his captive fast by the arm, while Reginald secured him on the other side. "Why, what's this, May? rouse yourself up; don't give in, man. No, you ain't mad, not a bit of you. Come along, wait here at Tozer's for me, while I do my business; and then I'll look after *you*. Come on."

There was a violent but momentary struggle; then all at once the struggling man yielded and allowed himself to be dragged within the garden-door. Was it because an ordinary policeman, one of the most respectful servants of the law, who would have saluted Mr. May with the utmost reverence, was just then coming up? He yielded; but he looked at his son with a wild despair which made Reginald almost as desperate as himself in maddening ignorance and terror.

"Ruin! ruin!" he murmured hoarsely, "worse than death."

CHAPTER XLIII.

THE CONFLICT.

THE day which had intervened between Phœbe's morning walk, and this darkling flight along the same road, had been full of agitation at the house of the Tozers. Phœbe, who would willingly have spared her lover anything more than the brief intercourse which was inevitable with her relations, could find no means of sending him away without breakfast. She had escaped from him accordingly, weary as she was, to make arrangements for such a meal as she knew him, even in his most sentimental mood, to love—a thing which required some time and supervision, though the house was always plentifully provided. When she had hastily bathed her face and changed her dress she came back to the room where she had left him, to find him in careless conversation with Tozer, who only half-recovered from the excitement of last night, but much over-awed by a visit from so great a personage, had managed to put aside the matter which occupied his own thoughts, in order to carry on a kind of worship of Clarence, who was the son of the richest man he had ever heard of, and consequently appeared to the retired butterman a very demigod. Clarence was yawning loudly, his arms raised over his head in total indifference to Tozer, when Phœbe came into the room; and the old man seized upon the occasion of her entrance to perform another act of worship.

"Ah, here's Phœbe at last. Mr. Copperhead's come in from the country, my dear, and he's going to make us proud, he is, by accepting of a bit of breakfast. I tell him it's a wretched poor place for him as has palaces at his command; but what we can give him is the best quality, that I answers for—and you're one as knows how things should be, even if we ain't grand ourselves."

"Have you palaces at your command, Clarence?" she said, with a smile. Notwithstanding the fatigue of the night, the fresh air and her ablutions, and the agitation and commotion of her mind, made Phœbe almost more animated and brilliant than usual. Her eyes shone with the anxiety and excitement of the crisis, and a little, too, with the glory and delight of success; for though Clarence Copperhead was not very much to brag of in his own person, he still had been the object before her for some time back, and she had got him. And yet Phœbe was not mercenary, though she was not "in love" with her heavy lover in the ordinary sense of the word. She went towards him now, and stood near him, looking at him with a smile. He was a big, strong fellow, which is a thing most women esteem, and he was not without good looks; and he would be rich, and might be thrust into a position which would produce both honour and advantage; and lastly, he was her own, which gives even the most indifferent article a certain value in some people's eyes.

"Palaces? I don't know, but nice enough houses; and you know you like a nice house, Miss Phœbe. Here, I haven't said a word to the old gentleman. Tell him; I ain't come all this way for nothing. You've always got the right words at your fingers' end. Tell him, and let's get it over. I think I could eat some breakfast, I can tell you, after that drive."

"Grandpapa," said Phœbe, slightly tremulous, "Mr. Copperhead wishes me to tell you that—Mr. Copperhead wishes you to know why——"

"Bless us!" cried Clarence with a laugh. "Here is a beating about the bush! She has got her master, old gentleman, and that is what she never had before. Look here, I'm going to marry Phœbe. That's plain English without any phrases, and I don't know what you could say to better it. Is breakfast ready? I've earned it for my part."

"Going to marry Phœbe!" Tozer gasped. He had heard from his wife that such a glory was possible; but now, when it burst upon him, the dazzling delight seemed too good to be true. It thrust the forgery and everything out of his head, and took even the power of speech from him. He got up and gazed at the young people, one after the other, rubbing his hands, with a broad grin upon his face; then he burst forth all at once in congratulation.

"God bless you, sir! God bless you both! It's an honour as I never looked for. Rising in the world was never no thought of mine; doing your duty and trusting to the Lord is what I've always stood by; and it's been rewarded. But she's a good girl, Mr. Copperhead; you'll never regret it, sir. She's that good and that sensible, as I don't know how to do without her. She'll do you credit, however grand you may make her; and if it's any comfort to you, as she's connected with them as knows how to appreciate a gentleman—" said Tozer, breaking down in his enthusiasm, his voice sinking into a whisper in the fulness of his heart.

"Grandpapa!" said Phœbe, feeling sharply pricked in her pride, with a momentary humiliation, "there are other things to be thought of," and she gave him a look of reproach which Tozer did not understand, but which Clarence did vaguely. Clarence, for his part, liked the homage, and was by no means unwilling that everybody should perceive his condescension and what great luck it was for Phœbe to have secured him. He laughed, pleased to wave his banner of triumph over her, notwithstanding that he loved her. He *was* very fond of her, that was true; but still her good fortune in catching him was, for the moment, the thing most in his thoughts.

"Well, old gentleman," he said, "you ain't far wrong there. She *is* a clever one. We shall have a bad time of it with the governor at first; for, of course, when there's no money and no connections, a man like the governor, that has made himself, ain't likely to be too well pleased."

"As for money, Mr. Copperhead, sir," said Tozer with modest pride, "I don't see as there's anything to be said against Phœbe on that point. Her mother before her had a pretty bit of money, though I say it, as shouldn't—"

"Ah, yes—yes," said Clarence. "To be sure; but a little bit of coin like that don't count with us. The governor deals in hundreds of thousands; he don't think much of your little bits of fortunes. But I don't mind. She suits me down to the ground, does Phœbe; and I don't give that for the governor!" cried the young man valiantly. As for Phœbe herself, it is impossible to imagine any one more entirely put out of her place, and out of all the comfort and satisfaction in her own initiative which she generally possessed, than this young woman was, while these two men talked over her so calmly. It is doubtful whether she had ever been so set aside out of her proper position in her life, and her nerves were overstrained and her bodily strength worn out, which added to the sense of downfall. With almost a touch of anger in her tone she, who was never out of temper, interrupted this talk.

"I think breakfast is ready, grandpapa. Mr. Clarence Copperhead wants some refreshment after his exertions, and in preparation for the exertions to come. For I suppose your papa is very likely to follow you to Carlingford," she added, with a low laugh, turning to her lover. "I know Mr. Copperhead very well, and I should not like my first meeting with him after I had thwarted all his views."

"Phœbe! you don't mean to desert me? By Jove! I'll face him and twenty like him if you'll only stand by me," he cried; which was a speech that made amends.

She suffered him to lead her into breakfast less formally than is the ordinary fashion, and his hand on her trim waist did not displease the girl. No; she understood him, knew that he was no great things; but yet he was hers, and she had always meant him to be hers, and Phœbe was ready to maintain his cause in the face of all the world.

The breakfast was to Clarence's taste, and so was the company—even old Tozer, who sat with his mouth agape in admiration of the young potentate, while he recounted his many grandeurs. Clarence gave a great deal of information as to prices he had paid for various things, and the expenses of his living at Oxford and elsewhere, as he ate the kidneys, eggs, and sausages with which Phœbe's care had heaped the table. They had no *pâté de foie gras*, it is true, but the simple fare was of the best quality, as Tozer had boasted. Mrs. Tozer did not come downstairs to breakfast, and thus Phœbe was alone with the two men, who suited each other so much better than she could have hoped. The girl sat by them languidly, though with a beating heart, wondering, as girls will wonder sometimes, if all men were like these, braggards and believers in brag, worshippers of money and price. No doubt, young men too marvel when they hear the women about them talking across them of *chiffons*, or of little quarrels and little vanities. Phœbe had more brains than both of her interlocutors put together, and half-a-dozen more added on; but she was put down and silenced by the talk. Her lover for the moment had escaped from her. She could generally keep him from exposing himself in this way, and turn the better side of him to the light; but the presence of a believer in him turned the head of Clarence. She could not control him any more.

"A good horse is a deuced expensive thing," he said; "the governor gave a cool hundred and fifty for that mare that brought me over this morning. He bought her from Sir Robert; but he didn't know, Phœbe, the use I was going to put her to. If he'd known, he'd have put that hundred and fifty in the sea rather than have his beast rattled over the country on such an errand." Here he stopped in the midst of his breakfast, and looked at her admiringly. "But I don't repent," he added. "I'd do it again to-morrow if it wasn't done already. If you stand by me, I'll face him, and twenty like him, by Jove!"

"You don't say nothing," said her grandfather. "I wouldn't be so ungrateful. Gentlemen like Mr. Copperhead ain't picked up at every roadside."

"They ain't, by Jove!" said Clarence; "but she's shy, that's all about it," he added, tenderly; "when we're by ourselves, I don't complain."

Poor Phœbe! She smiled a dismal smile, and was very glad when breakfast was over. After that she took him into the garden, into the bright morning air, which kept her up, and where she could keep her Clarence in hand and amuse him, without allowing this revelation of the worst side of him. While they were there, Martha admitted the visitor of yesterday, Mr. Simpson from the Bank, bringing back to Phœbe's mind all the other matter of which it had been full.

"Don't you think you ought to go and see about the horse

and the dog-cart?" she said suddenly, turning to her lover with one of those sudden changes which kept the dull young man amused. "You don't know what they may be about."

"They can't be up to much," said Clarence. "Thank you, Miss Phœbe, I like you better than the mare."

"But you can't be here all day, and I can't be here all day," she said. "I must look after grandmamma, and you ought to go down and inquire after poor Mr. May—he is so ill. I have been there all night, helping Ursula. You ought to go and ask for him. People don't forget all the duties of life because —because a thing of this sort has happened—"

"Because they've popped and been accepted," said graceful Clarence. "By Jove! I'll go. I'll tell young May. I'd like to see his face when I tell him the news. You may look as demure as you like, but you know what spoons he has been upon you, and the old fellow too—made me as jealous as King Lear sometimes," cried the happy lover, with a laugh. He meant Othello, let us suppose.

"Nonsense, Clarence! But go, please go. I must run to grandmamma."

Mr. Simpson had gone in, and Phœbe's heart had begun to beat loudly in her throat; but it was not so easy to get rid of this ardent lover, and when at last he did go, he was slightly sulky, which was not a state of mind to be encouraged. She rushed upstairs to her grandmother's room, which was over the little room where Tozer sat, and from which she could already hear sounds of conversation rapidly rising in tone, and the noise of opening and shutting drawers, and a general rummage. Phœbe never knew what she said to the kind old woman, who kissed and wept over her, exulting in the news.

"I ain't been so pleased since my Phœbe told me as she was to marry a minister," said Mrs. Tozer, "and this is a rise in life a deal grander than the best of ministers. But, bless your heart, what shall I do without you?" cried the old woman, sobbing.

Presently Tozer came in, with an air of angry abstraction, and began to search through drawers and boxes.

"I've lost something," he answered, with sombre looks, to his wife's inquiry. Phœbe busied herself with her grandmother, and did not ask what it was. It was only when he had searched everywhere that some chance movement directed his eyes to her. She was trembling in spite of herself. He came up to her, and seized her suddenly by the arm. "By George!" he cried, "I'm in a dozen minds to search you!"

"Tozer! let my child alone. How dare you touch her—her

as is as good as Mr. Copperhead's lady? What's she got to do with your dirty papers? Do you think Phœbe would touch them—with a pair of tongs?" cried the angry grandmother.

Phœbe shrank with all the cowardice of guilt. Her nerves were unstrung by weariness and excitement. And Tozer, with his little red eyes blazing upon her, was very different in this fury of personal injury, from the grandfather of the morning, who had been ready to see every virtue in her.

"I believe as you've got it!" he cried, giving her a shake. It was a shot at a venture, said without the least idea of its truth; but before the words had crossed his lips, he felt with a wild passion of rage and wonder that it was true. "Give it up, you hussy!" he shrieked, with a yell of fury, his face convulsed with sudden rage, thickly and with sputtering lips.

"Tozer!" cried his wife, flinging herself between them, "take your hands off the child. Run, run to your room, my darling; he's out of his senses. Lord bless us all, Sam, are you gone stark staring mad?"

"Grandpapa," said Phœbe, trembling, "if I had it, you may be sure it would be safe out of your way. I told you I knew something about it, but you would not hear me. Will you hear me now? I'll make it up to you—double it, if you like. Grandmamma, it is a poor man he would drive to death if he is not stopped. Oh!" cried Phœbe, clasping her hands, "after what has happened this morning, will you not yield to me? and after all the love you have shown me? I will never ask anything, not another penny. I will make it up; only give in to me, give in to me—for once in my life! Grandpapa! I never asked anything from you before."

"Give it up, you piece of impudence! you jade! you d—d deceitful——"

He was holding her by the arm, emphasizing every new word by a violent shake, while poor old Mrs. Tozer dropped into a chair, weeping and trembling.

"Oh! it ain't often as he's like this; but when he is, I can't do nothing with him, I can't do nothing with him!" she cried.

But Phœbe's nerves strung themselves up again in face of the crisis. She shook him off suddenly with unexpected strength, and moving to a little distance, stood confronting him, pale but determined.

"If you think you will get the better of me in this way, you are mistaken," she said. "I am not your daughter; how dare you treat me so? Grandmamma, forgive me. I have been up all night. I am going to lie down," said Phœbe. "If grand-papa has anything more to say against me, he can say it to Clarence. I leave myself in his hands."

Saying this, she turned round majestically, but with an anxious heart, and walked away to her room, every nerve in her trembling. When she got there, Phœbe locked the door hastily, in genuine terror; and then she laughed, and then she cried a little. "And to think it was here all the time!" she said to herself, taking out the little Russia leather purse out of her pocket. She went into the closet adjoining her room, and buried it deep in her travelling trunk which was there, reliev-ing herself and her mind of a danger. Then—Phœbe did what was possibly the most sensible thing in the world, in every point of view. She went to bed; undressed herself quietly, rolled up her hair, and lay down with a grateful sense of ease and comfort. "When Clarence comes back he will be dis-appointed; but even for Clarence a little disappointment will be no harm," said the sensible young woman to herself. And what comfort it was to lie down, and feel all the throbs and pulses gradually subsiding, the fright going off, the satisfaction of success coming back, and gradually a slumberous, delicious ease stealing over her. Of all the clever things Phœbe had done in her life, it must be allowed that there was not one so masterly as the fact that she, then and there, went to sleep.

All this had taken up a good deal of time. It was twelve when Mr. Simpson of the bank disturbed the lovers in the garden, and it was one o'clock before Phœbe put a stop to all Tozer's vindictive plans by going to bed. What he said to Mr. Simpson, when he went back to him, is not on record. That excellent man of business was much put out by the long waiting, and intimated plainly enough that he could not allow his time to be thus wasted. Mr. Simpson began to think that there was something very strange in the whole business. Tozer's house was turned upside down by it, as he could hear by the passionate voices and the sound of crying and storming in the room above; but Cotsdean was secure in his shop, ap-parently fearing no evil, as he had seen as he passed, peering in with curious eyes. What it meant he could not tell; but it was queer, and did not look as if the business was straight-forward.

"When you find the bill, or make up your mind what to do, you can send for me," he said, and went away, suspicious and half-angry, leaving Tozer to his own devices. And the after-noon passed in the most uncomfortable lull imaginable. Though he believed his granddaughter to have it, he looked again over

all his papers, his drawers, his waste-basket, every corner he
had in which such a small matter might have been hid; but
naturally his search was all in vain. Clarence returned in the
afternoon, and was received by poor old Mrs. Tozer, very
tremulous and ready to cry, who did not know whether she
ought to distrust Phœbe or not, and hesitated and stumbled
over her words till the young man thought his father had come
in his absence, and that Phœbe had changed her mind. This
had the effect of making him extremely eager and anxious, and
of subduing the bragging and magnificent mood which the
triumphant lover had displayed in the morning. He felt himself " taken down a peg or two," in his own fine language. He
went to the Parsonage and tried very hard to see Ursula, to
secure her help in case anything had gone wrong, and then to
Reginald, whose vexation at the news he felt sure of, and
hoped to enjoy a sight of. But he could see no one in the
absorbed and anxious house. What was he to do? He wandered about, growing more and more unhappy, wondering if
he had been made to fling himself into the face of fate for no
reason, and sure that he could not meet his father without
Phœbe's support. He could not even face her relations. It
was very different from the day of triumph he had looked for;
but, as Phœbe had wisely divined, this disappointment, and all
the attending circumstances, did not do him any harm.

It was late in the afternoon when Northcote called. He too
had acted on the information given by Betsy, and had gone to
Cotsdean, who made him vaguely aware that Tozer had some
share in the business in which Mr. May was involved, and who,
on being asked whether it could be set right by money, grew
radiant and declared that nothing could be easier. But when
Northcote saw Tozer, there ensued a puzzling game at cross
purposes, for Tozer had no notion that Mr. May had anything
to do with the business, and declined to understand.

" I ain't got nothing to do with parsons, and if you'll take
my advice, sir, it 'ud be a deal better for you to give 'em up
too. You're a-aggravating the connection for no good, you
are," said Tozer, surely by right of his own troubles and per-
plexities, and glad to think he could make some one else uncomfortable too.

" I shall do in that respect as I think proper," said Northcote, who was not disposed to submit to dictation.

" Fact is, he's a deal too well off for a minister," Tozer said
to his wife when the young man disappeared, "they're too independent that sort; and I don't know what he means by his
Mays and his fine folks. What have we got to do with Mr. May?"

"Except that he's been good to the child, Tozer; we can't forget as he's been very good to the child."

"Oh, dash the child!" cried the old man, infuriated; "if you say much more I'll be sorry I ever let you see her face. What has she done with my bill?"

"Bill? if it's only a bill what are you so put out about!" cried Mrs. Tozer. "You'll have dozens again at Christmas, if that is all you want."

But the laugh was unsuccessful, and the old man went back to his room to nurse his wrath and to wonder what had come to him. Why had his granddaughter interfered in his business, and what had he to do with Mr. May?

Phœbe got up refreshed and comfortable when it was time for the family tea, and came down to her lover, who had come back, and was sitting very dejected by old Mrs. Tozer's side. She was fresh and fair, and in one of her prettiest dresses, having taken pains for him; and notwithstanding Tozer's lowering aspect, and his refusal to speak to her, the meal passed over very cheerfully for the rest of the party, and the two young people once more withdrew to the garden when it was over. The presence of Clarence Copperhead protected Phœbe from all attack. Her grandfather dared not fly out upon her as before, or summon her to give up what she had taken from him. Whatever happened, this wonderful rise in life, this grand match could not be interfered with. He withdrew bitter and exasperated to his own den, leaving his poor wife crying and wretched in the family sitting-room. Mrs. Tozer knew that her husband was not to be trifled with, and that, though the circumstances of Phœbe's betrothal subdued him for the moment, this effect in all probability would not last; and she sat in terror, watching the moments as they passed, and trembling to think what might happen when the young pair came in again, or when Clarence at last went away, leaving Phœbe with no protection but herself. Phœbe, too, while she kept her dull companion happy, kept thinking all the while of the same thing with a great tremor of suppressed agitation in her mind; and she did not know what was the next step to take—a reflection which took away her strength. She had taken the bill from her trunk again and replaced it in her pocket. It was safest carried on her person, she felt; but what she was to do next, even Phœbe, so fruitful in resources, could not say. When Northcote came back in the evening she felt that her game was becoming more and more difficult to play. After a brief consultation with herself, she decided that it was most expedient to go in with him, taking her big bodyguard along with her, and confiding in his stupidity not to find out more than was indispensable. She took Northcote to her grandfather's room, whispering to him on the way to make himself the representative of Cotsdean only, and to say nothing of Mr. May.

"Then you know about it?" said Northcote amazed.

"Oh, hush, hush!" cried Phœbe; "offer to pay it on Cotsdean's part, and say nothing about Mr. May."

The young man looked at her bewildered; but nodded his head in assent, and then her own young man pulled her back almost roughly, and demanded to know what she meant by talking to that fellow so. Thus poor Phœbe was between two fires. She went in with a fainting yet courageous heart.

"Pay the money!" said Tozer, who by dint of brooding over it all the day had come to a white heat, and was no longer to be controlled. "Mr. Northcote, sir, you're a minister, and you don't understand business no more nor women do. Money's money—but there's more than money here. There's my name, sir, as has been made use of in a way!—me go signing of accommodation bills! I'd have cut off my hand sooner. There's that girl there, she's got it. She's been and stolen it from me, Mr. Northcote. Tell her to give it up. You may have some influence, you as is a minister. Tell her to give it up, or, by George, she shall never have a penny from me! I'll cut her off without even a shilling. I'll put her out o' my will—out o' my house."

"I say, Phœbe," said Clarence, "look here, that's serious, that is; not that I mind a little pot of money like what the poor old fellow's got; but what's the good of throwing anything away?"

"Make her give it up," cried Tozer hoarsely, "or out of this house she goes this very night. I ain't the sort of man to be made a fool of. I ain't the sort of man—Who's this a-coming? some more of your d—d intercessors to spoil justice," cried the old man, "but I won't have 'em. I'll have nothing to say to them. What, who? Mr. Copperhead's father? I ain't ashamed to meet Mr. Copperhead's father; but one thing at a time. Them as comes into my house must wait my time," cried the butterman, seeing vaguely the group come in, whom we left at his doors. "I'm master here. Give up that bill, you brazen young hussy, and go out of my sight. How dare you set up your face among so many men? Give it up!" he cried, seizing her by the elbow in renewed fury. The strangers, though he saw them enter, received no salutation from him. There was one small lamp on the table, dimly lighted, which threw a faint glow upon the circle of countenances round, into which came wondering the burly big Copperhead, holding fast by the shoulder of Mr. May, whose ghastly face, contorted with wild anxiety, glanced at Tozer over the lamp. But the old man was so much absorbed at first that he scarcely saw who the new-comers were.

"What's all this about?" said Mr. Copperhead. "Seems we've come into the midst of another commotion. So you're here, Clar! it is you I want, my boy. Look here, Northcote, take hold, will you? there's a screw loose, and we've got to get him home. Take hold, till I have had a word with Clarence. That's a thing that won't take long."

Clarence cast a glance at Phœbe, who even in her own agitation turned and gave him a tremulous smile of encouragement. The crisis was so great on all sides of her that Phœbe became heroic.

"I am here," she said, with all the steadiness of strong emotion, and when he had received this assurance of support, he feared his father no more.

"All right, sir," he said almost with alacrity. He was afraid of nothing with Phœbe standing by.

"Make her give me up my bill," said Tozer; "I'll hear nothing else till this is settled. My bill! It's forgery; that's what it is. Don't speak to me about money! I'll have him punished. I'll have him rot in prison for it. I'll not cheat the law— You people as has influence with that girl, make her give it me. I can't touch him without the bill."

Mr. May had been placed in a chair by the two young men who watched over him; but as Tozer spoke he got up, struggling wildly, almost tearing himself out of the coat by which they held him. "Let me go!" he said. "Do you hear him? Rot in prison! with hard labour; it would kill me! And it used to be hanging! My God—my God! Won't you let me go?"

Tozer stopped short, stopped by this passion which was greater than his own. He looked wonderingly at the livid face, the struggling figure, impressed in spite of himself. "He's gone mad," he said. "Good Lord! But he's got nothing to do with it. Can't you take him away?"

"Grandpapa," said Phœbe in his ear, "here it is, your bill; it was *he* who did it—and it has driven him mad. Look! I give it up to you; and there he is—that is your work. Now do what you please—"

Trembling, the old man took the paper out of her hand. He gazed wondering at the other, who somehow moved in his excitement by a sense that the decisive moment had come, stood still too, his arm half-pulled out of his coat, his face wild with dread and horror. For a moment they looked at each other in a common agony, neither the one nor the other clear enough to understand, but both feeling that some tremendous crisis had come upon them. "He—done it!" said Tozer appalled and almost speechless. "*He* done it!" They all crowded round, a circle of scared faces. Phœbe alone stood calm. She was the only one who knew the whole, except the culprit, who understood nothing with that mad confusion in his eyes. But he was over-awed too, and in his very madness recognized the crisis. He stood still, struggling no longer, with his eyes fixed upon the homely figure of the old butterman, who stood trembling, thunderstruck, with that fatal piece of paper in his hand.

Tozer had been mad for revenge two moments before— almost as wild as the guilty man before him—with a fierce desire to punish and make an example of the man who had wronged him. But this semi-madness was arrested by the sight of the other madman before him, and by the extraordinary shock of this revelation. It took all the strength out of him. He had not looked up to the clergyman as Cotsdean did, but he had looked up to the gentleman, his customer, as being upon an elevation very different from his own, altogether above and beyond him; and the sight of this superior being, thus humbled, maddened, gazing at him with wild terror and agony, more eloquent than any supplication, struck poor old Tozer to the very soul. "God help us all!" he cried out with a broken, sobbing voice. He was but a vulgar old fellow, mean, it might be, worldly in his way; but the terrible mystery of human wickedness and guilt prostrated his common soul with as sharp an anguish of pity and shame as could have befallen the most heroic. It seized upon him so that he could say or do nothing more, forcing hot and salt tears up into his old eyes, and shaking him all over with a tremor as of palsy. The scared faces appeared to come closer to Phœbe, to whom these moments seemed like years. Had her trust been vain? Softly, but with an excitement beyond control, she touched him on the arm.

"That's true," said Tozer, half-crying. "Something's got to be done. We can't all stand here for ever, Phœbe; it's him as has to be thought of. Show it to him, poor gentleman, if he ain't past knowing; and burn it, and let us hear of it no more."

Solemnly, in the midst of them all, Phœbe held up the paper before the eyes of the guilty man. If he understood it or not, no one could tell. He did not move, but stared blankly at her and it. Then she held it over the lamp and let it blaze and drop into harmless ashes in the midst of them all. Tozer dropped down into his elbow-chair sniffing and sobbing. Mr. May stood quite still, with a look of utter dulness and stupidity coming over the face in which so much terror had been. If he understood what had passed, it was only in feeling, not in intelligence. He grew still and dull in the midst of that strange madness which all the time was only half-madness, a mixture of conscious excitement and anxiety with that which passes the boundaries of consciousness. For the moment he was stilled into stupid idiotcy, and looked at them with vacant eyes. As for the others, Northcote was the only one who divined at all what this scene meant. To Reginald it was like a scene in a pantomime—bewildering dumb show, with no sense or meaning in it. It was he who spoke first, with a certain impatience of the occurrence which he did not understand.

"Will you come home, sir, now?" he said. "Come home, for Heaven's sake! Northcote will give you an arm. He's very ill," Reginald added, looking round him pitifully in his ignorance; "what you are thinking of I can't tell—but he's ill and —delirious. It was Mr. Copperhead who brought him here against my will. Excuse me, Miss Beecham—now I must take him home."

"Yes," said Phœbe. The tears came into her eyes as she looked at him; he was not thinking of her at the moment, but she knew he had thought of her, much and tenderly, and she felt that she might never see him again. Phœbe would have liked him to know what she had done, and to know that what she had done was for him chiefly—in order to recompense him a little, poor fellow, for the heart he had given her, which she could not accept, yet could not be ungrateful for. And yet she was glad, though there was a pang in it, that he should never know, and remain unaware of her effort, for his own sake; but the tears came into her eyes as she looked at him, and he caught the gleam of the moisture which made his heart beat. Something moved her beyond what he knew of; and his heart thrilled with tenderness and wonder; but how should he know what it was?

"Give my love to Ursula," she said. "I shall not come to-night as she has a nurse, and I think he will be better. Make her rest, Mr. May—and if I don't see her, say good-bye to her for me——"

"Good-bye?"

"Yes, good-bye—things have happened—Tell her I hope she will not forget me," said Phœbe, the tears dropping down her cheeks. "But oh, please never mind me, look at him, he is quite quiet, he is worn out. Take him home."

"There is nothing else to be done," said poor Reginald, whose heart began to ache with a sense of the unknown which surrounded him on every side. He took his father by the arm, who had been standing quite silent, motionless, and apathetic. He had no need for any help, for Mr. May went with him at a touch, as docile as a child. Northcote followed with grave looks and very sad. Tozer had been seated in his favourite chair, much subdued, and giving vent now and then to something like a sob. His nerves had been terribly shaken. But as he saw the three gentlemen going away, nature awoke in the old butterman. He put out his hand and plucked Northcote by the sleeve. "I'll not say no to that money, not now, Mr. Northcote, sir," he said.

CHAPTER XLIV.

PHŒBE'S LAST TRIAL.

"Now if you please," said Mr. Copperhead. "I think it's my turn. I wanted May to hear what I had got to say, but as he's ill or mad, or something, it is not much good. I can't imagine what all these incantations meant, and all your play, Miss Phœbe, eyes and all. That sort of thing don't suit us plain folks. If you don't mind following your friends, I want to speak to old Tozer here by himself. I don't like to have women meddling in my affairs."

"Grandpapa is very tired, and he is upset," said Phœbe. "I don't think he can have any more said to him to-night."

"By George, but he shall though, and you too. Look here," said Mr. Copperhead, "you've taken in my boy Clarence here. He's been a fool, and he always was a fool; but you're not a fool, Miss Phœbe. You know precious well what you're about. And just you listen to me; he shan't marry you, not if he breaks his heart over it. I ain't a man that thinks much of breaking hearts. You and he may talk what nonsense you like, but you shan't marry my boy; no, not if there wasn't another woman in the world."

"He has asked me," said Phœbe; "but I certainly did not

ask him. You must give your orders to your son, Mr. Copperhead. You have no right to dictate to me. Grandpapa, I think you and I have had enough for to-night."

With this Phœbe began to close the shutters, which had been left open, and to put away books and things which were lying about. Tozer made a feeble attempt to stop her energetic proceedings.

"Talk to the gentleman, Phœbe, if Mr. Copperhead 'as anything to say to you—don't, don't you go and offend him, my dear!" the old man cried in an anxious whisper; and then he raised himself from the chair, in which he had sunk exhausted by the unusual commotions to which he had been subjected. "I am sure, sir," Tozer began, "it ain't my wish, nor the wish o' my family, to do anything as is against your wishes—"

"Grandpapa," said Phœbe, interrupting him ruthlessly, "Mr. Copperhead's wishes may be a rule to his own family, but they are not to be a rule to yours. For my part I won't submit to it. Let him take his son away if he pleases—or if he can," she added, turning round upon Clarence with a smile. "Mr. Clarence Copperhead is as free as I am to go or to stay."

"By Jove!" cried that young man, who had been hanging in the background, dark and miserable. He came close up to her, and caught first her sleeve and then her elbow; the contact seemed to give him strength. "Look here, sir," he said, ingratiatingly, "we don't want to offend you—I don't want to fly in your face; but I can't go on having coaches for ever, and here's the only one in the world that can do the business instead of coaches. Phœbe knows I'm fond of her, but that's neither here nor there. Here is the one that can make something of me. I ain't clever, you know it as well as I do—but she is. I don't mind going into parliament, making speeches and that sort of thing, if I've got her to back me up. But without her I'll never do anything, without her you may put me in a cupboard, as you've often said. Let me have her, and I'll make a figure, and do you credit. I can't say any fairer," said Clarence, taking the rest of her arm into his grasp, and holding her hand. He was stupid—but he was a man, and Phœbe felt proud of him, for the moment at least.

"You idiot!" cried his father, "and I was an idiot too to put any faith in you; come away from that artful girl. Can't you see that it's all a made-up plan from beginning to end? What was she sent down here for but to catch you, you oaf, you fool, you! Drop her, or you drop me. That's all I've got to say."

"Yes, drop me, Clarence," said Phœbe, with a smile; "for in the mean time you hurt me. See, you have bruised my arm. While you settle this question with your father, I will go to grandmamma. Pardon me, I take more interest in her than in this discussion between him and you."

"You shan't go," cried her lover, "not a step. Look here, sir. If that's what it comes to, her before you. What you've made of me ain't much, is it? but I don't mind what I go in for, as long as she's to the fore. Her before you."

"Is that your last word?" said Mr. Copperhead.

"Yes." His son faced him with a face as set and cloudy as his own. The mouth, shut close and sullen, was the same in both; but those brown eyes which Clarence got from his mother, and which were usually mild in their expression, looking out gently from the ruder face to which they did not seem to belong, were now, not clear, but muddy with resolution, glimmering with dogged obstinacy from under the drooping eyelids. He was not like himself; he was as he had been that day when Mr. May saw him at the Dorsets, determined, more than a match for his father, who had only the obstinacy of his own nature, not that dead resisting force of two people to bring to the battle. Clarence had all the pertinacity that was not in his mother, to reinforce his own. Mr. Copperhead stared at his son with that look of authority, half-imperious, half-brutal, with which he was in the habit of crushing all who resisted him; but Clarence did not quail. He stood dull and immovable, his eyes contracted, his face stolid, and void of all expression but that of resistance. He was not much more than a fool, but just by so much as his father was more reasonable, more clear-sighted than himself, was Clarence stronger than his father. He held Phœbe by the sleeve, that she might not escape him; but he faced Mr. Copperhead with a dull determination that all the powers of earth could not shake.

For the moment the father lost his self-control.

"Then I'll go," he said, "and when you've changed your mind, you can come to me; but—" here he swore a big oath, "mind what you're about. There never was a man yet but repented when he set himself against me."

Clarence made no answer. Talking was not in his way. And Mr. Copperhead showed his wondering apprehension of a power superior to his own, by making a pause after he had said this, and not going away directly. He stopped and tried once more to influence the rebel with that stare. "Phœbe—Phœbe—for God's sake make him give in, and don't go against Mr. Copperhead!" cried Tozer's tremulous voice, shaken with weakness and anxiety. But Phœbe did not say anything. She felt in the hesitation, the pause, the despairing last effort to conquer, that the time of her triumph had nearly come. When he went away, they all stood still and listened to his footsteps going along the passage and through the garden. When he was outside he paused again, evidently with the idea of returning, but changed his mind and went on. To be left like this, the victors on a field of domestic conflict, is very often not at all a triumphant feeling, and involves a sense of defeat about as bad as the reality experienced by the vanquished. Phœbe, who was imaginative, and had lively feeling, felt a cold shiver go over her as the steps went away one by one, and began to cry softly, not knowing quite why it was; but Clarence, who had no imagination, nor any feelings to speak of, was at his ease and perfectly calm.

"What are you crying for ? " he said, " the governor can do what he likes. I'd marry you in spite of a hundred like him. He didn't know what he was about, didn't the governor, when he tackled *me*."

" But, Clarence, you must not break with your father, you must not quarrel on my account—"

" That's as it may be," he said, "never you mind. When it's cleverness that's wanted, it's you that's wanted to back me up —but I can stick to my own way without you; and my way is this," he said, suddenly lifting her from the ground, holding her waist between his two big hands, and giving her an emphatic kiss. Phœbe was silenced altogether when this had happened. He was a blockhead, but he was a man, and could stand up for his love, and for his own rights as a man, independent of the world. She felt a genuine admiration for her lout at that moment ; but this admiration was accompanied by a very chill sense of all that might be forfeited if Mr. Copperhead stood out. Clarence, poor and disowned by his father, would be a very different person from the Clarence Copperhead who was going into parliament, and had " a fine position " in prospect. She did not form any resolutions as to what she would do in that case, for she was incapable of anything dishonourable ; but it made her shiver as with a cold icy current running over ; and as for poor old Tozer he was all but whimpering in his chair.

" Oh, Lord ! " he cried. " A great man like Mr. Copperhead affronted in my 'umble 'ouse. It's what I never thought to see. A friend of the connection like that—your father's leading member. Oh, Phœbe, it was an evil day as brought you here to make all this mischief! and if I had known what was going on ! " cried Tozer, almost weeping in his despair.

"You are tired, grandpapa," said Phœbe. Don't be frightened about us. Mr. Copperhead is very fond of Clarence, and he will give in; or if he doesn't give in, still we shall not be worse off than many other people." But she said this with a secret panic devouring her soul, wondering if it was possible that such a horrible revolution of circumstances and change of everything she had looked for, could be. Even Clarence was silenced, though immovable. He went away soon after, and betook himself to his room at the Parsonage, where all his possessions still were, while Phœbe attended upon her grandmother, whose agitation and fear she calmed without saying much. Tozer, quite broken down, retired to bed; and when they were all disposed of, Phœbe went out to the garden, and made a mournful little promenade there, with very serious thoughts. If Clarence was to be cast off by his father what could she do with him? It was not in Phœbe to abandon the stupid lover, who had stood up so manfully for her. No, she must accept her fate however the balance turned; but if this dreadful change happened what should she do with him? The question penetrated, and made her shiver to the depths of her soul; but never even in imagination did she forsake him. He was hers now, come good or ill; but the prospect of the ill was appalling to her. She went up and down the garden-path slowly in the silence, looking up to the stars, with her heart very full. Phœbe felt that no usual burden had been put upon her. Last night her occupation had been one of the purest charity, and this Providence had seemed to recompense in the morning, by dropping at her very feet the prize she had long meant to win; but now she was down again after being lifted up so high, and a great part of its value was taken out of that prize. Was she mercenary or worldly-minded in her choice? It would be hard to say so, for she never questioned with herself whether or not she should follow Clarence into obscurity and poverty, if things should turn out so. She would never abandon him, however bad his case might be; but her heart sunk very low when she thought of her future with him, without the "career" which would have made everything sweet.

Mr. Copperhead, too, had very serious thoughts on this subject, and sat up long drinking brandy-and-water, and knitting his brows, as he turned the subject over and over in his mind, recognizing with disgust (in which nevertheless there mingled a certain respect) that Clarence would not yield, he was as obstinate as himself, or more so. He had gone to the inn, where he was alone, without any of his usual comforts. It was perhaps the first time in his prosperous life that he had ever been really crossed. Joe had never attempted to do it, nor any of the first family. They had married, as they had done everything else, according to his dictation; and now here was his useless son, his exotic plant, his Dresden china, not only asserting a will of his own, but meaning to have it; and showing a resolution, a determination equal to his own. His mother had never shown anything of this. She had yielded, as every one else had yielded (Mr. Copperhead reflected), to whatever he ordered. Where had the boy got this unsuspected strength? A kind of smile broke unawares over the rich man's face, as he asked himself this question, a smile which he chased away with a frown, but which nevertheless had been there for a moment roused by a subtle suggestion of self-flattery. Where, but from himself, had his gentleman-son (as the millionnaire proudly held him to be) got that strength of obstinacy? He chased the thought and the smile away with a frown, and went to bed gloomily nursing his wrath; but yet this suggestion which he himself had made was more flattering to himself than words can say. As for Clarence, the only other person deeply concerned, after he had asked for Mr. May, and expressed his regret to learn how ill he was, the young man smoked a cigar on the doorsteps, and then went peaceably, without either care or anxiety, to bed, where he slept very soundly till eight o'clock next morning, which was the hour at which he was called, though he did not always get up.

When Mr. Copperhead began the new day, he began it with a very unwise idea, quickly carried out, as unwise ideas generally are. Feeling that he could make nothing of his son, he resolved to try what he could make of Phœbe; a young woman, nay, a bit of a girl not more than twenty, and a minister's daughter, brought up in reverence of the leading member—any resistance on her part seemed really incredible. He could not contemplate the idea of giving up all the cherished plans of his life by a melodramatic renunciation of his son. To give up Clarence whom he had trained to be the very apex and crowning point of his grandeur, was intolerable to him. But Mr. Copperhead had heard before now of young women, who, goaded to it, had been known to give up their lover rather than let their lover suffer on their account, and if this had ever been the case, surely it might be so in the present instance. Had he not the comfort of the Beecham family in his hands? Could not he make the Crescent Chapel too hot to hold them? Could he not awaken the fears of scores of other fathers very unlikely to permit their favourite sons to stray into the hands of pastors' daughters? There was nothing indeed to be said against Mr. Beecham, but still it would be strange if Mr. Copperhead, out and away the richest man in the community, could not make the Crescent too hot to hold him. He went down the Lane from the " George," where he had slept, quite early next morning, with this purpose full in his head, and, as good luck (he thought) would have it, found Phœbe, who had been restless all night with anxiety, and had got up early, once more walking up and down the long garden-path, reflecting over all that had happened, and wondering as to what might happen still. What a piece of luck it was ! He was accustomed to have fortune on his side, and it seemed natural to him. He went up to her with scarcely a pause for the usual salutations, and plunged at once into what he had to say.

" Miss Phœbe, I am glad to find you alone. I wanted a word with you," he said, " about the affair of last night. Why shouldn't you and I, the only two sensible ones in the business, settle it between ourselves ? Old Tozer is an old ass, begging your pardon for saying so, and my son is a fool—"

" I do not agree to either," said Phœbe gravely, " but never mind, I will certainly hear what you have to say."

" What I have to say is this. I will never consent to let my son Clarence marry you." Here he was interrupted by a serious little bow of assent from Phœbe, which disconcerted and angered him strangely. " This being the case," he re-sumed more hotly, " don't you think we'd better come to terms, you and me ? You are too sensible a girl, I'll be bound, to marry a man without a penny, which is what he would be. He would be properly made an end of, Miss Phœbe, if he found out, after all his bravado last night, that you were the one to cast him off after all."

" He cannot find that out," said Phœbe with a smile ; " un-fortunately even if I could have done it under brighter cir-cumstances my mouth is closed now. I desert him now, when he is in trouble ! Of course you do not know me, so you are excused for thinking so, Mr. Copperhead."

The rich man stared. She was speaking a language which he did not understand. " Look here, Miss Phœbe," he said, " let's understand each other. High horses don't answer with me. As for deserting him when he's in trouble, if you'll give him up—or desert him, as you call it—he need never be in trouble at all. You can stop all that. Just you say no to him, and he'll soon be on his knees to me to think no more of it. You know who I am," Mr. Copperhead continued with a concealed threat. " I have a deal of influence in the connection, though I say it that shouldn't, and I'm very well looked on in chapel business. What would the Crescent do without me ?

And if there should be an unpleasantness between the minister and the leading member, why, you know, Miss Phœbe, no one better, who it is that would go to the wall."

She made no answer, and he thought she was impressed by his arguments. He went on still more strongly than before. "Such a clever girl as you knows all that," said Mr. Copperhead, "and suppose you were to marry Clarence without a penny, what would become of you? What would you make of him? He is too lazy for hard work, and he has not brains enough for anything else. What would you make of him if you had him? That's what I want to know."

"And that is just what I can't tell you," said Phœbe smiling, "It is a very serious question. I suppose something will turn up."

"What can turn up? You marry him because he is going into parliament, and could give you a fine position.

"I confess," said Phœbe with her usual frankness, "that I did think of his career; without that the future is much darker, and rather depressing."

"Yes, you see that! A poor clod of a fellow that can't work, and will be hanging upon you every day, keeping you from working—that you will never be able to make anything of."

"Mr. Copperhead," said Phœbe sweetly, "why do you tell all this to me? Your mere good sense will show you that I cannot budge. I have accepted him being rich, and I cannot throw him over when he is poor. I may not like it—I don't like it—but I am helpless. Whatever change is made, it cannot be made by me."

He stared at her in blank wonder and dismay. For a moment he could not say anything. "Look here," he faltered at last, "you thought him a great match, a rise in the world for you and yours; but he ain't a great match any longer. What's the use then of keeping up the farce? You and me understand each other. You've nothing to do but to let him off; you're young and pretty, you'll easily find some one else. Fools are plenty in this world," he added, unable to refrain from that one fling. "Let him off and all will be right. What's to prevent you? I'd not lose a moment if I were you."

Phœbe laughed. She had a pretty laugh, soft yet ringing like a child's. "You and I, I fear, are no rule for each other," she said. "Mr. Copperhead, what prevents me is a small thing called honour, that is all."

"Honour! that's for men," he said hastily, "and folly for them according as you mean it; but for women there's no such thing, it's sham and humbug; and look you here, Miss Phœbe," he continued, losing his temper, "you see what your father will say to this when you get him into hot water with his people! There's more men with sons than me; and if the Crescent ain't too hot to hold him within a month—Do you think I'll stand it, a beggarly minister and his belongings coming in the way of a man that could buy you all up, twenty times over, and more!"

The fury into which he had worked himself took away Mr. Copperhead's breath. Phœbe said nothing. She went on by his side with soft steps, her face a little downcast, the suspicion of a smile about her mouth.

"By George!" he cried, when he had recovered himself, "you think you can laugh at me. You think you can defy me, you, a bit of a girl, as poor as Job!"

"I defy no one," said Phœbe. "I cannot prevent you from insulting me, that is all; which is rather hard," she added, with a smile, which cost her an effort, "seeing that I shall have to drag your son through the world somehow, now that you have cast him off. He will not give me up, I know, and honour prevents me from giving him up. So I shall have hard work enough, without any insults from you. It is a pity," said Phœbe, with a sort of sympathetic regret for herself so badly used. "I could have made a man of him. I could have backed him up to get on as well as most men; but it will certainly be uphill work now."

She did not look at the furious father as she spoke. She was quite calm, treating it reflectively, regretfully, as a thing past and over. Mr. Copperhead tried to burst forth again in threats and objurgations; but in spite of himself, and though she never said another word, the big, rich, noisy man was silenced. He went away, threatening to appeal to her father, which Phœbe, with a last effort, begged him smilingly to do. But this was the last of which she was capable. When she had closed the door after him, she rushed upstairs to her room, and cried bitterly. Everything was very dark to her. If he did appeal to her father, the appeal would spread confusion and dismay through the pastor's heart and family; and what was to become of herself, with Clarence on her hands, who could do nothing that was useful, and could earn neither his own living nor hers? All this was very terrible to Phœbe, and for a moment she contemplated the unheard of step of having a headache, and staying upstairs. But she reflected that her poor old grandfather had done *his* duty, at no small sacrifice, according to her bidding, yesterday; and she bathed her eyes heroically, and collected her strength and went down to break-fast as usual. It was her duty, which she must do.

As for Mr. Copperhead, he took a long walk, to reflect upon all the circumstances, which were complicated enough to cause him much trouble. He could not give up his cherished scheme, his Member of Parliament, his crown of glory. It was what he had been looking forward to for years. He tried to realize the failure of his hopes, and could not—nay, would not, feeling it more than he could bear. No; without his gentleman son, his University man, his costly, useless production, who was worth so much money to him, yet brought in nothing, he felt that he must shrink in the opinion of all his friends, even of his own sons, the "first family," who had so envied, sneered at, undervalued Clarence, yet had been forced to be civil to him, and respect their father's imperious will as he chose that it should be respected. What a sorry figure he should cut before all of them if he cast off Clarence, and had to announce himself publicly as foiled in all his plans and hopes! He could not face this prospect; he shrank from it as if it had involved actual bodily pain. The men who would laugh at his failure were men of his own class, to whom he had bragged at his ease, crowing and exulting over them, and he felt that he could not face them if all his grand anticipations collapsed. There was nothing for it but to give in. And on the other hand this girl Phœbe was a very clever girl, able not only to save the expense of coaches, but to cram the boy, and keep him up better than any coach could do. She could make his speeches for him, like enough, Mr. Copperhead thought, and a great many reasons might be given to the world why she had been chosen instead of a richer wife for the golden boy. Golden girls, as a general rule, were not of so much use. "Fortune ain't worth thinking of in comparison with brains. It was brains I wanted, and I've bought 'em dear; but I hope I can afford it," he almost heard himself saying to an admiring, envious assembly; for Mr. Copperhead so far deserved his success that he could accept a defeat when it was necessary, and make the best of it. When he had nearly ended his walk, and had reached in his thoughts to this point, he met his son, who was walking up from the Parsonage to No. 6 in the Lane. Clarence looked cheerful enough as he walked along, whistling under his breath, towards his love; but when he saw his father, a change came over his face. Once more his eyelids drooped over his eyes, and those muddy brown orbs got fixed in dull obstinacy; once more his upper lip shut down sullen and fast upon the lower. The entire expression of his face changed. Mr. Copperhead saw this afar off, from the moment his son perceived him, and the sight gave to all his thinking that force which reality gives to imagination; the risk he was running became doubly clear.

" Good morning, Clarence," he said.

" Good morning, sir," responded the other, with lowering brows and close-shut mouth.

" I suppose you were coming to the George to me? Come along, I've had no breakfast; and let's hope, my boy, that you're in a better mind than last night."

" Look here, sir," said Clarence; "you might as well ask one of those houses to walk with you to the George, and show a better mind. I'm of one mind, and one only. I'll marry Phœbe Beecham, whether you like it or not, and no other woman in this world."

" Is that your last word? " said the father, curiously repeating, without being aware of it, his question of the previous night.

" That's my last word," said the son, contemplating his father sullenly from under the heavy lids of his obstinate eyes.

" Very well," said Mr. Copperhead; "then come along to breakfast, for I'm hungry, and we can talk it over there."

CHAPTER XLV.

THE LAST.

This is how Phœbe's difficulties ended. Contrary to her every expectation, Mr. Copperhead made a great brag of her powers wherever he went. "Money is money," he said, " but brains is brains, all the same—we can't get on without 'em—and when you want to make a figure in the world, sir, buy a few brains if they fall in your way—that's my style. I've done with stupid ones up till now; but when I see there's a want of a clever one, I ain't such a fool as to shut my eyes to it. They cost dear, but I'm thankful to say I can afford that, ay, and a good deal more." Thus everything was satisfactorily arranged. Tozer and his wife cried together for joy on the wedding-day, but they did not expect to be asked to that ceremony, being well aware that Phœbe, having now completely entered into the regions of the great, could not be expected to have very much to say to them. "Though I know, the darling, as she'd just be the same if she was here, and wouldn't let nobody look down upon you and me," said the old woman.

"She's a wonderful girl, she is," said old Tozer. "Wind us all round her little finger, that's what she could do—leastways, except when there was principle in it, and there I stood firm. But I've done things for Phœbe as I wouldn't have done for no other breathing, and she knew it. I wouldn't give in to her tho' about church folks being just as good as them as is more enlightened. That's agin' reason. But I've done things for 'em along of her!—Ah! she's a wonderful girl is Phœbe—Phœbe, Junior, as I always call her. There ain't her match between here and London, and that's what I'll always say."

But we will not try to describe the glory and joy that filled Mr. Beecham's house in the Terrace, when Mrs. Clarence Copperhead went back there with all their friends to the wedding-breakfast, which was in the very best style, and regardless of expense. Even at that moment it gave Phœbe a little pang to see her mother in the bright colours which she loved, but which made her so much pinker and fatter than was needful. Little Mrs. Copperhead, in dim neutral tints, looked like a little shadow beside the pastor's buxom wife, and was frightened and ill at ease and sad to the heart to lose her boy, who had been all she possessed in the world. Sophy Dorset, specially asked for the purpose with Ursula May, who was a bridesmaid, looked on with much admiration at the curious people, so rich, so fine, and so overwhelming, among whom her father had found it so remarkable to meet not one person whom he knew. "Now, Ursula," she said, "if you had played your cards properly that beautiful bridegroom and that nice little house in Mayfair, and the privilege, perhaps, of writing M.P. after your name some time or other, might all have been yours instead of Miss Beecham's. Why did you let her carry off the prize?"

"Cousin Sophy!" cried Ursula indignantly. "As if I ever thought of him as a prize! But I know you are only laughing at me. The strange thing is that she likes him, though I am sure she knew very well that Reginald—Oh, when one thinks how many people there are in this world who do not get what they wish most—and how many people there are—" Ursula paused, involved in her own antithesis, and Sophy ended it for her with a sigh.

"Who do—and the one is no happier than the other, most times, little Ursula; but you don't understand that, and as you are going to be one of the blessed ones, you need not take to making reflections; that is my privilege, my dear."

"Oh, Cousin Sophy, why were not you one of those blessed ones too?" cried Ursula, clasping her arms suddenly round her kind friend. This, be it understood, was after the breakfast was over, and when, in the deep gloom which generally concludes a wedding day, everybody had gone home. The two were in a magnificent large bedchamber in Portland Place, in the vast silent mansion of the Copperheads, where at present there was nothing more cheerful than the bridegroom's soft-eyed mother, taking herself dreadfully to task for not being happy, and trying not to cry, though there was to be a great dinner and entertainment that night.

"Don't you know?" said Sophy, putting her aside with a certain proud coldness, and a momentary laugh, "he I loved proved false; that is to say, in simple language, he turned out so poor a creature that it is very good of me not to despise humanity for his sweet sake. Never mind. If all had gone well, and he had been a real man instead of the sham image of one, I don't suppose I should have ever been among the blessed ones. Anne is, who never thought of such mysteries at all; and so you will be, my little Ursula—very happy. I am sure of it—though how you can manage to be happy, my dear, marrying a man who is not a good Churchman, it is not for me to say."

"Cousin Sophy, have I been brought up in a way to make me so fond of Churchmen?" said Ursula solemnly. She could not have told how much or how little she knew about her father's behaviour, and the "shock to his mental system;" but vaguely and by instinct there was a great deal that she did know.

"You have been behind the scenes too much perhaps," said Sophy Dorset, shrugging her shoulders, "but don't think any worse of the world than you ought, if you can't think very much better. No class is good or bad, Ursula. Men are but men all over the world."

This made Ursula cry, though it is difficult to say why. She thought it cynical, and probably so will the reader. Perhaps Sophy Dorset abandoned the cause of mankind too easily, as most people of her temperament and age are disposed to do. Anyhow the evening entertainment took place and was very fine, and every honour was done to Clarence Copperhead's marriage, especially by his mother, who appeared in the most lovely satin that eyes ever saw, and diamonds—and almost succeeded all the evening in keeping herself from crying, but not entirely.

She did break down when the health of bridegroom and bride was drunk as it ought to be; but recovered herself hastily when the mother on the other side gave her a kiss of sympathy. Though it was an honest kiss it filled poor little Mrs. Copperhead's mind with the most unchristian feelings, and gave her strength to keep up for the rest of the evening, and do her duty to the last. Nevertheless Phœbe was the best of daughters-in-law, and ended by making her husband's mother dependent on her for most of the comforts of her life. And Clarence got into Parliament, and the reader, perhaps (if Parliament is sitting), may have had the luck to read a speech in the morning paper of Phœbe's composition, and if he ever got the secret of her style would know it again, and might trace the course of a public character for years to come by that means. But this secret is one which no bribe nor worldly inducement will ever tempt our lips to betray.

Northcote was released from the charge of Salem Chapel directly after these events, by the return of the minister safe and sound from his holiday, to the great delight of the congregation, though they had not been very fond of their old pastor before. Now they could not sufficiently exult over the happy re-instalment. "The other one never crossed our doors from the day he came till now as he's going away," said one indignant member; "nor took no more notice of us chapel folks nor if we were dirt beneath his feet." "That time as the Meeting was held, when he spoke up again' the sinecure, was the only time as my mind was satisfied," cried another. "And a deal came of it after, making friends with the very man he had abused." "All his friends was Church folks," said a third; "he was a wolf in sheep's clothing, that's what I calls him; and a poor moralist as a preacher, with never a rousing word in them things as he called his sermons. We're well rid of the likes of him, though he may be clever. I don't give much for that kind of cleverness; and what's the good of you, minister or not minister, if you can't keep consistent and stick to your own side." The chorus was so strong that the echo of it moved Tozer, who was a kind of arch-deacon and leading member too, in his way, where he sat twiddling his thumbs in his little room. "I'm one as is qualified to give what you may call a casting vote," said Tozer, "being the oldest deacon in Salem, and one as has seen generations coming and going. And as for Church and Chapel, I've served 'em both, and seen the colour of their money, and there's them as has their obligations to me, though we needn't name no names. But this I will say, as I'm cured of clever men and them as is thought superior. They ain't to be calculated upon. If any more o' them young intellectuals turns up at Carlingford, I'll tell him right out, 'You ain't the man for my money.' I'll say to him as bold as brass, 'I've been young, and now I'm old, and it's my conviction as clever young men ain't the sort for Salem. We want them as is steady-going, and them as is consistent; good strong opinions, and none o' your charity, that's what we wants here.'" Now Tozer had loved clever young men in his day more well than wisely, as everybody knew, and this deliverance carried all the more weight in consequence, and was echoed loudly by one general hum of content and applause.

Northcote took this very quietly, but he retired, after he had married Ursula, from the office of pastor, for which he was not fitted, and from the Liberation Society, and various other societies, coming to see that Disestablishment was not a panacea for national evils any more than other things. He was in the habit of quoting his brother-in-law, Reginald May, as the best man he knew; but this did not make him a Churchman; for naturally he could not say the same of other members of the same class and family. He was shaken out of his strong opinions; but it is doubtful how far this was good for him, for he was a man of warlike disposition, and not to have something which he could go to the stake for—something which he could think the devil's own stronghold to assail, was a drawback to him, and cramped his mental development; but he was happy in his home with his pretty Ursula, which is probably all the reader will care to know. He paid Tozer's hundred and fifty pounds. And he made no inquiries, and tried not to ask himself what all that strange scene had meant—and whatever it did mean it was over for ever, and nobody asked any further questions or made any revelations on the subject. As for Mr. May, his mysterious illness went on for some time, the doctors never venturing to put any name to it. It was "mental shock," and perhaps aberration, though he was sane enough to calm down after that incomprehensible scene. Mr. Simpson of the Bank had a good guess at the secret of the enigma, but even Tozer got hazy about it after a while, and though he knew that he had done Mr. May a wonderful service, could scarcely have told what it was—and neither, when it was all over, could the culprit have told. He got better and worse for about a year, and then he died, his strength failing him without any distinct reason, no one could tell how. Reginald got the living and stepped into his father's place, making a home for the children, which sharp Janey rules over, not so softly or steadily as Ursula, with a love of theories and experiments not quite consistent with the higher graces of housekeeping, yet with an honest meaning through it all. As the times are so unsettled, and no one can tell what may become within a year of any old foundation, the trustees have requested Reginald to retain his chaplaincy at the old College; so that he is in reality a pluralist, and almost rich, though they say the hardest-worked man in Carlingford. He has his vagaries too, which no man can live without, but he is the kindest guardian to his brothers and sisters, and bears with Janey's freaks with exemplary gentleness. And he has a curate, whom in the course of nature Janey will probably marry—though this has not yet been revealed to either party, who have reached only the first stage of hating each other up to this time. It is not thought in the family that Reginald will ever marry. She was never worthy of him, the sisters say; but he thinks differently, as yet at least. However he is young, and things may mend.

THE END.

VIRAGO MODERN CLASSICS

The first Virago Modern Classic, *Frost in May* by Antonia White, was published in 1978. It launched a list dedicated to the celebration of women writers and to the rediscovery and reprinting of their works. Its aim was, and is, to demonstrate the existence of a female tradition in fiction which is both enriching and enjoyable. The Leavisite notion of the 'Great Tradition', and the narrow, academic definition of a 'classic', has meant the neglect of a large number of interesting secondary works of fiction. In calling the series 'Modern Classics' we do not necessarily mean 'great' — although this is often the case. Published with new critical and biographical introductions, books are chosen for many reasons: sometimes for their importance in literary history; sometimes because they illuminate particular aspects of womens' lives, both personal and public. They may be classics of comedy or storytelling; their interest can be historical, feminist, political or literary.

Initially the Virago Modern Classics concentrated on English novels and short stories published in the early decades of this century. As the series has grown it has broadened to include works of fiction from different centuries, different countries, cultures and literary traditions. In 1984 the Victorian Classics were launched; there are separate lists of Irish, Scottish, European, American, Australian and other English-speaking countries; there are books written by Black women, by Catholic and Jewish women, and a few relevant novels by men. There is, too, a companion series of Non-Fiction Classics constituting biography, autobiography, travel, journalism, essays, poetry, letters and diaries.

By the end of 1988 over 300 titles will have been published in these two series, many of which have been suggested by our readers.

Also of Interest by Mrs Oliphant

Chronicles of Carlingford
THE RECTOR AND THE DOCTOR'S FAMILY

"She watched him as women often do watch men. . . The incomprehensibleness of women is an old theory, but what is that to the curious wondering observation with which wives, mothers and sisters watch the other unreasoning animal . . !"

These two short novels raise the curtain on an entrancing new world for all who love Jane Austen, George Eliot, and Trollope's "Barsetshire Chronicles". The setting is Carlingford, a small town not far from London in the mid-1800s. The cast ranges from tradesmen to aristocracy and clergy . . .

The Rector opens as Carlingford awaits the arrival of their new rector. Will he be high church or low? And – for there are numerous unmarried ladies in Carlingford – will he be a bachelor? After fifteen years at All Souls the Rector fancies himself immune to womanhood: he is yet to encounter the blue ribbons and dimples of Miss Lucy Wodehouse.

The Doctor's Family introduces us to the newly built quarter of Carlingford where young Dr Rider seeks his living. Already burdened by his improvident brother's return from Australia, he is appalled when his brother's family and sister-in-law, Nettie, follow him to Carlingford. But the susceptible doctor is yet to discover Nettie's attractions – and her indomitable Australian will.

Chronicles of Carlingford
SALEM CHAPEL

"As he walked about Carlingford . . . He pictured to himself how, by-and-by, those jealous doors in Grange Lane would fly open at his touch, and how the dormant minds within would awake under his influence"

Arthur Vincent "fresh from Homerton, in the bloom of hope and intellectualism", arrives in Carlingford to take up the reins as Dissenting minister of Salem Chapel. A mixture of hope and ignorance prompts him to imagine that he will take his place amongst the cream of Carlingford society. But a six-o'clock tea at the home of Mr Tozer the butterman, senior deacon of the Chapel, throws cold water on the young man's aspirations. For there he meets Mrs Tozer and her daughter Phoebe, "pink, plump and full of dimples", and his congregation of greengrocers, dealers in cheese and bacon, milkmen, dressmakers and teachers of day-schools. To add to his problems he falls head-over-heels in love with "a beautiful, dazzling creature", Lady Western, only to find himself caught up in a crime most horrible to contemplate . . .

Chronicles of Carlingford
THE PERPETUAL CURATE

"For nearly a year past Mr Wentworth had had things his own way in Carlingford ... Now, to be looked upon as an unauthorised workman, a kind of meddling, Dissenterish, missioning individual, was rather hard upon the young man"

Frank Wentworth, Perpetual Curate of St Roque's, has basked in the popularity of Carlingford, beloved in the gracious homes of Grange Lane and the slums of Wharfside alike. But there are some among the sober-minded citizens who would see him as a "dilettante Anglican, given over to floral ornaments and ecclesiastical upholstery" – a verdict shared by the new Rector who regards the presence of a young and energetic rival as an intolerable encumbrance. Imperceptibly, the tide starts turning against Frank Wentworth: his love for Lucy Wodehouse is threatened by his lack of prospects; his Evangelical aunts, in charge of a family living, disapprove of his high church ways, and rumours about a pretty shopgirl begin circulating. Slowly it dawns on Frank that he may well be doomed to a life of perpetual – and single – curacy.

Chronicles of Carlingford
MISS MARJORIBANKS

"In such a case as hers, it was evidently the duty of an only child to devote herself to her father's comfort, and become the sunshine of his life"

From the moment of her mother's death, Lucilla Marjoribanks knows her vocation – a conviction based on the influence of morally uplifting novels and the "sublime confidence in herself which is the first necessity to a woman with a mission". The usurping of Dr Marjoribanks as master of his own table and the assuaging of Nancy, his formidable housekeeper, are but small steps in Lucilla's scheme, for she intends nothing less than the transformation of Carlingford society. Lucilla's "Evenings" become the talk of this quiet country town: not only are they an essential source of gossip and entertainment for old friends and neighbours of Grange Lane, but they are also the setting for some of Lucilla's most startling accomplishments. For it is on these occasions, under the watchful eye and guidance of this magnificent young woman, that reputations are made and lost and romances are pursued and undone . . .

HESTER

" 'The little firebrand!' she said, 'the little spitfire! facing me on my own ground, defying me. Catherine Vernon, in the very Vernonry, my own creation!' "

Catherine Vernon is the head of the family bank, reputed in the Home Counties to be "solid as the Bank of England." Loved and revered by the people of Redborough, she is nevertheless seen as a none-too-benevolent despot by those of her family who, dependent upon her charity, live in the nearby "Vernonry". Catherine is a proud businesswoman, in firm control of her life, her work and her family. She lives with her young cousin Edward, grooming him to succeed her in the bank, loving him like a son. Then fourteen-year-old Hester and her widowed mother join the tenants of the Vernonry and Catherine finds she has met her match in this strong-willed girl. We watch as Hester grows up through the 1860s and 70s and as their silent confrontation comes to a head over their love for the same man: an absorbing struggle which alters forever the fortunes of Hester and the Vernon family.